THE SKELETON PALMS

Cary Watson

THE SKELETON PALMS

To Sam

Teardrop

I'm impaled by the heat.

I squint and imagine that the pool lying between us is the narrow arm of an ocean, its sky-blue waters lapping at a coastline of tile and concrete. I'm wearing sunglasses, but still have to shade my eyes against the bombarding desert light to look across at Autumn and Enoch. She, her lounger positioned to catch the sun, wears her tanned skin like an expensive dress; her slim, coppery body lies as if at attention, neatly divided in three by a yellow bikini. He, his chair as close to her as possible without leaving the sun umbrella's shade, is looking closely at his white flesh, possibly doing an inventory of what new growths and blemishes have come to barnacle his seven decades of life; his red swimming trunks are a garish divide between his veiny, skinny legs and a belly that hangs down like melted wax.

It's almost silent. At the very edge of my hearing there's the occasional and distant whine of trucks on highway 111. The sun is slipping behind the San Jacinto Mountains, and the dying light tints the slopes and gullies in warm shades of pink and red. Enoch scrapes his chair across the patio stones as he stands up and the harsh sound makes Autumn flinch. She lowers her sunglasses a fraction to see where Enoch's going. He moves stiffly, and as he comes closer, I notice the faded scars on his knees that look like creases in a piece of parchment. I can't decipher his expression. His resting face is always sad, and when other emotions visit it they behave like unwanted visitors.

He stops in front of me, slaps his hands on his stomach, and says, "Tom, I'd like you to do me a favor."

I won't be able to refuse whatever he asks. It would be in bad taste to turn him down when I'm both a house guest and the man sleeping with his wife.

"What did you have in mind, Enoch?"

"We'll talk in my office,"

"Okay. I'll meet you inside."

I get up from my lounger, stretch, and walk to the edge of the patio to take in the view. I won't be rushed. He indirectly pays my salary but I'm not going to trot after him. Besides, I want to linger and let Autumn compare me to her husband. I'm less than half his age and hold every other kind of advantage over him, barring wealth. I'm being arrogant and shallow, but it feels justified after what I didn't do to him last night.

The faint smell of barbecuing meats in the air is the only reminder that there are other houses in Bighorn Estates, all of them hidden and moated by acres of sun-shattered rock and unearthly-looking desert plants. To the west, the lights of Palm Springs are coming on, glowing orange and white in the dusty heat haze, while across the Coachella Valley the hills of Joshua Tree National Park are darkening into purple, a moving necklace of white lights marking out I-10's path in front of them. Enoch slides open the glass door leading into the kitchen; his flabby, bent figure is a sad contrast against the glass and gleaming white brick of his sprawling home that angles and dips around the property like a cubist caterpillar. I shouldn't think of it as his, though; it was Autumn's creation, and if the eccentric design has any life it's because of her. Enoch will probably golf tomorrow, so Autumn and I will tell him we're going to Agua Caliente Casino and spend the afternoon at the Capri Inn.

"Coming?" asks Enoch from the doorway.

I follow him into the house.

The air conditioning is an electric shock to the skin and makes me gasp. We go through the kitchen where Maria and Oribe are standing at the island eating cheese sandwiches. I've only ever seen them taking a break at the end of their shift, after all the housework and maintenance is done. I've never seen them sitting down. Oribe looks at me with cold eyes and an ingratiating smile. I wonder how they'd react if I told them I speak Spanish? It would probably hurt Maria if I did; she pretends to be married to Oribe, but the truth, as far as I can tell from overhearing their conversations, is that she has to share his bed to keep a roof over her head. It makes sense; she's about my age and he looks like he's pushed past fifty after a hard struggle.

Enoch leads me into his office. I remember the first time I came here he invited me in to watch a football game and proudly called it his man cave as though he'd invented the term. Autumn says it's the tomb of a pagan king who's gathered all his prized possessions together to take into the next world. The office is stuffed with heavy, dark furniture, its walls covered with framed photos and plaques, a huge TV, autographed sports jerseys in glass frames, and mounted heads from his hunting days in Africa. A gun cabinet sits in one corner, the lion's head on the wall above it staring longingly out the window at the sun-varnished landscape. He's only at ease in this room. Just this morning he was casting baleful looks at the rest of the house—all those large white rooms stocked with spidery furniture in bright, primary colors placed at odd angles annoy Enoch, while the art on the walls infuriates him. He must feel he's trespassing when he leaves this room. His sleeping bag is balled-up on the office couch. I wonder why he doesn't turn down the air con instead of draping it over himself while he watches sports, or when he sleeps here on the nights Autumn doesn't want him in her bedroom. I expect he finds his own bedroom cold in other ways when he's not surrounded by his memory walls.

Enoch sits at his desk and waves me towards a chair. I remain standing and study the photos on the wall.

"I got some lousy news from the housekeeper at the Malibu house," says Enoch.

"What's that?"

"The dog's been taken and they want ten thousand to return him. I don't want Autumn to know about it; you know what she's like about Emoji."

Enoch's photos are all of himself: Enoch in camo gear kneeling on an African plain, a rifle held at a jaunty angle in one hand, the other holding up the head of a leopard, the animal's tongue lolling out of its mouth and dripping blood, while in the near background four of Enoch's buddies hold their rifles up in the air like successful revolutionaries; Enoch waist-deep in a river, shirt off, fly fishing; a very young Enoch and his volleyball teammates posing outside an Olympic venue; and Enoch on a construction site laughing at the camera. None of the pictures show him when he was older than forty or so. He was a fit and handsome bastard, once upon a time, and now he has a dog called Emoji that could fit in a purse that's worth ten large to him.

"What do you want me to do, Enoch?"

"The money's to be dropped off near here. Tonight. I would, but the drop is up a hiking trail, and my knees…"

"Okay. You think you'll actually get the dog back?"

"What else can I do?"

"You have the money?"

Enoch reaches into a desk drawer and hands me a thick envelope. "I'll get changed," I say.

I go to my room and put on jeans and a dark, loose-fitting shirt. This kidnapping smells like a scam, but that money is going to be mine. I look out my window at the pool where Enoch is speaking to Autumn. Making excuses for me, I guess. I return through the kitchen where Oribe stares at me. His dark, Mayan face breaks into a smile that counts for nothing.

"Are the keys in the Maserati, Oribe?"

"Yes. You going out?"

"Yeah. Tell Enoch I'll meet him at the car."

I go to Enoch's office, open his gun cabinet and look for something small. His handgun collection has been put together based on what he's seen in movies or read about in thrillers: mostly big caliber pistols from Sig Sauer, Walther, and Smith & Wesson. I need something to tuck in the back of my jeans that will prove my exclusive right to the ten thousand I'll be carrying. There's a Beretta that will do the job.

I exit the office and take the stairs down to the garage where Autumn's white Range Rover is parked between Enoch's Yukon and the Maserati. I could use my Civic—it's parked in the driveway—but whoever's waiting for the money will be expecting one of Marsden's cars to show up. I sit in the Maserati and watch a scorpion dart and juke across the garage floor.

Enoch comes into the garage and says, "It's the Broken Rock Trail in Palm Springs. A few hundred yards up the trail there's some kind of signpost, one of those things with a picture and writing to tell you what you're looking at. You put the envelope under a rock at the base of the post. That's it. Think you can find it?"

I point to the car's GPS screen. Enoch steps away as I hit the remote for the garage door. I turn off my phone as I leave the garage; I'll need quiet if I'm going to surprise this dognapper and I don't want unexpected sounds announcing my presence when I'm on the trail. Autumn is standing at a window watching me as I go down the driveway, the room behind her so brightly-lit she looks like a shadow puppet. She waves at me in a strange way and I remember that she wanted me to watch a film with her later tonight. I shouldn't be gone very long.

The heat of the day is dying a quick death, and the air, previously baked and tasteless, carries stray scents of flowers and grass from the sundown watering of lawns and golf courses. Broken Rock Trail is on the outskirts of Palm Springs at the base of the mountains. There's a small parking lot for it on Busby Road, and I drive by twice to scope it out. No cars in the lot, but there's an empty and elderly pickup parked on the street about one hundred yards away. Busby has no homes or businesses, but a large sign staked into the lifeless soil promises the arrival of a 'privileged enclave' called SunDesertSky.

I pull into the parking lot and kill the engine, half-expecting someone to leave the shadows and ask for the money, but it looks like they're going to make me walk. I put the cash in my pocket, stuff some tissues in the envelope, then grab a flashlight out of the glove compartment and start out. It's nearly dark, and I sweep the flashlight beam over the trail to check for obstacles and rattlesnakes. The path is smooth and rises steadily. I crest a ridge and look down at some massive homes, each forming its own glittering constellation of house lights, patio lights, and yard lights that float in the darkness. I recognize one of them; Autumn drove me past it once and told me it was built in the seventies for a comedian who was famous in the forties. It looks like an airport terminal. The adjacent house has an enormous oval pool, its bottom decorated in tile with the outline of a cock.

I find the signpost and pass the flashlight beam around the clearing. There's nothing but brittlebushes and a startled kangaroo rat that scuds out of sight. A curved slice of yellow moon is a brooch pinned to the night sky. I turn the flashlight off and put the envelope under a stone at the base of the post. I'll hurry back and hide near the pickup for the appearance of the disappointed thief. I'll take his ID, put a hurt on him, and tell him to return the dog unless he wants worse down the road.

I finish fooling with the rock and see a man standing on a rise fifty feet away. The moonlight has turned the world black and white, and the man's rifle casts a long, sharp shadow as he brings it up to his shoulder. I whip the Beretta out and drop to one knee. His shot strikes the signpost as I fire four rapid rounds that don't miss. He flails his arms and falls backwards, his last shot aimed at the Cheshire cat grin of the moon.

I stay frozen in place, listening for an accomplice running away or moving into a firing position. The gunman takes a few gagging breaths and then stops. The faint sound of music drifts up from a house—a female jazz singer. I don't move for five minutes and only hear an owl hooting and something small scratching in the dirt. I go to the body and roll it over.

He could be Oribe's twin. His green T-shirt is printed with the Mexican tour dates for a band called Pesado. Three bullet holes form a neat line up his chest. The fourth wrecked his lower jaw. His clothes are dirty and ragged, the heels on his cowboy boots worn down to nothing. He looks like any day laborer you see on a corner. There's a teardrop tattooed under his right eye.

His pockets hold a cheap cellphone and car keys. No wallet, no ID. I take the phone and keys and walk over to a ridge overlooking the city. No flashing lights to be seen. Most likely no one heard the shots; everyone's behind closed doors staying cool. I think about phoning the cops, but I want the money, and, besides, I'm almost sure Mr. Pesado wasn't trying to kill me for the ransom money. He was promised the money for gunning me down. By Enoch. So now I have a lever to get big money out of Enoch, and I don't want the cops interfering.

Josh, I recall, once told me that killing a man is the easy part—it's getting rid of the body that's a pain in the ass.

Chaparral

"Tom?"

I woke up slowly, my father shaking me gently until my eyes were wide open.

"What?"

"We're going on an adventure, Tom; a big adventure!"

My bedroom curtains weren't closed, and I was surprised to see that it was still dark out.

"Where?" I whispered.

"California."

"Where's Mom?"

"She'll come out later, but we've gotta go right now, get an early start."

Levi hugged me. His touch was jolting, as though an electric charge had passed from his tall, thin body to mine. He'd patted me on the head, even held my hand sometimes, but there'd never been a hug. He still smelled of suntan lotion from our trip to the beach the previous day for a July 4th party. I sensed that something in my world was coming undone.

Levi had our Taurus sedan packed and ready to go. He let me sit in the front seat, which was a rare treat, and as we pulled out of the driveway, I fully expected to see my mother come out and call us back, or at least wave. I was excited, but also felt I was somehow being naughty. We got onto the interstate and I fell asleep listening to Levi talk about the Red Sox, his favorite breeds of dogs, and how only people who've been in the army know what real work is. That was how Levi talked most of the time: zigzagging like a bee from one subject to another to pollinate them with his wisdom. Even at the age of seven I thought it was strange behavior; no other adult I'd ever encountered talked that way. My next memory is of crossing the Mississippi and seeing a string of barges leave a white V of wake against chocolate-colored water as they fought the current.

We'd been living in and around New London, Connecticut, since I was born. I can remember three homes that we lived in, but there were more. Levi had theories about how businesses should be run, and he let the managers and owners where he worked know exactly what they were doing wrong. He'd come home and tell my mother he was only trying to point something out and if that dude isn't interested in success that's his fault and the guy was a fucking moron anyway. And then we'd have to move.

My mother's name was Anne Charlebois. She and Levi weren't married, so I suppose she could have given me her last name but I ended up as Tom Bridger. She was from Brattleboro, Vermont, but her ancestors had come from Quebec. She pronounced her last name the French way, not "Charlie-boys," which is how she said Vermonters like to say it. Her sister would tease her about this when she came to visit. Gail was Anne's only relative and was always urging her to move back to Vermont. Levi would hear this and say that he couldn't leave the ocean. Gail would stare at him for a while and then go back to talking to Mom.

Anne worked at a Stop & Shop grocery store, picking up shifts at all hours and on any day. There may have been family pictures of the three of us, but if there were, Levi didn't bring them out west. Years later I found some high school yearbook pictures of Anne online. She wasn't pretty—I got my looks from Levi—but it could have been that her severe expression muted her attractiveness.

Often, before she went to work, we would sit together outside and talk, and it's those moments that left me with the clearest physical memory of Anne. She had short, short hair that was naturally dirty blonde, but often dyed bright red, or sometimes blue. A band of freckles ran across her nose, and when she smiled, really smiled, I could see that one of her side teeth was missing. She had a tattoo of me as a baby on her right arm, with my birth date, January 14, 1986, done underneath. She liked to tell me about random events that had taken place at work: rude or weird customers, shoplifters, funny things people said or did. She'd ask me about school, try and draw me out, but I'd usually just mumble something boring and wish that I had a story to tell as interesting as hers were. My last sharp memory of her came from our day at the beach on July 4th. I had begged her to come in the water with me, but she told me that she couldn't swim and I'd have to wait for Levi. I remember being bitterly disappointed that I couldn't play with her in the ocean. Years later, as my memory of her faded, I began to think that perhaps I'd only ever seen and talked with my mother on a handful of occasions, and that she was mostly absent from my life. I knew this couldn't be true, but the thought of it still crushed me.

When we were somewhere in Nebraska, eating lunch at a highway service area, Levi told me that Anne had left us. He explained that she'd gone away to start a family with another man and we wouldn't see her again. He said that his was sad, but we should look at it as an opportunity: we were free men now! We could eat and sleep when we wanted to and watch nothing but sports. Then he told me that we were going to be living in the Wild West, in a town called Hexum that was in chaparral country. *Chaparral* was a magical word for Levi. It only describes a type of semi-arid landscape, but to Levi it was redolent with the promise of complete freedom.

After three or four days of driving we got to our new home: a dusty white clapboard bungalow two miles outside of Hexum and up a dirt-track off a secondary road. It was in the middle of a half-acre square of beaten-down dirt mottled with engine oil stains and littered with the sun-faded plastic shards of broken toys. Its windows were milky with discoloration, stalactite-shaped stains ran down the outside walls, and various bits and pieces of it were loose or sagging. The poky interior was beaten up, smelled of cigarettes, and had a variety of furniture that looked as though it had been picked up from the curb. An empty beer bottle left on the kitchen counter was full of dead flies. I hadn't been inside the house more than a minute or two before I began to cry.

The place was a shithole, but Levi had found his chaparral Nirvana. The Sierra Nevada mountains rose twenty miles to the east, and between them and the house was a rippled carpet of sagebrush and stunted oak trees. When we'd first driven up to the house I hadn't taken in the scenery, my anxiety about where we'd be living blinding me to the wilderness all around us. I stared at the mountains and felt choked with questions about what this new world offered, both good and bad. Levi bounced around the property talking dirt bikes, hunting, clean air, room for a pool, no neighbors, and a dozen other things he thought recommended the place.

The chaparral was, indeed, beautiful. It was the one thing Levi got right. Most of the locals found the landscape dull or hostile, but I came to appreciate its tortured trees, the way the sunrises and sunsets played drunkenly with every color, and, most of all, the land's disregard for the horrors that it witnessed. It comforted me to think that the chaparral, unlike the people on it, could never be harmed by the things I saw and did there.

Levi threw himself into fixing up the place. It was the hardest I ever saw him work. He moved us into a motel called the Palomino that had a pool with a slide that kept me entertained while he was away cleaning and repairing the house. He also swapped the Taurus for a used pickup truck. For a week he cleaned the house and the property. Floors and walls were washed down, the moldy carpets and ratty furniture were hauled to the dump and replaced with new, and the area surrounding the house was picked clean of garbage, even the innumerable bottle caps trampled into the dirt that made the ground look like the pebbled skin of a lizard. He did it all himself. Levi never asked me to help. He wanted everything in his new life to be done with his own hands, to be his own creation. I'd roam around while he worked, making tentative forays into the wilderness, scared back to the clearing by sudden movements in the bushes or animal noises.

The first night we moved in, Levi built a campfire out of brushwood. We sat by the fire and speared hot dogs on the ends of sticks and cooked them over the flames.

"When's Mom coming?" I asked.

"I told you, Tom, she's not interested in us. She's gone off on her own. Got a new boyfriend. We'll be okay, though." He reached over and gave me a light, chummy punch on the shoulder. "This is some kind of life we're going to have. All this is ours." He swept his arm around dramatically in a broad gesture that took in the land and the misty, speckled carpet of stars over our heads.

"I want to see Mom."

Levi picked up his bottle of Captain Morgan and added a shot of it to the bottle of Coke he was drinking.

"One of these days, Tommy. I'm sure you'll see her again; you just have to be patient."

The yammering howls of coyotes drifted on the wind from somewhere far away. It was the first time I'd heard them and it froze my blood.

Levi punched the air and shouted, "Yes! That's what I wanted to hear!" He laughed to himself and added, "It's going to be our theme tune."

He picked up the rum bottle and walked to where the chaparral began. I was sure something was going to rush out at him from the jerking shadows thrown on the brush by the firelight.

"A toast to our coyote neighbors," said Levi, and whipped the bottle around in the air, the liquid arcing out in a stream that glittered like gold in the firelight before it flew into the brush.

I woke up the next morning to the sound of Levi talking outside with two men. I came out of the house and saw Levi standing next to a man his own age and a cop in his fifties who was leaning against a police car.

Levi waved me over and said, "Tom, I'd like you to meet my buddy Spencer Jones, and this is Sheriff Reinhart."

Spencer looked at me intently and said, "So, you've got one of these."

Spencer was easy to dislike at first sight. He was lean like Levi, and the same age, but pale and soft-looking, like someone who's been kept immobile and indoors too long. His tall, broad forehead was chasing his receding hairline, and his face, with its small, pinched features, was a bland afterthought. He wore a red Chicago Bulls tank top and matching shorts that hung on him like a pair of flags waiting for a windy day.

Reinhart came over to me, bent down a little, and shook my hand.

"I'm Sheriff Joshua Reinhart, son. You can call me Josh. And you're Tom? Or do you prefer Tommy?"

"Either's fine, either's good," piped Levi.

"I'm asking your son, Levi."

"Tom," I said. "It's Tom."

Levi used to call Reinhart the Marlboro Man, but that was because Levi had no imagination. Reinhart was not handsome. He did wear a cowboy hat and boots, but he was average height and had a pot belly. His tan went right down to his bones, and whenever he took off his hat to wipe his brow, his chalk-white hair was revealed as a kind of mad surprise.

Reinhart went back to leaning on his cruiser—a Suburban wearing a skin of mud and dust—and Levi resumed talking with he and Spencer. I sat on the front steps of the house, watching. I can't recall anything Levi said, but it dawned on me that he wanted to be liked by these men—he was the new kid in school trying to ingratiate himself with the big kids.

Reinhart wasn't paying much attention to Levi, just grunting or nodding when asked something. He scanned his surroundings like a lazy predator until his eyes suddenly locked on something: a snake was heading towards the house, its body leaving faint comma marks in the dirt. Reinhart unholstered his automatic in a motion as smooth as the snake's and fired a shot that exploded its body from a distance of at least thirty feet.

"Jesus fucking Christ, Josh, give a guy a head's up when you fire that cannon!" howled Spencer.

Levi was crouched down, his hands held loosely in front of his face. He was shaking.

Reinhart crossed the yard and kicked the snake's body deep into the bushes.

"It was a rattler," said Reinhart calmly. "You don't want one of those in the yard with Tom."

As Reinhart walked back to his vehicle, he looked my way and nodded appreciatively. I hadn't flinched or cried out at the sight of the snake, or at the sound of the gunshot, and he'd noticed that. It was then that I felt a connection with him, and a muddy feeling that I wanted to be his friend.

Fish

I pick Pesado up by the heels and drag him away from the trail. As his head bounces over the ground, his ruined jaw opens and closes as if he's trying to say something but can't find the right words. After a couple of hundred yards I tip his body over the edge of a ravine that isn't visible to the road or any homes. There's an excellent chance he won't be found. In this heat he'll only stink for a few days before his body becomes an odorless husk, and hikers don't have any reason to stray this far off the trail, or even come out here in these temperatures.

I kick dirt over the most obvious bloodstains and drag marks, and retrieve Pesado's rifle and the spent shell casings. In the parking lot I put the casings down a storm drain, then walk down the road to what I assume is Pesado's pickup and slide the rifle behind the seat. The key fits in the ignition, so it is his. The truck bed holds shovels, a pick, bags of fertilizer, and a five-gallon gas container. I leave the keys in the ignition and prise the licence plates off with a shovel. The gas can's half-full. I pour some on the car seat and ignite it with the lighter I found on the dash, then empty the rest of the can around and under the vehicle. With the truck burnt down to the rims the cops won't be able to lift DNA or prints to lead them to Pesado. Joyriders will get the blame for torching the vehicle. I jog back to the Maserati with the plates and leave.

Traffic is light. Tourists aren't around in August, and the domestics and outside workers are already home. Everyone else is indoors, letting their sweat evaporate in the air conditioning. I stop briefly to dump the licence plates in a trash can outside a mall.

It's nearly ten when I drive up to the house. Most of the interior lights are off and the place looks like an abandoned base on a hostile planet. Enoch's office door is closed and I can hear a play-by-play voice on his TV. He doesn't come out of his office, which means he's too alarmed to face me and is trying to imagine how badly things have gone. He'll probably be sleeping on his couch tonight, if he hasn't already passed out with fear. Autumn's closed her door as well. I go to my room and hide the Beretta under the mattress—I'll have to put it back in the morning—then wander to the kitchen and microwave a frozen dinner of butter chicken and rice, and take it and a beer out to a lounger by the pool. I turn my phone on and see some missed calls from Autumn. A slight wind shivers the water in the pool. A meteor draws a quick white line across the blackness, and farther up a pair of satellites glimmer as they pass behind the mountains.

Pesado's phone rings in my pocket. I wait for the ringing to stop. No message left. A few seconds later a text arrives: DONDE ESTAS? FUE BIEN? Somebody's looking for Pesado, wondering if he got the job done.

A patio door off the living room opens and Autumn steps outside. She's wearing tartan flannel pajamas as protection against the arctic chill of the house; they make her look like a child who's stayed up late. She sits by my side and looks at me without any expression. Her angular face is framed by long, dark red hair that she lifts a hand to adjust as the wind flips it around. She's eight years older than me, but washed in this light from the moon and the stars she looks that much younger.

"I'm sorry," she says.

And before she admits to it, I realize the shooter was hers.

"You really thought Enoch would go out there?"

She shrugs. "He's crazy about that dog."

"Funny, that's what he said about you."

"He gave it to me so I'm supposed to be nuts about it. You know that's how it works with Enoch; he gives me something and I owe him a pleasant emotion." She stretches her arms out as though she wants to hold me but then quickly draws them back, sensitive that Enoch might be watching. "I tried to call you when I realized he'd sent you in his place, but your phone was off." Her eyes grow moist. "I was waiting here expecting to hear from the police, thinking that I'd never see you again, and when you came in I had to get myself calmed down. I was worried Enoch might see me looking like this when I saw you."

I chance a quick squeeze of her hand.

"Why kill Enoch? You told me the will leaves everything to his kids."

"And his foundation."

"He has a foundation?"

She laughs as she dries her eyes. "The American Merit Institute, otherwise known as Greenpeace for billionaires. There's lots of reasons to kill Enoch: when he dies, I get a million for every year we've been married. That's fourteen million."

"Did you get Oribe to arrange the hit?"

"Yes. He said he knew someone who would do it. I was going to pay him 30k."

"A bargain. What was the other reason?"

"For what?"

"Killing Enoch."

"It doesn't matter. Something like Enoch doesn't need to keep living. You know what his death would mean in the end? A shuffling of money; a series of transfers to me, some lawyers, the foundation, and his kids who barely talk to him. No testimonials, no tears, just a ripple of accounting activity."

I walk to the edge of the pool. Insects, drawn by the underwater lights, have landed on the water and oar in circles with their wings, impatiently waiting to drown. I'm sensing that Autumn has another reason for killing Enoch that she's keeping from me.

"What are you going to do about Oribe?" I ask.

"He can't say anything. I'll give him the money anyway. What happened out there?"

"The hitman? He never showed up. Oribe just wanted to rip you off. So where's the dog?"

"I have a friend who has keys to the Malibu house; she picked it up this morning and put him in a kennel."

"Why didn't you ask me to kill Enoch?"

She joins me beside the pool and whispers, "Would you have done it?"

"Maybe. I would have organized it better. The loose ends you and Oribe left would close this case in twenty-four hours."

"So, better luck next time."

"Do it the old-fashioned way: make him eat more and exercise less. He already looks like he's only good for another couple of million to you."

She takes a small step closer to me and says, "I'd give a million to have you sleep with me tonight. I want you in the worst way."

"Tomorrow."

Autumn walks slowly back to the house. The patio door makes a delicate hissing sound as she opens and closes it.

I lie down on the lounger, fold my arms behind my head and stare at the sky. I shouldn't be surprised by Autumn's actions, her ferocity.

She's feral. It's what draws me to her. When she's bitten, she bites back. I can feel that Enoch's world is at a tipping point, about to topple over into utter ruin like an ancient city struck by an earthquake, and I want to be around to pick up the most valuable pieces and guide Autumn out of the wreckage.

I'll sleep here out here tonight, away from the cold of the house. I'm drifting off when a bobcat steps out from behind an ocotillo cactus and moves cautiously towards the pool, then bends down and drinks. It raises its head to snarl silently at me before returning to the desert.

I wake up a few hours later and look towards the house. The living room is lit by a blue glow from the lights in the pool. Autumn, followed by Enoch, strides quickly into the room. Their small, quick gestures tell me that they're arguing. It's like watching two fish in an aquarium dart around with sharp movements of their fins. Autumn suddenly leaves the room in the direction of Enoch's office. Enoch stares after her and shouts something. She returns quickly and raises her hand. She didn't go for something light, like the Beretta, she grabbed one of the big boys, a Glock, by the look of it. I jump up as she fires at Enoch, the muzzle flashes bringing three violent sunrises to the room, the shots audible through the thick, double-glazed windows as muted cracking noises. Enoch drops to the floor.

Autumn places her weapon on a table and comes out to the patio.

"What the fuck did you do that for?" I ask.

She isn't shaken by my question. She isn't shaken by cutting down Enoch.

"Oribe blew everything. He told Enoch weeks ago about my plan. Enoch sent you to die to punish me. He came into my room and told me to get out in the morning. I kind of lost it."

"What are you going to do now?"

"Disappear."

"Your plan's light on details."

"There's still money to be made. You ever hear Enoch talk about the Selous Group?"

"Yeah, once or twice, maybe, when he was on the phone. It sounded like a business thing. Why?"

"It's some investment thing he's part of, but they seem to want to keep their affairs very secret."

"Some kind of insider trading bullshit?"

"Perhaps. Squeezing his partners might be worth a lot. I'll take his laptop; I know he's got information about it there. I guess I should have thought of all this sooner."

"And not put holes in Enoch."

She grins wickedly. "Yes, but I enjoy having no impulse control—it's like having sex with the future."

"And where does that leave me?"

"Give me half an hour before you call the cops."

"Give me an hour and I can make this look like self-defence or an intruder. You're not going to get away with it by running."

"And spend months or years answering questions from cops and lawyers? And maybe end up in jail anyway, despite your best efforts? I don't want to take you down with me, Tom. Tell the cops you woke up to the sound of shots and let them take it from there. Maybe let them think I've been abducted; that should give me enough time to get out of the country. Hey, maybe I'll enjoy being on the run."

She puts her arms around me and we kiss. Time slides to a halt as I fill my mind with memories of the other times we've touched like this.

"I'll let you know when I'm safe," she says before running into the house.

I want to follow her, but instead I pace by the pool, clearing my mind, thinking of a story to build for the cops that will clear her. I hear the garage door open and go to the edge of the patio to get a view of the road. She leaves in the Range Rover, its headlights coning into the darkness and illuminating a confetti storm of flying insects.

The air in the living room is sharp with the smell of cordite. I'll tell the cops I was sleeping, heard the shots, but was too terrified to come out until I heard a car driving away. Enoch is lying on his back beside a black, kidney-shaped coffee table that Autumn paid five figures for in Italy. He's wearing a red bathrobe and dark green boxer shorts. He fits in well with the house's vibrant color scheme. There's a glistening patch of blood on the side of Enoch's head, but no other marks on his body that I can see. She must have put her first round in his head, the others going down the hallway he was standing in front of. I go and retrieve the Beretta from my room. The police will do an inventory of what's in the gun cabinet and I don't want any difficult questions about missing weapons.

On my way back to the office through the living room I find Enoch struggling to his feet, one hand pressed gingerly to his head.

Blood

A few weeks after we had arrived in Hexum, Levi and I were driving through town and passed a schoolyard filled with kids playing outside at recess. The cacophony of their voices and shouts was a Siren's call to me.

"When am I going to school?" I asked.

Levi had been jabbering about chemtrails, and my question silenced him.

He fidgeted, pulled some faces, and then said, "You're going to be home-schooled."

"What's that?"

"*I'll* teach you. You think I can't do a better job than some shit-for-brains government employee? I'll teach you cool stuff."

Levi began my education the next day. He went to the local Goodwill and brought home two bags filled with books. He dumped them out on the floor of my room and waved an arm at the mess as though revealing a shining treasure.

"I asked a woman at Goodwill to help me pick out books for a smart kid."

There were slim novels about talking animals and kid detectives, and thicker, illustrated books about dinosaurs, cars, the human body, and countries I'd never heard of. Some of them smelled of mold.

"You work your way through this pile and then I'll get you some more," said Levi, then left me to it while he watched TV.

That was Levi's home-schooling program. When I was finished with my books, he'd make another trip to Goodwill, sometimes with me along to choose, and more bags of books would come home. The "cool stuff" Levi taught me included changing the oil in our truck and learning the secret to starting a fire by rubbing two sticks together until you get bored and use a lighter.

If I was tired of reading or watching the few TV channels we got, I'd wander into the chaparral. In the daylight I wasn't too scared of the surrounding wilderness. Eventually, I set myself the challenge of going out a little further each day, memorizing landmarks, and daring to investigate the noises and movements made by the local wildlife. I was under the influence of all those kid detective books.

Within a year I could go a mile in any direction without fear of getting lost. I found a coyote den and watched the male bringing limp rabbits back to his family; I knew where mule deer liked to bed down in a narrow, bushy creek bed, their black-edged ears revealing their positions as they twitched away flies; and I explored the devastated interiors of abandoned buildings. One ancient, wooden ranch house, its holey roof letting in brazen pillars of sunlight, hummed loudly with the sound of bees that had built a massive hive in the ruins of the chimney.

If I walked far enough to the south I came to a ridge that stretched out like a root from the Sierra Nevadas to the east. I thought of this point as the limit of my land. From the top of it I could see more miles of chaparral, the road that led past our home, and, half a mile away, a sprawling, one-storey roadside building that was surrounded by parked cars and trucks. A neon sign on top of a phony oil derrick by the road in front of the building read J.J.'s in hot red letters. For no clear reason I felt that this place was an intrusion on my domain.

Discovering Hexum took more time. A sign just outside of town read 'pop. 40,600', and it annoyed me for a long time that it didn't go up by two to account for myself and Levi. Hexum was a place defined by where things used to be. Ask someone directions and they'd say something like, "It's near where the wire factory used to be," or "You know that vacant lot that used to be the bowling alley? It's next to that," or "It used to be a hotel, but now it's a storage locker business." Even the colors of the town were used up and faded. Buildings that had started life as red were now dusty pink, white walls became dirty gray, and other structures seemed to bleed and blend into the sagebrush prairie that surrounded much of the town. Hexum wasn't destitute, but it had aspirations in that direction. The local economy was kept going by a copper mine to the north, a small army base that tested non-combat vehicles, the county government offices, some ranches and farms, and, most importantly, lots and lots of marijuana plots and meth labs.

My childish perspective was very impressed by the width of Hexum's Main St. Levi said it was designed like that back in the old days to allow a team of horses to do a U-turn. That image captivated me until, a few years later, I read a slim volume of local history which revealed that the street had been widened to allow trucks from the mine to barrel through town with their strategic cargo during World War Two. The same book revealed that Hexum took its name from a Swedish prospector who was the first to find gold in the area.

For the longest time Levi would only take me into town on weekends because he was afraid of people asking why I wasn't in school. He needn't have worried; Hexum wasn't a curious place. No one inquired about all the Asian and Latino faces in town, or the cold-eyed white guys who employed them and drove around in SUVs and pickups blinged-out with chrome and extra lights. Hexum knew how to turn a blind eye.

The town and the land were relatively easy to explore and understand. Discovering and knowing Levi was harder.

For the first couple of years, Levi was almost always in a good mood, greeting each day as another express delivery of happiness. He kept busy by buying used cars, fixing them up in the yard and then selling them on. He even built an open-sided garage/carport so he could work out of the sun. On days he wasn't tinkering with a car, he'd take me with him to parts stores or to check out junkers he was thinking of buying. As we drove around he'd take the role of teacher and question me about what I'd learned from the last batch of books I'd read. But that would only hold his interest temporarily. He'd soon be singing along to the radio or yelling insults at the hosts of sports radio shows. It was when Levi was around other people that he unfurled his true colors.

He had two narratives that were the pillars of his existence: his life in the army, and the story of his Bridger ancestors, or his "folks," as he liked to call them. Around friends and acquaintances, or even clerks on the other side of sales counters, Levi would hook stray facts or allusions from the stream of other people's conversations and use them as starting points for his own self-involved chattering. He'd been deployed to Kuwait to repair and refit heavy vehicles during the first Gulf War but never saw action. He was happy, though, to recycle every war story he'd ever heard over there, with himself artfully wedged into the tales as a witness or peripheral participant. When we were alone I'd sometimes ask him for more details about his stories, and he'd casually reveal that he was just repeating something he'd heard. Levi made no effort to lie to me about his service, but it was important to him that the rest of the world thought he'd strutted on the world stage. I eventually became aware that he needed these stories to chock the gaps in his weak and fearful personality. They also gave me early training in the character and technique of his lies.

If Levi's time in the military was a winning poker hand he liked to flash, his ancestry was the castle he retreated into when the world was against him. It was his last redoubt against criticism or his own sense of failure, and he pulled up the drawbridge more often as he got older. He claimed to be a descendent of Ezra Bridger, one of the first settlers of Massachusetts. The subsequent Bridgers became mill owners, politicians, judges, land barons, and proudly saw their name attached to landmarks across New England. Levi said his Bridger blood made him a "true" American, and when he felt he'd been taken advantage of, slighted, or ignored, he'd come up with a reason to do a roll call of famous Bridgers. It comforted him to think that his DNA had a high historical credit rating.

It took me several years to piece together the bare facts of what had brought us to Hexum. Levi had inherited three hundred thousand dollars from his last living grandparent, which more than paid for our house and its 600 acres. It was Spencer, whom he'd known in the army, who had persuaded him to come out west. Spencer was from Hexum, and after his discharge he convinced Levi there were a lot of opportunities available in the area.

I was ten when I saw opportunity come knocking for Levi. He'd been letting his car business slip away recently, preferring to spend his time on the couch watching TV and complaining about money. One day he said he was going to do some work for Spencer and would be away for a while.

I was out in the yard and he was sitting on the front steps smoking a joint, cocking his ear every time he heard a car go by on the highway. The sun was lowering, and a wind coming down from the mountains was teasing little dust devils out of the ground. I crouched by a pile of bald tires that Levi had let accumulate on the edge of the yard and studied a coachwhip snake that had its jaws locked on the head of a small lizard. Neither animal moved. I figured both of them were too frightened of me to conclude their drama.

A crew cab pickup barreled into the yard, Eminem blasting from its stereo. Spencer was driving. He was wearing San Jose Sharks gear this time. I had never seen him not decked out in bright colors and logos.

"Let's go, Levi," shouted Spencer, then turned to stare at me, as he usually did, with a look of mild fascination.

In the seat next to Spencer was a man in his forties wearing a faded plaid shirt and mirrored sunglasses. His hair was steel gray and capped a face that tapered severely to a sharp, protruding chin. His sunglasses, I thought, made him look like an alien, and when he whipped them off to watch Levi getting off the steps, he revealed hooded blue eyes that didn't give a shit about anything. This was my first look at Jubal Jones, Spencer's uncle and the owner of J.J.'s.

Jubal pointed at me and said, "What are you doing with the kid, Levi?"

"Tom's okay on his own." Levi came over and kneeled beside me. "You'll be alright, buddy, isn't that so?"

I could see Levi was scared, so I nodded and smiled.

"Yeah, he'll be fine, Jubal," said Levi, who squeezed my arm and then hurried into the truck, shouting over his shoulder that I should go to bed at my regular time.

Levi wasn't worried about me being alone. He'd been wandering off into town on his own for months, sometimes until late at night, and he didn't worry about me when I went trekking for hours in the chaparral. He was unsure about being with Jubal and Spencer.

He returned some time after I fell asleep, and when I got up the next morning I found a fist-sized wad of $20 bills, tightly bound with elastic, on the kitchen table. I didn't touch it, but I couldn't stop staring at it as I ate my cereal. I put away my dishes, started a pot of coffee, and then went to Levi's bedroom and gave him a poke.

"There's a big bunch of money on the table."

Levi opened one eye, yawned like a lion, and said, "There sure as hell is. Did you start the coffee?"

"Yup."

"Thought so."

He swung his feet to the floor, gave himself a shake, and headed straight for the coffeemaker. He whistled tunelessly as he filled his cup and dosed it with a ton of sugar.

"So what did you do last night?" I asked.

Levi sat at the table and pretended not to look at the money. "Did some driving."

"Where to?"

"San Francisco."

"That's a long way, isn't it?"

"Yup."

"And that's what you got paid?"

"Uh huh."

"How much is it? Is it a lot?"

"It's a lot, but it's not easy money. It's like every other dollar I've ever made; there's blood and sweat in it. People used to tell me that working on trucks and Humvees didn't make me a soldier, that I was only a mechanic in camo, but the army's just a big goddamn machine from back end to pointy end, and each piece has to work hard and true for the whole thing to stay together. I've earned my money better than most people."

"Who was that guy with Spencer?"

"Jubal. He's Spencer's uncle."

"His face is shaped like a slice of pie."

Levi spit out his coffee laughing.

Once or twice a week for the next few months, Levi would take off in the evening with Spencer, sometimes other guys, and leave me to my own devices. He'd come back in the middle of the night, a few times not until the next morning. Each trip produced a wad of cash. Once he'd collected enough of those wads he got himself a brand new F-150. It was red with chrome running boards and a light bar over the cab. The day after he got the truck we drove over to J.J.'s to show it to Jubal and Spencer.

J.J.'s had originally been a motel built in the fifties. I once saw an old postcard picture of it when it had been called the High Country Motel. Where the oil derrick stood had been a tall neon sign of a smiling cowboy and cowgirl, their hands holding up a rectangular section of the sign bearing the motel's name. Jubal had bought the place when it was derelict, painted it black, and turned it into a bar. Over the years, random, boxy extensions were added to the building until from above it looked like a game of dominoes. The outside was windowless and decorated with neon beer company signs.

Levi came out of J.J.'s with Jubal and Spencer in tow. Even at a distance I could tell they didn't give a shit about Levi's new truck—the parking lot was full of similar vehicles. They glanced at the truck and started talking about some upcoming jobs. I was reading *The Mysterious*

Island and wasn't paying attention to what the three were saying until I heard my name. I looked up and saw Levi motion towards me and caught him saying to Jubal, "...shaped like a piece of pie."

Levi's barking laugh was very lonely. Jubal's hooded stare went from Levi to me. Spencer grinned. Levi cleared his throat as if he was about to say something else but was sent to his knees by Jubal head-butting him in the face. Blood poured from his nose, turning his white T-shirt into a Halloween costume.

Spencer giggled and lit a cigarette.

Jubal came to my side of the truck, reached through the window, grabbed a fistful of my hair and held my face horribly close to his.

"Your old man," said Jubal, "is a fucking moron. He repeated something that disrespects me. But you're the cunt who said it. Consider yourself lucky I don't beat up kids, even ugly little faggots like you. He's taking your punishment for you now, but when I see fit, I'll give you what he just got."

Jubal kept holding my head. Out of the corner of my eye I could see Spencer. He sighed and looked at his watch, a cartoonishly large thing with a jeweled wristband. I relaxed in that moment. Spencer knew nothing more was going to happen, and I realized Jubal was putting on a show for me. I imagined I was looking down on the scene from high above, and suddenly it all looked absurd: Levi on the ground moaning; Spencer in his long, baggy Oakland Raiders shorts and T; and Jubal doing an angry act while holding the hair of a kid.

I smiled at Jubal and he pushed my head away with a disgusted sound.

"Your kid's as goddamn witless as you are, Levi."

Jubal walked back to the bar.

Spencer stared at Levi for a moment and then said, "I'll pick you up at the usual time."

He sauntered over to his truck, cranked the stereo and drove off.

Levi looked at me helplessly, his blood-splattered hands held out in front of him.

"I can't get blood in the truck," he whined.

"I'll drive. You get in the back."

He stared at me wide-eyed as fat, crimson drips fell from his nose, and said, "Give me your T-shirt."

I took it off and tossed it to him as I got out to lower the tailgate. Levi had let me drive off-road as soon as I could reach the pedals, and our place was only a few miles away. He wrapped his hands in my shirt and pressed it against his face as he climbed onto the truck and lay on his back.

"Don't bounce me around. Take it slow."

I drove us home without bouncing.

I lowered the tailgate and he went into the house without saying anything. I sat on the steps, wondering if it was better if I went in or waited until Levi came out. I didn't think he'd want me to see him cleaning himself up, so I stayed outside. A hawk surfed the thermals low over the house, its tawny head and black pearl eyes taking the measure of the world below. I watched it until it was out of sight and then went inside.

Levi was sitting on the couch holding a paper towel to his nose, pretending to be concentrating on a baseball game on TV.

"You okay?" I asked.

He didn't even turn towards me.

I went to my room and poked around in a pile of *National Geographic* magazines. Levi came along a few minutes later. His breathing was rapid and he wasn't making eye contact with me. I was sitting on the edge of the bed and didn't move, even though I sensed what was up. He slapped me hard across the side of the head. He'd never really hit me before, just a swat every now and then, and he appeared unsure of how to follow-up this initial clout. After some hesitation, and despite my cries, he tried out a variety of other blows to my head and body. His technique would improve rapidly over time.

Standard Station

I slip the Beretta into a pocket before I help Enoch off the floor and dump him on the couch. His eyes are unfocused and he's making grunting noises of pain that sound like a small animal calling for its mother. There's a blood stain and some hairs on the edge of the table. He must have fainted or thrown himself backwards at the sound of the first shot and clipped the edge of the table on the way down.

"Are you okay?" I ask.

"Where's Autumn?"

"Gone. I was asleep in my room. By the time I got out here she was already driving away."

"Get me a drink. A scotch."

"No. You're concussed. You'll have some water, some ice for your head, and then we'll get you to the hospital. Should I phone the cops?"

He won't say yes; he doesn't know what went down on the Broken Rock Trail, so cops asking me questions is too risky for him. I need to make him think I'm on his team if I'm going to clean up this mess for Autumn and come out with a profit.

"You'd phone the police on her?"

"I heard shots. I don't know what happened here, but I'd say the police would want to know about it. What did happen?"

He's confused and nervous, and I can see in his eyes that he's trying to stitch together what the night's events mean and how they'll warp his future. He makes a fist and pounds it into his palm.

"No," he says. "I need some time to think."

"Okay."

I go to the kitchen and get him some water and put ice cubes in a Ziploc bag for his head. When I come back to the living room he's sitting up on the couch, trying hard to look composed. I put the glass of water and ice bag on the table and slide them over to him. He sips the water as though he's afraid it's going to burn his lips and puts the bag against his head, but only holds it there for a few seconds before putting it down. He doesn't want to acknowledge the injury.

"So?" I ask.

"Autumn and I had a fight."

"Yes, the gunshots were a giveaway."

"She's a dangerous bitch."

"But not usually armed and dangerous. Take it from the top."

He stalls for time by drinking water and using the ice bag again. Suspects I had in Grange County would fidget like this as they frantically engineered alibis and explanations in their heads.

"Oribe phoned me tonight, after you'd got back, and said Autumn had asked him to hire someone to kill me when I dropped off that money for the dog."

"Really. So he had a sudden crisis of conscience?"

"He was doing it because of Maria. Autumn said she'd report her to ICE if he didn't do it. She also promised him some money. He never did anything about it. You didn't have any problems dropping off the money, did you?"

"No. So the business with the dog was a pretext to get you out there."

"Right, right," said Enoch, with exactly the note of happiness in his voice that perps use when they think you're buying their bullshit.

"But why would Oribe phone you and admit to this?"

"He wanted my help in trapping Autumn. He wanted to know how he should go about recording her when he told her he hadn't gone through with the plan. He figured he could get her to admit to planning my murder."

Enoch is leaning forward, his eyes wide and pleading, hands waving, trying his hardest to sell his story—he's a desperate stand-up comedian trying to win over a reluctant audience with nothing but manic energy.

"I couldn't believe Oribe's story," continues Enoch, "so I went and woke Autumn up and told her what he said. She admitted it all, and then she just went off the deep end, screaming and yelling, none of it made sense. Then she went into my office and came out with a gun, and that's the last I remember."

I want to laugh at him. He gave everything away when he didn't come out of his room when I returned earlier. He should have been anxious to see what had happened, but instead he crouched in his office, panicking over how badly things might have come unstuck, and whether I had figured out that he was behind the shooter.

"Should we call the police?" I ask for the second time, pressuring him to say no before he's had time to think things through.

He runs his hand through his thick grey hair and inadvertently leaves a bloody red stripe through it. He hasn't had a chance to think through this part and he's looking desperate.

I decide to nudge him along: "The cops won't be happy you didn't call them right away after Oribe told you what Autumn had planned. And they'll come down really hard on Oribe, ask him why he went to you instead of them."

He clearly doesn't like the thought of Oribe being asked tough questions.

"Also," I continue, "it's going to be tough to prove Autumn did anything. It's your word against hers. All we've got here are some bullet holes in the walls. Autumn can say she fled the house because you were shooting at her and she fled for her life."

Enoch looks alarmed as he realizes Autumn could already be two steps ahead him, maybe talking to the cops right now.

"That's ridiculous," he bleats. "Look at me, I'm injured. And why would she run away if she didn't think she'd killed me?"

"Maybe she checked you over after she fired, saw you were okay and decided to play things differently. She could tell the cops she knocked you down as she ran for the car, pushed you out of the way to save her life and you hit your head. That's not a bullet wound you've got."

I point to the blood-stained edge of the table in front of him. He raises the ice bag to his head and sits quietly. I go into the kitchen and get myself a can of soda, leaving Enoch some time and space to sift through his options and see that he has none.

"What should I do?" he asks plaintively when I return.

Enoch knows he has no control over the situation. He sees me as a beacon to guide him out of the darkness, and I will, but along the way I'll bleed a rich future for myself and Autumn.

"You have to decide what you want to do about Autumn." I look at my watch. "At this point we can assume she hasn't contacted the law—they'd be here by now—but that could change. Do you want her found?"

Enoch puts the ice bag to his head and leans back on the couch. "I have to think."

I go to the far side of the room and look out the window at the valley. There's a thin red streak on the eastern horizon and the lights of a small plane descend towards Palm Springs Airport. I have to get in touch with Autumn. She doesn't need to run, but I don't think she'll want to stop now that she's started.

"Why did she want to kill me?" asks Enoch, but I'm not sure if he's asking himself or me.

"It's usually money, isn't it?"

"She has money. She has all this. You see that painting?"

He points at a wall which is almost entirely taken up with an enormous painting of a gas station at night, the old-fashioned kind, from the fifties or sixties. The painting is all diagonal lines and sharp wedges of red and black and white. It's like an architect's abstract drawing or a geometry puzzle—count how many triangles you can see. Autumn told me it's called *Standard Station,* and often says it's the only thing that makes living in the house tolerable. I asked her what she meant by that and she said, "The painting is screaming so I don't have to."

"That thing," shouts Enoch, "cost me over two goddamn million!"

"You're rich. She does what rich people do: buy rare and beautiful things, own houses, waste money. Enoch, you have to think about what you're going to do next, not what Autumn bought on your dime. Do you want to hear how I see things?"

He nods and burrows into his bathrobe. The adrenaline is wearing off and he's looking tired and very, very old.

"Once Autumn realizes you're not dead, she's probably going to position herself to take you to the cleaners in court."

"I have a pre-nup. It's watertight."

"Not divorce court, civil court. She could bring a charge of attempted murder against you. It wouldn't stand up in trial court, but in civil court? Much lower standard of proof, and odds are a jury will be happy to trim the fat from someone like you. And she might get Oribe to say you ordered the hit on me in return for a piece of the action. We should get hold of Autumn as soon as possible and offer her a deal, a financial settlement in return for which she signs an agreement to give you an uncontested divorce and never bring any civil suits against you. But it'll take a big number."

"Give her money? No fucking way."

"Your choice: some money or a lot of publicity. Do you want that scrutiny? Do your businesses need that attention? Does Autumn know anything about you, business or personal, that she could use against you?"

He stares at me, his face mournful and slack. His body's a declining asset and he's built a gleaming carapace for it of homes and cars to hide the soft, decrepit flesh within. Autumn, the young, beautiful wife, was supposed to be the glue that held it all together by giving soul and charm to this collection of shiny objects from the billionaires' gift catalogue. And now that she's gone, Enoch's a hermit crab that's lost its shell, scuttling around to find another haven.

Enoch smiles and says, "Can I trust you, Tom?"

His smile sits awkwardly on him, like a child's first attempt at drawing a face. Enoch only smiles when he wants to take something; it's why I clean him out at poker.

"Of course, Enoch."

"I do love her, Tom," he says, and puts on a hangdog expression that's meant to convey sincerity, but only makes him look nauseous. "I don't show it in the usual ways, but look at what I surround her with." He waves his hand at the art and the furniture and the view and the square footage, and maybe all of America. "I gave her an environment that tells her how I feel. She's walked and breathed and swum in the best, the choicest, ever since she met me. I've given Autumn heaven, the only real heaven there is. Her life is the best it will ever be and I created it for her, all of it, and she didn't have to do a thing. And then she just throws it all away. No one walks away from paradise."

"You have to come to an accommodation with Autumn. Things aren't going back to normal. If you don't want the world to hear about this and end up in court, you need to let me find her and broker a deal."

Enoch stares at his hands and makes fists with them like he's doing some kind of isometric exercise, then stares at me with the cold, emotionless intensity that's the sum of his personality and asks, "What's in this for you?"

He's far from stupid, but well short of clever. Enoch's world is a binary construction divided between wants and needs on one side and suppliers on the other. Everything else is a howling void. He can't see or believe that my need to be paid by him, to be in his good books, could be outweighed by a relationship with Autumn.

"Whatever the payout to Autumn is, I get ten percent of it on top. In cash."

"Your math is fucking aggressive."

I go and stand in front of *Standard Station* to remind him that if he has the right motivation, he's not shy about dropping seven figure sums on something he doesn't like.

"If you don't want that deal," I say, "I'm walking out of here right now. You clean up the mess. You'll have to start by coming up with a story for the bullet holes Autumn left in the walls. Maybe it would be more profitable to find Autumn and work for her. I can corroborate any story she dreams up for the right fee."

Enoch frowns, but I can tell he appreciates this kind of reasoning.

"And why are you the best broker for this job?" he asks sharply.

I sit across from him and put my feet up on the table that cost the same as a car, and say, "Because you know where I came from, what I used to do. If Autumn's difficult or too demanding, I can persuade her in ways no lawyer can."

Enoch thinks about it a bit before a crippled, traitorous smile staggers onto his face. "Okay. You find her and talk to her. Find out what she wants, and if it's a deal I can live with, you get your ten percent."

He's probably counting on screwing me over, keeping me busy and on his side while he works on a plan that costs him less or nothing at all.

"Good," I say. "Now let's get your head looked at by a doctor. You might need stitches."

Enoch grunts his assent, says something about getting showered and changed, and heads to his bedroom. I text Autumn: ENOCH HAD A FALL BUT HE'S FEELING FINE NOW. TAKING HIM TO THE LA QUINTA CLINIC FOR STITCHES. There's no answer.

From where Autumn was shooting, the bullets would have travelled down a hallway that leads to the guest bedrooms. I find two of the slugs buried in a teak table that sits in the hall. The other bullet went through an open door into a bedroom, passed through a mattress and buried itself in the box spring. Throwing out some furniture will sterilize the crime scene. I go to put the Beretta back in the gun cabinet but then decide not to. There's a better place for it.

Enoch has changed into khaki cargo shorts and a salmon-colored polo shirt; he wants his clothes to say that he's relaxed and that it's business as usual. On the way to the garage he ducks into his office and then swears. I look in and see him staring at his desk.

"She took my laptop," he hisses.

He's even paler now, and his hands shake a little.

"All the more reason to find her quickly. Let's go."

He leaves the room looking fearful. Some bodies must be buried in that laptop, and now that Autumn has it, Enoch will be all the more pliable and generous.

We take the Yukon and I tell him we'll go to the La Quinta Clinic, a 24-hour medical facility for people who can afford to not even bother with health insurance. During the Coachella festival it does big business in trust fund kids who've OD'ed on drugs and sun and booze.

I wave at the guard inside the gatehouse at the entrance to Bighorn and pull out onto the highway as the sun clears the horizon to begin another day of punishment. A Rancho Vista cop car goes past and I glance in the mirror to see it make a U-turn and catch up with us. Its lights come on and there's a single whoop from its siren.

"What the fuck?" says Enoch.

As I pull over and stop I say, "Be calm, be friendly, stick with the story about falling over, and don't talk too much."

Two cops get out of the patrol car, one coming to my window, the other to Enoch's. The Beretta tucked into the back of my pants feels cold and heavy. I power down the windows. The cop at my window is young, Asian, and looks at me with a mix of curiosity and amusement, like this is going to be an odd and fun start to his shift. CHUNG is printed on his name tag. The cop at Enoch's window is a white guy in his forties with a goatee and an old scar across his ear that looks like it was done with a thin blade. His embossed name tag reads HACKETT. He looks concerned.

"Was I speeding, officer?" I ask Chung.

He looks across at his partner.

"Mr. Marsden, isn't it?" asks Hackett.

"Yes?"

"I'd like to talk to you about your wife."

Game Boy

By the time I passed my twelfth birthday, I knew that Levi was a coward. What was worse, for Levi, was that he had the pathetic bravery of the pure coward; he was so terrified of standing up to Spencer and Jubal, so afraid of facing their wrath and scorn, he let them put him in the most dangerous and ugly situations. I suppose Spencer had spotted Levi as a malleable fool as far back as their time in Kuwait, and once he got him on his own turf he trained Levi up to be a service animal for himself and Jubal.

Levi was now almost always out on some errand for one or both of the Jones'. When he was home he'd curl up on the couch with a blunt or a succession of Jack Daniel's and Cokes. I'd learned that if he hit the booze it was time for me to find something to do outside, or face the chance that he'd want to belt me around. The beatings had turned into an awkward, spastic dance with rules we both followed. Levi would begin by accusing me of insulting or disrespecting him. Sometimes his opinion that I was ignoring him was reason enough to launch an attack. The rules of the dance were simple: I could parry his kicks and punches as long I let some through and made convincing noises of pain and anguish. As for him, he would only keep up the hurting until I fell to the floor. That was the ceasefire signal. So was blood. If I dropped too early he'd add some stomping to the mix, and that really hurt, so I tried to time my falls carefully. Levi had a set number of calories he had to burn during these sessions, and it was my job to gauge when he'd reached the minimum required.

It was when Levi was stoned that I learned about the world he worked in and cowered from. Half to himself and half to me, his lap covered in bits of weed from his badly-rolled joints, he would dissect and rehash the events that made him smoke and drink. And as time went on, instead of just listening to his bitter ramblings, I'd gently tease more information out of him.

Jubal was, as Levi liked to describe it, the FedEx of the local drug business. He didn't operate grow ops or meth labs, but his crew moved the stuff to market for Grange County's producers. That was the meat of the business. He also had a hand in moving illegal immigrants, as well as running the local brothels. Jubal was the boss, end of story. Spencer was number two, and under him were Levi and a rotating collection of guys, maybe three dozen in all, who did the deliveries of dope and illegals.

Jubal was the all-powerful and fearsome deity of his business, but he was a god whom Levi loathed and feared. He showered Levi with money—tightly wrapped wads of twenties, sometimes hundreds—but demanded sacrifices of Levi's thin supply of nerve and daring. There were the hours on the road dreading the sight of flashing lights in the rear view mirror, and the clammy terror of a drop-off that might become an ambush. And when Jubal's business was impaired or trespassed upon, his anger had to be appeased with blood.

One morning in late July I got up and heard Levi talking in a low voice outside. I peeked through the door and saw him lying on the bed of his truck, a ribbon of smoke rising up from the joint in his hand. He was talking to himself, a droning mutter that was only interrupted when he'd take a long puff.

"Did you sleep out there last night?" I asked from the doorway.

"Yeah. Didn't want a roof over my head." His voice was slow and thick, as though each word weighed a pound and had to be expelled by force. He was wasted to his core.

"How come?"

"That's what I felt like." He paused for a toke. "Spence thinks I'm not up for anything he asks, but what he doesn't realize is that I…I like to think things through. I did it, and it was done the way it should have been done," said Levi,

"What'd Spencer want you to do?"

"They needed to be hurt. That was what he told me. But you have to look big picture. What are you trying to accomplish?" Levi sat up a little, stared at me as though trying to identify my face, and then beat one fist into his chest. "I did it. I hurt them. I'll get my hands dirty. My people have never been afraid of kicking ass. You know we got an island named after us because we fought well? Cleared out the whole island, hundred and hundreds of years ago. Bridger fucking Island, it's right there on the map. And that slug Spencer gives me shit because I try and use some strategic thinking. He's…"

Levi never finished his ricocheting thoughts about Spencer. He curled up on his side and nodded off.

The pattern was simple: after Levi had done or seen something nasty he started smoking. When he knew Jubal or Spencer had something savage or risky on the menu, he hit the bottle. And sometimes me. I had begun to regard Levi solely as a problem that needed to be managed. He was a car that needs constant maintenance just to run badly. When he was drunk I was living in a minefield, and when he was stoned I had to manage meals, cleaning, and badger him to do chores that were beyond me. My feelings toward him were neutral; there was no affection, and no hate. He was a condition of my existence.

Levi could be funny, generous, and from time to time he made an effort to be a parent. If he was feeling flush and relaxed, we'd hop in the truck and spend a couple of days at Disneyland. And he was a maniac about keeping me supplied with books for my "home schooling." It was his way of proving that he was a caring and involved parent. He wouldn't read a book himself if he was paid to, but his guilt over not putting me in school, or perhaps his fear that an ignorant child would draw attention, goaded him into making me acquire and read books. But the books, gifts, and trips were just things Levi saw as the minimum necessary to keep things stable. I was a pet that's grown into a task or a burden, but still needs to be fed and watered and exercised. And, of course, I was a Bridger. He often told me I'd be carrying the Bridger name into future, but he wasn't clear on what I was supposed to do with it.

What Levi wanted from life was to have all his time to be his own. Time spent on caring for me was a grave imposition on him. When he wasn't out working for Jubal he watched TV and thumbed through automotive, gun, and DIY magazines he bought by the dozen. He'd sometimes pause in his reading and tell me about grand plans he had for our land: a one-acre pond stocked with largemouth bass; a shooting range with exotic weapons for rent; a dirt-bike track that people would pay for by the lap; or perhaps a ranch stocked with game animals for fancy restaurants in San Francisco. He was sure his pocket kingdom could be a goldmine, if only he could come up with the right plan from his couch. Sometimes, if he was mellow enough, I'd ask Levi why he didn't do something else, like go back to his car business. He always answered by patting the pocket he kept his wallet in.

I left Levi lying in the truck and had breakfast. He was still there when I came outside and went for a ride on my dirt bike. Levi had splurged for it on my last birthday. It allowed me to venture out for miles in all directions, although I was under strict orders from him not to go near town. His fear of discovery had seeped into me, and I willingly kept away from Hexum. By this point I was aware that Levi didn't want me known to the kind of institutions that keep records. I didn't know why that was bad, but I worried that it would result in me being taken away. And as shitty a parent as Levi was, I couldn't face having no one at all.

When I returned a few hours later, Levi was waiting for me outside, pacing the yard and taking sips from a vodka cooler. His hair was wet from the shower and he'd changed his clothes. He didn't seem drunk yet, but I still gave him a wide berth as I headed to the house.

"Get in the truck," Levi said suddenly.

Something felt very off about his tone and abruptness. He was scared. It was only working for Jubal that frightened him, so why was he taking me along?

We drove right through town and a few miles beyond to where Main St. hooked up with the interstate. A plaza with large and small chain stores, and a scattering of motels and restaurants clustered at the junction like trees growing around a desert spring. The area was called Mission Commons, and we drove out there at least once a week to shop or eat.

"Are we going to Denny's?" I asked hopefully. I was obsessed with trying everything on their menu at least once.

"No," said Levi, and took a last sip from his cooler bottle before pitching it out the window.

We went a couple of miles further to a big, brick box of a building sitting in a parking lot that was furrowed with cracks and dotted with slag heaps of dumped trash. Dangling wires and rusted bulb housings vomited from the top of shattered and vandalized light poles. It was, rumor had it, a Wal-Mart that had been built but never opened. Some said it was because the population of the town had dropped too low, others thought it was because the company suddenly realized they'd be selling a lot of merchandise to equip and defend drug operations, and they decided that there was probably bad publicity in that.

Levi drove around to the back of the building. The rear wall was mostly gone, and viewed from the back, the structure looked like an aircraft hangar. People had busted down the wall to haul out scrap metal, and now the building was a dark cavern, its mouth guarded by a berm of broken bricks.

Reinhart's cruiser was parked at the back, as well as a Hummer I didn't recognize as belonging to any of Levi's acquaintances. Levi stopped the car behind Reinhart's and got out. He looked at me for a moment as though trying to make up his mind. I was queasy with the kind of feeling that comes with the anticipation before the big drop on a rollercoaster.

"You come, too," said Levi.

"What for?"

"Just come!" he barked.

We climbed over the pile of bricks, the cave black as night to us as we stood outside in the sun. I didn't want to go in there. Levi didn't notice me lag behind and walked ahead into the darkness.

"Let's go," he called, his voice echoing inside the building.

I stumbled over the bricks and into the gloomy cavern. A hundred feet inside the building, Levi was standing with Reinhart and Spencer, and slightly apart from another man I didn't recognize who was sitting on a pile of wooden pallets, his legs crossed under him and his hugely bearded face illuminated by the Game Boy he was playing. I drew closer and kept my eyes on him. Spencer fixed his curious eyes on me. The bearded man was grunting as he focused his entire attention on playing with his console. Swallows were arcing in and out of the building to their nests built onto the ceiling, their metallic chirps echoing and re-echoing. The air smelled of burnt plastic and piss.

The bearded guy looked up from his game and said, "Who's the midget dude?"

He thought that was funny and laughed as he hopped off the pallets. He was wearing bib overalls and a pair of Timberlands. It didn't look like he did any kind of work in them. He was young, mid-twenties, and the way he moved over to the other men announced that he felt in charge of the situation.

"It's my son," said Levi.

"Why's he here?"

"I dunno. He always comes along with me."

"I dunno, I dunno," mocked the stranger. "Like you didn't know what the fucking hell you were doing last night? Like that?" He turned to Spencer. "Listen, Spence, if you want shit stains like this working for you that's your goddamn business, but don't send them out on jobs I hire you for. You and Jubal running a halfway house for retards or something?"

Spencer straightened up from his usual slouch. "You got what you wanted, Mickey, so I don't know why we're having this meet. Money paid, job done."

"Bullshit, man, bullshit. I wanted those gooks' asses kicked, not put in the fucking hospital. Now the rest of those yellow rats are pissed and scared and working like shit. Two of them skipped town and the others might go all Vietcong and stick me in the back if they get the chance. Who's gonna be making my stuff if they all leave? And all because you went and hired some bum buddy from your army days."

Spencer gave Mickey a hard shove and Reinhart shouted, "Hey!"

We all looked at Reinhart, who slowly and emphatically dropped a hand on his sidearm and said, "I'm policing this meet, boys, so we'll keep it Robert's Rules of Order all the way. I'm guessing you've never heard of that, so I'll keep it simple for you: next person to make it physical gets a big dose of hurt."

Mickey laughed and stroked his rust-colored beard. "Sure, Josh. No fucking problem."

"It's Sheriff Reinhart to you, Mickey, always and forever."

Mickey switched his gaze to Spencer and said, "You know what I asked for—a few guys skimming a little doesn't call for what your guy did."

"So what do you want, a refund? Did you save your receipt?"

Mickey pulled a small digital camera out of his pocket and held it up like a prize. "Keep your money. I want this guy's face fucked up to show to my little worker bees; it'll make them happy knowing their boss is standing up for them. It doesn't have to be permanent, just messy."

Levi looked at me pleadingly and I understood why he'd brought me along: I was his shield. He'd figured he was in trouble and thought his punishment would be lighter if his little kid was there to elicit sympathy. He didn't say anything to Mickey or Spencer, he just gawped at me as though expecting me to intercede or weep and thereby save the situation.

"No fucking way, Mick," said Spencer.

Levi grinned feebly.

"Okay," said Mickey. "How much business do I do with you and Jubal? What's that worth to you? My people in Oakland would already prefer I work with their bikers, but I told them these locals are good, they're trustworthy. This isn't about money, Spencer. I need to see some commitment to me from you. You want me to be a satisfied customer, you gotta clip my loyalty card, man." Mickey looked from Spencer to Reinhart. "You want bikers on your turf, Sheriff? They don't get along great with the law."

I was willing Levi to say something, to find some word or gesture that would derail Mickey. Spencer and Reinhart said nothing. Mickey studied their faces with a smile on his lips. As I watched the three men deciding Levi's fate they suddenly reminded me of a kids' picture book I'd once had; it had been about professions or jobs, and one illustration had shown a lineup of men, each in clothes that accorded with their calling: fireman, doctor, and so on. And, like the picture, here was Mickey in his faux workman gear, Spencer in bright orange athletic gear, and Reinhart in his crisp uniform. Levi was the odd one out. His faded jeans, dusty Converse sneakers and wrinkled yellow T-shirt marked him out as nothing at all. He was the man standing to one side of the illustration who was left to ponder what career should be his.

Spencer stared appraisingly at Levi before saying, "You did fuck up, Levi."

Mickey faced Levi and said, "It won't be anything drastic, dude. Nothing life-changing. Just...showy."

Levi finally found his voice: "No, Spence. How about showing some fucking loyalty to me?"

Spencer smirked, which was always a sign things weren't going well for someone. "I'm loyal when people don't put me in the shit, Levi."

Levi turned to Reinhart, his arms extended, palms up in supplication. "This isn't fair, Josh. And my kid's here, I mean..."

I could see Reinhart didn't like the weakness in Levi's voice and words.

"Levi," he said, "it's not my decision, but I'll see everything's done fair."

Levi gasped slightly, and I think it was that sound, that audible sign of fear that decided Spencer. "Alright. Levi takes a beating from you and Josh decides when he's had enough."

Mickey gave Spencer a thumbs-up and took a pair of leather work gloves—as pristine as the rest of his outfit—out of a back pocket and began putting them on. No one moved. We just watched him handle the gloves. Everything had happened too fast for me. I felt like I'd turned on a TV during the climax of a movie. I needed time to sort out what was happening. Levi stared at Spencer as if expecting him to say it was a joke or a test.

"Just wait," said Reinhart, "I'll take Tom out to the car."

It was then I knew that it was all going to happen exactly as that bearded prick wanted it to go down, and I also knew that Levi would be broken by it—what they were about to do to him would come crashing down on me tenfold. Levi would either become a greater tormentor or so crippled with dope and booze he'd slide gently off the side of the Earth. I'd be alone.

I walked towards Reinhart like an obedient and scared child. Mickey was wiggling his fingers in his gloves. Levi stared at the ground. I looked down and saw bits of broken brick and a short length of steel pipe. I scooped up the pipe, held it in both hands and took a baseball swing at Mickey. I missed, and he hopped back with a panicky yelp and fell against the pallets. He tried to block my second swing with his forearm but he was in an awkward position on his back and his arm wasn't in time to slow the pipe before it connected with the side of his head above the ear. He made a sound like water going down a drain, and his legs started to writhe as if he was pedaling an imaginary bicycle. His arms went stiff at his sides, and he blinked in slow motion as a bit of drool started to come out of his mouth.

"Fuck," said Spencer.

"Fuck," said Levi.

"Oh, my," said Reinhart.

Mickey's eyes showed mostly white and he wet his pants.

Reinhart stepped forward and took a closer look at Mickey, being careful to step around his pumping legs.

"He's not coming back from this, men," said Reinhart. "You two get to clean up this mess. I'll take the boy home."

Reinhart put a gentle hand on my shoulder and led me out of the building. Spencer was cursing. Levi said nothing. I didn't look back at them, and when I got in the cruiser I began to shake. As we drove through the parking lot, I asked Reinhart to stop so I could throw up. I heaved while Reinhart radioed in to ask if anything was going on. Everything was quiet.

"Am I in trouble?" I asked as we got near home.

"No. Maybe your daddy'll be in a bit of trouble; we'll have to see how that shakes out. I liked what you did back there, Tom. I don't mean hurting that bearded fool so badly, but you took a stand. You claimed that moment when it mattered. Do you know what I mean?"

I shook my head.

"Levi's probably told you lots about your ancestors, hasn't he? He's certainly told *me* about them. Your people are like my people—we made this country. And they did it by not being afraid of making hard decisions. It didn't matter if they chose right or wrong, there has to be somebody to make a choice, to move things in a different direction, to kick everything over so things change. If you're the one seizing the moment, making the hard choice, you get to choose how things change and what direction the world moves. It's a rare quality, Tom, but I think you and I share it. With respect, I don't think Levi does, but it's in your blood, that's for certain."

Reinhart didn't say anything else until he dropped me off at the house. He told me to wait an hour and then have some clear soup, if we had any of that around. I thanked him and he drove off.

I went inside, turned on the TV, and tried to fold my attention into a baseball game. I had no memory of falling asleep, but I woke up shouting when Levi and Spencer crashed through the front door just before dawn.

"I'm getting a change of clothes," said Levi.

"Okay," I answered.

He went into his bedroom. Spencer got a Mountain Dew out of the fridge. He'd insisted we always keep some of his favourite soda in the fridge for when he dropped by. Occasionally he'd stop at the house for the sole reason that he was thirsty, or so he said. For once, Spencer wasn't staring at me.

Levi came out of the bedroom and said, "I'm going to be gone for a while, Tom. You can look after yourself, right?"

"Sure."

"You going to be back tomorrow?"

"Maybe tomorrow, yeah."

They left as quickly as they entered and drove away in Levi's truck.

I suddenly got the idea that the police were going to be after me, which was irrational since Reinhart was the only law around, but I couldn't stop obsessing over the idea that soon or in the future uniformed men would be barging into the house. I'd seen enough true crime shows on TV to know that I needed to get rid of evidence, and I figured my clothes were probably loaded with clues. I put a change of clothes in a backpack that I normally used to carry food and water when I was out all day in the chaparral, then left the house.

It was a hot day with a hotter wind, and I rode my bike east, farther than I'd ever gone before. I went along ridge lines and game trails, dry washes and the tenuous threads of long-abandoned mining roads. As I got closer to the mountains the air grew cooler and the trees taller. I followed a zigzagging trail up a steep slope which ended at a perfectly level plateau that might have been flattened by a giant's hand. A regiment of Jeffrey pines held the sky up, and the ground underneath was cushioned like a mattress with their needles. I got off my bike and looked back to the west as a delegation of crows flew to a nearby tree and squawked and muttered about me. A spur of the mountains blocked my view of Hexum, and all I could see was an eternal, tawny landscape held under a pale blue dome speckled with a few thermal-sailing buzzards. A white veil of smoke far to the south marked a brush fire that the news had said was burning out of control. I'd never felt so completely alone, and I told myself that if I could stay there forever, nothing bad would ever happen to me.

I gathered handfuls of pine needles and built a great heap of them in a spot where flames couldn't spread, then stepped out of my clothes and added them to the pile. I thought about sacrificing my Air Jordans but set them aside and told myself they could just be given a wash. I took a lighter out of the backpack and ignited the needles. The fire popped and hissed, the burning fabrics adding random streaks of color to the orange flames. I stood there, naked, watching the fire until the flames died down. For the first time in many months I thought about my mother and wondered how often she thought about me. A gust of wind that carried a sliver of cold from the high mountains hurried me into my extra set of clothes.

A gleaming moon had replaced the burning sun by the time I returned home. I made a meal of instant noodles and hot dogs and tried to watch TV, but without Levi this felt uncomfortable. TV was his sparring partner and best friend, and I always felt I was trespassing by watching it alone. I went to my room and picked up where I'd left off in *The Three Musketeers*.

Spencer turned up late the next day. I was sitting at the kitchen table thinking about a trip to the grocery store for supplies. He walked in without saying anything, just headed to the fridge for his can of Mountain Dew and sat down across from me.

He opened his drink, took a long sip, and said, "Levi's gonna be away for a while."

"How long?"

"Don't know. Could be months."

"What happened?"

"He's busy. Doing stuff."

"Is it about that guy?"

"What guy?"

"Mickey."

"Mickey had a car accident. They found his Hummer in a ditch. I guess it was too much car for the dumb bastard and he rolled it. Josh found him."

I couldn't tell if Spencer was lying about everything he'd just told me or only part of it. His looked at me with an intensity that made me shiver. I'd always steered a wide path around him, rarely even glancing at him in order to avoid his strange looks, and now his face was right there in front of me. The wispy moustache he was growing looked like mold on a cheese.

He drew an elastic-bound wad of hundreds out of his jacket and tossed it on the table. "This should keep you going."

I took the money and put it in my pocket.

"You could say thanks, you know," said Spencer softly.

"It's what Levi would have got for his work, right? So it's not a gift, it's what's due to him."

Spencer smiled. "Due to him? You a junior lawyer now? Where'd you learn to talk like that?"

I wanted to rain obscenities down on Spencer, but all I said was, "This is mine and Levi's money."

Spencer shrugged. "Whatever."

I wanted him gone but wasn't sure how to move him along. He sat there comfortably, sipping his drink like he was in a restaurant waiting for his meal to arrive.

"You gonna be okay on your own?" he asked.

"Yeah."

I wasn't worried about money: I knew where Levi had several wads of cash squirreled away on the property.

"You get lonely," he said, "you can come over to my place. I got a Nintendo and every game for it you can think of. That sound fun?" I didn't respond. "It wouldn't be only you and me. I have boys your age come over sometimes and you can play with them. I like kids, you know. And I got a pool, an above ground one. We go for a swim, have a barbeque, it's fun. Sometimes we let off fireworks, real big ones. How's that sound? You could come over tonight; it'd take your mind off things. I could even let you have some booze. Make you feel better. Sleep over, if you want—I do a mean stack of pancakes for breakfast."

My mouth went dry and my voice sounded funny when I said, "Wait a sec."

I went into the bathroom and prised up a loose section of floorboard beside the toilet. I knew where Levi kept his money hidden, and I also knew about the snub-nosed revolver he kept under the bathroom floor. I came back to the kitchen with the gun held at my side. Spencer's mouth sagged open and he knocked his soda over. The pale yellow liquid hissed as it spread out on the table. He didn't move after that. His terror was almost palpable, like a wave of heat from an opened oven door. It relaxed me.

I pointed the gun at him and said, "Spencer, I think you'll be the second man I kill."

Shrine

Hackett looks at me and says, "If you would excuse us, sir, I'd like to talk alone with Mr. Marsden."

Chung opens my door and I follow him behind the Yukon. If they frisk me, I won't have any good excuse for having a Beretta tucked in the back of my jeans.

"Mind if sit?" I ask. "My knee's acting up."

Before Chung can answer, I park myself on a boulder that's in the ditch. I can watch Hackett listening intently at the car window and see part of Enoch's face in the side mirror. If Chung stops looking at me, I'll reach around and drop the gun behind the rock.

"What happened to your knee?" he asks, but not in the usual deadpan tone cops like to use on civilians. This guy's actually interested, or just bored.

"I went up for one too many lay-ups in high school. It didn't bother me for the longest time, but now I think I'm going to have to have it scoped."

"That's the shits."

"And it isn't cheap."

He keeps looking at me like I'm going to add something more, so I rub my knee and gaze into the distance behind him as though there's something fascinating back there. He finally decides I'm not going to extend the conversation and pivots for a change of view. I casually reach around like I need to scratch my back and slide my hand down to my waist.

"Mr. Bridger," says Hackett as he turns towards me.

"Yes," I answer, and make a show of scratching an itchy back.

Hackett ambles back, that blank expression on his face I've used myself a thousand times during pull-overs. I get to my feet, and the Beretta shifts so that it's almost falling out of the back of my pants. If I put my hand back there again Hackett is going to draw on me or bring Chung over to pat me down.

"My partner and I," says Hackett, "stopped Mrs. Marsden early this morning on Gene Autry Trail doing twice the speed limit. She was clean and sober, she got a ticket, but something didn't seem right about her."

"How so?"

"She was too happy to get the ticket. No fuss, all politeness, like she was anxious to get on her way. Too anxious, maybe."

Unlike his partner, Hackett is no fool. He knows an overly cooperative and friendly civilian is sometimes hiding something, and a few hours ago Autumn thought she'd blown holes in Enoch. Hackett picked up on that.

"She was fine, last I saw her."

Hackett nods, stares at me, and starts stroking his goatee like some kind of mastermind. A standard cop tactic: use uncomfortable silences so the suspect begins to sweat, maybe start babbling. I stare back at him. A breeze carries the sweet smell of something dead nearby, probably roadkill. It makes me think of Pesado, who should be pretty ripe by later today.

"You work for Mr. Marsden?" he asks.

"I work for a security company that Mr. Marsden uses."

"Personal security?"

"No. Loss prevention."

"But he says you're staying at his house."

"I'm friends with the Marsdens, as well as working for them."

"I see," he says, but clearly doesn't. "I was on my way up to Mr. Marsden's to check if everything was alright and I recognized his car. I do some work at his golf club on weekends sometimes; special events and so on. If people around here have problems, I like to help them nip it in the bud. I was a little concerned about Mrs. Marsden, considering how late at night it was."

So he's a moonlighting cop who's eager to do favors for the sun-basking aristocracy, sniffing around for a soft gig at a resort or golf club, or even just a thick envelope for looking the other way. Now that he thinks I'm friends with Marsden, he wonders if I can put in a good word for him. He's decided his long-term future is best served by being a concierge to the people who drive cars worth more than his own house.

"She was probably just getting an early start back to L.A.," I say.

Hackett smiles. He's happy with that idea. "What security company you with?"

"Hessian Security."

His eyes go cold but the smile remains, like the last guest at a bad party. Only two kinds of ex-cop work for Hessian: the corrupt and the vicious, and Hackett obviously knows that. He gets back in his cruiser after waving at his partner to come along.

Chung comes closer to me and asks, "I thought I recognized Mrs. Marsden from somewhere. Has she been on TV or anything?"

"Beats me."

"She's hot, man; I mean, for an older lady."

"Uh huh."

"Is she like one of those trophy wives or something?"

I have a quick, hot urge to say something sharp, but I have to keep things cool, send him away happy. "A trophy? Guys like Marsden see them as participation ribbons."

Chung snorts with amusement and goes to fist bump me but Hackett honks the horn and waves at him impatiently. The cruiser U-turns away as soon as Chung gets in, and I go back to the Yukon. Enoch is drained, his head lolling back against the seat, some streaks of sweat tinged pink with blood coming down his temple. He's too tired to say anything to me.

La Quinta Clinic is a sleek, two-storey glass building set back behind a solid and discreet wall of palm and yucca trees. I stop in front of a pair of sliding, smoked glass doors marked URGENT CARE and come around to open Enoch's door.

"You want me to go in with you?"

"No. Your job is Autumn. Get it done quick."

"I'll see you back at the house."

He shuffles towards the doors which open with a silky noise and then swallow him.

I lean my forehead on the steering wheel. I'm too tired. I need time to sort out all the pieces, think about my best moves. But first I need to find Oribe and get him off the board. He lives in a community called Bitter Furnace down near the Salton Sea past Indio. I remember Autumn once said, "Imagine how fucking awful a place had to be that you would call it Bitter Furnace, and how foolish or desperate people were to stick around long enough to bother naming it."

I take highway 86 down the west side of the Salton Sea and then turn up into the hills. It's a half mile to Bitter Furnace, which is strung out along the crest of a ridge, about fifty houses in total, half of them abandoned, the others working on it. I park in the shade of a big, rusted water tank that sits a little above the town and leave the car. I can see most of Bitter Furnace from here. A trio of collared lizards soaking up the early morning sun on top of a rusted engine block watch with me. The houses are bungalows, mostly stucco, all of them bleached white or gray. No one's visible, but I can hear air conditioners humming and a radio playing Spanish talk radio. A rotten egg smell drifts up from the Salton Sea, which gleams like a new coin dropped in the middle of the desert.

I take out Pesado's phone and text Oribe: ENCUENTRAME EN EL TANQUE DE AGUA. ESTOY LASTIMADO. A minute later the side door of a house with a partially collapsed front porch opens. Oribe looks out cautiously, one hand shielding his eyes from the sun. The Yukon's not visible from his angle and the shade from the water tank hides me from his sun-blinded gaze. His house is about a hundred yards to the north, with eight other houses between it and me. Oribe turns and speaks to someone inside and then starts in my direction along the town's single street. He keeps glancing around, not sure what's up, but probably thinking that Pesado's text saying that he's hurt somehow explains his long silence since last night. When he briefly passes out of sight I move behind a nearby house with a missing roof and pull out the Beretta. He'll pass by the corner of the house on the way to the water tank. I hear his steps approaching and then slow down.

"Benito?" he murmurs.

He's stopped just out of sight in front of the house. He might be able to see the Yukon from where he's standing, and that'll spook him.

"Benito?" he says more loudly.

I groan and say, *"Ayuadame."*

He comes quickly around the corner of the house, answering my call for help, and yelps when he sees the gun leveled at his head. I thought he might have a weapon, but he's unarmed. He's wearing his usual outfit: plain white shirt buttoned to the neck, dark, stovepipe jeans, and tan, square-toed cowboy boots. His breathing becomes rapid and he tries to form words, but his brain hasn't caught up with the situation yet.

"Let's go for a walk, Oribe."

I motion towards the water tank and stay well behind him. He stops in its shade and I say, "Further." I point south, away from the town. He walks slowly, and I let him take his time, allowing his imagination to summon up the blackest fears. The ground is littered with sharp-edged rocks and occasional brittlebushes, and our progress is slow. I keep him going until we're out of sight of Bitter Furnace's houses. There's something odd about the way he's walking, a kind of limp, and I tell him to stop and empty out his boots.

"Why?" he asks.

"I think you're carrying."

He stands there looking like a child that's been caught out in a lie. He takes off his right boot and tips it over. A flat, black-handled throwing knife falls out.

"Keep going," I say.

Oribe puts his boot back on and I keep him walking for a few hundred more yards until we reach a shallow depression shaded by some ironwood trees.

"That's far enough."

He looks back at me and I see he's starting to shake.

"Lie down on your stomach, arms at your side."

"Where's Benito?"

"Underneath some vultures."

Oribe closes his eyes and sways a bit. "I have a brother in Guatemala, in Jalapa. Please let him know I'm dead."

"I'm probably not killing you today, Oribe. I'm going to ask questions, and you're going to be very polite and truthful. Get down."

He does as he's told, and I move out of his view. He's lying with the side of his face on the ground, whispering prayers in Spanish, and his panicky breathing is making little clouds of dust jump from the ground.

"Who paid you more, Enoch or Autumn?"

"Enoch."

"How much?"

"Forty thousand. Mr. Marsden gave me all the money up front; his wife, she only give me half. But it's all yours, amigo."

"*Pinche estúpido*, of course it's mine. You have nothing anymore except your life, and maybe not that. You tell me where the money is later, first you tell me the exciting story of how you tried to get rich by killing me."

"It was maybe a month ago. She ask me if I know someone who would kill a guy. She says there's big money in it. So I tell her yes, I got a friend who can do that sort of thing. She give me half the money and tells me how it's going to go down, with her dog being taken and everything. Mr. Marsden wasn't at the house then, he was back in L.A, As soon as he gets back I tell him the whole thing, how he's going to get a call about the dog being stolen and the ransom and everything. Mr. Marsden, he ask me if I really can get someone to do a hit, and I say sure. He tells me to go ahead and do it only…it'll be you going instead of him."

"Did you hear what I said about truthful, Oribe? Autumn just asked you out of the blue if you could handle a killing? Why would she come to you?"

"She's a *Yanqui*. They all think we're killers."

"Why did Marsden want me dead?"

"He said it was a way to punish her, and he could force her to do something for him because he'd have proof that she arranged the hit."

"Proof?"

"I recorded her when she paid me money the first time. That was Marden's idea."

"Where's the recording?"

"On my phone."

"Throw it over here."

He takes his cell out from his back pocket and tosses it to me. I scroll through the phone and find a video taken in Marsden's garage. Oribe must have propped the phone up and out of sight on one of the shelves where he keeps his tools and cleaning stuff. For the first minute it's just Oribe standing near the camera, pretending to be interested in moving things around on the shelves. Autumn comes in from the right carrying a small plastic bag from Walgreen's. She hands it to Oribe and says, "There." He responds: "Why you want Mr. Marsden dead?" She answers, "None of your fucking business." He says, "Only maybe I should get more." She says, "You get that or nothing. Or maybe I get someone who'll do you and Enoch for the same price." He smirks and says, "I'm kidding." "Anyway," says Autumn, "there may be more money for doing someone else." "Who?" asks Oribe. Autumn says, "Never mind." She walks away quickly and the video ends a few seconds later.

"Who was this other person she was talking about?"

"I don't know. She don't like telling me anything."

"Does Enoch have a copy of this?"

"No. I was going to ask for more money before I give it to him."

"What was Autumn supposed to do for Enoch?"

"I don't know. Marsden don't let me know all his business."

"So what happened last night when you didn't hear from Benito?"

"Nothing. Marsden, he phoned me and said you'd come back and asked what was up. I tell him I let him know when I see Benito."

"You were all set to kill Benito this morning, right?"

"No!"

"What was the knife for, then? You figured to get him away from here, somewhere down by the Salton? Tell him that's where the money is? Lots of abandoned buildings to dump a body in down there. No way you were sharing that money, Oribe, and Benito couldn't be wandering around telling people how he got rich."

Oribe says nothing, but I notice his body relax and his eyelids droop. He's probably hyperventilated himself into a near faint.

"It's too hot to spend time threatening or torturing you, Oribe, so tell me where the money is. That way we both get out of the sun quicker."

"You want to take everything from me." He sounds almost drunk, even weepy. "How you think I ever get this kind of money again? This was my lottery win. This was where my life suppose to change so I can be my own man, not have to call other people 'sir.' You might as well kill me. I got nothing, now. I'm dead."

"I'll leave you ten large, Oribe, but only as a favour to Maria. Where?"

He sighs deeply. "In the house next to mine, the abandoned one, in the kitchen cupboard inside a can of Folgers."

"Okay, good. Now I've got some plastic ties and I'm going to do your feet and your hands. If I don't find the money, I'll come back here and go to work on you: start on your face and finish with your balls."

"It's all there."

"Roll over on your back with your arms crossed under you." He does what he's told. "Now put your feet up and together on that rock so I can pass the ties around."

He obediently puts his feet on the rock. He's so relieved that he's escaped death he hasn't noticed I don't have any ties. His boots lie solidly on the rock, about a foot off the ground, his legs at a perfectly straight angle. I stomp down hard and fast on his right knee. His leg U's down and his scream is piercing enough to alter the course of a hawk that's flying overhead. They say you can hear ligaments pop, but I've never noticed that. He's effectively crippled now. It should take him a couple of hours to stagger and crawl back to his house, and after that there'll be a trip to the hospital where they'll tell him the bad news about how little Medicaid covers. He won't walk properly ever again.

"I've fucked you up good, Oribe, but if you try and talk to Marsden or Autumn, or if I even happen to see you again, I'll kill you. I wanted to kill you when I came up here, but there wasn't enough time to make things neat. You understand? Tell me you understand."

He screams yes and begins sobbing. I start walking away and Oribe somehow finds the strength to throw a rock at me that goes yards wide. His curses fade into the distance. I should have killed him, but at least now he won't be sneaking around trying to put a bullet in my back.

Bitter Furnace has no sidewalks, so I walk down the middle of the street on buckled and riven asphalt. A brindle pitbull chained up outside a house runs to the end of its chain and wags its tail. At another house a man and a woman sit together on their front steps looking anxiously past me down the street. They're gaunt and haunted-looking, like refugees on the wrong side of a border fence. They're probably waiting for a connection to arrive with meth or crack. Oribe's stash house is missing all its windows and doors, and I find the Folgers can as full of money as Oribe promised.

I go to Oribe's house, the can tucked under my arm, and knock at the side door. Maria opens it, her expression fearful yet questioning.

"Hi, Maria."

She lets me in without saying anything. The bungalow is tiny: a living room, bathroom, kitchen, and bedroom. I go down a short hall to the living room and stop in my tracks. It's Autumn's house on a reduced scale: the armchairs, lamps, couch and side tables are the sort of items I've seen in the glossy interior decoration magazines Autumn leaves everywhere. The framed prints of effusive saints on the walls jar with the furniture's minimalism and cool eccentricity.

"Autumn gave you these?" I ask.

"Yes. When she get rid of something she always ask me first if I want it."

"Of course."

I ask Maria for the biggest glass or bottle of water she can bring me. I'm dehydrated, my head is splitting, and I need to sit down out of the heat and sun for a while. She goes to the kitchen and brings me a liter bottle of water and then sits in an armchair made of brass and tropical hardwood. I sit on a couch covered in three different colors of leather and put the coffee can on the floor at my feet. I tell her that we can speak in Spanish, and she smiles a little.

"I thought you could speak Spanish, or at least understand it," she says.

"How did you know?"

"Sometimes I'd see you reacting to things Oribe said."

"He liked to say some stupid things."

"Liked?"

"He's alive, and he'll be along in a while, but I think it'd be best if you moved on. You can stay if you like, but I always got the sense you didn't want to be near Oribe. I know he's not your husband."

I peel the plastic lid off the can and take out the money. Maria doesn't react; she'll have seen Oribe waving it around and boasting.

"I'm giving you half, just over twenty-two thousand. If you know of any other money he's got stashed you're welcome to it. You've earned it."

She lets out a sigh that's almost a sob and turns her eyes away as I count out the bills.

"Thank you," she says.

"Do you have some place to go? I can take you to the airport or the bus station."

"San Diego. I have a cousin there. She's legal."

"Why haven't you gone to her before this?"

"My cousin's husband isn't legal. Oribe told me he'd report her husband to ICE if I ever left. Also, he takes all my money."

"How did you end up here with Oribe?"

She sags in the chair and takes a deep breath. "I came across at a place called Calexico fifteen years ago. They took a whole bunch of us in a truck up to Las Vegas. The *coyote* told us we'd be getting jobs as chambermaids. He lied. When we got off the truck in Vegas, a man put me and some other girls in a van and took us to a big house in Henderson. I didn't leave the house for two years; the men came to us. One night a customer shot up the place, killed two of the girls, and we all ran away when the cops came. Three us stayed together and found an abandoned house full of people like us. Everyone slept on the floor. I got the usual jobs: housekeeping, kitchen work, sometimes handing out those awful cards on the Strip, but never more than a couple of days work at a time. Anyway, Oribe came through town to visit someone at the house—he was already working for Marsden—and said he could get me a proper job here in a big house with rich people."

"And you didn't find out about the living arrangements until he got you here, right?"

"At first he let me sleep in the living room, and then he told me I had to…"

I finish my water and give her time to collect herself.

"Do you know who Benito is?"

"Oribe's friend. He deals drugs around here when he isn't using them. Can I ask you something?"

"Sure."

"You and Autumn are, well, involved, right?"

"It was obvious?"

"Not at first. You started coming for weekends with her other friends about, what, a year ago? I noticed that the groups of friends would change but you were always one of them. Can you tell me what's happened?"

"Nothing good. Autumn's left Marsden, but there are complications, Oribe being one of them. We should go now."

"I'll pack."

I pass the rest of the money to her. "Here. You keep it all."

She's shocked. "Why?"

"San Diego's expensive."

She goes into the bedroom to pack and I close my eyes, letting exhaustion roll over me like a vast and gentle wave that drowns my memories. I snap awake when Maria gently touches my shoulder about fifteen minutes later. All that she wants to take with her, or owns, is in a small duffel bag.

"Ready," she says.

I tell her to wait outside while I look for something of Oribe's. She hesitates as though wanting to say something, but then goes outside and stands close to the door as if she's afraid of letting me out of her sight. I go into the kitchen and use a dishcloth to wipe my prints from the

Beretta and Benito's phone, then carry them in the cloth down the hall to the bedroom. The bed is neatly made and covered by a quilt with a Navajo design on it. On the wall opposite the bed is a shrine to the Virgin Mary. It's a shell-shaped sconce bearing a statuette of the Madonna in flowing robes, her right hand reaching out in a gesture of supplication. A small lightbulb hidden in the top of the shrine throws a yellowy light on her. Opposite, crudely taped to the wall above the head of the bed, is a collage of pages from magazines showing naked and nearly naked women. Most are from porn magazines, others from celebrity rags. The pictures reach right up to the ceiling.

I toss the gun and the phone on the bed for Oribe to find and pick up and get his prints on. If Benito's ever dug out of the ravine and identified, the story will be that Oribe killed him with a gun stolen from his employer. I could even tip off the cops myself. Of course, he might sense he's being set up and ditch the weapon, but I think I can count on Oribe being stupid and angry enough to keep the gun in case he ever gets a chance to use it on me. The closet door is open and something catches my eye: leaning in a corner is a Benelli M4, a ferocious-looking shotgun with a pistol grip that's usually only in the hands of Marines or cops. Oribe must have decided to splurge on something to guard his golden hoard next door.

Maria and I walk down the street towards the Yukon. The haggard couple are still on their front steps, the woman now with her face buried in her hands. Benito won't be bringing their fix. We reach the car and I look to the south where I left Oribe. He's barely visible as a wavering stick figure in the heat haze, his jerky, hopping movements making him look like a wounded insect.

Maria follows my gaze. "Is that Oribe?"

"Yes. He's getting used to his new pace of life."

"You hurt him?"

"He tripped."

"You see what he put on the bedroom wall?"

"Yes."

"When he had sex with me he'd stare at the pictures all through it. He called it his motivational wall. You didn't hurt him enough. Take me to the bus station."

As we drive back down to the highway my phone rings. It's Autumn.

Ghost

Spencer got up slowly from the table, his hands held out with the palms facing me in a gesture of abject surrender. He'd either pissed himself or the soda had spilled from the table onto his lap.

"We're cool, buddy, we're cool," he said.

I waved him towards the door with my gun hand. He backed all the way out of the house and tried not to hurry to his truck. I stood on the steps as he got behind the wheel and made a show of putting on his sunglasses as though nothing out of the ordinary had happened. He drove calmly out of the yard, but a minute later I heard the screech of tires once he got onto the highway. I cleaned up his mess in the kitchen and then threw up for the second time in 24 hours.

For the rest of that day I lay on my bed, feeling almost bolted to it. I ran Mickey's death through my head over and over, sometimes seeing it as a terrible accident, other times imagining he had recovered and had had the car accident Spencer described. I populated my imagination with a multiverse of scenarios in which Mickey didn't die at my hand or was somehow killed by another person. I knew I had killed him—I could still remember how the bar felt in my hands as it met the gentle resistance of his skull—but I spun out increasingly elaborate fictions that absolved me or put the weapon in someone else's hands. But like a rogue wave the detailed, crushing memory of killing Mickey would suddenly pound into me and my breaths would shorten and my heart would turn to a stone that felt as if it was gong fall away from my body. And then, worst of all, I would think that I did it to shield someone who didn't deserve protection.

For three days I barely moved from my room. I ate and drank a little, tried to watch TV or read, but mostly I lay on my bed, staring at the walls and numbly expecting to have something worse befall me. On the morning of the fourth day I was awoken by the sound of rain pounding on the roof. The light coming in from my bedroom window threw writhing water shadows against the wall. I opened the front door and a carnival of scents rushed in: wet earth, sage, pine and a dozen other plants and flowers that were trying hard to be noticed. The chaparral was a wet dog shaking its coat and throwing off fragrances. I stood there until the rain stopped. As the last drops fell, every bird within earshot began talking loudly about the weather.

I replayed Mickey's death for what felt like the thousandth time, and the memory of it began to harden into something small and remote, one of a billion, trillion incidents that happen everywhere and at every second of the day, an endless deluge of incidents that I could or could not choose to care about or remember. I wouldn't forget Mickey's spastic, foolish death, but I could choose to remember it as an incident that had swirled around and past me, and then joined the rushing stream of other events that are lost in time.

I took my dirt bike and rode into town along the edge of the highway. Small, tardy rain clouds scampered after the bigger storm still rumbling to the east, their gray, wet tails dragging across the land. I was going into town for groceries, something I'd never done solo, and it made me tense. Levi's fear of being questioned about me was part of my psyche as well, and I went into the Safeway feeling twitchy and ready to run. The place was packed and I remembered it was Sunday, so there were no worries about people wondering why I wasn't in school. The aisles were busy with people checking lists and telling kids "No." I forgot what I'd come in for and just cruised up and down the aisles, making a grand tour of the store. I felt a lightness come over me as I realized that what I had done didn't leave a stain or scar that people could see. I was unremarkable and unknown—one of the herd browsing the shelves.

Back at home, I cleared the fridge of Spencer's soda and took them out to the yard along with the revolver and a box of bullets Levi kept under the kitchen sink. I positioned the cans of Mountain Dew on the tire pile on the far side of the yard, walked ten paces back and fired a gun for the first time in my life. I missed the can I was aiming at and frightened something in the brush that ran away with a high-pitched squeal.

There were a hundred bullets in the box and I used most of them in the next hour. By the time the cans were all holed, I judged myself an average shot, but, more importantly, I no longer flinched at the sound and violence. I put the loaded gun on my bedside table and recalled the way Spencer's pallid face changed when he saw my gun barrel pointed at him.

The weeks rolled away and there was no sign of Levi—no phone call, no letter, no word from one of his buddies. I fell into a routine of spending the mornings out on the land, extending my explorations ever further, usually on foot, sometimes on my bike. I'd come back home in the afternoon and read, do some chores, and when it got near six, I'd bike into town for groceries or a meal at a fast food place. On weekends I'd go into town during the day, reasoning that a kid by himself wouldn't seem suspicious then. I usually went to a movie or visited a used book store that was run by a sallow-faced man in his fifties who always wore the same gray cardigan; he smelled of mints and sweat, and only ever spoke to tell me what I owed him.

By October the stores were filled with Halloween crap. I had a ragged memory of going out on Halloween with my mother, her hair dyed orange for the occasion, and me in zombie makeup. Levi made a point of staying in on Halloween when we moved west, although he was happy to watch horror movies with me instead. That first year in Hexum I'd bugged him about going into town to trick or treat, but he deflected me with some story about newcomers like ourselves not being welcome: "They won't give you anything," he had said.

I decided to go into Hexum on Halloween night. I wanted to see what a Halloween night looked like, and whether it would be anything like my memories of it.

In all the time that Levi had been away, I had never felt so apprehensive as when I went into Hexum in the late afternoon of that Halloween. It was overcast, but stiflingly hot and dry, as though the town was sitting in a kiln. I sat outside a 7-Eleven on Main Street drinking a Slurpee and waited for dusk to fall. The light in the sky finally drew away to the west and I walked down one of the residential streets that ran off Main.

The first couple of blocks were lined with two-story wooden houses in obvious ill health, most of which held the Asians and Latinos who worked in the town's businesses, legit and otherwise. The workers were outside their houses, sitting on the porches or standing on front lawns sharing cigarettes. They looked exhausted and subdued, like people in a hospital corridor waiting for bad news. Through the open windows and doors of the houses I could see that every room, even some hallways, were filled with bunk beds. No one was trick or treating around here.

In a few more blocks the streets began to fill with children and their parents. Kids my age and older were going around in loud, happy gangs, dressed in half-assed costumes. I got curious looks from a few people because I wasn't in costume or carrying a bag of candies. The wind suddenly picked up and sent waves of leaves down the street and I began to feel jittery. I didn't belong here. Every face I saw was happy and accompanied by family or friends, while I was a wild animal that had wandered into town and was trying not to be spotted.

The revelry began to die down and soon there were only stray packs of teenagers on the streets laughing hysterically as they stole pumpkins from porches and smashed them on the ground. I drifted along the sidewalks from where I could see in the windows of homes where people were watching horror movies or sorting through heaps of candies. This was better. It reminded me of being alone out in the chaparral watching wildlife. I tried to imagine the sort of conversations people were having on the other side of the windows, or speculated on what they did for a living. I imagined myself as a new kind of ghost that's too afraid to do his haunting indoors but has to roam outside and peek in windows at the living.

In another hour the houses were almost all dark, and I went back to Main St. to a sub shop that was open. A couple of Asian guys were counting out change to buy one sub for the two of them. They stared at me with innocent curiosity when I paid with a fifty for my sandwich. I took it outside and sat on a bench to eat it. The few vehicles that rolled past left behind the scent of weed or the reverberations of stereos. A few men walked by, their heads and shoulders sagging as if ashamed of being on foot. At eleven o'clock the sub shop closed its doors and switched off the lights, the owner coming out a few minutes later and giving me some side eye before hurrying away.

I knew I should go home, but the stillness and emptiness of the night pinned me where I sat. The moon, fat and mushroom-white, hung low in the sky, filling my vision with stark, geometric shadows. I left the bench and walked down the middle of the wide street. I was heading for the 24-hour gas station on the edge of town where I'd left my bike, but I was in no hurry to get there; I felt invisible and invulnerable. A few apartments above closed stores showed some lights, but no one was witnessing my solo parade except a cat sitting on the roof of a car. It lashed its tail furiously as I drew near and jumped away into the shadows.

I passed a school and heard a rhythmic, metallic squeaking sound. The noise was coming from a playground sitting in the shadows at the back of the schoolyard. The squeaking continued. I considered moving on, but a movement in the playground caught my eye. Someone was on the swings. The dim figure pendulumed back and forth, their legs gently pumping. They were facing away from me, so I moved quietly into the yard for a closer look. It was a boy my own age wearing denim bib overalls that were streaked with paint. His face was turned up to the sky as he swung, his lips puckered into a whistle that I couldn't hear. I was rooted to the spot, fascinated that there might another ghost like me in Hexum.

"Hey," I said.

The boy jerked his head towards me and dragged his feet in the ground to come to a quick stop. He had a narrow, hungry face and blonde hair that was the victim of an amateur barber. He stood up from the swing I could see that he was my height, but thin as a stalk of corn.

He squinted and asked, "You go to this school?"

"No."

"Nor me."

"You home-schooled?" It occurred to me that perhaps wandering around at night was something home-schooled kids did.

"I am. By Founder."

"Who?"

"My father. We call him Founder."

"His name's Founder?"

"No. He is the founder and provider of our family and its holy wealth, so he must be called Founder. He says."

"Okay. I'm Tom.

"I'm Malachi Gaunt. Do you want to swing with me?"

"Sure."

I sat on a swing and kicked my legs back and forth, and as I swung up in the air it dawned on me that I hadn't done this since leaving New London. The sensation of rising and falling, the air rushing against my face, and the strangeness of this night enthralled me, and I felt an urge to laugh. I looked across at Malachi who was sitting in his swing, watching me with narrowed eyes.

"I can swear, you know," he said.

"So?"

"You want to hear me swear?"

"Alright."

He took a deep breath and then whispered a stream of "Shits" that ended when he had to take another breath. He looked at me expectantly, and when I didn't react, he frowned and turned away.

"So why are you out so late?" I asked.

"Founder put me in my own house last month, after I turned fifteen. He said I couldn't be under the same roof as the Eves since I was now a man. So now he can't know what I do or where I go at night."

"What the fuck? You've got your own house?"

Malachi got off the swing and sat on a round metal bar that supported a nearby teeter-totter.

"I do. It's not a real house, it's like a wooden tent. He locks himself and the Eves in the house at night and won't open the door until morning."

"What are Eves?"

"His brides," said Malachi matter-of-factly. "Why are you out here?"

I brought the swing to a stop, "My dad's gone away for a while, so I live on my own. It's not bad; I watch what I want, eat what I want, and I can go where I want—like here."

"But Christ is always with you, so you're not really alone."

I laughed. "You're one of those, huh?"

Hexum had lots of people—often cashiers—who liked to tell Levi and myself that Christ was with us. Levi would sometimes answer that Christ was indeed with us, but we'd dropped Him off earlier at Safeway and hoped to see Him later. Levi had a small arsenal of jokes, but that one always made me smile.

"Don't you believe in God?" asked Malachi, his voice low and tense.

"Don't know, don't care."

Malachi reacted to this as if it was a physical blow. He jumped up and ran behind a play structure that had slides and a rope ladder, then peeked out at me, his hands held up to his mouth as though stifling a scream.

"Can I tell you something?" he called out.

"Yeah," I said, and moved a bit towards the street.

"Sometimes I don't either!" he shouted. He stayed where he was, hidden from sight, and then added, "I've only ever said that to myself, that's why I came back here; I couldn't be looking at you and say it. It's a terrible thing to say and other folks shouldn't be made to hear it. I'm sorry. I just hope on the day I die it's on one of the days when I really, truly believe in God."

"You think you're going to die soon?"

"Oh, yes," he said eagerly. "You see, I feel wrong all the time, like living is a pair of shoes that don't fit me. That's a sign, I think, that I'll be gone soon."

"Bullshit."

Malachi giggled. "Maybe."

He came back to the swings and in a few moments was back up in the air, his head tilted back and a grin on his face as though he was sharing a joke with the Man in the Moon. That Malachi was a bit nuts didn't particularly alarm me; some of the men Levi worked with were far more disturbed. There was Atomic Dog, who frequently answered questions with barks, and Travis, with his imaginary brother Kyle. Anyway, I didn't know any other kids that I could compare to Malachi. Perhaps, I thought, this is what kids in Hexum were like. I didn't immediately like or dislike Malachi, but I badly wanted to be with someone my own age.

"So," I said, "you come here every night?"

"Mostly. Sometimes I just wander around. I like to look in people's windows."

"I'm gonna go now. I'll catch you back here sometime."

He got off the swing wearing a serious expression and came over and shook my hand. I'd never shaken hands with someone my own age, and it felt so odd that I laughed, which lit up Malachi's face with a grin.

"We'll be friends, Tom."

"Sure."

I went back out to Main St. and the swings started squeaking again.

I walked with my head down, debating whether I should seek Malachi out tomorrow night. The last stretch of Main before Hexum petered out was lined with shuttered and abandoned buildings. But some of them were only trying to look forgotten. Light, and the sound of raised voices seeped through cracks around shiny new metal doors set in battered brick walls, and exhaust fans nosing out of boarded-up windows hummed furiously as they exhaled choking chemical smells.

As I went past a two-storey building made of gray, chipped cinder blocks with a single metal door facing the street, a white Escalade pulled to the curb beside me. I quickened my pace and didn't look back as I passed it. One of its doors opened and quick steps came up behind me. I glanced back and then ducked and twisted to one side as a hand got the collar of my T-shirt and give it a mighty jerk that pulled me off my feet and dropped me in a kneeling position on the sidewalk. Another hand grabbed my hair and twisted my head around. It was Jubal. He was breathing heavily through flared nostrils, and his eyes were filled with a hungry rage.

"Little boy out for a stroll," he rasped, his breath carrying an ammonia reek. "Take a good look at my face, Tommy, and tell me what shape it is before I turn you into a fucking bloodstain."

He bent my head back so far, I thought my neck would snap. His mouth was twitching in and out of a grin like a faulty neon sign, and his pupils were dilated into glittering black buttons. I knew he was really going to hurt me this time; this wasn't for show or to put a scare in me. I grabbed his belt buckle with my left hand and, using it as leverage, drove my right fist up into his balls. He sucked in his breath with a hollow, whistling sound and released me. I scrabbled away on all fours, abject terror temporarily taking away my ability to stand. I got to my feet and Jubal tackled me from behind, his arms vised around my waist. He was keening with anger and threw wild punches at the back of my head. I kicked out at him with both legs and felt my feet hitting his chest and stomach. He reached to his side and pulled a knife from a scabbard hanging from his belt. It was an ugly, wide-bladed thing with a serrated edge along one side—it was like he'd magically produced a shark from a side pocket. He swung it at me, and its tip brushed across my stomach with no more weight than a feather.

We were suddenly bathed in flashes of red light, and from behind me there came the hiss of tires on pavement and the brief blare of a siren. I looked over my shoulder and saw Reinhart getting out of his cruiser, one hand resting on his holster. I scrambled to my feet and saw that my shirt was sliced open and the skin underneath was bloody.

"Get the hell out of here, Josh," bellowed Jubal.

Reinhart roared back, "To hell yourself, Jubal!"

Jubal picked himself up and took a firmer grip on his knife. "This isn't any business of yours, Josh; this little shit is owed a beating by me, and he's going to get it even worse if you hang around."

"I don't see a beating," said Reinhart, "I see someone who's been eating too much of their own cooking coming after a child with a damned machete."

Reinhart walked over to me and lifted my shirt. The blade hadn't cut me deeply, merely skipped across my stomach leaving a Morse code message written in scarlet dots and dashes.

"You've made your point, Jubal," said Reinhart, "now run along and cool down before your heart kicks its way out of your chest."

Jubal was sweating heavily and his knife hand had a tremor to it.

"No, Josh. I got a right to damage that kid. He mocked me!"

Reinhart laughed. "He *mocked* you? Man, you are one delicate flower." He turned to me. "So, what did you say that put that giant pickle up Jubal's ass?"

"I told Levi that Jubal had a face shaped like a slice of pie and Levi repeated it to him later."

Reinhart looked sternly at Jubal. "Is this true, Pieface?"

Jubal made a guttural noise and took a step towards Reinhart, who flicked the safety strap off his gun.

"This is over now, Jubal. You're higher than a kite; you're not thinking properly."

"You don't tell me what to do, Sherriff Joshua Reinhart. We're partners. Equal partners."

"Partners in business, Jubal. This isn't business, so you behave like a Boy Scout unless I give you permission to do otherwise."

"Fuck that!" yelled Jubal. "This is all open land and I do what I want on it and fuck up who I want."

Reinhart walked quickly up to Jubal and slapped him across the face. Jubal looked shocked, as if he'd seen something wildly indecent.

"Jubal, you're acting and talking like one of those mouth breathers that work for you. Cool your jets. Be better. This boy is under my protection. He goes where he wants, does what he wants, and if he gets a bump or a bruise, then it'll cost you two of your best men."

Jubal puffed out his cheeks and looked down at the ground. Reinhart said something to him in a low voice that I didn't catch, and

Jubal put his knife back in its scabbard. Another cop car pulled up with two deputies inside. The driver leaned out and asked Reinhart if everything was okay.

"Just a half-assed knife fight, boys." He came over to me and put his hand on my shoulder. "This is Tom. He's a friend of mine, so you'll let him mind his own business if you see him around town."

The deputy gave me a big smile and a wave before driving off.

Reinhart led me to his car and dug out a first aid kit. He cut my shirt off, rinsed away the blood with saline solution, sprayed the cuts with a stinging antiseptic and applied some Band-aids.

"You okay, Tom?" he asked kindly.

"I'm fine."

He held my shoulders and looked at me intently. "Yes, you are fine, aren't you? I can see it in your eyes. There are grown men who'd have pissed themselves, but you're a rock, Tom, a damn rock. I know you've had some tough knocks and that you're out there on your own, but it's forming you into a different, stronger person. You're like a diamond that's being cut into something special and rare. It's a salty life you've been handed, but one day you'll be glad of it."

The only thing I felt was numb. Jubal would probably stay away from me now, but I knew that Hexum was roamed by similar monsters, and I couldn't count on Reinhart to save me from all of them. I felt cold as it dawned on me that, in the future, I would have to slay some of these monsters or be slain myself.

Reinhart took off his cowboy hat and rubbed his scalp vigorously, his white hair rising up in erratic tufts. He looked at Jubal who was leaning against his Escalade mopping his face with a green handkerchief, and asked, "You okay now, Jubal?"

Jubal grunted. "Tell your little sidekick to keep his smartassery to himself in future, or I'll let Spence make him one of his fuck puppies."

I knew that this was Jubal signalling a ceasefire; his tone was grumbly and without venom.

"I know it's Halloween, Jubal, but you didn't come into town just to scare kids, did you?" asked Reinhart.

Jubal sighed with annoyance, tucked his handkerchief away, and said, "Got a goddamn delivery."

As if on cue the metal door in the cinder block building swung violently open and the dark street was violated with a throbbing bass beat and a yellowish light that thrust apart the darkness. A group of men, all of them laughing and yelling, spilled out onto the sidewalk. I could see more men inside the building, which was one big open space filled with a random collection of couches and easy chairs, refrigerators, and some trestle tables covered with liquor bottles, beer cans and pizza boxes. There was a Confederate flag hanging on one wall. I had seen some of these guys at the house, coming and going with Levi. Atomic Dog was one of the men on the sidewalk.

One of the crowd shouted, "Where's our goddamn dessert, Jubal?" Another cried, "Whatcha brought us?"

"You're getting strawberry fucking shortcake," growled Jubal.

Jubal went to the back of his car, raised the hatch and dragged out a girl. Duct tape covered her mouth, as well as binding her ankles and wrists. She had long, pale blonde hair and milky skin. Her blue, short-sleeved blouse was torn at the collar and her denim skirt was streaked with dirt. She might have been a teenager. Jubal picked her up and cradled her in his arms as if carrying a child to bed. Some of the men chanted "strawberry shortcake."

"What's the dessert's name?" someone yelled.

"Crystal," barked Jubal.

"A stripper name!" hooted Atomic Dog, and then yipped like a coyote.

Her head was arched back, eyes wide open, and as Jubal passed her off to the men on the sidewalk, she twisted her head around so that she was looking up into the sky rather than the circle of shouting, grinning faces. They carried her into the building and the door slammed shut, entombing the light and sound.

Reinhart pointed at the building. "Are you putting her back where you found her, Jubal, or what?"

"She's doing a home movie tomorrow, but after that I'll have her shipped out."

"Good, because I've got too much on my plate already to be doing extra paperwork."

Jubal closed the Escalade's hatch and drove off without a glance in our direction. Reinhart put away the first aid kit and got behind the wheel of his cruiser.

"You need a lift home, Tom?"

"No. My bike's just up the street."

"I never asked: did you come into town for Halloween, for some candy?"

"I just wanted to look around, see what it was like. I'm kind of too old for it."

"I love Halloween. Kids get more excited and happy at Christmas, I guess, but unless you have a child you don't see much of it. With Halloween, all that pleasure is out there in the open. We all share in the fun." He started the engine. "Remember, Tom: you have the freedom of this town. I'll spread the word to all the deputies."

"Thanks."

He pulled away and his taillights become tiny red eyes in the distance. Silence and darkness crept softly back onto the street. I approached the building and put the flat of my hand on the door that the girl had disappeared behind. It was cool to the touch and vibrated slightly with the beats of the music. I stepped away and headed for my bike and home.

John Daly

I pull the Yukon over to the side of the road and get out.

"Where are you?" I ask.

"At loose ends," says Autumn.

"Well, you could go to a firing range and put in some practice."

She laughs. "Not even close, huh?"

"Nope."

"I'm excellent with rifles, not so hot with handguns. I'm by the pool at the Capri."

"You didn't get very far."

"I was halfway to Vegas when I got your text. You didn't mention the law, so I assumed it meant that Enoch hasn't either, so I turned around and came here. I could claim he shot at me, or he just decided to fire off a gun in the house because he was drunk or angry, and I decided to come here while he cooled down. If I ran to Vegas or L.A., that's halfway to a guilty plea."

"Your mind is way sharper than your aim. That's essentially the argument I put to Enoch. I've got him thinking he's more at risk from this shit show than you, and he's willing to come to a generous divorce settlement, with me as the middleman. I anticipate a number with eight figures in it."

Autumn doesn't answer. Maria is glancing nervously at her side view mirror, worried, probably, that Oribe is going to suddenly appear with his Bernelli. I really should have killed him.

"So you're taking a cut?" asks Autumn.

"No, ten percent on top."

"And Enoch agreed to this?"

"Yeah."

"We need to talk, but not over the phone. Can you come here?"

"Not right away. I've got to clean up the house, probably see Enoch again. Tonight?"

"Okay. See you."

She hangs up, and I wonder why her tone became tense and thoughtful.

Maria relaxes as we drive away, even singing a little under her breath. I drop her off at the Greyhound bus terminal in Indio. As she gets out of the car, she goes to say something but then changes her mind. I don't know what to say either. I suspect that this is the second time I've chauffeured her, and I hope this trip has a better ending. We wave goodbye to each other as though we're going to meet again later in the day.

Enoch calls me just as I'm parking the Yukon back at the house. "Are you still at the clinic?" I ask.

"No. I got one stitch and some pills. I'm going to stay overnight at the club. No one to go home to, is there?"

I'm not surprised he retreated to Royal Palms; it's his prized possession. He'll be in one of the luxury bungalows they call "casitas" that are scattered across the property for the use of premium club members.

"Have you reached her?" he asks anxiously.

"Yes, she took my call."

"Where is she?"

"She wouldn't say, but she said she'd phone tomorrow to arrange a meeting with me."

"You have any guess where she'd be?"

"Back at the L.A. house? Does it matter?"

"Just curious. So, she'll do a deal?"

"I didn't get into specifics. I'd like to meet her first and get a read on what she's planning to do. If she's scared, panicky, you might end up paying out a lot less."

"Bad for your bottom line."

"Whatever I get, it's all profit to me."

Enoch chortles. "You got it, Tom; any profit is a good profit. Oh, I need you to bring me down a change of clothes and my pills."

"Sure. It'll be in a while; I've got to tidy things up here."

"Is Oribe there?"

"That's a funny thing: he and Maria never showed up."

Enoch clears his throat. "Oh, well; just tell them to do their normal stuff if they come by."

I don't think Enoch has any idea what their "normal stuff" is—Autumn managed the staff—but I tell him I'll take care of it. We end the call and I take out Oribe's phone and place it on the kitchen island. It lights up a minute later and the screen shows an incoming call from *Jefe* that matches Enoch's phone number. Enoch doesn't leave a message; he's worried now, wondering if Oribe's silence means he's gone rogue.

I've never been in the house when it's unoccupied. One of the appliances hums softly and the air conditioning whispers in the background. It never felt like a place people lived in—these kinds of houses never do. It has the air of a gallery that's more walls than art, or a hotel with a statement lobby and an Instagrammable pool. The air has its usual sterile chill and it's making me even sleepier. I go to my room, collapse on the bed, and set my phone alarm for four hours from now. As sleep reaches out for me, I imagine filling the house with C4 and watching it explode; a big bang turning its clean lines into an ever-expanding cloud of dust and glass shards that glint like a million stars.

The alarm snaps me awake. I feel okay, and even better after a shower and some fresh clothes. I drag the bed and box spring down to the garage and dig the bullets out, and then the same with the hall table before putting all three pieces at the end of the driveway. Bighorn's maintenance crew will be along tomorrow morning to haul everything away. After that I grab some clothes for Enoch from his bedroom. Something about the house has changed. There's been some subtle alteration I can't put my finger on.

It's while I'm crossing through the kitchen that I see it: high up on a wall is a small security camera. I've always known it was there, as well as others in the house that watch the entranceways, but now a green light is glowing just below the camera lens. I can't remember if I've seen this light being on before, and perhaps my unconscious is telling me it shouldn't be there. I go through the house checking the other cameras. They all have the same light illuminated. I retrace the route Autumn took when she got the gun and then shot at Enoch. None of the cameras would have caught her movements.

I pack my bag and put it in my own car and then circle around the house to the pool. There are several cameras that cover the exterior of the house and I make it look as though I'm checking the perimeter like a conscientious security man. The pool isn't covered by any cameras, so I take out Oribe's phone and hold it underwater for a minute to let the saltwater do a thorough job, then take out the SIM card, crush it under my heel and sweep the remains into the water.

I take my Civic for the drive to Royal Palms and stop at a McDonald's to get a soda and dump Oribe's phone in a trash bin. I sit at an outside table and think about the security cameras. It's possible that they were remotely activated to livestream somewhere. I don't know much about the house's security setup other than the code to set or disable the door alarms, and I can't even recall the security company's name. Enoch could be accessing the cameras from his phone. Autumn? She has Enoch's laptop, which is likely to contain all the essential information on the security system. I can't see why she'd look in on the house. Also, any remote access might be logged or flagged by the alarm company, which would let Enoch know that Autumn is spying on the house. It's probably Enoch. He'd want to know if Autumn had come back to the house, and, if she did, how she was acting with me.

The entrance road to Royal Palms twists through its three different courses, its rich, green fairways contrasting brutally with the bare, lunar mountains that surround the club. Sprinklers are misting the air and the setting sun yellows the puddles forming on the road. I stop in front of the clubhouse and let the valets take my car. They recognize me but raise a collective eyebrow at my Civic. They'll probably stick it in the staff parking lot. The clubhouse is long and low and done in a Pueblo Revival style, or so Autumn says. Golf carts are toing and froing from it like bees around a hive, and I have to dodge them as I follow the path to Enoch's casita.

His casita is a smaller version of the clubhouse and has a flagstone patio that faces the mountains. Enoch is on the patio, sitting at a glass-topped table and looking through a pair of binoculars.

"Hey, Enoch."

He lowers the binoculars as I join him at the table and hold up the gym bag I've brought.

"Clothes and meds are in the bag. How are you feeling?"

"Better. I slept."

I point at the binoculars. "What are you watching?"

"Bad golfers."

From the patio we can see four greens and as many tee boxes. The play on the course is being loudly commented on by jays up in the palms.

"Do you want something to eat?" asks Enoch.

"Yes, actually, I'm starving."

He calls the clubhouse restaurant on his cell phone and we order steak sandwiches, mine with a salad, his with mashed potatoes and cherry pie. He leaves his phone on the table.

Enoch gestures towards the greens. "I can't tell you how much I love this place."

"Yes, it's lovely."

"Lovely? I suppose. Building this club gave me everything. You know how? In 1976 I had nothing: no reputation, no track record that I could handle something as big as this. But building a golf course is, in the end, just a logistical process: find financing, get an architect, a course designer, planning permissions, marketing, and so on. It was impressive, but it's just another construction project. I never saw it as a golf course, though. I wanted a watering hole for rich bastards like me." He tries to laugh heartily but it sounds like he's breathing hard after some exercise. "The kind of watering hole a hunter sits at to bring down game. You see, I wasn't in the golf business, I was in the pleasure business, and when you give pleasure to men who control L.A. and California and America, you have their attention and respect, and even their affection. All my deals, everything I grew, sprang from the favor I gained with those men through this club."

"So, you had them by the balls, but in a way that they enjoyed."

Enoch laughs again, and this time it sounds honest. This must be the sixth time I've heard him tell his origin story. He must think no one knows that he inherited a hundred million from his father, who had himself inherited and later sold a chain of gas stations in the Midwest. Autumn told me that Enoch lost a quarter of his inheritance within three years by bankrolling films that were D.O.A. at the box office before sobering up financially and partnering with two minor investors in building Royal Palms. After that, he was always the junior partner in different ventures. Autumn says that his only true talent is finding men who know what they're doing and sticking to them like a tick.

"You want a drink, Enoch? Why don't I make us a pitcher of something?"

Enoch thinks it over, undoubtedly concerned about the colorful collection of pills he takes every day that alcohol apparently doesn't agree with. I need to get something down his throat that'll make him sleep.

"Sure, why not?" he says affably.

I go into the bungalow and check out the bar. It's well-stocked by the club and has everything. I make a tall pitcher of John Dalys. As I bring it out to the patio, a golf cart arrives with a waiter from the club's restaurant. He has our meals under covered trays as well as linen napkins and heavy, ornate cutlery. He lays out the food on the table with crisp, servile efficiency, wishes us a "delightful" evening, and departs.

We don't talk while we eat, and I notice Enoch has almost chugged his first drink. I top him up and take a few sips of my own. By the time he finishes his pie, Enoch has had three drinks to my one. I've never seen him drink so much, so quickly. He must be trying to rinse off the last 24 hours with booze.

Enoch drags a stool near his chair, puts his feet up on it, then refills his glass and sighs contentedly. One of the courses is illuminated at night, and the lights, positioned in the palm trees, come on with a noise like a distant door closing. Enoch takes this as a signal to start reminiscing. He goes back in time and drags me with him to revisit past triumphs. As usual, he takes an oblique approach to his self-celebrations. He talks about the border wall, which leads him to Mexico City and then to his being part of the U.S. Olympic team in 1968. Another six or seven anecdotes are constructed in the same fashion. He likes to pretend that conversations have serendipitously stumbled across yet another one of his moments in the sun. We eventually reach the Hall of Fame portion of his memory: the famous people he's met at the club over the years. As the booze unfetters his ego more completely, he recites their names in a reverent monotone as though listing the animals entering the Ark.

He ends the roll call of past glories and stares fixedly at the purple sky over the mountains that's fading to black. There's an anger in his eyes that's aching to leap out.

In a slurred voice he says, "All this should be gone after me."

"All what?"

"What I've created. My land, my businesses, everything. Why should the success and happiness I've built be here after me? It's all mine. It's as much a part of me as my bones or skin or lungs, and when I'm dust it should be too."

"You have kids."

Enoch waves his hand dismissively. "Children are just other people, like you are, or one of those golfers over there. We have them to be like everyone else. Anyway, children are for women; it's something

we give them to keep their biology in order. What I'm talking about..."
He pauses to corral his thoughts. "What I mean is that I've created my
own world, one that's bigger and better than most. If my creation is used
and enjoyed after I'm gone, then that's theft. And trespassing. Can you
understand that?"

"You want to finish on a funeral pyre of your possessions? Raze
your homes and salt the earth?"

He looks at me warily, unsure if I'm joking or serious. I'm not
sure myself.

Enoch holds his hand up and makes a fist, like some prophet
about to abuse or coerce a crowd. "What's mine is mine. It begins and
ends with me. Anything else is...not right."

He settles back in his chair, his eyelids drooping, and I welcome
the urge to smash his life out on the patio stones. It would be so easy. So
pleasurable. I roll the idea around in my mind and savor it, like a
sommelier tasting wine. Enoch is an endlessly thwarted child crying "no
fair" when the world puts things forever out of his reach.

"You look tired, Enoch. You should go to bed. Last night and
today have taken a toll; I certainly feel like crap."

"You didn't say if you understand me."

"I understand your frustrations, Enoch, but not why they exist."

He's too tired and drunk to unpick what I've said, so he contents
himself with nodding thoughtfully in a charade of comprehension. As he
gets to his feet, I move the empty pitcher so that it blocks his phone from
view. I ask him if he needs any help, and he waves me off and shuffles
into the bungalow. I wait ten minutes and then step inside the bungalow.
He's snoring lightly in the bedroom, so I go back to the patio. His phone
isn't locked. There's no app from a security company on his phone that
would let him operate the cameras. I go to the recent calls screen and use
my phone to take a picture of his calls from last night and today. There
aren't many calls, and I take pictures of each call's information screen as
well as his contact list.

When I get back to the clubhouse a large group of bros in their
twenties are waiting for their cars. They're shouty and playfully pushing
each other. I instinctively tense up with the muscle memory of dealing
with crowds like this in Hexum. These guys aren't in that league. They
quieten down as they get into their Audis and BMWs and follow the
club's posted speed limit of 15 mph on their way out. My Civic is the

last to arrive. The club has a no-tipping policy, but I need to celebrate the last time I'll have to come here so I slip the valet one of the hundreds from the ransom money. He's pushing fifty and shouldn't have to be doing this job, which is why he doesn't mention the policy as he jams the bill in his pocket and whispers his thanks.

Partway along the road out of Royal Palms I see a golf cart about to cross the road. The driver waits for me to go by and moments later I hear the howl of brakes on the asphalt. I stop and look back. A shabby-looking silver Mazda 3 has stopped just short of the golf cart. It must have been going at a fair clip to produce that much tire squeal, and golf cart guy is giving it to the driver about the speed limit. Mazda man is a bald white guy in his thirties wearing a bandage on his left forearm. He's half out of his car shouting "Sorry" repeatedly in a thick accent I can't place. The decrepit car and the accent mean he's staff, and he was probably racing to his second job. It'll be his only job now.

I get to the Capri just after eleven. It's discreet, retro neon sign glows invitingly at the end of a cul-de-sac called Jimmy Durante Drive, casting a pinkish light on a house that was built in the fifties to look like it had arrived from the future, and is now the hotel's reception area, bar and restaurant.

The woman at the front desk smiles at me and says, "Number four."

I walk through to the pool area. Nine cottages, mostly hidden by lush shrubbery, flank the large pool, but only number four has lights on.

Autumn's in a chaise longue on the patio in front of the cottage. She puts down her book and leads me by the hand into the bedroom. We can't be bothered to get fully undressed before we start making love. Afterwards, we take the rest of our clothes off and lie on the bed watching the ceiling fan turn, its breeze making us shiver pleasantly. I start to talk about what's happened since last night, but she silences me with a look. We make love again, and after that I slide into a sleep that feels like it's been months in coming.

I wake up in the morning and hear Autumn out on the patio ordering us breakfast. The bed has an iron grip on my will, and I would happily lie here until the sun burns out. My bladder disagrees. I shower, dress, and go outside. Autumn is in a white bathrobe, her hair wet from the pool or the shower, sitting at a low table. I kiss her neck and get a smell of lavender. Not the pool.

"Morning," I say.

She smiles, and it strikes me that hers is one of the few smiles I've never had to take the measure of.

"You look better," she says.

"Pour some coffee into me and I'll have my nine lives back."

"Good. Before you tell me what you've been up to there's a statement I'd like to read out to the court: when I shot at Enoch it was the most intense experience of my life; a come to Jesus with a loaded Glock moment. Like sex and Christmas morning rolled into one. Ever since you told me I'd missed, all I've wanted to do is recreate that moment more perfectly. I want his money and his life."

"The money's not enough? Is his death worth that much to you?"

"When I pulled the trigger on him, I lifted a curse; the curse was that I had never done the same to other men like Enoch. If I'd known how easy it is to feel this right about something, I would have killed my first man at sixteen. But I'm free now, and the least I can do for myself is enjoy watching Enoch's face as he sees me bringing death to him."

"You're overcomplicating this. The money's out there for you, no need to risk everything."

She looks at me with carnivorous intensity. "Are you with me? I can't promise to be rational or to tame my impulses. Since the other night I realize that I've got a taste for destruction that I didn't know I had. I'm saying that I'm a poor bet, but I desperately want you with me."

I want to say no. I have an overpowering sense of doom that I've felt before when I know that I might die. I don't want to feel this about Autumn, but I know that if I say no, she'll go it alone. She might die, she might get rich, and either way I'll be left without her. I used to be able to manage being alone—it defined my life—but now it's a harsh color I can see and a bitter flavor I can taste.

I take her hand. "I'm with you."

"Good. Now give me all the gory details."

I wait until our breakfast arrives and then tell her everything, including the death of Benito. She only interrupts to ask why I didn't tell her before about killing Benito. I explain that I didn't want her to be an accessory if the cops managed to connect me to him. When I finish she leans back, her fingers steepled in front of her face as she concentrates on what I've revealed.

"Why are you smiling?" she asks.

"You look like Sherlock Holmes considering a case."

"Fuck off," she says with a laugh. "But there are some things you may have missed, Watson."

"Such as?"

"The security cameras. I'm sure those lights you saw have never been on before, which means they were remotely activated. Are you sure the camera couldn't have seen me with the gun?"

"Positive. What about the feed?"

"It goes to a local security company. They don't monitor it, but it's kept on their server for a week. Only the customer can access it."

"Enoch doesn't have anything on his phone to do that."

"It's not an app. You go to the company's website and put in a password that lets you view or download what's been recorded or, apparently, activate the cameras for remote viewing. But Enoch is fucking helpless with technology and passwords. He can just about manage his laptop and that's it. But he could have given the password to a third party, someone who looked for him."

"Yes, the cameras would have to be monitored continuously if they were hoping to catch you at the house with me, and I don't think Enoch was in any shape for that kind of concentrated effort. He said he had a nap during the day and I believe him. No way he could have powered through the day after the previous night."

"Let's check the pictures you took of his phone, see if he called someone. If he made a call it'll be some time after you dropped him off at the clinic."

I get my phone out and we look at Enoch's recent calls.

There are two calls to a Los Angeles area code just after I dropped him off. The first call wasn't picked up. The second lasted eleven minutes. Then there was a call to a Las Vegas number at 7:36 that lasted twenty minutes. After that there was the call to Oribe that I saw and two calls to the golf club. About an hour before I got to the golf club the Las Vegas number phoned Enoch and they talked for eight minutes.

Autumn points to the Los Angeles number. "That one seems familiar."

We look at Enoch's contacts list. The number belongs to a Gideon Newcastle.

Autumn jumps up and paces around patio, her hands clenching into fists.

"What's the matter? You know this Newcastle?"

"I lied to you the other night when I said Enoch told me to leave because Oribe revealed everything."

"Oribe said something about Enoch forcing you to do something if he had proof of you paying for a hit."

"That was what Enoch came into my room that night for—to tell me that he had me dead to rights and that it was time for me to behave."

"Behave?"

"He wanted to lend me to Gideon Newcastle. His choice of word: *lend*."

"What the actual living fuck does that mean?"

Autumn sits beside me. "It means Newcastle has a thing for me; has had for a long time ever since he saw my movies back in the day. And now as a commission or reward for letting Enoch be part of this Selous Group, for getting a piece of whatever the big deal is, Gideon is demanding a taste of me. Enoch said it would only involve a month in Europe with Newcastle, and I would get to choose the destinations. Fun on a yacht in the Mediterranean. Sounds like a great time, right? How could a girl say no?"

I have to take a few moments before answering her. "So, this Gideon Newcastle; he's young and handsome, athletic build, and spends his free time volunteering at hostels?"

Autumn puts her arms around me. "Shockingly, no. He likes to massacre African animals and looks like someone stuck a pair of Mr. Potato Head eyes on a very old penis. By the way, you do a so-so job of not looking full of rage. Does any of this surprise you?"

"Not really. In my experience some men are relentless explorers of their vices."

"You sound like a second-tier superhero."

"No, a second-rate P.I."

We heal the moment by sitting there and holding each other for a while.

"You know why I didn't tell you about Newcastle after I thought I'd killed Enoch?"

"Why?"

"You would have done something stupid like try to cover for me. I didn't want you involved."

"Thanks, but we're well past that now."

"Indeed. Back to business: what do you make of that call to Vegas after the two calls to Newcastle?"

"First, who and what is Newcastle?"

"Gideon is Enoch with smarts and hunger. Sharper teeth, too. He's a landowner and developer—apartment and office buildings, planned communities, industrial parks, even some vineyards and farms. All of it's in California. I'd say he's worth north of two billion. You know what his favorite joke about himself is? He says, 'I'd like to describe myself as a shark when it comes to business, but the sharks would sue me for defamation of character.' What you said about some men being explorers of vice? He's fucking Magellan."

"Oribe recorded you saying that you might want someone else killed. Newcastle?"

"Uh huh."

"So why does Enoch reach out to him first thing? Newcastle doesn't sound like the kind of guy whose sleep you disturb without a good excuse."

"Same reason a child runs to a parent: comfort, explanation, support. And to warn him that I've got the laptop?"

"And maybe Newcastle gives him this Vegas number; it's some kind of 911 call for billionaires, or at least it is for these two."

"Enoch gives them the passcode or PIN or whatever for the security system and they start watching the house to see if we're colluding."

"And phone back after I leave to report to Enoch. I'd like to phone this Vegas number, but not on either of our phones. I'll go out and get a burner and call it. Have you had a look through the laptop?"

"Not yet. If Enoch did contact some kind of security outfit, then I'm guessing he's not interested in a payoff or deal. Gideon probably changed his mind on that."

"We'll just have to get more creative, and I think the way to our money is through that laptop. I'll be back as soon as I've got the phone."

"Tom."

"Yes?"

"This is going to be fun."

"It's more likely to be scary."

"Both are fine with me."

I leave Autumn on the patio with Enoch's laptop and drive to a Best Buy to pick up a phone. I get back in my car with the burner and give the Vegas number a call. No answer, just an automated voice asking me to leave a message. It's possible Newcastle told Enoch not to go forward with any deal. Or did he suggest something more vigorous?

I turn onto Durante and see a car parked on the side of street about a hundred yards from the Capri. This isn't the kind of neighborhood where people street park. The driveways and garages are generous, and the police are quick with parking tickets. I glance at the car as I go past. It's a silver Mazda 3, and the man with the bandage on his forearm is behind the wheel, watching the Capri.

Settlement

Two nights after Halloween I went back to Hexum. I was afraid, but
Reinhart's vow of protection gave me some confidence, and so did
Levi's revolver, which I carried in my backpack.

The night air tasted burnt and almost gritty from a big wildfire
that was burning far to the east near the coast. I went to the playground
and found Malachi sitting on the bottom of a slide staring at the ground
between his feet. He looked up as I approached, and half his face broke
into an eager grin. The other half was too bruised and swollen to do
much of anything.

He rushed up to me and shook my hand. "You came back," he
said happily, as a few tears, vivid against the yellow and purple bruises,
ran down his face.

"Shit, what happened to you?"

Malachi raised a hand to his wounded face. "Founder hit me with
a plank."

"Why?"

"I spoke wrongly to one of the Eves."

It made perfect sense to me because it made no sense. Levi hit me
for no reason that I truly understood, so there was a strange satisfaction
in learning that someone much like me was getting kicked around. It
must be normal. I told Malachi about my beatings and it thrilled him that
I was a fellow victim. We moved over to the swings and, as we sailed
back and forth, started comparing thrashings we had taken in the past.

"Why did he use a plank on you?"

"That's what he was holding at the time. One of the Eves had
come into the workshop with his lunch—he always has a big lunch—and
I told her she should have two of those lunches because she's so skinny.
It was kind of a joke. He walloped me good then, and said my language
and thoughts were carnal. I think he was right. Is your father going to
come back?"

"If he wasn't, I think someone would have told me by now."

"You miss him?"

I had to think about this. "I want to miss him, but that's not the
same as really missing him."

"You don't hate him?"

"Same sorta thing: I want to hate him, but..."

We swung in silence for a few minutes and then got off.

Malachi suddenly hugged himself with excitement and said, "You want to go looking?"

"For what?"

"In windows."

This didn't sound interesting, but I agreed to go along with him. He led me into a part of town with big, well-kept homes sitting on wide, grassy lawns. It was approaching midnight and very few windows were showing light. I asked Malachi what he wanted to see, but he only giggled and headed towards a house that was shielded from the street by trees and tall shrubs that grew close to its walls. I suspected Malachi wanted to see girls undressing or undressed. Levi often watched movies in which women would be getting out of their clothes or taking a shower while men secretly watched. Malachi moved to the side of the house and slipped between a gap in the bushes and carefully approached a darkened window. I moved silently behind him and looked in the window over his shoulder. It was a living room: couches, chairs, television, tables, lamps, a gas fireplace, pictures on the wall, some magazines on the floor, a ceiling fan, and dozens of other bits and pieces. My heart was pounding as I scanned the room, fully expecting to see something shocking.

"What do you see?" I whispered.

"Look at all that stuff," Malachi whispered back. "If I lived here I'd sit in that chair, the one closest to us, because you'd be able to see the TV and fireplace at the same time without moving your head. And I'd have more pictures on the wall—pictures of animals and pictures of me—and I'd put something on that fan so that it made a funny noise or waved something when it worked. Let's try over here."

He led me to the back of the house and we looked in at an equally dark kitchen. There were glass-fronted cabinets on the walls filled with dishes, boxes of cereal, cans, spices, bowls, and a few small appliances.

"What's that, Tom? Beside the sink."

"A food processor."

"And the box beside it?"

"Uh, dishwasher powder. Calgon."

"How about that box over there?"

"Pancake mix. Aunt Jemima."

"Oh, pancakes," he said excitedly. "I've had those."

"Can't you read?"

"I can read; I just don't know what's in things. Why's that pancake mix got a nigger woman on it?"

A light came on in a window above our heads and we bolted from the yard, crashing through bushes and running a block away before we slowed down. I followed Malachi to several more darkened houses that night, standing beside him as he described the things he'd do in the different rooms, answering his questions when he saw something unknown to him. I didn't ask Malachi why he didn't know about common things. His ignorance was fascinating to me, and I found it deeply satisfying to describe the fragments of the world that puzzled him. Malachi was living in an incomplete jigsaw puzzle and I was helping him connect one piece to another.

By two in the morning I was tired and hungry. Malachi was still filled with a feverish desire to press on and look in more houses.

"I'm done, Malachi. I gotta eat and sleep."

He pouted and begged until I offered to give him a ride home on my bike.

"You got a motorcycle?" he said incredulously.

"A dirt bike."

We weren't far from where I had parked the bike, and Malachi peppered me with questions about it the whole way. There was barely room for him on the back of it, and when I told him to hang on tight, he practically crushed my ribs. He directed me to go north of town to a secondary road that ran off the road to the mine. I didn't take it very fast through town, but it was still a thrill ride for Malachi. He gasped with shock or pleasure at every turn or sudden acceleration.

A cop car with two deputies inside pulled alongside us, and I slowed down. One of them lowered his window and asked, "You're Reinhart's guy, ain't you?"

"I am!" I shouted.

"Okay. Watch out for potholes, there's some real monsters up ahead."

"Thanks."

He raised his window and the car U-turned sharply, like a fighter jet breaking formation.

Malachi's place was half a mile out of town. When he shouted in my ear to stop, I thought he was fooling around. On the left side of the road was a big Quonset hut workshop made of dull gray steel. The front of the workshop had tall sliding doors, and near the apex of the hut a single light that formed the nucleus for a cloud of moths illuminated a sign that read: GAUNT SMALL ENGINE REPAIR. The area immediately around the hut was paved, and yard tractors and Bobcats were parked in neat rows on either side of it. A wire fence ran around the property and the driveway into it was blocked with a low metal gate that was locked. There were no other buildings in sight and no neighbors, just flat fields covered in brush and a stand of trees.

"You live here?" I asked, thinking that Malachi had tricked me into doing some more looking in windows.

"I do. My home is around the back of the workshop. Do you want to see?"

Malachi was subdued, and I wasn't sure he actually wanted me to follow him onto the property. I parked by the gate and Malachi led me around the back of the workshop. The land behind sloped down into a shallow depression about an acre in size that held a scattering of buildings made of raw-looking lumber. It reminded me of pictures I'd seen of old logging camps.

With a slight tremor in his voice Malachi said, "This is the Settlement."

The biggest building looked like a letter L laid on its side. The long part didn't have doors or windows, and was attached to a narrow, two-storey house that had a door on the ground level and a big picture window on its second floor. There was also a small barn, an A-frame building, a large storage shed, and, nearest to us, what looked like an elongated dog house that was surrounded by bits of scrap wood and sawdust. Four sodium lamps mounted on tall poles at each corner of the area cast a burning light. Bats picking off insects drawn to the lamps cast swift, erratic shadows on the ground and buildings.

"That's mine," said Malachi, pointing to the dog house.

It was about four feet high, with a small door that looked like it belonged on a playhouse. I walked over to it, squatted down and pulled the door open. There was a rolled-up sleeping bag, a foam pad, a pillow, and a small electric heater.

"Don't you have any games or books or anything?" I asked.

"There are some play blocks in Founder's house for the little ones."

"You've got brothers and sisters?"

"Five. They're all lots younger than me."

Malachi was nervous having me here, but he also had a pleading look in his eyes. I guessed that he wanted to show me more, to take his turn being the guide to a new world.

"What are these other buildings for?"

"The big house, the one with the long bit on the side, that's Founder's dwelling. He sleeps on the bottom floor, and his office's on the top floor, the one with the windows."

"What's in the other part on the side?"

"That's where the Eves and the children sleep. And also the bathrooms."

"These Eves are like wives, right?"

"Yes. He has four. Thursday told me he wants to have six, one for each day of the week except for Sunday because that would be blasphemy."

"They're named for the days of week? Those their real names?"

"Now they are. Founder named them when he got them."

"Is Thursday your mother?"

Malachi's expression changed. He withdrew into himself for a moment and become older.

"No. My mother left when I was five and became a hellion apostate."

"A what?"

"That's what Founder calls her."

"What was her name?" I was curious to learn which day of the week she was named for.

"I don't know. I can't remember," said Malachi in a thin voice that made me think he was lying.

I asked about the other buildings and he told me that the barn was where the kitchen and dining area was. The A-frame doubled as a church and school. According to Malachi, the reason there was only one door in the big house was to prevent anyone sneaking in or out at night. The only exit from the house led through Founder's bedroom, where he took a different wife to bed every night. During the day, which began at seven, Malachi helped his father in the workshop. At eight sharp every evening

Founder retired to the house with the women and children and locked the door.

I was itching for a closer look at this bizarre encampment, and Malachi followed me nervously, whispering that we had to be dead quiet, as I walked past the barn and then the church. The buildings looked no less rough and ready at close range: boards were loose, joints had gaps, and nails had been hammered in at all angles. Malachi, with his sunken cheeks and ill-fitting, dirty clothes, looked very much at home here.

"Your dad's a Mormon, right? Don't they have lots of wives?"

"No. We're that." Malachi pointed to a wooden sign above the church door. In letters burnt into the wood it read: REFORMED CHURCH OF THE RIGHTEOUS FATHERS.

"You the only ones in this church?"

"No. A few men come to Sunday services, and Founder's people belong, but they're back in Oregon. That's where we came from—there's lots more of them up there."

"Let's look at the place where the women and kids are."

"No," said Malachi with quiet panic. "Founder might hear us. I shouldn't have let you get this close."

"Okay."

We went back to Malachi's sleeping box.

"Will you be at the playground tomorrow night, Tom?"

His hunger for companionship, like all his emotions, shone in his face. He was a cartoon character animated by the warped little world he'd just shown me.

"Maybe," I answered. "I've got some things to do."

That was a lie, but I needed time to think about how well I wanted to know Malachi and estimate how far his craziness might go. He shook my hand sadly and watched me as I walked back towards the gate.

I drove my bike a short distance down the road and stopped on a rise. Looking back through some leafless trees, I could see Malachi crawling into his wooden burrow. A faint glow was coming from the window in the big house. I revved my motor a few times. A man's silhouette moved in front of the window, and even from that distance I could tell that he must be huge. I didn't leave until he moved away from the window.

I spent the next two days in my usual routine and began to think about what would happen if Levi never came back. I turned the idea of going to school over in my head, even though I was leery that it would somehow cause trouble for Levi, and maybe me, if I went someplace that asked for birth certificates and signatures and addresses and so on. But then, what would be so bad about that? If they took me to an orphanage or foster home, couldn't that be better? I might be put somewhere far out of the reach of Jubal and Spencer. Down the road I knew I'd have to get a high school diploma. I didn't know why, exactly, but I knew I needed it.

On my next trip to the book store I stared at some shelves of math and science books. This was the sort of stuff I needed to know if I went to school, and then it occurred to me that maybe I wouldn't even be allowed to go to school; I hadn't been in a classroom in five years, so they might bar me or make me take a test.

"Why are you looking at those?" demanded the owner of the store.

I was shocked that he spoke to me. He normally sat behind the store's counter buried in a paperback, always science fiction, and only looked up to give directions or make a sale. He was in his usual uniform of a battered Padres baseball cap and the severely baggy gray cardigan that made him look like an emaciated elephant.

"Just looking," I said.

"You're normally a novel and history guy, so I thought you were looking for something special."

"Do you know about what they test you for to get into school?"

"You home-schooled?"

"Yeah."

"Then why do you want to go to school?"

"Well, I mean, what do you have to do to get a high school diploma?"

"You pass a kind of exam called the equivalency test. You don't do it until you're eighteen, I think."

This was good news. I had years to learn some of these subjects. I opened a thick book about physics, read a random section and felt dizzy. A chemistry book was equally alarming.

"So which church you belong to?" the man asked.

"None."

He reacted with surprise. "Really? The home-schooling folks who come here to get stuff for their kids always belong to some kind of church."

"A friend of mine is home-schooled and theirs is the Reformed Church of the Righteous Fathers. Ever hear of it?"

"No, that's a new one on me. But there's others with names like that around here. In my experience the longer the name of the church, the more batshit crazy they are. Pardon my French."

"My friend's father has four wives."

"Oh, it's one of those I-can't-get-laid-any-other-way churches, is it? Pardon my French, again."

"They have a place north of town; his father has an engine repair business."

"Caleb Gaunt? I took an air conditioner out to him a few months ago. He's good at what he does, but you can tell he's got the stink of almighty God on him. Doesn't stop him from fixing every piece of gear the growers and cookers bring his way." He paused, as though worried that he had said too much. "Anyway, why don't you try learning Spanish? That might count for something in getting a diploma."

A few minutes later I brought a Spanish textbook up to the counter.

"What's your name?" I asked.

He was taken aback by my question. "Latimer."

"I just wondered. I mean, your store doesn't have a sign out front."

"Fell off years ago. No point in replacing it; there's only one book store in Hexum and everyone knows where it is and who owns it."

When I got home I took a stab at the textbook. It was tolerable. For the next few weeks I devoted time each day to learning Spanish. Unless there was a hockey game on TV that I really wanted to watch, I'd go into Hexum every night. Not always to see Malachi, but often. If Latimer thought Caleb had the stink of God on him, I knew his son had an air of imminent disaster about him. His carousel of emotions was entertaining and intriguing, but there was a menace that shadowed him. Someone that mercurial was, I judged, bound to flame out.

I'd meet up with Malachi at the schoolyard and we'd cruise around town. Looking in windows was his main pleasure, but I found it tiresome. I'd stay out on the sidewalks, keeping watch, and let him gawp.

If he didn't get to look into at least a couple of homes a night he'd get moody. He had no money of his own, so sometimes I'd take him to a burger place or doughnut shop, but those environments always overwhelmed him. He'd cram his food down quickly and in silence, and then the second we were back outside he'd release a torrent of questions about the food and the other customers. I put up with all this because I could tell Malachi anything and he would listen with keen attention and never pass judgment. I told him my father was a criminal, my mother had left us, that my father's friends did terrible things, and that I had done some bad things myself. He said he felt sorry for me and that no doubt my "natural goodness" would see me right in the end. I didn't disclose that I was a murderer.

The main reason I spent time with Malachi was that the pocket universe he lived in behind the Quonset hut fascinated me, and I slowly got him to give me a more complete picture of his life.

Malachi had grown up in a compound outside Bend, Oregon. It was much like the one he was in now, but larger and shared with two other families, all of them Righteous Fathers followers. They called their piece of land and its buildings the "Settlement." His mother's name was Dawn and came originally from a Righteous family in Idaho. Caleb had been working as a clerk in a convenience store and had saved up twelve thousand dollars—the bride price for Dawn. She was fourteen and he was thirty-seven. Caleb changed her name to one of his choosing— Verity—as was church custom. She ran away in a car stolen from one of the other families when Malachi was five. Caleb had to pay for the stolen property. Malachi couldn't recall what his mother looked like, but he remembered that she never let him call her Mom or Verity, only Dawn. But not when Caleb was around. After she left, Malachi was raised by the other families while Caleb worked two jobs to pay off his debt and acquire enough money to buy another wife. Although Malachi was schooled and ate with the other children in the compound, they weren't allowed to play with him. He was what the Righteous called "marred" by his mother's sin. Three years ago, Caleb inherited enough money to build his own settlement in Hexum, as well as buying four brides. Two came from the same family in Colorado, the other two from Montana and Nevada.

Day began in the Settlement with the women and children leaving their sleeping quarters and filing past Caleb in his bedroom. He'd get a "Good morning, Founder," from each of them before they went over to the kitchen/dining barn where two of the women would prepare breakfast, while the others took care of the children. It was oatmeal and scrambled eggs every morning except Saturdays, which was pancake day. Lunches were sandwiches, usually peanut butter, and dinners were spaghetti, or occasionally meatloaf. The smallest children had milk, everyone else drank water. Twice a week Caleb would go into town to get groceries. Twice a month or so he'd drive to a larger town and buy a big supply of fabric and sewing supplies for the women. When the wives weren't cooking or cleaning or teaching the kids, they made quilts that Caleb would sell on eBay. Their own clothes came from what Caleb picked up in thrift stores. None of the Eves or the children were allowed to leave the Settlement. Except, it seemed, Malachi.

"Why," I asked him one night, "does Caleb let you off the property? He's gotta know you go out at night, doesn't he?"

The question distressed him. We were sitting on a bench in a small park that held a fountain and a statue of a soldier from World War Two. Malachi leaned his elbows on his knees and stared at the ground. He stayed like this for so long that I began to wonder what was wrong with him. The park was full of fallen leaves that scratched and hissed as a sudden gust of wind gave them life and broke Malachi's reverie.

He looked up at me, and in the quietest voice I'd ever heard him use, he said, "I've thought much on that too, and I think Founder would like me to go away."

"How come?"

He shook his head slowly. "I'm marred, and Founder thinks I'll cause the Eves or the little ones to become like me."

"Bullshit."

"Something of my mother is in me. Why would I want to wander at night? I shouldn't, but I do. She left me behind because she knew I was as wrong as her. My bloodstock is poor and Satan has painted a black stripe on my soul." Malachi tapped his chest gently and whispered, "I *am* marred."

"So why hasn't he just kicked you out?"

"Founder's merciful."

"Founder's fucking cheap, you mean; you work for free in the workshop. Think he wants to pay a stranger to be around all his wives?

And don't call him Founder when you're with me. He can't hear you. Call him that cheap fucker Caleb."

Anger flooded my body. Malachi looked at me as though I was telling him to grow wings and fly.

"Go on," I yelled, "call him that cheap fucker Caleb."

I didn't know if he was going to run away or hit me.

"I've heard you say 'fuck' before, Malachi, now just add two more words to it."

He said it, but it sounded like a cat bringing up a fur ball.

"Again," I urged him.

He said it with more confidence. And said it again. And then began to chant it as the ecstasy of rebellion took hold of him. He leaped to his feet and ran around the park, his arms held out from his body like wings, his bellows echoing through the night. He even climbed the statue and shouted his curse in the soldier's bronze ear. After that night he never said Founder in front of me again.

In late November I told Malachi that I was going to take him the next night to an actual sit-down restaurant—Applebee's—instead of going to a burger place. He practically danced with excitement and shook my hand so energetically it was sore the next day. I arranged to pick him up at the end of the road to his place after it got dark. Malachi had no means of telling time in the Settlement—he didn't have a wristwatch or clock—so he generally judged time by how long it had been dark or light.

I waited at the end of the road, and when Malachi hadn't showed up after half an hour I walked to the Settlement and tapped on the door of his wooden hut and whispered his name. There was no answer, but I could hear a slight movement from within.

"You there, Malachi?"

"I am," he replied, his voice raspy like someone who's been crying or shouting too much.

"You coming out or what?"

"No."

"Why? We're going to Applebee's. You were going to try ribs."

"No."

"Did that bastard hurt you? You okay?"

"I'm well in body, Tom."

I pulled the toy door open. The light was faint, but his face was unmarked and he stared back at me from the far end of his sleeping chamber with eyes that were red from crying.

"What's the matter?"

"I've sinned, Tom. I've added to the black mark on my soul."

"What did you do?"

"I can't say. It would cut my mouth like glass and thorns just to speak the words to describe it."

"Can't be that bad unless you killed Caleb."

Malachi said nothing and put his head on his pillow.

"So, you going to stay in here forever?"

I waited a minute or more for him to speak, but when his eyes began to close I said, "Well, maybe I'll see you around then."

I closed his door and took a look at Caleb's Settlement. Nothing was changed from the first time I saw it. The four floodlights hummed faintly, a dim light came from the house's second floor window, and a pair of pants left on a clothesline moved in the breeze as though trying to run away. I walked towards the house, watching my steps carefully so as not to step on or kick something that would make a noise. I moved around the extension housing the women and kids, stopping twice to see if I could hear something from behind the windowless plank walls. The main house had a low porch on the front that looked like it would squeak and groan just by looking at it. I stepped slowly onto it and moved to the door. It was faint, but I could hear a rhythmic slapping noise and intermittent murmurs from inside the house. I listened for a few moments and then moved carefully off the porch. A few minutes later I was back on my bike.

For the next week, I regularly checked the schoolyard as well as driving through the neighborhoods where Malachi usually did his "looking." He never appeared. I decided to forget about him, telling myself he'd probably gone full religious nutjob.

As I traversed the town at night, I became aware that very few ordinary citizens were out after dark. Some would be around at dusk, walking their dogs or telling their kids to come inside, but by ten o'clock the streets were empty. It wasn't hard to figure out why: at night Hexum belonged to shiny SUVs and pickups bedecked with gleaming accessories that roamed through town calling out to each other with their thudding stereos like beasts on a plain. The men who drove them would often slow down to check out people on foot, then sometimes lower a window to shout instructions or abuse. A few times I saw them chase people and drag them back to their vehicles, the slam of a door cutting off cries of fear or calls for mercy. Later in the night I might hear shots crack apart the night. They left me alone. News of Reinhart's benediction had travelled swiftly. The only people who regularly walked late at night were Asian and Latino men coming and going to labs or fields, their faces hungry for something the town couldn't give them.

My rambles around Hexum had no particular purpose; I enjoyed studying the town as though it were a large and living diorama laid out for my pleasure. The houses that had permanent parties became familiar to me, as did the brothels and anonymous buildings where men went to work at all hours of the day and night. Strange dramas often played out on the darkened streets: once I saw a pair of deputies laughing as they chased an Asian woman running barefoot down Main St., and another night I witnessed a deranged addict having a bloody fistfight with a telephone pole.

I'd sometimes run into Sherriff Reinhart at Maxi Donuts, an all-night coffee shop out by Mission Commons. He'd ask how I was doing, offer to buy me something to eat or drink, and introduce me to whomever he was sitting with. He was always with one or two men. Most of them were the nocturnal drivers of the big cars, their mounts making ticking sounds of cooling metal as they rested outside the shop. The men would acknowledge me but remain silent until I'd moved away from their table, then lean forward and resume intense conversations. Reinhart always appeared to be amused by whatever was being said to him.

One night I ran into Reinhart as he was coming out of the coffee shop and cramming a thick envelope into a jacket pocket. As usual, he looked happy and relaxed.

"How's it hangin', Tom?"

"Fine, Josh. It's getting cold out now."

"It certainly is but can't complain; winters are a hell of a lot worse back where you're from. You keeping okay?"

"Yeah, no problems."

"Money holding out?"

"Yup."

"And you're keeping up your education? Levi was very firm on that last time I heard from him."

My stomach lurched and I said, "You heard from him."

"In a roundabout way. Before you ask, no, I don't know when he's coming back. But you're doing fine, Tom. I think, no, I *know* that any other boy in your position would not manage like you have. Latimer tells me you're in his place buying the right kinds of books all the time, and my deputies say you keep your nose clean at night. You have manned up to the situation, Tom. I even hear you put the fear of God into Spencer." I started to say something but he put his hand up and said, "Spence can be bumptious, and his hobbies can cloud his judgement, but he knows his job, and the way he bitched about you told me that you'd shown him more grit and backbone than he knew how to deal with. I'm proud of you, Tom. You were made for this life and this part of the world. You keep on like you are and you've got a place at my side."

Reinhart's speech left me both proud and alarmed. I didn't like that Spencer was complaining about me, but Reinhart's promise of some vague, future role with him I found comforting. Whenever I imagined a future for myself, I could only see chaos.

"Thanks," I mumbled, and then asked, "Do you know Caleb Gaunt?"

"Caleb? Oh, yeah, he's that repair guy. I hear he's got himself a harem in that stockade behind his shop. Why?"

"I'm sort of friends with his son, Malachi, and I'm worried about him. I haven't seen him for a while and I know Caleb beats him pretty bad sometimes, and so..."

Reinhart spat on the ground, removed his cowboy hat, and ran a hand through his hair.

"Beats him, huh? Well, I know fathers have their rights, but I am not a believer in corporal punishment. My daddy was quick and determined with his belt, and all it taught me was how to run and hide and tell lies. One sin just births another, I guess. I'll tell you what: lets you and me go out there tomorrow afternoon and see how your friend is. And I should probably have a word with Caleb about that business of his—I hear it's profitable."

Reinhart picked me up at the house the next day in his cruiser and we drove out to Gaunt's. The sliding doors on the front of the workshop were open and we could hear the scream of an angle grinder as we got out of the car. The workshop was crammed with shelves loaded with disembowelled engines, tools, parts, paint cans, and containers of degreasers, WD-40, and a dozen other liquids. An engine crane in the front of the shop held a motor that wept slow black tears. The air smelled sharp and infernal.

Josh reached back into the cruiser and made the siren yelp a few times. The angle grinder was turned off and a man emerged from the far end of the shop and moved unhurriedly towards us. He was tall and wide and fat. His weight didn't make him look weak or soft; it was armor plating on something slow and powerful. He was well over six feet tall, with a broad head covered in short, salt and pepper hair that sat on a throne of a double chin. His stiff, dark green workpants and shirt were blotched with sweat, and he took a handkerchief out of a back pocket and patted his glistening forehead with a surprisingly delicate gesture as he studied us. His tiny eyes were alive with interest, but his face was immobile; a ruddy Easter Island statue with an appraising stare. He could be a shaved bear, I thought.

"Can I help you?" he asked tonelessly in a voice as heavy as his body.

"Mr. Gaunt? I'm Sherriff Reinhart, and this is my friend Tom. I thought I'd drop by and say hello. I like to introduce myself to new businesses, let them know how we can help each other do our jobs. And it turns out Tom is friends with your son Malachi, so, Tom, why don't you cut along and find him while Caleb and I talk about some of our mutual friends in the agricultural business?"

Gaunt's expression didn't change as he said, "I'd rather my son and my family not be disturbed. We have a great many chores and tasks taking place here today and Malachi is responsible for many of them. Also, we are a Christian community with a deep and lonely calling; mixing with outsiders, people not of our church, is something we shun. I am the bulwark of my family's faith and must protect them from worldliness. It's a rocky path we've chosen, but we take it alone."

"Did you like that James Bond movie?" I asked matter-of-factly.

Gaunt blinked rapidly. "What?"

"*The World is Not Enough*. I saw you at it last week at the Regal Cinema out at Mission Commons. You sat down front and I was at the back. You were at *The Matrix*, too. That was really good, wasn't it? Did you go to Denny's afterwards? I've seen you in there a few times when I was with my father."

As soon as Gaunt had trudged into view I'd recognized him. Over a year ago Levi and I had been in Denny's and seen Caleb come rolling into the place. Levi had leaned over to me and whispered, "Here comes a buffet's worst nightmare." I'd laughed then and I smiled now. One look at Caleb and there was no forgetting him. I'd seen him since then at least a dozen times during the day at the movies and fast food places.

Reinhart saw that Gaunt was off-balance and said, "The movies, huh? Don't find time myself to go to them, but it's nice that you take advantage of what Hexum offers. So, maybe I should take a mosey around your shop. We get reports of stolen equipment all the time, not that I think you'd be doing anything like that, Caleb, but the stuff can turn up most anywhere. Tom, you go look for your pal."

Caleb tried to say something, but Josh put a hand on his massive arm and steered him into the workshop, asking as he did so: "What's a bulwark, Caleb?"

I hurried around to the rear of the building. Two of the wives were sitting on white plastic lawn chairs in front of the kitchen peeling potatoes. Another was inside the church holding a baby and talking to three young children who sat on the floor in front of her. I looked in Malachi's hut—empty—and then walked over to the women in front of the kitchen. When they noticed me approaching they jumped up and gasped. Like Malachi, they were skinny, even though one of them was pregnant. They both had long ponytails, and wore plain, knee-length floral dresses that were the frayed ghosts of their original colors. The pregnant one wore a puffy yellow jacket over her dress. Her slim body made her perfectly rounded belly look like a cartoon version of a pregnancy. Their tired faces made it hard to estimate their age. No more than twenty, I guessed.

"Hi," I said. "Is Malachi around?"

They looked at each other and said nothing. I asked again.

The pregnant girl pointed somewhere behind her and in an uncertain voice said, "He's helping Thursday put out the laundry."

The clothesline was at the back of the property, hidden behind the A-frame. No one was there. The line was crowded with dripping clothes that should have ended their lives at Goodwill. Two empty laundry baskets lay on the ground. A little farther back on the property was an old panel truck facing towards me that, from the look of it, had been abandoned decades ago. It sat low to the ground on its tireless rims, its back doors hanging open, rust eating away at its sides. A sound come from the truck and I moved towards it at an angle that let me see into the back from about fifty feet away.

A girl was lying the floor of the truck on a brown wool blanket. She was naked. Her eyes were open, but she must have blinded by the sunlight that shone in her face because she didn't see me. Malachi, wearing only a shirt, was on top of her, thrusting into her slowly. She had his face cupped in her hands and smiled each time he moved against her.

Bernelli

Autumn is swimming laps in the pool. The water's striped with shadows from overhanging palm trees, and her body appears to flicker as she slices rapidly through bands of sun and shade. She sees me but continues swimming, her clean, precise strokes barely making a splash. When she has to do some serious thinking she often goes for a swim. I go inside the cottage and lie on the bed. She comes in a few minutes later, out of breath and wrapped in a white bathrobe.

"We have company," I say.

"Oh?"

"A guy I saw last night when I was leaving Royal Palms is parked down the street watching this place."

"He tailed you here?"

"He was held up leaving the course, but he might have caught up with me. I wasn't paying attention. Did you use your credit card here yet?"

"Yeah. Shit. Enoch has access to my credit card accounts. He'd see where I was."

"Doesn't matter how they found us, it's what comes next that's important."

"Why follow us?"

"To prove we're having an affair? He might think that counts towards paying out less money to you, or maybe giving you nothing at all."

Autumn tosses away her bathrobe, strips out of her swimsuit, and gets a towel from the bathroom and starts drying her hair. She sees the way I'm looking at her.

"Later," she says with a smile, and then says decisively: "I don't think Enoch is behind this. He's too slow, too cautious. That's why he's always had to find ambitious men with energy to partner with. It's got to be Gideon. Enoch phoned Gideon, then the Vegas number, and then we're followed. Gideon put him in touch with whoever's following us, or Gideon gave the orders for it to happen."

"Because of this Selous Group, right?"

"Right."

"You have any luck with his laptop?"

"Some. I'm still trying to piece it together. So how do we find out who's out there?"

"I've got his licence plate number, and I think I might have a friend on the local force."

"Really?"

I call the main number for the Rancho Vista Police and ask for Hackett. I'm transferred to his office phone but there's no answer, so I leave my number and a message that I'm calling on behalf of Mr. Marsden.

Autumn finishes with the towel, drapes it around her neck, and stands at the foot of the bed.

"You don't have someone at Hessian who could put a name to the licence plate?" she asks.

"Yes, but they couldn't do it as fast, and who's to say that it isn't a Hessian guy out there? He may have contacted Hessian from a different phone, told them I was a problem. Marsden is more important to them as a client than I am as an employee."

"So, until we found out who's following us, you can't trust Hessian."

"Uh huh."

"I'll work on that laptop in the meantime."

"That's a plan. Is it later now?"

She throws the towel away. "Yes indeed."

Afterwards, she lies on her side studying me, her hand resting lightly on my stomach. I don't want to look at her; I'm afraid that something in my face will give away what I'm feeling.

"You were different just now," she says.

"How so?"

"It's hard to describe…Like you wanted to drink me in…put me inside you. Is there something wrong?"

"Not with us."

I can't tell her how sure I am that those who come close to me live on borrowed time. I should try and send her away, or convince her that she should meekly offer favorable terms to Enoch and quietly leave the field of battle. But that would break us apart. Autumn is committed to vengeance like a character from mythology.

My phone rings. It's Hackett.

"What can I help you with, Mr. Bridger?" His voice is cold. He doesn't want to be friendly with someone from Hessian, but he just as badly wants to be on Marsden's team.

"Thanks for returning my call, Mr. Hackett. Uh, how I should I put this? When you stopped Mrs. Marsden the other day you stumbled into a bit of a family drama. Some years ago, before she knew Mr. Marsden, Mrs. Marsden was in another relationship. It ended badly. In the last month she's received communications about some videos from that relationship, and the inference was that she and Mr. Marsden might want to pay to get possession of them. The person who controlled the material never used the word 'blackmail.' He only offered it for sale. The Marsdens had a disagreement about how to handle this—a fight, in other words—and Autumn left for one of their other residences. She's since told us that she was approached by a man who showed her images from the videos. She doesn't know him, he didn't give a name, but she did get his licence plate number. Mr. Marsden was hoping you could give us the name that goes with that plate. After that, my company can take over the matter. Enoch would be very much in your debt if you could help him with this affair because he certainly doesn't want it getting into the public arena."

Hackett is silent. He's wise to be reluctant: police forces often log searches for licence plate numbers, and freelance searching can get you demoted or suspended. But there are work arounds. Autumn raises a questioning eyebrow at me and I shrug.

"I'll check," says Hackett. "And please ask Mr. Marsden to keep me in mind for any positions that come up at Royal Palms. I'll call back in a bit."

I end the call after thanking him profusely and mentioning how grateful Enoch will be.

Autumn fist bumps me and says, "Nice storytelling, honey."

"Thank you, dearest."

She gives me a kiss and hops off the bed. "First a shower, and then I'm doing a deep dive on that laptop. You?"

"Also a shower, and then a leisurely visit to the bar. I can see up the road from there and watch our watcher. If it's any kind of proper, organized surveillance, he'll be spelled off by someone. I want to see any extra faces or cars."

The hotel's bar is advertised as a 'reimagining of the Tiki bar concept.' It's a lot of dark wood, eccentric hanging lights, and cocktails that cost as much as meals. I get a bottle of Pacifico and sit at a table that gives me a view down the street. The Mazda is still there, a man's silhouette behind the wheel. I'm halfway through my beer when Hackett calls back.

"I got it for you," he says. "It's registered to a company called Lodestar in Las Vegas."

He gives me the address and ends the call before I even have a chance to thank him. He's scared, and I don't think I'll get a second chance to use him. I may have heard the name Lodestar mentioned at Hessian, but I don't want to contact the office to ask about them. Hessian might have some awkward questions for me if Enoch's gotten in touch with them. Not that it matters; my days with Hessian are over. I decide to call Leon Dooley; he retired from Hessian a few months ago so he won't have heard anything about me.

Leon answers right away and whistles when I mention Lodestar. "Oh, man, they are the security company you call when you want a final fucking solution to your problems. I mean, you know, we just scared people, bloodied some noses, broke a leg, but Lodestar is the goddamn major leagues. They mostly do contract security work over in Iraq and Afghanistan, close protection work for VIPs, a lot of really heavy shit. I was working a case up in San Jose once, an IT company that was sure one of its employees was leaking intel to a competitor. They thought we weren't solving things fast enough, so they dumped us for Lodestar. A week later the guy I had figured as the source turns up dead on Pescadero Beach. The cops said he went swimming at night, drowned, and then got run over by a fishing boat. Right. I started asking around about Lodestar after that. It's owned by some former general who was big news in the second Iraq War, and he's got all these ex-special forces guys working for him, mostly American, some from Britain and Israel. They make big problems die a quick death."

"Fuck," I say with feeling.

"You're not tangling with them, are you? I thought you were busy clearing the thieves out of that restaurant chain?"

"I am, but it got sidetracked. Thanks, Leon."

I finish my beer and signal the bartender for another. She brings it over with a bowl of cashews and is about to say something friendly but then catches the look on my face. Autumn was right: Enoch can't act this quickly or ruthlessly. It's got to be Gideon Newcastle, and he doesn't give a shit about Enoch's marriage; it's the Selous Group he's worried about. I try not to convince myself that he's worried enough to have us killed.

A dark green Tahoe with Nevada plates pulls up beside the Mazda. There are two men inside the Tahoe and the passenger hands a small box over to the Mazda driver. The Tahoe does a three-point turn and leaves. The Mazda driver gets out of his car holding something in his hand and disappears into the shrubs and trees that mask the wall around the property he's parked in front of. He's back in the car minutes later, empty-handed, and drives away.

I finish the cashews and most of my beer as I add up what I've just seen. The Lodestar guys can't be cancelling the surveillance, which means they have another way to keep tabs on us. They must have a tracker on one or both of our cars. Probably mine. Only mine. They didn't know where Autumn was until I led them here. The Mazda driver would have had time to plant one on my Civic back at Royal Palms, that's why it didn't matter that he was blocked from following me. So why leave now? The trip into the bushes has to be about monitoring us. They don't want to hang around in plain sight in case they're spotted or the police move them along.

I leave a twenty for the bartender and take a roundabout route to the hotel's parking lot that keeps me out of sight of the street. From there I climb on to the top of a fence which surrounds the property that borders the spot where the Mazda was parked. The large, Mediterranean-style house in front of me seems unoccupied: window shutters all closed, silence from the big air conditioning unit beside the house. I take a chance that no one's home and jump down into the yard and follow the wall to the driveway entrance, which is just past where the Mazda was parked. Looking down along the street side of the wall I can see a eucalyptus tree that has something small and black attached to it at shoulder height. It probably doesn't pick up sounds, but I still move over to it quietly. It's a surveillance camera, the same model I've used a few times with Hessian. Its lens is pointed towards the Capri. This is how they can see if the Range Rover leaves the hotel.

I retrace my route and sit on a lounger on the shady side of the pool. That camera has a top range of about a mile, but they're bound to be closer if they want to scramble after the Range Rover. I check the map on my phone. The Capri has only two road accesses to the main street, Palm Canyon Dr. One is about 300 yards away, the other double that. It's a perfect setup for Lodestar: one vehicle will be at each intersection, the drivers watching the camera feed on their phones. There's no way for the Range Rover to escape being followed. Lodestar's been quick to get men in place, but two cars with three men isn't enough to maintain 24-hour coverage. More will be coming. The only reason I can see for Lodestar being on the scene is to snatch back the laptop, and my instincts are saying that they'll also be taking Autumn and me. Whatever action they take will have to be soon, probably no later than tonight. They'll have a team assembled by then and will come right into the hotel under cover of darkness to do it—much easier than trying to organize an ambush on the roads.

I'm startled by the sound of the hotel maintenance man coming out to the pool with a kit for testing the water. He gives me a discreet "Good day" and goes about his work. It strikes me that I haven't seen any other guests. I go to the reception desk in the lobby. A skinny guy behind the counter looks happily at me like I'm his first break in a monotonous day.

"Can I help you, sir?" he chirps

"Yes, Mrs. Marsden just found out some of her friends want to come down to stay at the Capri today. Did they make reservations yet, or should she reserve for them? They may have booked last night."

"That must have been the reservation I took this morning: it was for a Mr. Cassidy and he booked three cottages for one night for a party of six. Is that who she was expecting?"

"It is. Did they say when they were arriving?"

"They said tonight about ten."

"Excellent."

So that's their play. Six Lodestar people check in to the Capri and take us and the laptop when it's dark and quiet. If they only wanted the laptop it could be done with two people, even one in a pinch. If we try and run now we'll be tracked until the rest of the team can catch up, and given that ten o'clock is only five hours away, the reinforcements might be quite close, getting geared up and going over their plan of action.

I go to our cottage and give Autumn the bad news. She puts the laptop aside and looks at me quizzically, as though I've told her it's raining rabbits outside.

"I've got my head so deep into this Selous business," she says patiently, "I can't spare a thought for anything else, so I'm going to leave this whole other problem for you. Any ideas?"

"One or two, but I'll have to leave you here for a while. I need to get a weapon."

"I'd say disable the camera, but that would be announcing we know that they're out there, right?

"Exactly."

"You're convinced they're going to take us out of here?"

"You don't hire a company like Lodestar to take incriminating photos of your wife and her lover, and you don't need six people to grab a laptop."

"What if the hotel reservation is legit?"

"It's over a grand a night here, right? So who books a place like this for one night only and arrives at ten?"

"Huh. It's all very dramatic, isn't it?"

"I admire your coolness."

"If you're not back when they arrive, I'll call the police and say one of them put his hand on my tits."

"That'll work for a delay, but they'll have five others to do the job."

"Okay. Give me a kiss and then get busy." I bend down and kiss her. "By the way, how will I be sure these guys checking in are Lodestar?"

"They won't look or act like the typical Capri guests."

"You mean not gay?"

"You're so judgy. But yes, probably not gay."

I go to the parking lot and check my Civic for a tracker, looking in the spots where I've put them in the past on other people's cars. I find it near one of the jack points underneath the car and hide it a few feet away in a bush. They'll see a Civic driving away from the Capri on their camera, but assume, I hope, that it's not the particular Civic they're supposed to be interested in because the tracker won't be moving. Even if they do recognize the car or me behind the wheel, I'm sure neither car will follow me; if one car goes after me it leaves a big hole in their net.

I spot the Mazda sitting in a CVS parking lot where Durante joins up with Palm Canyon. It doesn't move as I turn south on Palm Canyon. The run down to Bitter Furnace takes forty minutes. I park in the same spot, beside the water tank, and circle behind the houses, away from the street, to get to Oribe's place. The heat has climbed into the triple digits, and there isn't a window in an inhabited house that doesn't have its shades or shutters down, including Oribe's. I move quietly to the side door and put my ear against it. Nothing, not even the tell-tale vibration of an air conditioner. He might not be at home, and it's a long shot that he saw me coming, but I can't assume he isn't on the other side of the door with the pistol I left behind. The door is flimsy and sits crookedly on its hinges. It should pop right out of its frame after a hard shove with my shoulder, and the bedroom closet and the Bernelli that I want is only a few strides away from the door. If Oribe is in there, the element of surprise should get me to the shotgun before him.

As I turn my shoulder towards the door I catch a whiff of something vile and familiar. I put my hand on the doorknob and give it a slow turn. It opens, and with it comes a superheated exhalation of air that smells of rot and death. I look inside and see a pair of legs sprawled on the living room floor. It's Oribe. His body has swollen up so much he's halfway to being a novelty hot air balloon. They put one shot in his chest and one to the head. Lodestar is losing no time in cleaning up Enoch's mess. I grab the shotgun and a box of shells I find on the floor of the closet and hurry back to the car.

The Mazda is in the same position in the parking lot when I turn onto Durante, and Autumn is still frowning in concentration at the laptop when I get back to the cottage.

"Well?" she asks.

I tell her about Oribe.

"They're taking this way too seriously, but good riddance to Oribe; I should have known there was something wrong between he and Maria. When do we get away from here?"

"As soon as it's dark," I say, and then go over what else is involved. It doesn't faze her. "You ready for this?"

"Oh, yes. It's like I told you before: I should have pulled a trigger when I was sixteen."

"Why sixteen?"

Autumn sits on the sofa and tucks her legs under her. "I got my first role. The part was actually for an eighteen-year-old, but I could pass for that and mother faked my ID. You ever hear of Bob Beaton?"

"A stand-up, wasn't he?"

"That's right. He was the hot new thing for a few years back in the early nineties. So he gets his own sitcom called *Bob's Not Here*. The gag was that he was this super-lazy guy who finds crazy ways to get out of doing anything at home or at work. It was basically his act turned into a sitcom. I got the part of Steffi, the German au pair girl who lives next door and doesn't wear very much. Once or twice an episode I'd come barging into Bob's house, like they do in sitcoms, say something silly in a fake German accent, and then Bob or one his buddies in the show would crack a joke about me being an au *pair* and also having a great *pair* of boobs and legs. They cancelled it after five episodes. Anyway, one afternoon Beaton takes me to his trailer to go over some lines in a script for a movie he says he's being considered for. He said he wanted me to play his girlfriend in the movie. Guess what? It's a sex scene, and about ten minutes after I'm in his trailer he's pulled my clothes off and he's fucking me. Every time I said "No" he'd say, "But you've made me so horny." I told my mom what had happened and she asked if it was certain that I was going to get the girlfriend role. Beaton must have mentioned how much fun he'd had, because a few days later the producer got me in his office and made me give him blowjob. He was rougher than Beaton. The day after that I brought a knife with me to the studio. I told myself I'd pull it out if anyone came near me. But then I thought, why not just stab Beaton or the producer? I wasn't going to kill them, just sneak up behind them and shove it in their ass. It made me giggle thinking about one of them running around screaming with a knife in their ass. Then I thought about going further, actually putting it between Beaton's ribs. In my fantasy he wouldn't die; he'd be scared shitless and turn into a bloody, weeping wreck. I was going to do it on the day we taped, a Saturday. I came in that day and was told we were cancelled. I saw Beaton about ten years later at a comedy club in Venice Beach. He wasn't even top of the bill, and after the show I was at the bar and he came up and hit on me. He didn't recognize me. I told the guy I was with that night that Beaton had said something really disgusting to me. He decked Beaton, smashed his nose almost off his face, but afterwards I realized what a pathetic revenge that was. No beating would

108

knock Beaton's memory of what he did to me out of his head. In some corner of his mind there's a happy place for him where he remembers what I looked like naked with his cock in me. He'll always be having fun with my body in his memory. As long as he's alive he can go back in time and rape me again and again and again. That's when I really regretted not killing him. It wouldn't have been murder, it would be taking back what's mine."

I go to sit beside Autumn on the sofa, but she puts a hand up to stop me. "I don't need to be comforted," she says evenly. "I want to be understood."

An hour later it's dark enough. I go out to the parking lot while Autumn is packing our stuff and transfer the shotgun from my car to hers, then put the tracker back on the Civic. Autumn comes out to the lot a few minutes later with the bags. We stow them in her car and then go to the lobby where the skinny guy is looking twice as bored.

"Hi," says Autumn. "I was hoping you could help me. One of my friends is arriving at the airport and we need to drop his car for him there. Could we borrow one of your staff to take it to the airport? We have to go out and we aren't going in that direction. Will this cover the cab fare back?"

She slides four hundreds across the counter. The staff is used to guests who live in the certainty that all inconveniences will be dealt with by concierges, lawyers, and domestics. He makes a pretence of refusing the money but takes it at Autumn's insistence and says one of the maintenance men will be glad to do it.

The maintenance guy I saw earlier at the pool meets us in the parking lot and I tell him to park the Civic in the short-term lot at the airport and leave the keys under the floor mat. He gets behind the wheel whistling a happy tune, so he must have got at least a hundred out of the deal. The fastest route to the airport will take him past the Mazda. As soon he pulls out of the lot we follow in the Rover and take the longer route that will go past the Tahoe. The two cars will be communicating with each other right now, finalizing whatever plans they made earlier should both our cars leave before the rest of the team arrives. I'm counting on the guy in the Mazda not noticing who's behind the wheel in the dark. Autumn's driving, and I crouch below the windshield so the camera can't see me as we drive away from the Capri.

The Tahoe is parked on Palm Canyon and immediately moves into position behind us. The streetlights will give them a good view into the car, so I stay down until we get to the I-10 and turn east. The highway is quiet and the Tahoe drops well back; he doesn't want to announce his presence.

"Is there a chance we're driving towards the main team?" asks Autumn.

"No. They'll be coming from the opposite direction: Vegas or L.A. We're heading towards Phoenix, and I doubt Lodestar has people down there."

Autumn sighs. "I normally love driving at night. My favorite memory might be of driving by myself down highway 1 south of Carmel at four in the morning with all the windows open. No other drivers on the road. The surf was drowning out the sound of the car and I kept taking in deep breaths of misty-salty air like it was some kind of delicious, invisible food."

"Driving at night in Hexum was either dull or terrifying."

"Sometime you're going to have to explain to me exactly how fucked-up that place was."

"Do you want to fill me in on the laptop?"

"Not now. If we don't get through the next few hours there's really no point, is there? Let's enjoy the drive."

We say nothing until the exit sign for highway 277 appears. The Tahoe is still the same distance behind us. Autumn takes the exit and we head south.

"How long?"

"Probably twenty minutes," I answer.

It's been at least ten years since I was last on this road, riding point for trucks full of illegals. It wanders through 80 miles of desiccation before arriving at another interstate down by the border. Almost no one drives it at night. I can't imagine why it was built; one glance at a map tells you it can't take you anywhere. This country loves to tattoo itself with asphalt.

The Tahoe has dropped even further back. He'll have checked his map and seen that there's no turnoff, no escape for miles and miles. All he needs to do is keep the glow of our lights in sight. He might be calling for clearance to ambush us right now. My phone is only showing two bars of signal strength, and as I look at it another bar disappears. I climb in the back and load the Bernelli. Oribe has kindly provided me with shells loaded with buckshot, which is overkill, but welcome. I glance at my phone every minute or so waiting for the last bar to go. The remaining bar is finally replaced by a NO SERVICE message. If things don't go exactly our way, the Tahoe won't be able to call for help.

"As soon as you see a piece of cover beside the road," I say, "brake quickly and I'll jump out. They'll think you're avoiding a pothole or some animal. After I'm out, floor it. I want them going fast when they pass me. Keep going for five minutes. If you don't see their headlights behind you, turn around and come back for me."

"Don't miss."

We both see the junked car close by the right side of the road at the same time. Autumn brakes hard but without any tire squeal or fishtailing. I dive out of the Rover and get behind the wreck as Autumn speeds away. The lights of the Tahoe are five hundred yards away. I pump a shell into the chamber and crouch behind the car. I'll be shooting from the driver's right side, so he'll instinctively jerk the wheel to the left when he sees the muzzle flash and hears the blast. The Tahoe's engine begins to rev higher as the driver realizes he's falling behind his quarry. I take a bead on his right front tire when he's sixty yards away. At thirty yards I fire, pump in another shell, and fire again.

Snow

Malachi's ass and thighs were cross-hatched with thin red lines from a whipping—the flesh doodles of a sadist. I found this almost as startling as Thursday's naked body. Their conjoined moans covered any sound I made while walking back to the clothesline, where I waited until I heard Malachi's hushed voice and some quiet laughter.

"Malachi," I called out.

He leaned around the corner of the truck, his face a picture of shock. His hair was sticking out at odd angles and he was doing up the top buttons on his red and white check shirt with one hand while holding a raggedy pair of jeans in the other. Thursday spilled out of the truck, busily adjusting her ponytail and smoothing down her frayed, greenish dress around her spindly body. They were a pair of scarecrows that had been frightened into life.

"Don't worry," I said, "Caleb's busy with Sherriff Reinhart."

The two of them came towards me slowly, round-eyed with alarm. Thursday was as skinny as the other wives and a bit taller than me. Her eyes were the bluest I'd ever seen, and she looked at me as though I was a new and remarkable landscape. I couldn't decide if she was pretty or not; her gaze was so intense and searching I had to look away from her.

In a trembling voice Malachi asked, "Why are you here, Tom?"

"Just checking on you. Caleb put those stripes on your ass?"

He nodded, and Thursday suddenly moved towards me and put a hand on my shoulder as though testing my solidity. Something about the swiftness and lightness of her touch made me gasp and I let myself be held by those searching blue eyes.

"You're Tom," she said breathlessly.

"Yes."

The anxiety left her face like a curtain suddenly pulled aside to reveal a blindingly bright window to the outdoors. She clapped her hands and laughed. The idea of someone being so delighted at the sound of my name made me blush, and I suddenly couldn't stop looking into her eyes.

"You're Malachi's great and good friend!" she said.

I nodded dumbly.

She lowered her voice to a thrilled whisper and said, "He told me what you said about not calling Caleb Founder. And that bad word. I like that. You could teach me things to call him. I want my own special curse I can say to myself when I need it. Do you dwell nearby? You have to come amongst us again and tell me the things you've told Malachi, about houses and food and other kinds of people. Do you have a pet? Can you tell me about them?"

The words continued to pour out of her, a pent-up list of things she wanted me to describe and explain, and as she spoke, different emotions played across her face like actors on a stage. As with Malachi, her speech was off-kilter, peppered with odd phrases and words. She also shared his sudden shifts in mood, and I became aware that in the presence of myself, an outsider, both of them became untethered, like beasts of burden let free for the first time to madly, happily, paw the ground and sniff the air.

Malachi begged Thursday to leave in case Caleb appeared.

Thursday turned to me. "You will return, won't you? Come to us on Saturday! That's the day Caleb goes into town. Will you?"

"I will."

She cupped my face in her hands as I'd seen her do with Malachi and planted a burning kiss on my forehead before dashing away. Malachi said something to me, and I had to have him repeat it twice. He was worried about Caleb.

"Don't sweat it," I said. "This is Reinhart's country. Your fat fuck of a father is finding that out right now."

Usually when I cursed out Caleb, Malachi would grin or laugh. Now his shoulders sagged.

"What's the matter?"

"You saw what Thursday and I were doing?"

"Yeah. That why you haven't been coming out at night?"

"I couldn't look into your face when I've become such an unholy creature by betraying my father."

"For fuck's sake! I thought you didn't care about him anymore?"

"I've gone too far, Tom. I was only a wayward child before, and there was a path I could have followed to be saved, but now I've plunged into darkness. I am marred through and through, forever and ever. My blood and my soul are deepest black and I sail on a lake of sin that has no shore and no ending."

Tears began to roll down his face and he wiped them away with shaking hands. I wanted to yell at him or knock him down, anything to bring back the manic fool I liked.

"Come with me," I said.

I led him to the workshop where we found Reinhart perched on a workbench looking through a stack of papers while Caleb watched, his face impassive but his hands busy knotting and unknotting his handkerchief.

"I found him, Josh," I said loudly.

Reinhart gave me a thumbs-up, and continued leafing through what appeared to be receipts. Caleb threw a look at me and allowed a spasm of anger to contort his face.

"Caleb, you should take Malachi and the girls to Denny's with you some time," I said innocently. "You're in there often enough, so why not bring them? Or the Regal. Take Malachi to that Bond movie; you'd probably enjoy it a second time." I turned to Malachi. "Your dad loves movies, and he always gets the biggest bucket of popcorn they have. You should see it; it's big enough to stick your head in." I mimed lowering a bucket over my head. "That big, really."

Caleb looked slowly from me to Josh and back to me again. "We are a poor family and there isn't enough—"

Reinhart laughed, waved the sheaf of papers like a fan, and hopped down from the bench and handed them to Caleb. "You're doing just fine, Mr. Gaunt, just fine. It's nice that Tom'll be seeing more of Malachi in the future. Boys need other boys; it keeps them out of trouble. And be nice to Tom, Caleb, he's a particular friend of mine. A pleasure meeting you, sir, and I'll drop by in a few days for that tax payment."

Reinhart tipped his hat to Caleb and gestured for me to follow him to the car. Malachi hurried back towards the Settlement. As we drove away, I could see Gaunt slowly tearing the handkerchief in half.

"That was a worthwhile visit, Tom."

"He gave Malachi a whipping."

"I don't doubt it. But, like I said, it isn't up to us to decide how a man raises his children. You had him off the rails, Tom. That was good work, made it easier for me to explain Hexum's tax code to him. Try and keep your eyes peeled for a safe or strong box. Gaunt runs his business on a strictly cash basis, and I'd like to give him some pointers on how to keep his money secure."

Saturday was two days away, and I spent that time in a fever of anticipation. I was desperate to see Thursday again. Her voice, her eyes, and her body filled my imagination. I tried not to lust after her. She was, I told myself, Malachi's girlfriend or Eve or something else. I'd seen them fucking, but I couldn't convince myself that that meant anything. They lived in a distorted world and what they were doing had to be equally strange and warped. I wasn't jealous of Malachi, and when I flirted with the idea of my body being on top of Thursday's, it seemed as bizarre and unlikely as her lying under Malachi. I simply wanted to be with her. I wanted to listen to her and have her reach out and touch me.

By Friday I couldn't think about her anymore. I was a glutton who suddenly turns against his favorite food after stuffing himself with it. The day was unusually mild, and I decided to explore some new territory. I normally went east, towards the mountains, on my odysseys. The land was wilder and empty of people. To the west the country flattened out a bit, ranches and farms were more common, and there was a greater chance of running across a marijuana plot guarded by some armed and twitchy grower.

I set off on foot from the house, following a dirt track that was the ghost of a road that once led to a silver mine. Trees and bushes crowded in on the path and startled rabbits dashed ahead of me. The old mine was in a circular clearing, and what was left of it had been stripped of its scrap metal years ago. All that remained was a dusty litter of weathered planks and a tall wooden headframe that leaned to the south and supported a ghetto of swallows' nests. Lying on the ground near the headframe was a rattlesnake coiled like a length of gleaming rope. I'd lately become addicted to watching *The Crocodile Hunter*, and I'd caught various snakes, but never a rattler. Without stopping to think or worry, I found a suitable stick and managed to pin its head down, then grabbed it behind the head as I'd seen Steve Irwin do dozens of times on TV. As I lifted the snake, I told myself that now I'd have something interesting and dramatic to tell Thursday when I saw her next; something that Malachi would never have done. I tossed the snake away, feeling slightly queasy at the thought of how reckless I'd been.

I continued hiking until I was stopped by what sounded like coyotes quarreling. It was coming from behind a ridge to my right, and when I scrambled to the top I could see down onto a section of flat land that was emerald green with a triangle-shaped plot of weed one-third the size of a football field. Two men and a boy were facing in my direction on the edge of the patch, about seventy yards away. Reinhart and Spencer were opposite the trio. The men had full garbage bags of grass at their feet, maybe seven or eight in total. The boy was young, no more than eight-years-old. All three of them looked raggedy and washed out, like people who'd stepped out of a sepia picture into the wrong century. Reinhart was in uniform, as always, and Spencer wore a gold and purple tracksuit that had a logo on the back I couldn't make out.

The men were shouting at Spencer and Reinhart and pointing emphatically at the bags of weed. Spencer was yelling something back at them. Reinhart was silent. I couldn't make out their conversation, just odd words that caught the right air current and came to me as clear as a bell. I got the sense the men were claiming that they had rights to the crop. Their strident shouts and gestures were a pantomime of people losing an argument. They fell silent and looked towards Reinhart, who must have been speaking in a normal tone. The scene stayed like that for a minute, and I figured that things were about to end with the men slinking away or being handcuffed. The boy looked bored and was kicking something in the dirt with the toe of his shoe. The man on the left reached down by the garbage bags and slowly picked up a double-barreled shotgun. He barely got it two feet off the ground before Reinhart drew his gun and fired four shots that sounded like one. The man dropped in a compact heap on the ground. The boy covered his ears and wailed, a piercing cry that sounded like a hawk's call. The dead man's partner shouted "Fuck" loud enough for me to hear and then bent over the body. He was looking down at the corpse, his hands held out as if expecting the dead man to grasp them and get to his feet, and didn't notice or move when Reinhart came up behind him and put a bullet in his head. The boy continued his keening.

Spencer and Reinhart had a short talk and then walked over to the boy, who was kneeling in the dirt and letting out little shrieks like an animal sending out an alarm. Reinhart patted him on the head and lifted him to his feet. Spencer took the boy by the hand, and the three of them walked out of my sight around the corner of the weed field. Two engines started, and moments later Reinhart's cruiser drove into view with Spencer's yellow Silverado following close behind. The boy was with

Spencer. The vehicles bumped slowly over the rough terrain before crossing over a rise and disappearing from sight.

I hiked home and turned on the TV. The Kings and Flames were playing, and I focused my mind on the action. It worked for a while. I took apart what I'd seen and tried to strip the horror from it and turn it into a logical chain of events. The men had been trespassing or stealing. One of them had gone for his gun. Josh had defended himself. The second man was probably making a grab for the fallen weapon when Reinhart stopped him. He and Spencer had undoubtedly taken the boy away to a hospital or orphanage. The dead men were entirely at fault. It was all making sense now, and I congratulated myself on reaching this conclusion. I went to bed, thinking only of the next day when I would be able to see Thursday.

The temperature plummeted during the night, and, in the morning, there was snow on the ground and more falling. I was on my bike by seven o'clock. I didn't know when Gaunt would be leaving on his errands, so I wanted to be there early to see him leave. I hid my bike well away from the Settlement and worked my way through the brush to a concealed position where I could see the buildings. The windows of the dining hall were steamed up and vague shapes moved behind them. The Gaunts were at breakfast.

I didn't have to wait long before the door of the hall flew open and Caleb exited followed by a cloud of steam that licked the outside air before retreating. Malachi was trailing his father and not looking happy about it. They went to the far side of the workshop and left in a red mini-van that needed a new muffler. I was surprised that Caleb was taking Malachi with him, but I suspected it had everything to do with my visit earlier in the week.

I hesitated before walking over to the buildings. I didn't know what to say to Thursday, and even though she'd asked me to come, my expedition began to seem foolish and pointless. Two of the women came out of the hall holding hands with three small children, two girls and a boy, and led them inside the church. Thursday came to the door and stood there looking up at the sky and its silent fury of fat snowflakes. She turned her attention to the road for the longest time, and I imagined that she was looking for me. I tried not to break into a run as I went to her.

"Tom!" she cried, and hurried down the steps of the dining hall, catching me in a tight hug that made me laugh. "I thought of you and you came. Like a miracle."

"I said I was going to come back."

"You did, and you kept your word. Malachi's not here, though. He'll be grieved that he missed you."

"I saw him leave. Caleb probably won't be away as long as he normally is since he's got Malachi with him; he won't be taking him to any restaurants or films."

"Malachi told me what you said Caleb does on his trips. Is it true?"

"Yes, all of it. He has a good time when he's in town."

Thursday was thrilled with this news. "I want you to tell the others." She turned and shouted, "Abby, Linda, Sarah!"

"I thought you were all called after days of the week."

"My name's Rebecca," she said sternly. "We don't use those names when Caleb's not around."

The other girls came out of their respective buildings and gathered in front of us. They were nervous and shivered in the cold. None of them were dressed for the day. They wore thick, baggy sweaters over their dresses, but their legs were bare and their feet protected only by cheap, worn running shoes. They stood like pillars against the snow that whipped past them, their arms wrapped tightly around their chests.

"Tell them about Caleb, tell them," urged Rebecca.

"Can we go inside first?" I asked.

Fear passed across their faces. They were scared enough of being with me outdoors, but the idea of taking me into where they lived must have seemed worse.

"Yes," said Rebecca slowly. "We'll go indoors. The house."

She took me by the hand and led me to the house, the others following close behind, their voices whispering and then falling silent as we went through the door. The main floor was a single large room with walls that had been painted white and a plain, wooden floor mostly covered by a square of dark green broadloom speckled with stains that looked black against the green. A king-sized bed was against the far wall and next to a narrow staircase that climbed to a small landing and a closed door. There were no decorations, nothing hanging on the walls, and no other furniture. Two laundry baskets at the foot of the bed held heaps of men's clothing. Several smells were competing for space in the air, none of them good. A door on the left side of the room led to the quarters for the women and children. The women practically tiptoed through the first room, as if Caleb still had a presence there.

The women's room was effectively a wooden tunnel. The walls were unpainted and the roof was too low for a space that long. There were four bunkbeds, two cribs, and at the far end of the room a curtained-off area that held a toilet, sink, and metal shower stall. A mongrel collection of carpets and rugs lay on the floor. Everything looked like it had been salvaged from somewhere else. A dented galvanized tub held a jumble of wooden off-cuts painted different colors. Toys for the kids, I guessed. Two big space heaters sat at either end of the room but weren't working. I could see my breath. In one crib a baby was fussing quietly. The other held a toddler who was almost too long for his bed. The top of his crib was gated over with a piece of slatted wood that looked like it had come from another crib. It was hinged to one side of the crib and padlocked to the other. His face was chalky white and he silently chewed on his fist while staring at me.

I pointed to the imprisoned child and asked, "Why's he in there like that?"

"Daniel's dangerous," said the pregnant girl.

"How?"

"He bit Caleb. He's only allowed out when Caleb's not around."

"Well, let him out, then."

She shrugged, took a key out of a pocket in her dress, unlocked the crib and flipped the top back against the wall. The child put himself in a sitting position and continued drooling over his fist.

"Now tell us," pleaded Rebecca.

I wasn't sure the others were that interested in what Caleb got up to away from home, but as I described each time I'd seen him, they became more fascinated and shocked. I enjoyed casting a spell on my audience, so I made-up some stories about Caleb hanging out in a bar, playing golf, and walking hand-in-hand with a woman his own age on the street. When I finished, the girls looked confused and stricken.

"Thank you, Tom," said Rebecca.

The others took this as a signal to leave and filed out quickly. The boy in the crib clambered out of his prison and trotted after them, his fist still in his mouth.

Rebecca sat on the bottom of a bunk bed and indicated I should sit beside her. "I want to ask you about out there."

"Sure, anything," I said as I sat next to her.

Her questions were much like Malachi's. She had a dim recollection of living in a home with all the usual things in it—TV, phones, appliances, pets, books, junk food—but those memories had become fragmentary and distorted. For Rebecca, my answers must have been like looking in a kaleidoscope that, when turned, becomes less chaotic. The more I told her, the more the light went out of her eyes. I began to feel that what I was doing was dangerous in some way.

When she finally ran out of questions, she was looking tired. The baby mewled, and Rebecca went over and began changing its diaper.

"Is it yours?" I asked.

"No. It's Abby's. She and Linda are sisters. The pregnant one is Sarah. Daniel belongs to her. I don't have any children. I never will, by Caleb."

"How long have you been his wife?"

"I was thirteen when I was wedded. Four years ago. My family wasn't always part of the church. My father swore us to the church when I was...six? Seven? We were living in Kansas, but he lost his job, sold our house, and delivered us all to a Righteous Settlement in Colorado."

"What about your mom?"

"She died when I was two. Dad had two wives in Colorado."

"And he sold you to Caleb."

"He did. I had an older sister who was sold to a Righteous man in Guatemala. She got to fly on a plane."

"They don't sell boys, do they?"

"No," she laughed. "Sarah says boys toil for fathers so fathers can buy brides, and fathers have brides to have daughters to sell. Boys have to leave Settlements when they're eighteen."

"Why don't you and Malachi go away? It would be easy."

Rebecca finished with the baby, who grunted contentedly as she set it down in the crib and then sat beside me.

"I don't lie with Malachi because I love him. I like him, but I want to betray Caleb. When I'm with Malachi I'm hoping that Caleb will find us. I imagine how he'll feel when he sees his son with me, when he sees me enjoying being with a man. Malachi is very cautious, though, or we would have been found by now."

"Caleb might kill you."

"And burn in hell because of it. That's what I want. I've sinned, but he'll have done so much worse if he kills me. To see him below me in the fires of hell would make it a paradise."

"But it's all bullshit! Why do you believe in this crap? You haven't done anything wrong; you're not going anywhere awful."

She nodded at my words and smiled. "Malachi told me you're an unbeliever, and he has doubts of his own. His faith wavers in the storm. I'm sorry I seduced him and made him sin, but I think God will give me his punishment in the end."

"Why do you want to die? Leave this shithole and stay with me; I have a house all to myself. Why are you so interested in what things are like outside of here if you don't want to run away?"

A wistfulness came over Rebecca, and the hope that she was considering my offer made my heart pound.

"I'm weak," she said calmly. "I should ignore the worldliness you describe, but I'm weak. God *can* be found in our church, in our faith, but Caleb has marred everything with his bestiality. If a house is damaged in a storm you don't walk away from it, you repair and rebuild. Caleb is the storm. But God is still there behind the clouds and the wind and rain, and he wants me to follow this path. I'm sure of it."

"What's Caleb done to you?"

She turned away from me and paused before saying, "He takes us to his bed in twos and threes. He shows us hideous pictures in magazines and makes us copy them. He has us lie with each other while he watches and abuses himself. He hurts us if we don't follow his commands. He hurts us when we do follow his commands. He's made his bed an altar of sin and led his wives to damnation on it a hundred times and in a hundred different ways."

I argued some more with Rebecca, told her that Caleb was a criminal, that she could help the others by leaving and telling what she knew, but nothing swayed her. I knew her reasoning made no sense, but she bent and twisted all my arguments around the pillar of her faith. I couldn't find the right words to tear down her defences. I felt there was something I could say, but it was tantalizingly out of reach, like trying to remember a name for a vaguely familiar face. Rebecca, like Malachi, had a strand of madness in her that vined around her thoughts. The trinity of God, Caleb, and her father had shaken and worried her mind until now there was only a wisp of her that pined to escape. But she'd said she was weak, and I pinned my hopes on that.

I looked at my watch and stood up quickly. "Fuck. I didn't mean to stay this long. Caleb might be back soon and I don't want you getting into trouble."

I didn't think Caleb would get rough with me, but I wasn't so confident without Reinhart on the property.

Warmth came back to Rebecca's eyes as she said, "You were going to give me a bad name for Caleb."

The second she said this it crossed my mind that insults weren't enough for Caleb. He should be killed. I didn't immediately dismiss that thought.

"How about Fat Bastard?"

She snorted with laughter.

"It's from a movie," I said. "You should see it."

A truck growled by on the road outside and it reminded me that I should leave. As we went back through Caleb's bedroom I stopped and pointed up at the closed door.

"That's Caleb's office, right?"

"Yes," said Rebecca nervously.

"Do you know what's in there?"

"None of us are allowed in there. That's where the foul magazines come from."

I sprinted up the stairs to the door and Rebecca let out a gasp. It was locked.

"Do you know if he has a safe in there?"

"I don't."

"Where does he keep his money?"

Rebecca shrugged.

"And the key for the door?"

She shook her head. I came back down and we went out on the porch.

The snow had almost stopped, and the wind was shredding the clouds to reveal fragments of blue sky. Two kids were doing a clumsy job of throwing snowballs in front of the church. Daniel, his hand finally out of his mouth, stood by the dining hall trying to catch laggard snowflakes in his mouth.

"Goodbye, Tom. Please come back," said Rebecca, putting her arms around me and brushing my cheek with hers.

I returned the hug and held her close. I didn't want to let go. My breaths were shaky.

"You can hold me as long as you want, Tom," whispered Rebecca.

I held her until my breathing matched hers, and when it finally did, tears came to my eyes. She pulled away from me gently and wiped my face dry with the sleeve of her dress. I said goodbye and walked, then ran, to my bike.

I drove to Main St. and went into Latimer's store. He was buried in a copy of *Gormenghast* and only grunted when I came in. I wandered through the store feeling both happy and furious. I left without buying anything and walked down the street to the Hexum Diner. It had booths done in shiny red vinyl and a long bar with round, backless stools that spun around. I ordered a hot chicken sandwich and thought about trades the Kings could and should make. A Mountain Trailways bus was idling across the street and making the diner's windows vibrate slightly.

Including myself, there were three people sitting at the 12-seat counter. One booth at the far end of the restaurant was occupied, and a murmuring voice from that direction drew my attention. A young boy was sitting on the only side of the booth I could see, staring blankly at the person across from him, who was visible as a slightly balding head barely rising above the top of the booth. I recognized the voice. It was Spencer. His hand came into view holding a long spoon loaded with vanilla ice cream and dripping chocolate sauce. The boy opened his mouth and Spencer slowly fed him the ice cream, only removing the spoon when it was licked clean.

"That's it," cooed Spencer. "Sweet medicine for a sad boy."

It was the kid who'd been with the men Reinhart shot at the weed plot. He was dressed head to toe in brand new Miami Heat gear that was at least a size too large.

"One more errand today and then we can go back home. What do you want for dinner tonight? Pizza?" asked Spencer.

The boy said nothing; he barely even blinked.

"Now, how can you have what you want when you never speak?" chided Spencer. "I want to give you everything, you just have to ask. You're my special little dude."

He spooned another dollop of ice cream into the kid.

"You think about tonight, little dude, while I go to the can. We'll play some cool games and you'll have thought about what you want to eat."

Spencer got up and went down the basement stairs that led to the washrooms. I left a ten-dollar bill on the counter and hurried over to the kid in the booth. He didn't react or resist when I took his hand and pulled him out of the diner and across the street to the bus. Its destination sign read 'San Francisco.' The bus's door was open and I pushed the boy ahead of me while the driver raised an eyebrow at us.

I took a hundred out of my wallet and held it out to the driver. "Is this enough for him to San Francisco?"

"I can't take a kid that young by himself."

I took out another hundred. "Now?"

He hesitated slightly but then shook his head. "No way. I could get fired."

"You live here in Hexum, don't you? I've seen you around."

"Yeah, so?"

"If you don't take him, I'm going to find out where you live, and one night I'm going to empty a clip from my AR-15 into your house. You'd better be sleeping in the fucking cellar."

The driver blinked a few times as he thought about what was an entirely plausible threat in Hexum, then whisked the bills out of my hand.

I held the boy by the shoulders and said, "When you get off this bus in San Francisco you go up to a cop or go to the ticket counter and tell them you're lost. You understand? What are you going to do?"

"Say I'm lost," he said, his voice dry and cracked as if he hadn't spoken in days.

The driver slammed the door shut as soon as I hopped off, and I watched him drive down a few blocks and make the turn that lead to the interstate. I got on my bike outside Latimer's and headed home. Spencer was in front of the diner looking anxiously in every direction. As I drove past, I gave him the finger.

Starry Night

The first shot flattens the tire and sends the hubcap spinning into the air like a flipped coin. The second shreds the tire as the driver throws the wheel to the left, the rim biting into the road at a severe angle, throwing up sparks and chunks of rubber and a metallic howl as the weight of the Tahoe fulcrums on the rim and the back end lifts up and the vehicle stands on its nose before flipping over and rolling three times. It finishes up on its roof twenty feet off the road and facing away from me. One headlight is still working. I make a wide circle around the vehicle to check if any of the occupants have been thrown clear. The doors are hanging open and from the passenger side a man falls out on all fours clutching an automatic in his right hand. He's got a gash over his forehead that's pouring blood into his eyes which he tries to wipe away with his free hand.

"Drop the weapon!" I shout.

He's too concussed or hard ass to follow my command, so he pivots towards the sound of my voice and stands up, his weapon at the ready but pointing well off to my right. I aim at his gun and fire. The buckshot sends the weapon flying into the darkness along with part of his hand. He screams and falls to his knees. I continue around the Tahoe until I can see the driver. The windshield has come away entirely and he's lying in front of the vehicle on his stomach, unmarked and unconscious, but breathing badly.

I keep the shotgun levelled at the driver and wait a few moments until his partner has stopped swearing before saying, "What was the plan and who ordered it?"

He ignores me, gets his breathing under control, tears off a piece of his shirt with his good hand and his teeth, and starts fashioning a tourniquet. He's got to be ex-military; no civilian would be so quick to block out the pain and do what needs to be done. In the half-light from the Tahoe's interior lights, I can see he's about my age with a squashed nose, and a wiry, athletic build.

"Answer, now." Still no reaction. "Lodestar pays you enough to make it worth your while dying out here? You're looking forward to your loved ones collecting a big insurance check?"

"We were only supposed to follow you," he says in a thick Scottish accent.

"You always go armed when you're tailing someone?"

"My personal weapon—makes me feel safe. Dangerous place, America."

"And what about the crew who were checking into the Capri tonight?"

"I don't know about that."

He finishes his tourniquet and lies on his side, panting with the pain and exertion. I walk over to him, put my gun barrel in his face and rest one foot on his wounded arm. What's left of his hand looks like a mop that's been dipped in blood. He moans as I step down slightly.

"The tough guy chit-chat stops now," I say, "or you lose more than a hand."

"Cassidy was in charge of the snatch team," he says reluctantly. "We were surveillance and backup."

"Snatch to where?"

"There's supposed to be a laptop to be found. We get the laptop then take you and the woman out in the desert and find out what you've got from it and who you've told."

"And after the torture session?"

He doesn't want to say, and I have to step down hard to operate his voice.

"Burial," he says, and then adds, "But I wouldn't have been part of that team."

He's offered up that piece of information so easily either because he thinks help is close at hand or because he's evaluated me as someone who'll be impressed by his honesty and let him lie there until aid arrives.

"Who's the client?"

"Ach, I don't know that. We get orders from Cassidy, and he gets them from higher up. Believe me, I'm at the bottom of the information ladder."

"I believe you."

I take a step back and shoot him through the heart. The shot barely echoes in this flat expanse of grit and pebbles and creosote bushes. A tiny bubbling sound comes from the Scot's body as his blood leaks into the thirsty earth, and I remember other times I've been in this position: standing above a man's cooling flesh with my ears ringing from the sound of my weapon. I can't recall when it last meant anything to me.

A mile to the south the headlights of the returning Range Rover wink into view. I gather the spent shotgun shells, put them in my jacket pocket and reload with the spare shells I brought with me. The used shells will have my partials and DNA on them, so I'll have to dispose of them elsewhere. Autumn pulls off on the other side of the road and hops out.

"Well?"

"One dead, the other dying. The dead one confirmed everything."

"Motherfuckers."

Autumn comes over to the Tahoe and sees the man with a hole in his chest. She looks at me and then the driver, who groans and pops his eyes open. Autumn jumps back and I rack the shotgun. The man on the ground looks around with unfocused eyes, and his hands claw at the dirt as he's seized by a coughing fit that brings pink froth to his lips.

"My back hurts," he says in a peevish tone.

I say to Autumn, "Wait in the car and I'll finish this."

She moves towards me and holds out her hand. "I'll do it."

"No. You really don't want to."

"I do," she says calmly.

"There's no need."

"For me there is."

"You don't come back from doing this. You're not the same person afterwards."

"I don't want to be the same person anymore. That person never made good choices. Maybe this new character will get things right."

"My back hurts," says the driver in the same aggrieved voice.

Autumn puts her hands on the shotgun and I let her take it as though passing a bouquet to the winner of a pageant. She takes a stance as if she's skeet shooting, then lowers the barrel and fires. Her technique's not great—she didn't bring the barrel to rest before pulling the trigger—but it gets the job done. I pick up the empty shell and put it in my pocket. Autumn passes me the gun and gets in the Range Rover on the passenger side.

To the north, headlights suddenly appear on the road. The vehicle is several miles away and I almost hold my breath waiting to see if it's only one car or Cassidy's whole team. The lights glide and bend along the distant shadow of the road and it could almost be a UFO skimming along the ground. There's only one car.

"Is it the Mazda?" asks Autumn.

"Most likely. He would have come after the Tahoe when he realized the trip to the airport was a decoy. When he gets close I'll shout 'Now' and you turn the headlights on and blind him."

"What if it isn't him?"

"We'll see."

I turn the Tahoe's lights off and drag the two bodies out of sight. It's a moonless night, but the blizzard of stars over my head washes the terrain with a pale glow. The sound of the distant car's engine falls and rises as it encounters dips in the road. I kneel behind a bush near the Range Rover and raise the shotgun. If it's not the Mazda, I'll hope the driver keeps going and assumes there are some abandoned vehicles by the side of the road. The car crests a rise a few hundred yards away and slows down. The Tahoe might have a satellite tracker that the Mazda driver can access; there's no other reason for a car to slow down. The car crawls forward and when it's fifty yards away I can see that it is the Mazda. No need of headlights for this: there's a phone mounted on the Mazda's dash and its light reveals the man who followed me from Royal Palms.

The driver is staring to the right, which is where the tracker signal on his phone is telling him to look and doesn't see me rise up and walk swiftly towards the edge of the road. I'm ten feet away when I fire through the windshield and see his face cratered by the slugs and a red cloud fill the back of the car. His body slides below the dash as the car rolls past me and off the road. I pick up my shell, put the Benelli across the back seat of the Rover and get behind the wheel.

Autumn points to my left. "Look."

The Mazda is still rolling across the desert. The land for miles around is flat and featureless, and there's nothing to stop the car as it heads west with its last passenger. A jackrabbit darts into the funnel of light thrown by the headlights and runs ahead, zigzagging furiously but staying within the illumination like an insect trapped in a jar. We should leave, but I'm transfixed by the shrinking plume of light slowly sailing away on a dark, sandy sea, its course taking it to where the arch of the Milky Way comes down to meet a distant, jagged horizon.

I start the car and we head north without speaking.

We reach the I-10 and turn back towards Palm Springs. I pass Autumn the burner phone and she texts local TV stations to alert them to a fatal shooting on highway 277 involving Lodestar security personnel. The name won't immediately mean anything to them, but it should end up in the initial news reports. Every mile or so I toss one of the used shells out the window.

"You okay?" I ask.

"Never better," she answers. "So, about the laptop: Gideon would be shitting himself if he realized how catastrophic Enoch is about basic internet security. They communicated via email, and several times Gideon expressly tells Enoch to delete his emails, which of course he doesn't because he's lazy and uses assistants, or me, to do anything more technical than turn on his devices. Gideon's not much better in that regard as well, because he tried to disguise that it was him sending them by using some anonymous-sounding Hotmail account. The only problem is that the emails contain personal information only Gideon could have known. In one he reminds Enoch we're invited to his son's birthday party! This is what happens when computer-illiterate septuagenarians attempt a criminal conspiracy."

"What's the criminal part?"

"That's the tricky part. They use the term Selous Group in a jokey way, or as if it's shorthand for something else. I don't think it's an official name. Gideon and Enoch at least had sense enough not to name the others. The interesting part is that Gideon supplied Enoch with a list of companies he's supposed to have his companies sign contracts with."

"So?"

"These companies are to supply Enoch's with services starting in November; not goods, only services. Gideon listed the exact dollar value for each contract, six in total, and they range from five million up to twenty-three million, nearly a hundred million in total. Here's why this all smells: Enoch's businesses don't need these services. The biggest contract is for a new software program for the restaurants. That's bullshit. I know that part of his business inside out and it only needs and uses the industry standard programs. The other contracts are for things like cleaning and maintenance, employee training, marketing, and so on."

"His companies have those services in place already."

"Exactly. It gets smellier: the companies the contracts were signed with barely have an internet presence, only basic websites that don't really tell you anything." She rhymes off a list of company names. "You ever hear of those?"

"No. How long ago were the contracts signed?"

"It varies, but no more than three months ago. The last email from Gideon indicated that the Selous Group would be celebrating this September, October at the latest. Enoch's reply was a picture of a superyacht he wants to buy. I'm amazed he managed to attach a picture to his email."

"That's all there is to it?"

"That's it."

"What do you think it adds up to?"

"You give me your ideas first."

"We have some shell companies being set up for Enoch and others to place contracts with, contracts that are actually worthless. These contracts aren't going to be fulfilled, but Enoch's apparently going to earn a big pay day because of that. Gideon's half of the deal is to set up the fake companies, and I'd guess he came up with the whole scheme. He's got to be getting half of all the profits, which is a multiple of how many people are in the Selous Group. Make sense so far?"

"So how do you monetize an unfulfilled contract from a bogus supplier?"

"No way that I know. Some kind of tax avoidance scheme?"

"Not likely. Enoch and Gideon have people whose religion is finding tax loopholes; no need to be all cloak and dagger about it. But think about this: why bring in Lodestar? What is the Selous Group doing that has them so nervy they'd be willing to have us killed? It has to be something so putridly illegal that it would put them in a penitentiary no matter how rich and well-connected they are."

"It makes me think Lodestar has an equal share of this. They're at the very dirty end of the security business, but it's still a big ask to go out and waste people."

"If that's the case, then three dead employees and their name in the news might not be enough to back Lodestar off. They could keep coming for us."

"We stick with the original plan: hide out until we can squeeze money out them. Only now we ask for even more."

Autumn chews on her knuckle and stares out her window at the desert flashing past. I can sense she's about to balk.

"No," she says finally. "We're going to keep a high profile. We're going to make it hard for them to kill us without getting way too much attention. We're going to find other ways to put Lodestar on a leash. We're going to figure out exactly what this scam is and then we'll ask for Enoch's share. Fifty million, let's say."

"So where do we go now?"

She smiles. "The Malibu house. We can get there in time to have a swim when the sun comes up."

I want to tell her that this isn't a good idea, but I'm beginning to feel that the last few day days—fuck, most of my life—has been nothing but bad choices, so why not keep surfing this wave of recklessness and see where it takes us? It can't leave me on a shore I didn't think I was going to anyway.

Ahead of us the lights of a low-flying aircraft are closing rapidly. It's a helicopter, and it thumps by no more than 500 feet overhead as it follows the path of the highway and then breaks right a few miles later, roughly where 277 begins.

"Police?" asks Autumn.

"Or a TV news chopper."

"Let's stop and eat at the casino."

"You hate the food there."

"I want lots of noisy people around me."

The casino is thronged with gamblers, and the exultant lights and sounds of slot machines. We walk through to an Italian-themed restaurant that overlooks the casino floor and don't really talk until we've finished eating our overcooked and under-flavored pasta dishes. Autumn drinks her coffee and seems to find relaxation in observing the animation below.

"You feeling okay?" I ask.

"You mean, how do I feel about killing a man?"

"That and other things."

"You ever hear the term *la petite mort*?"

"Uh huh. The little death. It describes the momentary loss of consciousness during an orgasm."

"Ooh, look at you with your fancy book learnin' talk."

It feels good to laugh.

"I was thinking," she continues slowly, "that we should welcome death and obliteration. If our keenest moment of pleasure, the thing we chase most of our lives, is when we stop being ourselves, lose self-awareness, then death must be...not so bad. Or is that the logic the executioner uses to allow himself to sleep at night? Those people down there are all looking for little deaths at the slots and tables—I do when I gamble. An hour of blackjack is full of little deaths. I lose myself completely when I look at my cards, when I see a card come out of the shoe, and when the dealer flips over his hole card. One hand, three deaths. You add up all the vices people have, all the ways we have of distracting ourselves into *not* being, and you have to think that most of life is an eager sprint from one little death to the next. I pulled a trigger tonight and put the last link in the chain of deaths that man had forged for himself. I saved him the effort of looking for the next one."

"Do you believe any of that?"

"I don't want to, but..."

"Don't. The people who did the killing in Hexum knew that ending a life was another form of ownership. They murdered for money and power, or to protect those two things, but also because *taking* a life, like it was something you grab off a shelf, is the ultimate act of greed for the guy who pulls the trigger; everything that a person was, all those years of life, translates to nothing more than a brick of cash or a deadlier reputation. They took lives to increase their net worth."

"Isn't that what we just did?"

"We killed killers."

"So you're claiming self-defence?"

"I'm saying there are different kinds of killing."

"Sorry."

"Sorry for what?"

"I'm acting like I'm the only person at the table who's had to try and rationalize killing. It was arrogant of me."

"Yes, leave the excuses to me—they're tried and tested and fit me like a glove."

I'm tempted to tell Autumn the full extent of my crimes in Grange County, but those horrors should stay hidden.

A riotous celebration breaks out at a craps table as someone hits their point. We decide to leave. There's something unsettling about their enthusiasm and pointless energy. As we get back on the highway, a thin orange line is writhing at the top of the San Jacinto Mountains.

"What's that?" asks Autumn.

"Brush fire; probably just an hour or so old."

"No. It's a dragon getting ready to fly down from his lair and ravage the city."

"Really?"

"If you squint."

"Then we better get going."

Autumn drives while I doze in the passenger seat. I drift off for an hour or so and wake up as we pass Splash Kingdom in Redlands.

I yawn and indicate the park. "Levi took me there just after it opened. It was called Pharaoh's Lost Kingdom back then."

"A good memory?"

"I have one or two."

"I've been thinking about it; I do feel different."

"I'd be worried if you didn't."

"I'm focused now," she says with a smile. "I haven't felt like this for a long time, not since before I met Enoch."

"Why happened then?"

"I stopped acting. After the sitcom crashed and burned, I had the market cornered on roles with names like Young Hooker, Girl at Bar, Stripper Number Two, or Naked Girl in Pool. I was busy, busy, busy. Mom was taking courses to become a real estate agent, so of course she couldn't work, and then when she got her licence she needed new clothes, of course, and her own car, of course, and then she needed an apartment closer to her office."

"Of course."

"So she eventually gets a chance for an exclusive listing on a house in Bel Air. The asking price would have been three million, the sale would be easy, and her commission would be huge. It would be the making of her as a real estate agent, she said. All she needed to close the deal was for me to go on a date with the guy selling. I said no, and she yelled and cried and explained how I'd been a burden to her over the years and now it was my time to help her just this once, and back in her day things were worse, and pretty please, pretty please. I went on the *date* and it was as rapey as I'd expected, but he did list the house with her and she sold it in two weeks. A month later she asked me to go another date seeing as how successful the last one had been. I didn't bother to say no, I just moved out, no forwarding address, nothing. That's when I did my first film for Excalibur."

"They made those thrillers?"

"Please, *erotic* thrillers. I did six in a row for them and a bunch of similar stuff elsewhere. I was doing okay, moneywise. But I was a bad actor in bad films. It's hard to explain what that's like. I was choosing to do something that I knew I did poorly, I was with actors who were equally crap, the scripts were awful, and the end product was straight-to-video junk that people laughed at or whacked off to. I was a shining star in films sold in bins. But we all pretended that we had a morsel of acting talent, and nobody ever said the films were lousy. I felt like a zombie. Now, when the scripts for those films called for a mansion, they'd rent an empty house—the kind my mother wanted to pimp me out for—and furnish it any which way. On this one shoot I noticed what a shit job they'd done dressing the location. It was this amazing house designed by Richard Neutra—not that I knew who that was then—and they'd filled it with stuff that looked shiny and expensive but was actually cheap and tacky. On the next film I offered to do the set decorating along with my usual jumping in and out of beds and showers and pools, and all for the same fee. Naturally, they said yes. I spent about five years doing nothing but set design and decoration. For five years I knew I was doing something I was good at. The films were still just glossy, softcore porn or varsity league action films, but my little corner of them was fantastic. I felt like I was awake for the first time in my life. You know what I mean?"

"Maybe one day. Why only five years?"

She makes a disgusted noise. "Excalibur and the other mom and pop film companies I was working for all dissolved after 2008. Part of it was the crash, but also because the market for that stuff had died. I tried to get more work; my CV was lengthy, but when the credits include stuff like *Babysitter Passion IV* and *Blood Shot*, well..."

"Yeah. *Babysitter Passion III* was miles better."

"Bastard," she laughs, and gives me a slap on the arm. "I went back to acting for a while, but the parts and the pay were even worse the second time around. That's when I started at one of Enoch's restaurants, and you know the rest."

It's just past five o'clock, but the traffic is already starting to thicken as we pass the 605 interchange. A dumpster truck ahead of us scatters papers and plastic bags like flowers thrown before conquerors entering a city. I can't shake a feeling of futility, that it would make more sense for us to keep driving and driving until we fetch up in a place where no one would ever know us. I might as well wish for time to reverse itself. I often do.

"We'd better stop at my apartment," I say. "I want to pick up my gun; if I have the bad luck to be stopped by the cops, I'd like to be carrying a weapon that's actually registered to me. Speaking of which, we have to get rid of that shotgun."

"Bring your best suit, too."

"A suit?"

"I'll tell you after."

I tell Autumn to exit onto Arlington. We go a few blocks north, turn left on Alcott St and pull up directly in front of my place. All the houses on the street are dark, and I remember that it's Sunday, which means my neighbors won't be making their usual early start for work.

Autumn peers at the house. "Huh. It's an original American Craftsman, but someone's ruined it by adding that crappy outside staircase."

"You are such an architecture snob."

She sticks her tongue out at me. "Be quick, I want to go swimming."

I climb the staircase to my apartment and key the door open. The air inside is stale and stiflingly hot, and as I step into the hall, I see a small red light glowing in the living room. It's coming from a boxy old radio on one of my bookcases. I turn the radio around and take the surveillance camera out of the hollow interior. The red light only comes on when it finishes recording after detecting movement, so it isn't on because of me. Someone has been in the apartment. I take the video card out of the camera and put it into my laptop on the desk by the front window. I can see Autumn down below waiting impatiently in the car. The footage comes up on the screen. The camera is angled to catch a view of the front door. Anyone who breaks in would, logically, come into the living room and get close to the camera as they search for valuables or info on whatever I'm working on for Hessian.

The man on the video who enters my apartment is white, in his twenties, and wearing jeans, a red hoodie, and a small backpack. He puts away a set of lock picks in the backpack as he enters, locks the door, and I know I'm not dealing with an ordinary thief. In this neighborhood they use crowbars or lug wrenches to get into houses. He steps into the living room, puts his hands on his hips, and looks around appraisingly as though he's not sure what to do or where to start looking. He flinches slightly as if reacting to a sound and leans to one side to look towards the window. After staring outside for a moment, he mouths a silent curse, pulls out a gun tucked in the back of his jeans, darts down the hallway to the rear of the apartment, and not even thirty seconds later I see myself come through the door.

I mouth my own silent curse.

Archie

The next day was a Sunday, still cold, but now the clouds were gone, and the mountains were a row of broken white teeth against an infinite blue sky. I had woken up that day feeling elated. The memory of being with Rebecca, of holding her and being held by her, made me sick with longing. I was also pleased with how coolly and effectively I'd taken the boy away from Spencer. I felt emboldened, and confident that I could do something similar with Rebecca.

I went into town on my bike to get groceries, but I also toyed with the idea of driving by the Settlement, even though there was only a slim chance of seeing Rebecca from the road. I picked up a few things at Safeway and was cruising along Main on my way to Gaunt's, when I saw Malachi standing on the sidewalk staring in the window of a closed hardware store. I pulled over beside him.

He turned at the sound of my bike and struggled to put a grin on his face. "Hello, Tom."

"What are you doing in town during the day? You told me Caleb spends Sundays doing all kinds of church crap. Don't you have to be there?"

Malachi, always so quick to let his emotions dance across his face, stood there like a statue, his eyes blinking back tears, and said, "He's cast me out of our church."

Caleb had hewn away part of Malachi's soul. I understood that Malachi couldn't be reasoned with; there was no way I could make him see that what had happened was trivial and petty. I clumsily put a hand on his arm and gave it a squeeze, a gesture I'd seen someone in a movie make at a moment like this. Malachi sagged against me, his head resting on my shoulder and his howls of grief provoking a dog inside a parked car into a barking fit. Malachi pulled away from me when his sobs slowed down into tearful hiccups. My shoulder was soaked with his tears.

"He kicked you out of the Settlement?" I asked.

"He says I can still earn my room and board by working, but when I'm not needed, he wants me away from the Settlement or in my sleeping quarters. That's why he took me with him yesterday, to help with getting supplies. He never used to do that."

"Did he find out about you and Rebecca?"

"No. He thinks I've become corrupted by you, and he said I'd been speaking disrespectfully about him behind his back."

"Who told him that?"

"Sarah. She spies for Caleb. She only tells him little things, though. He gives her chocolate bars when she tells him stuff."

"This isn't bad news; you don't have to sneak around at night anymore. And you don't really care about that church stuff, do you?"

Malachi turned and leaned his forehead against the store window. There was a display of power tools decorated with Christmas wreaths and ribbons. This held his attention for a moment, and he put a hand against the glass as though he thought he could reach through and pick one of them up.

"I do care, Tom. When I told you that sometimes I didn't, I was lying. I wanted you to like me because you're an unbeliever. Caleb is a corrupt defiler, but God's sent him as a test of my faith. I see that clearly now. If I'm to unblacken my soul I must survive Caleb and keep my belief in the church. Our God has promised a paradise for men if we follow his path and protect his church. Where am I to honor and worship God if Caleb denies the church to me? That's the only place God will listen to prayers."

"Jesus fucking Christ, Malachi, don't you realize Caleb has this whole setup so he can make money and get laid? And what about you and Rebecca? How is that going to fix your soul?"

"I'm weak, Tom. I've told Rebecca we can't lie together anymore."

I didn't know what to say. Like Rebecca, Malachi's mind had been filled with fears and desires and confusions that flared like lightning before disappearing just as quickly. The idea of arguing any further with him made me feel weak. Words alone would never cut the leash that held him to his church.

"You hungry, Malachi? You want to go eat?"

I didn't need to ask; he was always hungry. We climbed on my bike and I took him to Applebee's. He was downcast when we went in, but the novelty of sitting in a real restaurant, and its gleaming, cheery environment, brought him back to life. I told him to order anything, and he squirmed like a puppy as he asked me about almost every menu item. He said he'd never eaten fish, so he ordered a salmon steak, which he followed with fajitas and three different desserts. The waitress complimented him on his appetite, and I thought he was going to faint with embarrassment. I insisted he have coffee afterwards. He wasn't sure he enjoyed it, but he liked the smell. I asked him if there were regular times that Caleb left the Settlement and for how long. Apparently, Caleb always went into Hexum for a few hours on Saturdays for shopping, and on every second Monday he'd go away for the whole day. Over the last month or more, however, Caleb had been making unexpected trips away from the Settlement. He usually went out in the evening after locking the women and children in the house, and never said where he was going or when he'd be back. Sometimes he'd be gone for only half an hour, other times it would be two or three hours.

When we left the restaurant, Malachi was closer to his old self. I offered to take him to a movie or anywhere else he wanted, but the prospect of another new experience made him anxious, and he asked me to drop him off at home. By the time I left him on the road outside Caleb's workshop, his spirit had drained away. He mumbled a goodbye and left without shaking my hand. As I rode away, I glanced at the Settlement: no one was outside, and yesterday's snow had been churned into tan mud. The place usually had a raw, pioneer look, but now it made me think of the Second World War.

I decided that the only way to free Rebecca from Caleb would be to spend more time at the Settlement, even if Caleb was there. I was hoping that the glimpses Rebecca got of the outside world through me would wear down her loyalty to that muddy patch of ground and its berserk church. If Caleb objected to my presence, I'd threaten him with another visit from Reinhart.

I went there on the following Tuesday, near lunchtime, armed with a phony story about wanting a new clutch for my bike. I found Caleb and Malachi in the workshop dealing with three customers who were clearly taking up all of their time. I mentioned the clutch to them and said I'd wait until they were finished. Caleb showed no emotion as I sauntered away from the workshop and towards the Settlement. Malachi looked worried.

Rebecca was in the church by herself working on a diamond-patterned quilt. Her smile shook me with pleasure. She put the quilt aside and gave me a hug.

"You're back! Did Caleb see you?"

"He did, but he's busy with people in the workshop. Malachi told me Caleb's been going out at night."

"Yes, and it's a blessing for us. We don't know where he goes, but often when he returns, he wants to be alone in his bed."

"Is there one night he's always out?"

"The last three Fridays he's been gone till very late. Other evenings he's been gone only a half hour or so."

"I'll be back then."

"He locks us in, you know."

"From the outside? What if there was a fire or something?"

"He cares nothing for our souls, so why should he care for our lives? Why do you want to come then?"

I was tempted to blurt out that being near her was the whole reason for my coming to the Settlement, but I didn't know how to say it without sounding weird.

"I want to get into his office."

"It's always locked," she said with disappointment.

I didn't want to tell her that I was looking for Caleb's money box so that I could give her money to run away.

"I want to try getting in the window upstairs. There's a ladder behind the workshop I can use."

"Oh." She turned and looked at the house as though seeing it for the first time. "You could, I suppose." She took my hands in hers and asked, "I'll always welcome you, Tom, but why do you want to be with us? We can't be very interesting to you; you have a bigger life outside of here than we'll ever have. Why?"

My blushes were so intense I was sure Rebecca could feel them as well as see them.

"I like you," I said. "I don't think you should be in this place. If you won't leave, then I'll keep coming here until you do."

Her smile was warm but uncertain. "I'll see you Friday night, then."

Rebecca sat down and picked up her quilt. I croaked out a "Goodbye" and went back to the workshop. There was only one customer in the place now, an elderly rancher, and he was battering Caleb with questions about water pumps. Malachi was standing at a worktable taking apart a rusted generator.

Caleb put up a hand to stem the customer's questions and half-shouted at me: "I don't have any parts for bikes. You'd best go elsewhere, and you cannot enter my property. I told you before, we must deny outsiders."

I was feeling happy and bold, and as I looked at Caleb, I became aware of the ridiculousness in him. There was danger in those massive arms and his hostile, statue-like gaze, but I could also see the fat man who preached God while dreaming of popcorn and porn. He was nothing but teenage appetites made flesh.

"Really, Caleb?" I said coldly. "I didn't think you've ever denied yourself anything."

I finally saw a strong emotion on his face: he turned red and puffed out his cheeks as though suppressing a mighty shout, and for a moment he became the image of a God of the Winds on an ancient map. If there'd been no one in the workshop I'm sure Caleb would have come for me. He stood there without moving, like a wrathful giant that's been turned to stone, and then turned to resume his conversation with the old man, who was too deaf to have heard what I said. Malachi looked stricken, and I realized he might suffer for my insolence. Guilt tugged lightly at me, but my mind was too full of Rebecca. While Caleb was looking away, I passed a twenty-dollar bill to Malachi. He smiled crookedly at me and went back to his work. I didn't know what use the twenty would be to him, but it made me feel better.

Caleb's evening trips away from the Settlement intrigued me; a half hour wouldn't allow him to see a movie, and it wasn't enough time for one of his restaurant feasts, although it was possible that he was just dashing away for a quick bite at KFC or White Castle. I decided to follow him on his nighttime excursions.

Early the next evening, not long after sunset, I waited on my bike on the edge of town beside a derelict motel. The road in front of me was the only one Caleb could use to go into Hexum. He didn't keep me waiting long. I heard his mini-van's vibrating muffler before I saw him, and I ducked out of sight as he passed my hiding spot. I stayed well behind him as he cruised into town and turned onto Pine St. It was lined with used car lots, small industrial businesses that sat behind fences topped with razor wire, and old houses that had become offices for doctors and dentists.

I pulled behind a parked SUV as Caleb stopped in front of a house with a huge picture window on the ground floor revealing an office furnished with a single, massive desk. The office's walls were white and sparsely decorated with framed documents and photos, and the overhead fluorescent lights blazed so brightly it seemed strange that the elderly man behind the desk wasn't wearing sunglasses. He wore a black suit over his skinny body and was so pale I wondered if the lights hadn't bleached him. The man saw Caleb coming up the steps and gave him a wave.

As soon as Caleb was in the office I ran across the street for a better look. The two shook hands, and Caleb sat down on the opposite side of the desk. They talked and passed papers back and forth, and, as they did, Caleb smiled and laughed, behavior that seemed unnatural to him, as though he'd become possessed or was playing a role. There was a wooden sign on the lawn in front of the house that was in deep shadow from the glaring office light, but I could make out the words: ELMER CRIPPEN, ATTORNEY. I didn't know what to make of Caleb seeing a lawyer, but I assumed it had something to do with running a business. Fifteen minutes later Caleb came out of the office and drove away. I didn't bother following him.

I didn't think Caleb was seeing a lawyer every night, so the next night I was back beside the motel waiting for his mini-van to appear. He turned up at almost the same time, only now he went to the Hexum Diner, ate leisurely for an hour, then drove to a 7-Eleven and came out with two full bags. He headed back in the direction of the Settlement, so I turned around and went home. The following night I waited for over an hour before giving up.

Friday was his night to be away from the Settlement for at least a couple of hours, so I got to my hiding spot even earlier—I didn't want to risk not seeing him go by. He came past sooner than usual and, instead of going for a meal or to Crippen's office, went down one of the streets that accommodated some of the ragged houses filled with bunk beds and tired-looking men. His mini-van pulled to the curb in front of one of the biggest houses, a dark, almost black, three-storey clapboard pile that bristled with porches, gables, and Juliet balconies. It's shape and air of weariness made me think of a haunted house from a children's picture book, with an interior filled with cobwebs, claw-footed furniture, and a wrinkled, hollow-cheeked owner.

Caleb jogged up the porch steps and walked right in the front door. The door stayed open and I could see a long hall garlanded with multi-colored Christmas lights. An eccentric variety of chairs, at least a dozen, lined the hall on either side. Half the chairs were occupied by Asian women talking to each other, and they barely glanced at Caleb as he disappeared up a staircase. One of the women in the hall came out on the porch to smoke a cigarette and closed the door behind her. As she did so, and as if by clockwork, a woman came out on a balcony above her and another leaned out of a large, sash window on the top floor. They were wearing brightly-colored dressing gowns with designs of flowers and birds done in reds and golds and greens. They looked like jewels displayed on the black velvet background of the house, or lonely ornaments hung on a misshapen Christmas tree.

I knew there were brothels in Hexum, some exclusively Asian or Latino, but I hadn't come across this one before. I wondered if Rebecca and the others would even believe me if I told them what Caleb was doing on his Friday nights. I rushed to the Settlement and found Malachi sitting on a stump under one of the floodlights that bordered the property. He was reading what looked like a slim magazine, and he had a lot more of them sitting on his lap.

His smile was a mile wide as I approached him, and he held up what he was reading and said, "Look what I got with that money you gave me, Tom."

He'd bought himself a thick stack of creased and dog-eared *Archie* comics.

"Where did you get those?"

"A place on Main St. that sells books."

I remembered that Latimer kept piles of comic books on display in his windows.

"There's better stuff than that you can read."

Malachi shook his head emphatically. "Oh, no. These are wonderful. They make me laugh so much, Tom. Archie is always being such a fool!" He became helpless with laughter for a few moments. "Haven't you read them? I don't think there can be anything funnier. Tomorrow I'll give them to Rebecca. She'll like them, won't she?"

I ignored his question. "I'm going to get into Caleb's office. You want to help me?"

He tried to put on a serious face, but his eyes kept drifting back to the comic he had open on his lap, and a grin pulled at the corners of his mouth. Malachi was truly, hopelessly lost. Before, I'd told myself that he was the warped shadow of someone who'd been beaten, deprived and brainwashed, and I was certain that he could be made 'normal' if I enlightened him about Caleb, or showed him more of the world outside the Settlement. But there was no coming back for Malachi; anything I did for him would damage him further, like a piece of metal that snaps after being bent back and forth too many times. It said everything about Malachi that all his fear for his blackened, marred soul had been whisked away for the moment by Archie and Betty and Veronica.

At that instant I considered going home and never coming back. It struck me that Rebecca was probably as far gone as Malachi, and that my ambition to detach her from the Settlement and her mad faith was futile. But then I remembered that in the past, like me, she'd had a regular life, with a mother and a home that wasn't a compound or dropped down in the back of beyond. Part of her, I was sure, wanted to go back to that. I was certain she could be saved as I'd saved the boy in the diner. And I was pretty sure I loved her.

"No, Tom," said Malachi distractedly. "You won't find anything up there, and I don't want to catch another whipping."

I left Malachi turning the pages of his comic, his laughter sounding like a bubbling kettle.

I got an aluminum extension ladder that was lying on the ground behind the workshop and carried it to the house. The front door was secured with a padlock and hasp, and I considered knocking on it to tell Rebecca that I'd arrived, but if the window in Caleb's office wasn't open, I'd just be disappointing her. I angled the ladder against the porch roof and scrambled up. The office was in total darkness and for a moment I had an irrational fear that Caleb was inside, waiting for me. The window slid up smoothly and quietly, as though it was waiting for my touch to bring it to life.

My heart was pounding as I stepped through the window. A desk and a chrome and leather office chair sat in the middle of the room on a thick, red carpet. There was a computer on the desk sitting like an island in a sea of papers and magazines. A low table against one wall held a TV with a pair of headphones plugged into it, both a VHS and a DVD player, and a stack of cassettes and DVDs. On the wall above there was a poster of John Elway throwing a pass. There were more football posters on the walls, and maybe twenty *Playboy* centerfolds. A bar fridge was next to the table. I opened it and found bottles of Michelob and Pepsi, chip dip, six different kinds of candy bars, and Ben & Jerry's ice cream. A tall bookcase on the other side of the rom held a stash of cookies, bags of potato chips, skin mags, two bottles of Dewar's scotch, some framed photos of Caleb in football gear as a teenager, and a few dozen paperbacks, most of them by John D. MacDonald. I turned on a standing lamp near the door that led downstairs. The light only made the room uglier. The floor was littered with bits of trash that Caleb couldn't be bothered to bend over and pick up: fragments of food, bottle caps, magazine inserts, and crumpled balls of paper. What I hadn't seen was anything like a safe or money box.

I sat at the desk and stared at the computer. I knew how to turn one on, but beyond that I was helpless. Levi had never bought one, and I'd really only seen them being used in stores and on TV. I gave up on the idea of using the computer and started going through the stuff on the desk. There were utility bills and all kinds of paperwork related to his business. None of it was interesting, and I didn't even know what I was looking for or why. A tall stack of magazines on the edge of the desk caught my attention. I'd assumed they were porn, but when I flipped over the top one I saw that it was a travel magazine. And so were the others. All of them had feature articles, or were entirely about, travel in Asia. I went through the desk drawers and found two file folders in a bottom drawer. The first was full of articles clipped from newspapers and magazines about red light districts in Thailand and the Philippines. I couldn't make sense of this; his visit to the brothel showed that he liked Asian women, but why was he reading about places he would never get to? The second file folder was half as thick and held articles about gold, and how it was the only safe investment to protect yourself from Y2K and the coming depression.

I put everything back the way I had found it and went to the door. I was eager to show Caleb's room to Rebecca and the others, and let them see how everything about the Settlement was a joke that only Caleb knew the punchline to. I opened the door quietly and stepped out onto the small landing. The girls were in the room below looking up at me like nestlings waiting for a feeding.

"We heard you," said Rebecca.

"Come up," I urged them. "You have to see this."

They hesitated, but then Sarah stepped forward, followed immediately by the others.

They moved into the office like cautious astronauts on a strange, new planet, and gasped quietly as they saw the centerfolds, the contents of the fridge, and especially the TV.

Rebecca pointed at the headphones. "What are these?"

"Headphones. He wears them so you don't know he's got a TV. Does he come up here for a long time on Sundays?"

They all nodded. It was hard to get a read on how they were reacting. They were shocked, Sarah maybe less so, but I didn't know what emotions that shock was producing. I told them about seeing Caleb go into the brothel, and then had to explain what a brothel was. This didn't surprise any of them, and Abby wondered if Caleb wasn't going there to add more wives to his collection. Linda began crying and said that she couldn't stomach the idea of lying with a strange woman, especially a foreign one. I told her I was certain Caleb wasn't adding more wives, he was just out having fun.

"We'd better go before he comes back," said Rebecca.

The others filed out as quietly as they'd come in. Rebecca lingered and took a last look around the room.

"I'm glad you showed me this," she said.

This is what I'd wanted to hear, but she looked sad as she said it. She closed the door softly behind her and I was left alone in the office. Now that Caleb's lair had been revealed, I felt awkward, like a child who's sure he's done something clever but ends up causing damage.

I went out the window, closed it carefully, and climbed down the ladder. Malachi was still on his stump, rocking with laughter. He didn't look up and I said nothing to him as I put the ladder away and left.

For the next week I haunted the area around the Settlement, hiding in the brush and watching for some kind of change. I thought that after all I'd done to undermine Caleb, I'd see a difference in the way Rebecca and the others acted. It didn't happen. The girls did chores, made quilts, taught the children, cooked meals. Malachi helped in the workshop or went into his hut. On Sunday it was mild enough for the door of their church to be left open, and I could hear Caleb's droning, heavy voice lecturing or praying or reading scripture, or whatever it was he did in there. Instead of going up to his office and watching football after church, he took off in the mini-van with Malachi. I scampered out of the brush and found Rebecca in the kitchen preparing a meal. The other girls were in the main house with the children. She greeted me with a hug, and her smile was warm, but there was something subdued about her.

"How's things been?" I asked.

She thought about this for a long while as she cut potatoes, and then said, "Caleb knows we think differently about him. We don't honor him the way he normally likes, and we don't..." she struggled to find the right words, "pretend to be as happy in his bed."

"That's good, right?"

"It's made him crueler. He hurls terrible insults about our bodies and the children. He never did that kind of thing before. And he doesn't seem to care about us."

"He never did care about you," I protested.

"No, not like you mean. He doesn't seem to worry that we're different now. Sarah laughed at something clumsy he did yesterday, and at first he looked angry and I thought he was going to strike her down— he's hit us for less reason than that—but then he laughed *at* Sarah, like the joke was on her. It scares me."

"Then leave."

She didn't immediately say no, but after a moment she shook her head. I didn't want to press her, but I hoped she was changing her mind.

"What does Caleb talk about in church?" I asked. "I could hear him going on and on."

"He reads from the Book of the Righteous Fathers."

"Is that like the Bible?"

"I think so. He reads parts from it that he says are from the Bible, and then he reads out what the Righteous Fathers say the Bible means, and then he tells us what the Righteous Fathers are saying."

"Haven't you read it?"

"Women aren't allowed to read it."

"How about *Archie* comics?"

Rebecca laughed ecstatically. "They're lovely! We have them hidden under our mattresses. Malachi said he got them with the money you gave him." She put her hands on my shoulders and looked at me as if I was an interesting package that needed unwrapping. "I don't know why you've come amongst us, Tom, but I'm glad."

Abby came into the kitchen and asked me if I could bring them some *National Geographic* magazines; she'd read some once and remembered them fondly. I told her I'd try, and that if I got any I'd hide them in the panel truck at the back of the property. They were happy with that plan, and I promised to do it soon.

As I drove back through Hexum, Reinhart flagged me down in his cruiser. We stopped in the middle of Main St. and the traffic politely went around our vehicles. None of the passing drivers made eye contact with us.

"You're going to a Christmas party tomorrow, Tom," Reinhart said cheerily.

Christmas was two days away, but I'd kept it out of my mind what with shadowing Caleb and thinking about Rebecca, and, besides all that, I had no reason to look forward to the day. I was planning to spend it watching a bunch of movies I'd rented from Blockbuster, and now I had a horrible feeling Reinhart was going to take me to some kind of kids' Christmas party.

"What kind of party?" I asked suspiciously.

"A Christmas Eve party at Jubal's place." Reinhart hooted with laughter at the astonished expression on my face. "Don't worry, I'm going with you. I figured with your dad away I should make sure you have a bit of Christmas fun. Jubal lays out a pretty fantastic spread for his crew, and it's time you and he buried the hatchet." He winked at me. "But not in each other's backs. I'll pick you up tomorrow afternoon."

I was too stunned say anything before he left. The book store was nearby so I went in and bought some *National Geographics*, *People*, and *Archie*. Latimer gave me a funny look and I told him they were for a friend.

"That Gaunt kid?"

"How did you know?"

"He introduced himself like he was gonna sell me on his church. Be careful with him."

"Why?"

Latimer shifted in his chair, adjusted his lanky, tired cardigan, and looked out the window. "When I was in the army, every unit had one or two guys who you knew were going to go off the deep end eventually; I mean, do something really goddamn freaky to themselves or the people around them. You could see it in their eyes and the way they talked. That kid's one of them. All the time he was in here I had a hand under the counter on my rifle."

"You keep a gun under there?"

"Yeah. This is Hexum. It only makes sense."

"Malachi's okay. He's messed up, but he wouldn't do anything."

Latimer raised an eyebrow and rang up my purchase.

About three o'clock the next day, Reinhart came by the house and we drove the short distance to J.J.'s. I must have had a grim look on my face, because Josh tried to cheer me up by cracking silly jokes. There weren't many cars in the lot, but I recognized many of them as belonging to men Levi worked with. Jubal's sprawling building didn't look Christmassy: neon beer logo signs glowed starkly against its black walls, and I wished I was wandering around the wild foothills that rose up in the background. But I didn't want to disappoint Reinhart.

We came through the main door into a rectangular, low-ceilinged, cavernous space that was almost identical to the outside: black walls, neon signs, and a drunken army of tables and chairs haphazardly crowding the room. The walls were unevenly decorated with promotional posters from beer companies, framed sports jerseys, and a scattering of American and Confederate flags. A raised stage at the far end of the room was bare except for some sound equipment piled into one corner. A bar ran half the length of one wall, and the opposite wall had a wide doorway to another, equally large space, filled with pool tables. Tables had been grouped into some kind of order near the bar, and Jubal's men, more than two dozen, were sitting at them and singing 'Rudolf the Red-Nosed Reindeer' along with a karaoke machine.

Jubal and Spencer were sitting at their own table, belting out the song enthusiastically. Spencer was wearing a Santa hat and a Dodgers jersey. We sat down at their table and Jubal, who was acting like he was having the time of his life, gave Reinhart a crisp salute and me a friendly nod. Spencer waved at Josh and ignored me. Everyone had a beer or a cocktail in their hand, although a few were sticking to soda. The song ended and the men began a jovial argument about which song to play next. They settled on 'Deck the Halls.'

"Josh," said Jubal, "I swear I have never seen you out of that damn uniform. You ever take it off?"

Jubal was right; in the dozens of times that I'd seen or met Reinhart, he'd always been in uniform.

Reinhart shook his head. "Why would I ever take it off, Jubal? I don't make any money or have any fun when I'm out of it."

Jubal roared with laughter. Even Spencer smiled.

Jubal pointed at me and asked, "Why did you bring along this little ball of piss and vinegar, or can I guess?"

I was startled by Jubal's friendly, joshing tone, and also by the implication that something was in store for me.

Reinhart clapped a hand on my shoulder. "Yes, Tom is going to be one of my boys down the road, and I think he's going to be one of the best. And I thought he could use some Christmas cheer."

Jubal stood up and, shouting over the noise of his men singing, said, "Hear ye, hear ye! I'm letting you bastards know that this young man, Tom Bridger, Levi's son, is going to be one of Josh's boys. So, treat him with respect, or he'll tap you upside the head."

There was applause and cheers, Spencer barked out a laugh, and there were confused questions about what Jubal meant by a "tap upside the head." I felt sick at the veiled mention of what I'd done to Mickey, and also by the awareness that his death was a trap that now held me in its jaws. But part of me took solace in now being part of a group that was going to give me a future, even if didn't have any clear idea of what being one of Josh's "boys" meant. I assumed I'd become a cop, like him, and wondered how that would ever come to pass.

The singing resumed, and the smell of cooking food began to fill the air. There were a set of swinging doors beside the bar with porthole windows through which I could see men moving around a kitchen. Jubal, Reinhart and Spencer joined in the singing, and I hummed along while studying Jubal's crew. It occurred to me that these were henchmen, like the ones in films, and that struck me as funny because they were such a scruffy, unhealthy-looking bunch. Movie henchmen looked ruthless and professional, but this crew were lumpy or scrawny, and a few were clearly stupid. All of them were white, most of them in their 20s or 30s, and as they sang, joked, and bantered, they couldn't stop glancing at each other with deadly seriousness. I thought of things I'd read about pecking orders and hierarchies, and I could see it happening right in front of me.

Every shouted joke or comment or anecdote was an attempt by one of them to either hold their place on the ladder, or climb up a rung by impressing with their wit, viciousness, or bravado. Atomic Dog had his barking routine going, but when he saw the others weren't laughing at it anymore, he tried to tell a story about stealing a tractor. He was ignored, and his expression became anxious even as his grin grew wider. They were all performing for each other, but especially for Jubal and Spencer, and they knew it.

Jubal banged on the table for silence and rose to his feet, the drink in his right hand slopping out a little as he did so. He made a comic show of gently putting it down on the table, which brought much laughter from his men.

"Boys," said Jubal, "we've had a fine fuck of a year." Cheers all round. "That's how I like to judge each year that's passed, like it was sex." Some hooting. "Was this year just a hand job in a restroom, or a fuckfest on silk sheets with champagne and a fat bag of coke?" Laughter and hooting. "This year," he said, and paused for dramatic effect. "This year has officially been a threesome with Sharon Stone and Pamela Anderson." Cheering and hooting. "Now, if we want to make next year as good a lay as this one was, there's some things we have to remember. First, let's behave a bit better in town. Sherriff Reinhart is busy enough keeping the gooks and greasers in line, he doesn't need you peckerheads breaking the china and putting your paws on the civilians. Have some fun with them, but don't leave a mess on the carpet. Second, I don't want to see anyone wasted when they're on my time and dime...except me." Roars of laughter. "Last, this is my land. No trespassing, no visitors allowed. If you get a hint, a rumor, a scent on the breeze that we have competition, you tell me or Spence." He paused for a long sip of his drink. "I am the king and you are my knights, and when you ride with me you share fully in the bounty of my table." Thunderous applause. "But it's my table, forever and always. If you're not sure what parts of this kingdom are mine, remember this: if I can see it, it's already mine or I want it to be mine. Remember that most of all, you dirty bastards. Now let's eat."

The men roared their approval, and I could see that they were genuinely thrilled with Jubal. His words had wiped away their anxious, evaluating glances and replaced them with rapture. They loved their king.

As Jubal stormed into the kitchen and started shouting at the cooks, Reinhart leaned over to me and whispered, "Jubal's got his knights and this big, ugly, black castle, but I've got the law, and I can smite him down any time I like. Sometimes he doesn't realize he's mortal."

Jubal ushered out a group of Latino kitchen workers who filled two long tables with roast turkeys, prime rib, a ham, and large serving pans filled with dressing, potatoes, corn on the cob, carrots, turnips, salad, and tubs of gravy. A third table held plates and cutlery. We crowded around the food tables and held out our plates for the kitchen staff carving the meats.

Spencer came back at our table with a plate holding only turkey and salad. Jubal looked at Spencer's food and said with a smirk, "You slimming again, Spence?"

"Just not hungry," Spencer said tersely.

Jubal turned to Reinhart. "Spence gets antsy when his love handles get too big for little hands."

Jubal and Reinhart chuckled while Spencer glared at his plate.

"I want to cut out a couple of the boys," said Spence coldly.

"Who?" asked Jubal.

"Atomic Dog and Lancey. They're getting weak. Ike told me Lancey got his ass kicked off a patch by two chinks last week. And Dog has done two deliveries for the Sutler brothers without getting our money; they gave him some bullshit about us owing them."

Jubal shrugged. "Okay."

"Retired or fired?"

Jubal glanced at me before answering Spencer. "We'll talk about it later. It's fucking Christmas, Spence."

"Just one more piece of business, Jubal," said Reinhart. "Remind your men to let me know if they see any blacks around town. I don't mean those army boys who work out at the base; it's Bloods and Crips from the cities I'm worried about. I want a cop uniform to be the last thing they see in Hexum."

Josh raised his drink in a toast. "To serve and protect, Josh, to serve and protect."

"Just trying to keep things calm, Jubal; we don't need any race relations in Hexum."

I hadn't eaten this well in months. Too many of my meals had been microwaved or handed to me in a paper bag. I was uncomfortably full when trays of desserts were brought out along with a coffee urn. I ate pie and cake until I began to worry my stomach was on the verge of splitting open like the husk on a ripe chestnut. I sat in my chair in a stupor, half-listening to Reinhart, Jubal and Spencer as they talked business while picking at the ruins of their meals.

The three were gloating about the state of their nation. They talked about problems solved, enemies driven off, and new clients who tithed them fat profits. But they still found time to grumble about money. They had no specific complaints about opportunities missed or denied, just a nagging suspicion that they could get more out of Hexum if only they knew how.

Jubal got to his feet and shouted, "You greedy cunts want your Christmas presents now?" This was answered with gleeful shouts, and Jubal went behind the bar and pulled out a clear shopping bag filled with sealed envelopes. "Come and get it."

The men went to the bar where Jubal handed each of them an envelope, which they only tore open when they got back to their seats. No one was disappointed with the amount of money in their envelope.

Jubal came back to our table and flipped me an envelope. I stared at it for a moment, unsure whether I should open it or put it in my pocket.

"It's your dad's, but I think you'll be able to guard it," said Spencer in a mocking tone.

I debated if now would be a good time to ask where Levi was and when, if ever, he'd be coming back. But I didn't; if they hadn't told me by this point in time, it was because they didn't know or had reasons for not telling me. I thanked Jubal, who made an it's-no-big-deal face, and stuffed the envelope in my pocket.

Reinhart cleared his throat and said, "I got something for you, too. Hold on."

He went out to the parking lot and came back a minute later holding a shoe box, which he set down in front of me. I took the top off and found an automatic pistol lying on a neatly folded towel with a box of 9mm rounds nestled beside it. The gun was sleek and dark with an oily sheen.

I must have been looking at it blankly because Reinhart said, "I figure you're old enough and smart enough for a gun. You should get used to handling one—you never know what the world's going to throw at you."

"Thanks, Josh," I said, and meant it. I took it out and hefted it in my hand. I liked its shape and weight, but I also felt that by accepting it I was swearing a kind of oath to Reinhart.

"You know what kind of gun it is?" he said eagerly. "It's a Walther PPK. I remember you said you liked that James Bond movie, right? That's the kind of gun James Bond uses. I got the idea when you busted Gaunt about seeing that movie."

"Gaunt?" said Jubal. "You mean that ham-faced holy roller out near the mine with the repair business?"

"That's him," agreed Reinhart.

"He just bought one of the girls from the house on Lincoln."

The brothel I'd seen Caleb going into was on Lincoln Ave.

"Bought?" asked Reinhart.

"You know: he bought her passport off me."

"He's got her out at his place?"

"No. She's still in the house and Gaunt pays her rent."

"What's her name?" I asked.

Jubal was surprised by the question. "I think she calls herself Monique or Mona. The name on her passport's some kind of Chinese shit: Ding Dong Kong, or something like that."

"We going to watch those movies now?" asked Spencer.

"Oh, yeah," said Jubal. "Let's get everyone in the back room."

"What are you showing?" asked Reinhart.

"I got a bootleg of *Any Given Sunday*," said Jubal enthusiastically. "Al Pacino, man, I love him."

Reinhart was disappointed. "Anything else?"

"Don't worry, Josh, we've got some home movies for dessert."

"You want to see this Pacino movie, Tom?" Reinhart asked me.

I said no, and he offered to drive me home since he didn't mind missing part of the Pacino movie, but I told him I preferred to walk and work off some of what I'd eaten. Reinhart and a few of the men wished me a Merry Christmas as I left. Shockingly, so did Jubal.

It was dark as I walked home through the chaparral. A coyote, made ghostly white by the moonlight, yipped once and sprinted away when it saw me, but otherwise the world was cold and silent and empty. Guiltily, I contemplated if it would be best if Levi never came back. I'd managed perfectly well on my own, and my only worry was running out of money, but that problem had been put off by the envelope resting in my pocket. Perhaps I could start working for Reinhart right now. I couldn't see why Caleb had bought Mona or Monique's passport, or why it was something that was up for sale. He wasn't going to add her to the Settlement, it appeared, but the change in his habits was disturbing.

I got home and noticed the stack of magazines I'd bought for Rebecca and the others and decided to drop them off that night. I pictured their excitement at finding them on Christmas morning.

Hexum was quiet when I went through it on my bike—the booming, thumping cars had taken the night off. I parked away from the Settlement in case Caleb was up and about watching TV, but his room was dark. Malachi's hut was empty and I wondered if he was in town waiting for me in the playground. As I passed the church, I saw a figure moving near the abandoned van. It was Caleb. I stepped out of sight behind the church and watched. He raised the van's hood and lifted out a box about the size of a serving tray, which he opened after fiddling with a lock. He shone a flashlight into the box, and I was expecting him to take something out or put something in, but he stood there, frozen, staring into it. Whatever was in the box cast a yellow reflection on his face. He stayed like that for more than a minute with a smile fixed on his face like a parent beaming at a newborn in its crib. He wasn't placing or removing anything, just enjoying what he'd hidden away.

Caleb finally closed the box, locked it, lowered the hood quietly, and walked back to the house. I made sure he was inside before going to the van. I raised the hood even more quietly than Caleb had and found a black metal box sitting on the engine block. It was about three inches deep and fastened with a combination lock, the kind with three rotating discs marked with numbers from 0 to 9. It seemed an unlikely place to keep a money box, but if someone wanted to steal Caleb's money, they'd check the workshop, the house, or one of the other buildings, but not a decayed van sinking into the ground.

I tried some simple combinations, like 000 and 123, but with no luck. I thought of movies where people listened for a telltale clicking noise as they spun the dial on a safe, and I tried that. Nothing. But movies made me think to turn the discs to read 007. It opened. Half the box was filled with rectangular gold wafers inside clear plastic covers. They were smaller than a playing card and stamped with a maple leaf and the words: ROYAL CANADIAN MINT 1 oz. I stared at them almost as long as Caleb had. On the other side of the box were four rolls of hundred-dollar bills held together with rubber bands and some papers inside a clear plastic bag. I carefully took the top sheet out of the bag. It looked like a diploma, but across the top it read: GOLD CERTIFICATE. The text below declared that the certificate was issued by the United Overseas Bank of Singapore and could be exchanged by the bearer for one kilogram of gold. The bag held thirty or more certificates identical to the one I was holding. I replaced the sheet I'd taken out, and as I resealed the bag, I felt something slide under it. Beneath the bag were two passports, one American and one Indonesian. The American passport belonged to Caleb and had been issued two months ago. I opened the other passport and saw a black and white photo of a young Asian woman wearing a delicate smile. Her name was Mo Chou Kong. Underneath the passports were plane tickets made out to Caleb and Kong. The tickets were one-way from Los Angeles to Singapore, and the departure date was January 10. Less than three weeks away.

Beau

I text Autumn: CALL ME RIGHT NOW. MAN IN APT. My phone rings seconds later.

"Hey," I say loudly, "I'm just on my way out the door. I had to pick something up. See you."

I mute the phone and walk over to the door, open and close it, and move noiselessly into the kitchen. The intruder will have to come past the kitchen entrance if he wants to leave. After a minute I hear slow, quiet steps from the hallway. He pauses halfway, presumably to listen for movement, then sighs with relief and moves quickly up the hall. As he passes the kitchen, I throw an elbow into the side of his jaw that buckles his knees and rolls his eyes back. I drag him into the living room, fetch a pair of handcuffs from my desk, turn him onto his stomach and cuff him. He moans as he begins to come to. I get a roll of duct tape from under the kitchen sink and bind his legs at the ankles and knees. He has a Ruger six-shot revolver tucked in his jeans. Inside the backpack are the lock picks and a Ziploc bag that holds an identical Ruger. I break open the cylinder without opening the bag; only four chambers are loaded. The missing rounds will undoubtedly be the two that killed Oribe. The Ruger won't have my prints, but Oribe's will be on it, and the cops could bring a strong case against me if it was found in my apartment. I go through his pockets and get his phone, car keys, and wallet.

Autumn will be wondering what's happened, and I have to check if this guy's got a partner waiting in a car outside. I take his gun, keys, and go out the door onto the staircase and almost shout as I see Autumn planted at the bottom of the stairs pointing the Bernelli at me.

"Well?" she whispers.

"It's under control."

I come down the stairs and show her the car keys. "We're looking for a Toyota. The guy upstairs might have a partner. We'll go out on the sidewalk and I'll hit the unlock button. When we see lights flash, we walk up on the car, weapons down at our sides, me on the street side, you on the sidewalk."

"And?"

"And I hope we get the drop on him."

I press the button and the fifth car along to the right, a sedan, flashes its lights. We move towards it at a fast walk. It's empty.

"Now what?" asks Autumn.

"I'll talk with the guy upstairs. Call me if another car shows up. He might have backup arriving if he hasn't returned soon enough or checked in."

I return to the apartment and find my burglar has wormed across the floor to the door. There's nothing that looks ex-military about him: he's skinny, with traces of acne on his face, and it doesn't look like he's ever lifted anything heavier than an extra-large latte. His stare reminds me of animals I had to put down that I found crippled beside Hexum's roads. I go through his wallet and phone. Lodestar's Vegas number is in his contacts list. The name on his driver's licence is Beau Manley.

"Well, Beau," I say softly, "there's two ways we can do this: you can tell me all about what Lodestar wanted you to do and what they're planning, or I can hurt you."

Beau's frightened voice goes through several registers as he says, "You should call the police. Have me arrested."

This tells me Lodestar lets its people know that getting arrested on dirty missions, or at least this particular mission, is an acceptable escape route because they have enough influence and skill to get them sprung.

I pick up the roll of duct tape, then drag him down the hallway to the bathroom and lift him into the bathtub.

"What are you doing? Why am I in the bathtub?" he asks breathlessly.

I tear a piece of tape off and hold it in front of his mouth. "It'll be easier to clean up the blood and piss here."

I slap the tape over his mouth as he draws in a breath to yell. He thrashes around and I pinch his nose shut. His chest begins to heave violently and I let go of his nose as tears come to his eyes.

"Ready to talk?"

He nods vigorously. I rip the tape off his mouth and he takes deep breaths in-between sobs and hiccups. "Fuck, fuck, fuck! This is bullshit, man. I didn't sign up for this shit."

I let him weep a bit more before asking, "What did they tell you to do?"

"Hide a gun somewhere here. I only do break-ins for Lodestar, that's all."

"You always go armed?"

"Just a precaution, man, just a precaution. I'm not one of their soldier boys, I'm a techie."

"What kind of tech work?"

"I plant bugs, cameras, steal some shit sometimes; you know, computers, phones, anything with data on it."

"What do you know about me?"

"Nothing, man. They gave me an address and said it was, like, one hundred percent certain you wouldn't be around. Fuckers."

"When did you get the gun and your orders?"

"Yesterday morning they called me and told me to be on standby, then I got the piece in the afternoon."

"Are you supposed to call in when you're done here?"

"Yeah," he says nervously. He's almost as afraid of his bosses as he is me.

I admire Lodestar's thoroughness. Killing Oribe silenced him and gave them the chance to frame me. Even if they had captured us at the Capri, they'd probably still want the police to draw a line from me to Oribe, make it look like a dirty ex-cop got involved in some drug deal. I bet if I'd searched Oribe's house after I found his body, I would have turned up a drug stash. Autumn's death or disappearance would have been passed off as collateral damage from her association with me.

"And who do you call, Beau?"

"Cassidy. He's, like, my boss."

"And does Cassidy have anything else planned for me?"

"I wouldn't know, man. I never heard of you until this afternoon."

"Lodestar's got something special, something big, coming up soon; what's your part in that?"

Beau hesitates before answering. "I haven't heard anything. I'm low man on the totem pole around there."

Beau's gaze wandered to his right as he answered me; it's the easiest tell in an interrogation room or at a poker table that someone's lying. I put the tape back over his mouth and pinch his nose. He screams from behind the tape a few times before I remove it.

"Lie to me again and I'll suffocate you just enough so that you wake up with brain damage. Okay?"

Beau whimpers and I give him a moment to collect himself. "All I know is Cassidy told me to be ready to go out every night for the next three weeks. It could be tomorrow night or weeks from now."

"Go where?"

"He took my phone from me and pinned five locations on Google Maps. He said when I got the call, I'd be told which location to go to, and when I got there someone from Lodestar would tell me what to do. But he also said I was only backup in case one of the guy's assigned to this job was unavailable. It must be a big deal, because Cassidy said I'd be in serious shit if I wasn't around when the call came or didn't make it there in time."

"Who did you call when you finish here and what do you say?"

"I'm supposed to text Cassidy."

"Is he in your phone's contact list?"

"Yes."

"And is he nearby?"

"Could be. I don't know. Lodestar's office is just a few miles from here."

"Where?"

He gives me an address near LAX.

"Beau, I'm going cover your mouth again and move you out to your car. You'll be in the trunk, keeping quiet, and I'm going to leave you in a parking lot and call the cops."

Panic floods his face as I put the tape back on and leave the bathroom. I go down to the Rover, tell Autumn what I'm planning, and move the Bernelli to the back seat of Beau's Corolla after wiping it clean of prints. We go upstairs and I take the tape off Beau's legs while Autumn collects his backpack, the revolvers he brought, the handcuff keys, a pair of binoculars, duct tape, and my Walther.

As I maneuver Beau out of the bathroom, I hear Autumn mutter, "Jesus Christ."

"What?"

"You've got a lot of books."

"So?"

"Nothing. Just saying."

At the bottom of the stairs I drape an arm around Beau like he's a drunk friend I'm helping. Autumn pops the lock on the trunk and puts his stuff on the back seat. I dump Beau in the trunk, tape his wrists together before removing the cuffs, and then close the trunk lid. He's hyperventilating as I close the lid, no doubt thinking he's just been put in his coffin. I get behind the wheel and wait for Autumn to get in the Rover.

I drive up to Pico Blvd. with Autumn following close behind and put the Corolla beside a clothing-for-charity drop box in an empty parking lot, then run across to a side street where Autumn's parked behind another car. I take Beau's phone and text Cassidy: DONE, BUT I HAVE PROPERTY OWNER WITH ME. CORNER OF PICO AND WILSON IN PARKING LOT. There's an immediate answer: ? I reply: NEED HELP WITH CAR. TRUNK IS FULL. There's a minute delay and then: COMING.

"He's on his way," I say.

"Maybe he'll send someone else."

"Very possible. Cassidy might not credit Beau with being smart enough to send coded texts on the spur of the moment and figure we're doing it. If he thinks it's a trap, he'll still come, but it'll be an oblique approach."

"If he thinks it's a trap he might come in force, have some men on foot or driving around looking for this car. We could be caught."

"I doubt he'd chance anything that noisy on such short notice. But we've got an opportunity to fuck him over, or at least see him so we can recognize him later. If he's at Lodestar's office, he shouldn't take more than fifteen minutes to get here. If he's much later than that we'll go."

My mind burns with acid memories from Hexum when I waited, gun in hand, for people I might kill or be killed by. Autumn looks keyed-up and alert, almost rapturous. I want to tell her not to feel like this, that I've betrayed her by letting her be touched by these emotions, but I lost the right to determine people's lives a long time ago.

"I still want to go swimming," says Autumn softly.

"I forgot to pick up my suit. I can't think why it would've slipped my mind."

"We'll go back and get it. Are you expecting any more visitors tonight?"

"No. Beau was my last appointment."

It's been twenty-five minutes and I'm about to tell Autumn we should go when a white guy on a bike rolls into the parking lot and stops near the Corolla. I look through the binoculars. He's in his mid-30s, fit, and wearing shorts, brightly-colored Nikes and a zipped-up black windbreaker, which is probably hiding a holstered gun. He glances at the car and I see his lips move as he says something. Beau must have made a noise in answer because the man flinches slightly and looks towards the trunk. I pass the binoculars to Autumn and use the burner phone to text 911 and tell them that I'm seeing a man being forced at gunpoint into the trunk of a car at Pico and Wilson. I describe the man on the bike as the assailant.

"That's got to be Cassidy," I say.

"Why?"

"It's what I'd expect someone special forces to do; he scouts the target area but doesn't make it obvious by coming in with a car or extra bodies. He's had someone drop him off a few blocks from here. He wouldn't want to bring a car into view in case there are surveillance cameras that can record a licence plate number. I was hoping he'd come by car so I could give 911 a licence plate number."

The man starts pedalling back the way he came.

Autumn takes the burner phone and says, "Let's be sure. What's Cassidy's number?"

I tell her and she punches it in. The man stops, pulls a phone out of his jacket and scans the area before answering.

"Yes?" says a calm voice.

Autumn says, "Don't move, Cassidy,"

"Why?"

"For health reasons."

"What do you want?"

"To talk,"

Cassidy looks to his left down Pico and pedals quickly back the way he came.

Autumn punches the dashboard. "Shit."

"Let's go, I think he spotted cops coming."

Autumn pulls onto Pico and flashing lights are coming toward us from ten blocks away. We return to my place to collect my suit, then get back on the I-10.

"So," sighs Autumn, "was that worth the detour?"

"We eliminated another Lodestar employee and got eyes on Cassidy. Plus, Lodestar's going to be scrambling after the cops find Beau, because he seems like the type who's going to talk once they start asking him about all those guns in his car. Lodestar might back out of this scheme entirely if the heat's bad enough."

"This won't stop them. If the guy who owns Lodestar is anything like Enoch and Gideon, he'll crawl over broken glass for a big payday. Enoch has his restaurants routinely break every labor law in the book just to add a million, tops, to his profits. I asked him once why he bothered, and he looked at me as though I'd suggested he eat roadkill, and he said in this really baffled way, 'Why should I pay them if I don't have to?' Men like that are black holes of greed. I've been around these people for fourteen fucking years, and for them, everything is never enough."

We get to Malibu as the eastern sky changes from black to gray-blue. Traffic on the Pacific Coast Highway is picking up—early birds looking to grab a parking spot near the beach and domestics heading to work in the big homes. Marsden's place is on the Carbon Beach section of Malibu, and as Autumn turns into the driveway it crosses my mind that Enoch will have had time to change the codes on the door locks. He hasn't.

We walk through to the main room and look out at the beach and the dark sweep of the Pacific through the windows. Autumn's visibly relaxing. This is her favorite house, one that she leaves with reluctance. Compared to its neighbors, it's ancient, built more than sixty years ago. It's all steep angles and rectangles, like an exploded deck of cards made of tropical woods and glass. I think the architect was called A. Quincy Jones, but that doesn't sound right.

Autumn throws herself down on a sofa and lets out a deep breath. "I'll have Enoch give me this house on top of the money."

"I'd say we've given ourselves some breathing room."

"How do we spend it?"

"Checking out those shell companies and the locations on Beau's map. Why did I need a suit?"

"Friday night we're going to Gideon's son's birthday party. It'll be full of A-listers from their world, and when Gideon hears me dropping the Lodestar name in front of them, he'll probably cut a check for us by midnight. But we'll still need hard facts on their side hustle. In the meantime, I'm going to keep this house filled with people; if Lodestar still wants us dead, they're going to have to go through a crowd of witnesses."

She hasn't said anything about killing Enoch. I hope she's lost her taste for vengeance after what happened in the desert.

"Can we go swimming now, Mom?" I whine.

We change into our swimming gear right there in the living room and go out to the teak deck that fans out from the back of the house. The beach is empty, not even an early morning jogger in sight. Some seagulls are still asleep on the sand, heads tucked under their wings, looking like pearl-feathered nautiluses left behind by the tide. The ocean is flat and wears a tenuous skin of mist. We run down to the water, the birds rising with sleepy squawks, and dive in. Autumn takes off like a seal released back into the wild. I splash and wallow while she dolphins around and away from me. Whenever we swim together, I feel like an intruder in her world.

By the time we leave the water and go up to the house, a few runners have appeared on the beach, as well as an elderly man unsteadily waving a metal detector back and forth over the sand. A young Filipino woman, his caregiver, accompanies him and keeps one hand ready to catch him if he stumbles. We lean on the deck railing and watch the old man maneuver in fits and starts down the beach. He's several unhealthy shades of white, emaciated, barefooted, and his pale pink shorts and shirt hang carelessly on his twig-like body.

Autumn points to him and says, "Remember what I said about greed? That's Lucas Petty. He owns banks and railroads, and here he is up at dawn searching for coins and jewelry. He looks like the ghost of a fucking crab."

We go to bed, too exhausted to do anything more than hold each other. The sound of the Santa Ana winds whistling past the house wakes us at noon, and as soon as Autumn's out of the shower, she calls the housekeeping staff and tells them they're needed, then phones some friends and invites them to come and stay. They're bound to come—no one turns down a chance to live on Billionaires' Beach. The place has seven bedrooms, and for each person who spends the night there'll be one or two more who'll stay for a day or an evening. It's going to be rammed in the house.

We're in the kitchen, trying to scrounge together a meal from the near-empty fridge, when Autumn says brightly, "I'm going to call Enoch. I mean, why not? We might learn something from him."

"Sure."

She puts the phone on speaker and calls.

Enoch's nervous voice fills the kitchen: "Autumn?"

"I'm at the Malibu house, Enoch, just in case you thought of turning up here. I have a shitload of friends staying with me, so there won't be any room for you or any of your Lodestar buddies. Where are you?"

There's a long pause before Enoch stammers, "The casita."

"Ah, yes, golf forever and always."

"I can't go to the house," Enoch says petulantly. "Oribe and Maria have disappeared."

"And so have I. I doubt we'll see each other again, but I will be wanting my paintings out of the Rancho Vista house."

"I don't have to."

"Enoch, thanks to your emails I can make the Selous Group very mad at you, so you'd better do exactly what I say. You let Gideon know that I'll be telling him what I need by way of a settlement at the party. Consider him my divorce lawyer. Was there anything you wanted to say?"

Enoch sighs mournfully, coughs, and says, "No."

"So long," chirps Autumn, and ends the call. "Well?"

"Interesting. He never tried to deny anything or play the concerned and shocked husband. He essentially conceded being involved with Lodestar and Gideon."

"That's what I thought. He was never very smart. Cunning, yes, in the way a casino cheat is, but he's never been able to see past short-term gain."

"Luckily for him the world's rigged for his type."

"True. I can't think that he's ever had a real setback since I've known him; although he'd say it was a shocking blow when I refused to get breast implants. So, mister hardboiled private detective, how do we drill down further on Gideon's scheme?"

"I'm going to go check those pinned locations on Beau's map and do some surveillance on Lodestar's office here in L.A. I want to be able to recognize as many of their people as possible if they come after us again. And how about you try and find out the ownership of those dummy companies. I forgot to ask: were there addresses for them on the websites?"

"Only phone numbers. I tried a few of them and got an answering machine every time. Gideon must have created the phony companies, but how to prove it?"

"Difficult. If their plan is as heinous as we think, he'll have insulated himself through false front businesses and bank accounts in places like the Virgin Islands and Malta, but let's see if the companies Enoch contracted with exist physically or not. By the way, I'm not hardboiled, I'm noir."

"Sorry, dear."

I leave a half hour later just as some of the staff arrive. The Range Rover is too well-known now, so I take the silver Audi Autumn keeps at the beach house and head for Lodestar's office. I also take Beau's phone and my Walther.

The address Beau gave me is in a business park in Culver City behind Westfield Mall that's filled with low-rise office buildings. The Lodestar building is two-storeys, fronted by a parking lot, and surrounded by neatly maintained lawns and flower beds. A LODESTAR sign sits on the grass verge in front of the office, and there are ten cars in the parking lot. A larger office building is across the street, and I find a spot in their lot that gives me a good view. I check on my phone to see if we've put Lodestar in the news cycle in the last 24 hours. We have. Palm Springs' media outlets are all over the mystery of two men found murdered "execution-style" in the desert, and they all quote "anonymous" sources that say the men were working for Lodestar, a "shadowy" and "controversial" security company. A Lodestar spokesperson has denied the men were working for them. Apparently Oribe hasn't been found yet, or, if he has, his death didn't rate a mention.

One story has a backgrounder on Lodestar and includes a picture, a head and shoulders shot, of its owner, ex-general Preston Gantry. The photo shows him in uniform, probably taken during one of the Gulf wars. He has a lean face, wispy blonde hair and eyebrows, and a savage-looking burn scar on his neck. He's gazing into the distance with that special, bird-of-prey-at-rest look senior officers like to affect when being photographed. I'm almost certain I've seen him before.

At five o'clock, a trickle of people begins exiting Lodestar. None of them look military, just regular types in office wear who wave goodbye to each other and leave in their cars. At ten past five, Cassidy comes out of the building with two other men, neither of whom are office workers. They're in T-shirts and shorts that show off muscular arms and chests, and some gaudy tattoos. They slouch against the wall and glance expectantly down the street to their left. A mid-sized delivery truck with a Ryder logo on the side comes into the Lodestar parking lot. Cassidy gets into a red Mustang while his two friends join the driver in the cab of the truck. The Mustang leads the way onto the street. I wait until they turn a corner before following them.

It's an easy pursuit. The truck is visible from a distance, and they go north on the 405 almost immediately, which is bumper-to-bumper. We stop and start in traffic until they exit onto the Ventura Freeway and continue north towards Thousand Oaks. I may be following them for nothing. Lodestar undoubtedly has other security jobs on the go, and I could be tagging after some mundane piece of business. But if Cassidy has been put in charge of ground operations for the Selous Group, then it's likely worth my time.

They exit at Kanan Rd. in Agoura Hills and head west. I drop back further. We're in the hills above Malibu, and there isn't much up here except hiking trails, scattered homes, and some small film production facilities. The hills are dense with trees and brush, and I have a flashback to wandering through this kind of country around Hexum when I was a kid. The two vehicles turn right onto a Blanco Canyon Rd. It's a dead end. I pull over past the turn and check my map. The road is about a quarter mile long and has at least twenty buildings on it. If I drive down the road, Cassidy might spot me, but there's no way to guess where he's gone and check it out later. I turn the car around and go down the road.

The first few buildings are homes, sprawling structures with barns, paddocks, and pools. A wedding/conference center is next, more homes, and then I get a glimpse of the Ryder logo through the brush a few hundred yards ahead. I'm passing a place called Jagged Ridge Vineyard, and I pull into their parking lot. The vineyard has a store and restaurant so I'm not the only car in the lot, which should make it innocuous-looking if Cassidy drives back and looks this way. I walk up the slope behind the store and into the vineyard to get a better view of the truck. The grapes are gone from the vines, and their curled, exhausted leaves, which look like they've been left in an oven too long, rattle and hiss in the dry, hot wind blowing down to the ocean.

The Ryder truck and the Mustang are parked in front of a white, three-storey wooden building that looks like something between an office building and a barracks. I can just make out Cassidy and the others unloading cardboard boxes from the truck and taking them inside. They finish the job in no more than twenty minutes, then stand around the truck listening to Cassidy, who appears to be giving them instructions. After his lecture they get in their vehicles and leave. I give it fifteen minutes in case one of them comes back, then start walking through the brush towards the building. Taking the road would be quicker, but dangerous if Cassidy returns.

I come out of the brush on the east side of the building and walk around to the front. It's a rectangular structure, about fifty feet across the front and half that deep. Up close, the place looks deserted. Weeds are emerging from cracks in the parking lot's asphalt, and the lowered Venetian blinds shielding every window are dusty and bent. It might have been part of a film studio's operation, back when westerns were being shot in these hills. The glass entrance doors are modern, as is the small lobby, which has a board on the wall listing the businesses inside. The doors are locked, so I take a walk around the outside looking for an easily forced window or door. The rear of the property is overgrown with sedge and wild rye, and oak and sycamore trees that come right up to the rear of the building. A wood-framed glass door in the back opens onto a central hallway leading to the front entrance. There's no sign of an alarm system at either entrance, so I find a rock and smash in the door's window. No alarm, but that doesn't mean Lodestar hasn't got a monitoring system that will send them here in a hurry. I'll have to be quick. I step into the hallway.

Drifts of dust on the floor stir in the breeze coming through the broken window. I open a door on my right that's signed SANTA MONICA HOSPITALITY SERVICES. The office faces the back of the building, and the pale, yellowy light that's leaking through the blinds reveals a random collection of desks and chairs, some wooden, some metal, all of them covered in a layer of dust. On one table there are some cardboard boxes. I lift the flaps and find computer towers, monitors, keyboards, phones, and a fax machine. All of them look used and dirty. I go into the office across the hall and find a twin of the one I was just in: more furniture, electronics in boxes, and dust on everything. The main floor has two offices in front, two in the back, and I find the same layout as I check the upper floors. Some offices have as many as a dozen boxed computers, others only two or three. The offices in the rear on the top floor have all their windows open, and stacks of old newspapers on the floor. An owl perches on the windowsill in one office and clacks its beak at me before flapping away. The Santa Ana wind punches through the open windows and rattles the raised blinds. I take out my phone and do a video tour of the office, then go to the front entrance and take a picture of the lobby board. There are twelve company names on it, six of them are the ones Newcastle told Marsden to sign contracts with.

I hurry out the back and return to my car the same way I came. No one comes to check on the building after fifteen minutes, so I can assume my break-in wasn't immediately noticed. I look on Beau's phone at the locations Cassidy pinned on the map. The five spots form a rough line less than a mile east of here, running just south of Thousand Oaks over to Agoura Hills.

It's only a few minutes' drive to the nearest location: the entrance to an unofficial trail used by dirt bikers. There's nothing out of the ordinary about it, just a beaten-down path hemmed in by trees and brush. The other four locations are the same: isolated, not on main roads, and walled-in by vegetation. I'm back at the beach house in twenty minutes.

Autumn's on the deck with four of her friends, all drinking wine, and a few others are down on the beach. Autumn's circle of friends— actors, artists, gallery owners, writers for arts magazines—have always been guarded around me. I don't blame them. They know Autumn and I are together, but my past and my job have a way of curtailing conversations. Once, when I was drunk, I told them a story about Hexum. Since then they're happier when I'm not in the room. They greet me warmly, but I can tell they're glad when I go to the kitchen for a beer and then retreat upstairs. Enoch has an office on the second floor that's pretty much a copy of the one in Rancho Vista, right down to a gun cabinet and walls covered with dead animals and pictures of himself. I sit behind his desk and look out the window at the ocean. A surfer stands nonchalantly on her board as a gentle wave brings her towards shore, and farther out a pod of dolphins moves steadily towards the setting sun.

Autumn comes in the room and I tell her what I've found out. She flops in a chair and thinks over my news. Most of the photos on the wall show Enoch shaking hands with business partners or grinning with celebrities on golf courses. I recognize Michael Douglas in one picture. A few show Enoch, gun in hand, posing with dead animals.

"The windows on the top floor were left open, right?" asks Autumn.

"Yup."

"Very odd."

"Fuck."

"What?"

"I'm looking at the Selous Group."

I take a photo off the wall and hand it to Autumn.

Gold

I locked and replaced Caleb's treasure box, lowered the hood, then sat on the ruins of the van's driver's seat. The rolls of cash made sense—they had to be the collected takings of Caleb's business—but I was confused by the gold wafers and certificates until, however, I remembered the clippings about Y2K and gold that I'd found in Caleb's desk. I had no idea what the certificates were worth, but there had to be a small fortune in the case. The source of the money was equally puzzling, as were the one-way plane tickets. I couldn't believe Caleb was going for good, but it was equally unlikely that he was taking some kind of vacation with Mona. I was sure he wouldn't abandon his wives and the Settlement, but, if he did, I'd be able to rescue Rebecca without any risk or special effort. Leaving the magazines in the van didn't seem like a good idea now, so I put them inside Malachi's empty hut before heading home.

Main St. was deserted, and I rode my bike in a lazy S-pattern from one side of the street to the other, smiling to myself and feeling thrilled about the great changes that were coming. Rebecca was at the center of the altered world I imagined, but not Malachi. He was, I reasoned guiltily, old enough to take care of himself. I'd tell Rebecca she could move in with me. By the time I got home I'd let some doubts creep into my mind. Caleb had to have some plan for the family he was leaving behind, and I worried that he would sell the women to other men or send them back to their families. Or perhaps his plan was to eventually take everyone to a new Settlement halfway across the world. It wasn't an impossible idea; Rebecca's sister had been sent off to Guatemala.

I didn't get to sleep until near dawn, and then awoke out of a horrible anxiety dream in the early afternoon. It was Christmas Day. I tried to settle down to watching movies, but my thoughts kept wandering to what Caleb was or wasn't doing, and my fear that I might be misinterpreting everything that I'd found and learned.

TV wasn't working for me, so I went outside with the vague idea of going for a hike. The air was sharp with cold, and the low clouds offered a dreary selection of raindrops, sleet, and random snowflakes. I paced around the yard for a while, willing myself to go for a tromp through the chaparral. What I really wanted to do was get some definite answers to the questions I had about Caleb. That's when I decided to go into town and speak to his girlfriend. I wasn't certain that she would want to talk to me, but I hoped some of the money I'd received in Jubal's Christmas envelope might persuade her.

The house on Lincoln was busy. Cars were parked tightly on both sides of the street, and small groups of men, mostly white, some Asian, stood on the house's front yard and porch, laughing and talking loudly. Lots of them had a beer or a joint in one hand, sometimes both. One man was wearing a Santa suit. They were happy and excited in the way children are when a special event is imminent. In the day's fading light, I could see that the house wasn't actually black, but a weathered forest green. There were no signs of life, no women looking out windows or standing on balconies. The house felt like it was closed in on itself, shunning the crowd outside.

I hurried to the front door to avoid the amused and curious looks of the men. A voice behind me said, "Someone's in a hurry to get their cherry busted." I opened the door and almost ran into a middle-aged Asian woman standing just inside the door. She was wearing jeans and a fleece jacket with a lurid drawing of a howling wolf on it. I'd interrupted her in the middle of eating a Payday bar.

She scowled at me and snapped, "Don't open for fifteen minutes. Girls not finished eating."

"I only came to talk to Mona about something…Monique?"

"Let him in," said a man's voice from down the hall.

It was Jubal. He was standing at the end of the hallway in the doorway to the kitchen. Behind him I could see a long table packed with women eating bowls of noodles. The kitchen was steamy, and a few of women were singing along to a stereo playing 'Last Christmas'.

Jubal grinned at me. "You here to dip your wick, Tommy boy?"

"No. I want to talk to the woman Gaunt bought."

He frowned. "Why you got a hard-on for this Gaunt fellow?"

"I'm friends with his son. He wants to know if Caleb's getting a wife for him."

"For his son?" he laughed. "Man, I wish my daddy had been in that church; there was no free pussy on offer for being a Methodist. You want to talk to her, you go right on up. What room's she in, Winnie?"

"Twenty-seven. Top floor," said the woman in the wolf jacket.

Jubal returned to the kitchen as I stepped past Winnie and started up the staircase.

I knew it was a big house, but I was still astonished by the number of rooms it had. Each landing had four or five doors leading off it, as well as corridors that led to more rooms. Most doors were closed. The open ones revealed tiny rooms with mattresses on the floor, and walls decorated with posters, decorative shawls, and framed paintings of mountains and seascapes. In one room a girl who looked my age was standing on a mattress tacking a map of Vietnam to her wall. The air was gummy with the smell and taste of perfumes and air fresheners.

At the top of the stairs there were four doors identified with adhesive number stickers, the reflective kind that usually go on mailboxes. I knocked on 27. The woman who opened the door didn't look much like her passport photograph. She was thinner in the face and looked older, and my first thought was that she was far too small for someone like Caleb—one of his legs probably weighed as much as her. Her room was slightly bigger than others I'd seen and had a bed that was off the floor on a bed frame, as well as a table and two chairs. Two shelves on the wall were piled with romance paperbacks.

She looked at me apprehensively and said, "I just live here, I don't work. You have to go with another girl."

"I'm not here for that," I said urgently. "I wanted to talk to you about Caleb Gaunt."

"You know him?"

"I know his family."

"He has a family?"

"Yes, but that's not really what I wanted to talk about."

Like anyone close to Gaunt, she was scared. She might be afraid that I was here on his orders and would report back to him on her. After some hesitation she waved me into the room and closed the door.

"He's not coming here tonight, is he?" I asked.

"No. He was here earlier." She pointed to one of the chairs. "Sit, please."

I took the chair while she sat on the edge of the bed. She was dressed in turquoise tights and a Denver Broncos T-shirt—undoubtedly a gift from Caleb—and wore her shining black hair loose down her back. I guessed her age was closer to thirty than twenty.

"Your name's Mona?"

"You can call me that."

"I saw your real name on your passport, only I'm not sure how to pronounce it."

Her eyes lit up and she leaned forward. "You have it with you?"

"No. But I could get it."

"Can you get it soon?" she whispered.

"Well, uh," I stammered, "not right away. It's tricky to get to and it's kept locked up." I pulled out my wallet and handed her two hundred dollars. "That's for you. I don't want Caleb knowing I was here."

Mona put the money on the bed beside her and looked at me with new interest. "You're so young. What do you want?"

"I want to find out what Caleb's doing. Is he really going away with you to Singapore?"

"Why you want to know?"

"He's leaving someone behind here, a friend of mine, and they'd like to know. I don't care where he goes or for how long, but they would."

"I don't want Caleb not to go with me," she said pleadingly. "I have to leave here. Tell Caleb I love him, please."

"I'm not a friend of Caleb's," I said with frustration. "I'll be glad he's gone; I hate that fucking pig."

"Oh," she said with surprise.

We sat in silence. She picked at her tights and stared out a small window that had a view of a bare oak tree. A faint cheer came from outside; apparently the front doors had been thrown open to the customers.

Mona moved to the chair opposite mine and said, "Tell me about his family."

I gave her a brief description of the Settlement, and especially of how Caleb treated the women and Malachi. She didn't react to anything I said, just nodded her head occasionally as though what I was saying was a confirmation of something.

"He didn't tell you any of this?" I asked.

"No. He told me he was an investor, that he plays the stock market."

I laughed, and, after a moment, so did Mona.

"All the men lie in here." she said bitterly. "They say they have big jobs or have done big, exciting things. I hate Caleb, too. I hate all the men here."

"Why is he taking you to Singapore?"

"Not Singapore. Bangkok. He said we'll fly there first because he has to do some banking. He says he'll be a multi-millionaire by the time we get to Bangkok."

"What's he want to do there?"

"Open a bar. A bar with girls. I'm going to help him run it."

"Are you?"

"No! I told him I speak Thai and could make it easy for him to get going in Bangkok."

"Where the hell did he get this idea?"

She sat straight in her chair and said firmly, "I made him think it. He started coming here last Christmas. He told me I'm his favorite and came once a week, sometimes more. Caleb said he'd likes Asian women because they treat men better, and that in Thailand women like being prostitutes and fucking white guys like him because their men are small. He said he wanted to go there some day. That's when I said I speak Thai and he should take me with him."

"Do you?"

She made a disparaging noise. "A bit. I have an uncle there we visit. So all this year I keep telling him he should buy a bar in Bangkok, that we can run it together. He just laughed, but he liked talking about it. Then four months ago he says he might do it, that one of his investments paid off real good. Last month he told me we are going and that he'd bought my passport for me."

"What's all this about the passport?"

Her reply was interrupted by the sound of feet pounding up the stairs. Two men stood outside on the landing arguing about which number room their girls were in. We heard doors opening and closing, muffled conversation, and then silence.

"They took away my passport when I got to this country."

"Who?"

Mona went and sat on the bed. "I'm from Indonesia. My family's Chinese, but we live in Indonesia. We have four restaurants in Jakarta. At college I took a business course so I could help manage our restaurants. When I graduated, a man came to our school, a business recruiter he called himself, and said he could get Chinese girls jobs in the West working in hotels as managers. He said there more and more Chinese tourists going to America, and hotels needed people who spoke Chinese. The pay was very huge. My family said I should go for a few years. I could send money back. The man who recruited me said I'd only have to pay back the airfare and his recruiting fee. Four of us from the school flew to San Francisco. Winnie and a man met us at the airport and took our passports and told us we'd get them back at the hotels. She said it was required by law. Two of us she left at a house in Oakland, I think. Then they drove me and the other girl here. Right to this house. That was two and a half years ago. They said I had to work here until I pay off my debts."

"Why didn't you run away?"

"I couldn't! When they first brought me here, they locked me in a room and had men take turns with me. They took videos of it and said they'd send them to my family if I didn't do what they said or tried to leave or call anyone. Once a month they let me send a postcard home. It has to be written in English. Some girls have run away, but if the police see a girl who looks like me on the streets, they grab them and bring them back here. Anyway, I can't get home without my passport. As soon as Caleb and I get to Singapore, I'll run away from him, go to the police. I could even leave now if I had my passport. Will you bring it to me?"

She was breathing heavily and trying not to cry when she finished speaking. I stared at the floor. A man in one of the other rooms started chanting "Yup" over and over again.

"Yeah," I said. "I'll bring it to you as soon as I can."

She covered her face with her hands.

I left her room, closed the door quietly behind me, and went down the stairs, trying hard not to look into any open doors or remember the lie I left behind with Mona. I wasn't bringing her passport any time soon; if Caleb checked his money box and found the passport missing, he'd move it beyond my reach, and I wanted to use the cash in it for Rebecca when the time was right. Mona hadn't made the fate of Caleb's family any clearer, but now I was certain he was leaving for good.

I rattled around the house for the next few days, unsure of how to proceed. I was tempted to do nothing until Caleb left in January—why not let him leave with Mona? That way Rebecca and the others would be free, as well as Mona once she landed in Singapore. Every time I grew comfortable with this idea the fear rose up inside me that Caleb would never just abandon the Settlement; he'd have some plan to screw over Rebecca and the others. His cruelty was all-encompassing.

Despite not being overly interested in football, the next day I went to the Regal Cinema to see *Any Given Sunday*. I needed a distraction. I was too early, but I went into the empty theater anyway and took a seat near the back. Not five minutes later Caleb walked in, his bearish arms cradling a bucket of popcorn and a jumbo soda. He settled himself in the very front row where he could stretch his legs out and started eating his popcorn by the fistful.

He hadn't noticed me when he walked in, and I didn't move a muscle or make a noise. I was initially horrified at the idea of being alone in the theater with him, and I thought about leaving. But as I watched him destroy his bucket of popcorn with the single-mindedness of a dog at a food bowl, I felt a glow of satisfaction that Mona, a key part of his grand scheme, was going to betray him. Fate was going to kick him in the balls, and it warmed me that he couldn't see the blow coming.

I cleared my throat and Caleb looked in my direction. I smiled at him, and he astonished me by smiling back and chuckling.

He turned his gaze to the blank screen and said, "Are you taking a break from pestering my family? I almost expected to see you turn up in my Christmas stocking. Why don't you go there now? You can circle the house and sniff like a raccoon at a trash can."

I could taste the pleasure I would get from seeing his shocked face if I told him I knew about Bangkok. I moved down and sat a few rows behind him. He didn't so much as glance in my direction.

"Why do you treat the girls like shit, Caleb?"

"Why? Because that's the natural order of things. If the Bible teaches us nothing else, it's that God made every man the sun at the center of his own little solar system. Just as the planets are born of the sun, women are born of Adam's rib, and thus my rib, and even your rib. That makes my wives part of my flesh, and if I want to work or beat or pleasure my flesh, then I'll do so."

"There's no fucking way you believe in the Bible."

He began laughing; great wheezing laughs that shook the loose bits of popcorn decorating his chest. "No, Tom," he said as he caught his breath, "I don't suppose I do, but damn it's a useful document. I was only quoting what the Righteous Fathers say. So, which of my wives is the one that's lured you in? This much attention paid to us can't be because of Malachi; he's a clod of earth that wears a simpleton's smile. Is it Monday? She's the pretty one. Thursday?'

"Her name's Rebecca."

"Aha! I hit the mark. I have to admit there's something about her. Those eyes. She has the kindest soul, to be sure. Not an eager partner in my bed, though. She needs strong handling, which, to be honest, can be entertaining. I know you think I'm a bastard, and I probably am, but you'll learn soon enough that life only puts so many tasty things within your reach, and if you don't gobble them up, then they rot away or someone else eats them first. I was born to a bastard and grew up poor, and maybe if I had got that football scholarship I'd be something better now, but I sure as hell have had more tail than I deserve, and, God willing, there'll be twice as much in the future."

He turned to look directly at me and winked slowly, like some kind of gross, outlandish automaton. He was so sure of his plans and future happiness he didn't care what he said to me. As far as Caleb was concerned, paradise was only weeks away, and his gloating confidence made me certain he'd planned something awful for the wives. There was no way he'd leave behind something he thought of as his, for someone else to use or profit from. His good humor was the twitching tail of a cat before it pounces. I was flooded with a hatred as all-consuming as an illness.

I got up and left the theater.

The following day I went looking for Reinhart. I checked in at the Sheriff's Office, but no one knew where he was. The deputy on the front desk said that if he wasn't on patrol, he was probably at home, but then said with a grin that Reinhart was "always" on patrol. I knew where Reinhart lived. On my drives around Hexum I'd seen his patrol car regularly parked outside a small, neat, stucco bungalow the color of honey that was surrounded by lilac bushes.

His car was parked in front of the bungalow and, with some reluctance, I knocked on the door. I was worried he might not want to be disturbed at home, but Reinhart seemed pleased to see me when he answered the door.

"Come in, come in," he said.

The front door opened right into the living room. It was a perfectly square room that must have been half the size of the house—a square within a square. Precisely in the middle of the room was a leather reclining armchair positioned in front of a big TV that sat in an entertainment unit covering most of one wall. The shelves in the unit were filled with small sports trophies in gold and silver, a potted barrel cactus, and probably every paperback copy of the novels of Louis L'Amour and Zane Grey. The other walls of the room were bare, as was the parquet floor. On one side of the armchair was a standing lamp, and on the other a small table that held a glass of water, a pencil, and a find-a-word puzzle magazine. There was no other furniture in the room.

"You caught me on my day off," said Reinhart. He was wearing his uniform, but not his utility belt. "Come through to the kitchen."

The U-shaped kitchen was reached through an arched doorway from the living room. There was a white Formica table with two folding chairs and completely empty countertops. The walls, the appliances, the cupboards, and the countertops were white as well, and I couldn't imagine that food had ever been cooked or eaten here. Reinhart opened the fridge, which held a loaf of bread, a tray of cold cuts, a mustard bottle, and dozens of cans of soda of every variety—it was like a cooler at 7-Eleven.

Reinhart waved a hand towards the open fridge. "Name your poison."

I asked for a Dr. Pepper. Reinhart took a Pepsi and we sat at the table.

"So, what brings you to my casita?" asked Reinhart cheerfully.

"I wanted to ask you a favor, Josh. Do you know a lawyer named Elmer Crippen?"

"Sure. He's been around Hexum forever and a day. You got some business with him?"

"Sort of. He's been doing work for Caleb Gaunt. Gaunt is going to be leaving the country. For good. He's going to open a bar in Thailand."

Reinhart leaned forward. "Really?"

"And I'm worried about what's he planned for his people. He's leaving them behind."

"He isn't taking them along?"

"No. The men in his church sell women to each other, so I'm wondering if that's what's going to happen."

"And you *don't* want that to happen?"

"No."

He took a long drink of his soda, let a burp slowly escape, and said, "Tom, you put the detective skills of most of my men to shame; you are a well-informed individual, and that is a damn interesting piece of news, no doubt about it. So, you want me to talk to Crippen?"

"No, no. I'll do it; it's just that...I figure because he's a lawyer and Caleb's his client, he won't talk to me or anyone else. I thought that I might have to...force him to. I don't want anyone but me to get in trouble over this, but I thought I should ask if it's okay by you. I won't do it if you say I can't."

Reinhart thought about my request. I couldn't read anything in his eyes. It struck me that his snow-white hair matched everything in the kitchen.

"Tom, I admire your grit and your—hold it, I just learned this word the other day, it'll come to me—your perspicacity! That's it. You are a shrewd one. But dealing harshly with a lawyer, especially Elmer Crippen, is another kettle of fish. Sometimes when fellows like that stub their toe, they shout so loud it's heard in Sacramento, if you catch my drift. Also, Elmer has been useful to friends of mine from time to time. Now, if it was almost anyone else in town, I'd say get at it, but I'm afraid I'm going to have to rein you in."

"I know where Caleb keeps his money. A lot of it's in gold."

"Oh," said Reinhart, and leaned back in his chair.

I could see what was in his eyes now: he was hungry and wary, a predator circling around a baited trap. The mention of gold had riveted his attention, but my unspoken offer to trade it for questioning Crippen had changed how he saw me. I worried that I'd overstepped some invisible boundary, that I'd gone from being a malleable recruit to a kind of competitor—a smaller, more furtive predator.

"You should take up poker, Tom, because I can't tell if you're bluffing or being straight."

"I found it. There are these little gold bars marked Royal Canadian Mint, and gold certificates from some place called the United Overseas Bank of Singapore. And rolls of cash. I'll let you know where it is if I find out what I need from Crippen."

"Why don't you tell me what your goal is, Tom? What do you want to come out of all this intrigue with Gaunt? I'd like to help you, just like I've helped you in the past."

I felt guilty for being evasive with Reinhart. I thought of how he'd handled things after I'd killed Mickey and when Jubal had tried to knife me. I owed him my life, so I told him that I wanted to save Rebecca and Malachi, but I also didn't want anything to stop Caleb from leaving.

"You don't have to say it, Tom; you're worried that if you reveal where X marks the spot, Caleb's loot might disappear and he'd be stuck in Hexum. Well, that's not going to happen. He's got a dream, and I'm not one to take that away from any man. I just need to know when he's going so I can visit him the day before and explain Hexum's leaving-town-in-a-hurry tax. I expect he'll squawk, but it's only a nominal fee, as they say, and you'll get a taste of it, too—you can use some of it for that girl and boy." He reached across the table and shook my hand. "You're as keen as a knife and bold as a lion, Tom, and I'm proud to say I think of you as a friend. Oh, and have fun with Crippen."

I was speechless with gratitude and an intoxicating feeling that I'd secured a better future for Rebecca. It was also in that moment that I knew I didn't want Levi to return. I didn't need him; I had Josh.

"Say, I just thought of something," said Reinhart. "You like reading, but I bet you've never read a western. You should take one of mine; I'll choose it for you."

I had read a western once and didn't like it, but I wasn't going to say that to Reinhart. He led me over to the entertainment unit and started rummaging through his paperbacks, hemming and hawing over which one to offer me. I was standing beside the shelves filled with trophies and began looking them over. They were for all kinds of sports and events: baseball, cross-country running, bowling, chess, even pie-making. Reinhart's name wasn't on any of them. I picked up one with the tiny, golden figure of a golfer swinging away on the top and noticed a piece of tape stuck to the bottom. Written on the tape in pen was JUNE 16/98 BENT CREEK. I checked the bottom of another trophy and found MARCH 3/86 TURLOW'S HOUSE. There were at least thirty trophies on the shelves.

He finally pulled a book off the shelf and handed it over. It was *The Call of the Canyon* by Zane Grey. Reinhart told me I could borrow others if I liked that one. I thanked him and asked if I could use his washroom. He pointed down a hallway and went back to rifling through his paperbacks, commenting loudly on his favorite titles. There were two bedrooms on the way to the washroom, both of which were empty; no furniture, no curtains on the windows, just a few tumbleweeds of dust on the floors. The clothes closet in one room was open, and inside it was a cardboard box with socks and underwear. Hanging above it on wooden hangers were six sets of Reinhart's uniform and his utility belt.

When I came back to the living room Reinhart was in the armchair working on his puzzle book.

"Don't you have a bed?" I asked.

"I sleep right here. I don't like lying down. You live longer if you don't lie down." He said this with the certainty of a scientist.

"I forgot to ask: does Crippen live alone?"

"Oh, yes. A carefree bachelor like me. His address is in the phone book."

I thanked him again and left. As I walked away from the stucco house, a sense of unease about Reinhart flickered in me, but was immediately replaced by satisfaction at having gotten his approval of my plan for Crippen.

My route home took me past the brothel on Lincoln. Caleb's mini-van was parked in front, so I changed course and went to the Settlement. I sat on my bike by the side of the road and looked through the leafless trees at the crude wooden buildings, the light poles that stood on the edges of the property like herons poised to strike, and, in the distance, the rusted hulk of the van that held Caleb's golden future. The girls were walking slowly from building to building, doing chores, and holding children in their arms. Even from that distance the way they moved told me they were bored and tired. I revved my engine and drove the bike down into the middle of the Settlement and stopped in front of the dining hall, where Rebecca was on the steps carrying a sack of potatoes. The other girls stopped what they were doing and stared at me with alarm. Malachi popped out of his hut holding a *National Geographic*. I was so tempted to double the surprise on their faces by telling them how their world was going to change, but I bit my tongue. I didn't want to risk word getting to Caleb through Sarah that his departure wasn't a secret.

"Like to go for a ride?" I asked Rebecca.

"But—"

"Just a short trip," I said quickly.

She must have read something in my eyes that said it was safe to come with me, that Caleb wasn't a threat. She set down the bag and carefully got on the back of the bike, her arms holding me tight and then tighter as I kicked it into gear and drove back up to the road. Her chin was resting on my shoulder and I heard her gasp as I opened the throttle and headed into town. I kept expecting her to tell me to turn back or stop as we tore down Main St, but she only gripped me harder, and out of the corner of my eye I could see her looking at the town like an explorer sailing past a lush and unknown shore. I had an urge to keep going until we were so far away we couldn't find our way back.

I drove all the way to my house. She got off the bike slowly, as if uncertain the ground would bear her weight.

"This is my place," I said.

She looked at the house for the longest time before saying, "Can I come inside before we go back?"

"Of course."

She walked cautiously towards the house as though she was approaching an animal she didn't want to startle.

I opened the door for her and she stepped into the kitchen. The place wasn't tidy, and I guilty realized it could smell a bit better, but the look on Rebecca's face said that it was a mansion. She went from room to room while I sat at the kitchen table, not wanting to rush or intrude on her tour. She returned to the kitchen and opened the cupboards and the fridge, making noises of astonishment or recognition at what she found.

"Do you want something to eat?" I asked.

"Yes," she said excitedly.

"You choose."

I didn't have much in the way of groceries in the house, but she ate a can of tuna, a banana, two oranges, a bowl of Alpha-Bits, two pieces of leftover KFC from the fridge, three scoops of Rocky Road ice cream, and two cans of Pepsi to wash everything down. I watched with fascination her reactions to foods she had never had or long forgotten. We hardly spoke, but when I mentioned that Malachi had had coffee at Applebee's, she insisted I make a pot. She loved it.

"Do you want to watch TV?" I asked.

We went in the living room and sat on the couch together. I showed her how to operate the remote and she flicked through the channels, gasping at each new program. She settled on an episode of *The*

Simpsons and watched it without laughing, but with hawk-like intensity. I was so happy to have her in the house I didn't say anything to break her concentration and make her think about going back to the Settlement.

The show ended, and she said with a yawn, "I'm so tired."

"It's all that food, probably."

"I think so." She yawned again. "No. I've been tired for a very long time. We don't get much sleep between Caleb and the babies. I had a cold once, and it was lovely to be in bed all day. Sometimes I pray to be ill again, but then I think God wouldn't want us to wish illness on ourselves."

"You should stay here tonight. Have a real sleep. You can have my room."

Rebecca looked at me steadily and without any expression. Her brilliant blue eyes froze me in place, and I didn't know whether I wanted to keep looking into them forever or run from the room. I was scared and enthralled.

"You like me, Tom, don't you?"

"Yes."

"A lot."

"Yes."

"Why?"

My heart was pounding so hard I felt Rebecca must be able to hear it.

"I've never really liked anyone before. Not since we came here. I want to like someone."

Even as I spoke, I wasn't sure that what I was saying would make sense to her—it barely made sense to me—but she smiled at my answer and said, "I'm the same, Tom. I'm the same." She leaned back against the couch and closed her eyes. "I have to go back. I can't let the others do my work, and who knows what Caleb will do. I can't believe I came here. That's how tired I am: I just don't care anymore. I like you very much, Tom, and I can feel part of me not wanting to move from this place no matter what, but I have to return."

"Caleb won't do anything," I said sharply.

"How do you know?"

"I guarantee it."

"You seem very sure."

"I am."

Rebecca squeezed my hand.

"I believe you. I still have to go back, but can I ask you a favor?"

"Sure."

"Before we go, I want to be alone in the house for a while."

"Why?"

"I haven't been by myself in…years. I want to feel what it's like to be in a room without other people. To have time to think without someone asking me for help or ordering me around. Does that sound strange?"

"No. For how long?"

"Just an hour or so."

"I'll go for a walk."

I left her sitting on the couch with the TV turned off.

The weather outside was getting colder again, but the sun was out and kept me comfortable as I moved quickly through the chaparral. The last snowfall had mostly melted, but ragged sheets of it, patterned with the tracks of small animals, remained in the shade of bushes. I couldn't think properly about Rebecca and Caleb and Mona and the Settlement anymore; it was all a riot of hopes and fears and unanswerable questions.

When I returned to the house, Rebecca was in the kitchen eating another bowl of ice cream. The sight of her with her mouth full and wearing a smile made me happy.

"You just wanted me out of the house so you could eat all the best stuff!"

She laughed, and some ice cream ran down her chin. She wiped it away with a napkin and said, "It's so good!"

We talked about food and the things she'd seen on TV for a little while, and then she said we should be going. Before we left for the Settlement, I took the Walther and put it in my backpack. I wanted it in case Caleb objected to Rebecca being away with me. When we got back, the mini-van was still absent. Rebecca hopped off the bike and stared at the Settlement like it was a field of battle she was about to enter.

"Things are going to get better, Rebecca. Very soon."

"I've always expected they will. Something as evil as Caleb is bound to burn itself out in the end. No one so far from God can last."

"Do you want to come back to my place tomorrow? You can come every day, if you want."

"No," she said with conviction. "It's hard enough coming back now. But please keep coming to visit me; you're the only face I look forward to seeing anymore."

Rebecca kissed me and then went quickly to the dining hall, where I could see that the windows were steamed up with the evening meal. As she went through the door, she turned and gave me a wave. On the drive back home, my thoughts were going in so many different directions I ran a stop sign and almost T-boned a truck. I spent the rest of the evening trying to focus my attention on reading *The Jungle Book*, but my mind kept turning to what life would be like when Rebecca was living with me.

I was anxious to get answers from Crippen. His office, with its giant picture window, was too public, so I'd decided to deal with him at his home. I went to his place the next day at about seven o'clock, the Walther in my backpack. Crippen's brick bungalow was painted white and peeked out from behind some cottonwood trees. There were lights on in the house, and as I stepped onto the porch and rang the doorbell, I took the gun out of my backpack and tucked it into my waistband under my sweater.

Crippen opened the door and greeted me with a look of mild curiosity, as if I was an unusual insect he'd found on a leaf. He was pale, with porcelain-white skin, and a pink blush on each cheek. His meager head of hair was dyed nut brown. I guessed he was in his sixties. He was wearing a black suit and tie with tartan slippers, and was holding a travel magazine in one hand.

"Hello?" he said, drawling out the word in an odd way.

"I want to talk to you about Caleb Gaunt," I said, and lifted my sweater to show him the Walther the way I'd seen it done in movies.

He raised an eyebrow, sighed deeply, and said, "I suppose you're the Ghost of Hexum Future."

"What?"

"Never mind. Come inside and threaten me in comfort."

As I followed him into a small living room stuffed with dark, old furniture, I caught a whiff of booze. He was drunk. Crippen slipped into a wingback chair that was tucked into a corner of the room. On the table beside him was a bottle of Southern Comfort and a shot glass. The rest of room was cluttered with a sofa, two more wingbacks, footstools, and bookcases loaded with leather-bound books. Two dirty white Persian cats, both as inert and round-eyed as a pair of stuffed owls, sat at either end of the sofa—the air was charged with their smell and drifting fur.

Crippen filled the shot glass, took a delicate sip from it, set the glass down and said, "This is my ingenious solution to controlling my drinking: small measures Now, you wanted to talk about Gaunt? But first, why don't you sit down? You can shoot me, if it comes to that, just as easily sitting down as standing up, and that way I won't die with a crick in my neck from looking up at you."

I sat on an ottoman that was half-chintz, half cat fur, and shifted the gun, which was now digging into my thigh.

"Oh, no," Crippen cried with mock alarm, "he's reaching for his gun already! And I was about to spill the beans!"

"I know that Caleb is going to Singapore in January," I said in a rush, "and that he's got all his money, a lot of money, in gold. He's not taking his family with him, so I want to know if he has plans for them. He doesn't care about his son, but I think he might try and sell his wives. That's what the guys in his church do."

Crippen stared at the ceiling for a bit, took another taste of his drink, then glowered at one of the cats before turning his attention to me and saying, "Congratulations on getting your junior detective's badge. I'm only sorry you had to earn it by following that lumbering bag of suet. Now, I'll tell you what *I* know: your name is Tom Bridger, and you're under the raven's wing of Sherriff Reinhart. That means you're here with his blessing, or perhaps at his urging." He paused for a thoughtful sip of his drink. "Joshua works in mysterious ways, but always for himself. Your interest in Caleb's wives makes me think you're the prime mover here. Joshua's interest in women is purely situational, or so I've been told. I'll guess that you're close to one of the girls and want to protect her? Save her? Buy her?"

"No. Keep her here. Let her go free."

Crippen's dry laugh sounded like leaves rustling. "That would be quite an achievement in Hexum. It's something I never managed."

"I need to know what he's doing about them. Nothing more."

"This is when you should pull out your gun and threaten me. Don't feel shy; you wouldn't be the first to do it. This town runs on threats, implied and otherwise. It's the fourth branch of government hereabouts. I do it myself, from time to time."

He finished his drink and grinned as he began to refill it, as if amused by the reappearance of liquid in his glass.

"Please," I said.

Crippen slopped a bit of his booze onto the table and looked at me with an exaggerated frown. "Please? That's the worst threat of all: appealing to my better nature. I don't have one anymore, and your 'Please' just echoes around in the space where it used to be and reminds me of what an old, empty, haunted building I am."

We sat there staring at each other. I didn't know what else to say, and the idea of doing anything with my gun felt absurd. Crippen took small sips of his drink like a bird at a puddle, and let his eyes wander towards the cats, whom he appeared to regard as intruders.

"You shouldn't worry about freeing other people, young man, it's yourself you should be worried about. Joshua and his allies are crocodiles, and Hexum is their swamp. Beware their smiles. A perfect analogy, don't you think?"

I stood up and Crippen looked at me with surprise as I moved towards the door.

"You're leaving? I didn't say I wouldn't tell you what you want."

I paused near the door and he waved me back into the living room, so I returned to the ottoman.

"I wouldn't normally offer up a client's secrets so easily or cheaply," said Crippen in a voice that was becoming slurred, "but Gaunt was made for betrayal, such is the loathsomeness of his character." He paused to gather his thoughts. "You're aware of the copper mine north of town? Good. In August they approached Caleb, through me, and inquired about buying his property. They want to sink a new shaft there. After the requisite haggling, they agreed to a price of half a million. The deal closed a few weeks ago, and the property will be theirs at the end of January."

"They paid in gold?"

"Yes. That only slowed the deal. Gaunt is convinced his gold will quintuple in value after Y2K destroys the global economy—idiocy can be added to his many other sins. I did ask him about his family, and I am aware that his happy band of cultists sells their women. He told me he's leaving them behind. As far as I can gather, he sees it as an enormous practical joke on them. Apparently, he tried to sell them, but the only prospective buyer who showed up said he thought the women were too worn-looking. He says he has no legal obligation to them since there are no actual marriages and the children's births are unrecorded. The mothers would have to go to court to prove he's the father, but, of course, he'll be long gone by then and they have no money. It's slash and burn agriculture practiced on people, which makes him a perfect citizen for this part of the world."

"Thanks," I said, and moved to the door.

"Come back any time, Tom; it's only ever me and my two captors," he said plaintively, waving a hand towards the two cats.

That night I celebrated by cooking a steak and watching the movies I'd put aside on Christmas Day. I finally had certainty that Rebecca would be free, and, even better, the mining company would be forcing her to leave the Settlement, and that would mean she'd move in with me. I figured on giving Malachi enough money so he could get a place in town, or possibly move away. The others I didn't think about much; I had a vague idea they'd be taken care of by some government department.

I avoided going to the Settlement over the next few days, fearing that I'd jinx things if I showed up too often. I ran into Malachi in town and he told me that Caleb wasn't bothering with his repair business anymore and spent most of his time up in his office or in town. I didn't enlighten him.

The next time I saw Reinhart was at Blockbuster on New Year's Eve. He was in uniform and studying a pair of VHS boxes as though they were evidence. He saw me approaching and held up the two cases.

"Hiya, Tom. I can't decide. What do you think?"

One was a Steven Seagal film, the other was called *Babysitter Passion* and had a semi-naked woman on the front. He held up the one with the woman and said, "It says this one's a thriller, but it looks kind of sexy to me."

I told him I'd seen the Seagal film and it was great.

"Did you see Elmer?" asked Reinhart.

"I did. Everything's good. Caleb's taking off without doing anything about the women; he's abandoning them."

"Huh. So, when's he going?"

"His flight's on January 10th, but maybe he'll go a day or two before."

"Could be. That makes things kind of tight." Reinhart took off his hat and ran a hand through his hair as he frowned in concentration. "You know what, Tom? I think I've got a better plan: you tell me where old Caleb keeps his gold and I'll swing by tonight and take it for safekeeping. I'll return it to him in a couple of days and say some remorseful thief turned it in. It'll be a touch lighter, but he'll be so happy to get it back he won't complain and he'll be on his way."

Apprehension hit me like an electric current as I weighed the likelihood of Reinhart taking it all for himself, and the consequences if I refused to tell him.

"It's under the hood of an old van at the back of his property."

The words had slipped out of me as though they had a mind of their own. I felt both nauseous and relieved.

"Not someplace I ever would've thought to check," mused Reinhart. "I'll let you know when I've given it back to him. You know, I think I'll take both these."

He gave me a friendly slap on the shoulder and went to pay for his rentals.

At midnight, I stepped outside the house to listen to the distant crackle of gunfire as Hexum greeted the end of the millennium. The sky was clear and its fierce blaze of stars gave a false warmth to the air. Coyotes howled in response to the shots and the odd crack or thump of fireworks. The lights in the house were still on, the TV was working, and I couldn't see any planes falling from the sky, so I guessed the whole Y2K thing had been a dud. I enjoyed the thought of Caleb waking up to the news that his gold wasn't worth anything extra.

A couple of hours later I was fighting to stay awake while watching *The Mummy* when the phone rang. It was Malachi.

"Hello, Tom,"

"What's up? Are you at the Settlement?" As far as I knew the only phone there was in the workshop, which was kept locked at night.

"No. I'm outside the 7-Eleven. I ran into town to call you."

"Why?"

"I think Caleb is going to kill the women and children."

Safari

The picture is of the same group of five men that I saw in the photo in Enoch's office in Rancho Vista posing with a dead leopard. Instead of a leopard, they're standing on the neck of a giraffe that's sprawled in an awkward heap, its chest smeared with blood. They have silly grins on their faces as though they're having trouble keeping their balance. Preston Gantry is one of them. He looks a good ten years younger than anyone else in the picture.

"Is Gideon there?" I ask.

Autumn points to the tallest man. "That's him. These two are Jasper Cordell and Roger Pinder. I don't know this one."

"That's Gantry."

"How did you decide this is the Selous Group?"

"Selous is a big game reserve in Africa. Tanzania, I think. Enoch ever talk about his days on safari, where he went?"

"You're right, it was Tanzania. When I was first with him he'd go there every year for one of his killfests, then his knees went and he caught a bug over there that knocked him on his ass for three months and the doctors told him not to go back."

"So, what are Jasper and Roger into?"

"Jasper is Cordell Meats. Probably a third of the beef you've eaten in your life has come through his family's meatpacking plants. Pinder is old oil money. He doesn't have oil anymore, just the old money. They're both billionaires, but we can't assume they're part of the group. I know there were others who went on those safaris, and Gideon may have only offered this deal to a chosen few."

I look down at the beach and see Petty doing another unsteady sweep of the sand with his metal detector. In the setting sun, his shadow is a blind man feeling his way along with a cane. The caregiver trails a good distance behind him. Maybe she's given up wanting to stop him from falling.

"I can see why Gantry is all-in on this," I say.

"Why?"

"He's desperate to join the club. The profile I read of him said that between Lodestar and his share of his wife's shipping business, he's worth a few hundred million—a smelly little pauper, really."

"How does he even show his face in polite company? So, we know who they are—probably—but we're not sure how they're going to get paid on this scheme."

"I'd bet Gideon owns the building I saw today, but let's find out for sure. Know any property lawyers?"

"Rachel Sebring. I'll call her tomorrow. And I want to take a look at that building and the locations Beau gave you. For now, let's lie out on the deck and drink too much. My mind's been sandpapered by thinking about these people."

It's probably after midnight. Autumn and I are sharing one of the big loungers on the deck, two empty wine bottles on the table beside us. Nearby, Yan, a retail design consultant, and Megan, who owns a gallery in San Diego, are describing their favorite hill towns in Tuscany in low, slow voices. Megan is slightly drunk; Yan is slightly stoned. He thinks it's odd I asked him to smoke down on the beach, but the smell of weed can bring me out in a cold sweat if I'm in the wrong mood. Autumn has her eyes closed, but every now and then she joins in their conversation. I'm enjoyably on the cusp of oblivion. I haven't drunk that much, but I was tired to begin with, and now I feel weightless and more relaxed than I deserve. The hazy night sky is freckled with the lights of planes going to and from LAX, and I think about getting on one with Autumn and flying across the ocean to live on a beach in a country where no one speaks English. Other people's words have only ever told me lies or revealed horrors. I never want to listen to another voice that isn't hers.

"This could be our home in another week or so," Autumn murmurs to me.

"You want all these things so badly?"

"What things?"

"The money, the house, the paintings."

"What you're trying to say is that I'm acting like the Selous men."

"No. If you were one of them, you'd still be with Enoch. Men like him take their triumphs after the field's been prepared for them by lawyers and politicians and hired muscle. They're tiger hunters who bag their trophy after it's been driven into the open by an army of beaters while they're on top of an elephant. And then they climb down and pose for pictures with a corpse and put on their hardest face. It's the bravery of cowards."

"I was a brave little coward when I married Enoch. I was terrified of falling further down the ladder, from ex-actor to restaurant hostess to I don't know what, but it gave me the bravery to become arm candy to a man I didn't care about, a man I knew I'd grow to hate. What I want more than the money and the rest of it is to take things away from Enoch. From Gideon, too. They've been wrapped in happy certainty all their lives. I want to take that away from them forever."

Tamsin, Inez and Will come up from the media room and tell us about the film they just watched. The deck is filled with chatter about directors and influences and gossip about actors. I let it wash over me— the pointlessness of it is soothing. Autumn wakes me when the deck is empty and the house is dark and quiet. We make love on the lounger like furtive teenagers and then stagger upstairs to bed.

We get up before ten and Autumn calls her property lawyer while I go for a run along the beach. The heat is such that every ten minutes or so I have to dash into the surf to cool down. I get back to the house after sweating last night's wine out of my system and chug some orange juice in the kitchen. Autumn is on the phone, and Inez and Megan are doing yoga on the deck.

Autumn ends her call and says, "That was Rachel, the lawyer. She knows the building on Blanco Canyon. One of her clients asked her to contact the owners about it four years ago. There's a lot of acreage attached to the building, and her client wanted to tear it down, clear most of the land and put up luxury homes. Gideon's company, Newcastle Holdings, was the owner. They couldn't agree on a price, but Newcastle wasn't reluctant to sell. Fast forward to the beginning of this year: the same client asks Rachel to try again. It turns out ownership passed from Newcastle to a company registered in Panama, and they never responded to Rachel's enquiries."

"Can she find out if that company owns more property in California?"

"I've already got her doing that."

We take the Audi up into the hills to Blanco Canyon. There are no signs of life around the building, but we park down the road and walk back. Autumn stares at the open windows at the back of the building, then turns and points in the other direction.

"That's east, isn't it? Where Beau's locations are?"

"Roughly. A mile and a bit as the crow flies."

"Do you have a theory? I do."

"Arson."

"Same here. What convinced you?"

"The computers and phones; burn down this building and investigators are going to comb through it, and if they don't find melted plastic and electronics, they'll get aggressively suspicious. What I don't get is how they can pass off the contents of these businesses as being worth millions."

Autumn looks very pleased with herself. She walks under the shade of a sycamore tree and sits on a low branch.

"You don't get paid for the contents; you get paid because you've got business income insurance. You can insure against loss of profit due to fire, flood and whatever. The contracts Enoch signed with these companies will have due dates for delivery of services; if the services aren't provided for any reason, the contracts will be null and void. That means the shell companies can claim the full profit value of the lost contract. When I was still working at Enoch's restaurants one of them was closed because of flooding and the loss was covered for the three weeks the place was shut down for clean-up and repair."

"It fits, but it's a high-risk gamble. You burn down this building and you've got fire marshals and insurance investigators taking the rubble apart piece by piece. And what if the fire department gets here in time to put it out? It's a quiet road, but it's not the boonies; there must be a half-dozen properties that have a view of this place. People around here are trained to call 911 if they see so much as a puff of smoke from a barbeque this time of year."

"You're so close," she says, holding her fingers an inch apart. "Why does the arson have to take place here?"

"Oh, shit."

"Yes!"

"A wildfire."

"It's fucking brilliant. They start a wildfire and burn everything in a few square miles around here."

"Those locations are where Lodestar's men are going to start fires in the brush."

"And this is when to do it; the Santa Ana winds are blowing, it's hot as hell and everything's bone dry." She jumps from the tree branch and pulls up some long blades of brown grass that crackle like cellophane as she crushes them in her hands. "They might not even have to start a fire themselves."

"The only arson investigation would be of who started the wildfire. If the fire's big enough there might be, what, hundreds of homes and buildings burned down? The insurance investigators would only come around to check that the building was gone; they might not even get out of their car."

"And here's the extra layer of genius in Gideon's scheme: one of his emails mentioned a company called Pacific Rim Insurance, so I read up on it. He bought it for a hundred million and change a year ago, then got the banks to give PRI a $700 million line-of-credit to cover, allegedly, an aggressive expansion plan. Based on Gideon's reputation, the banks were happy to open the vaults."

"So, all the insurance policies will be with PRI."

"Gideon would have put his own man on the inside to rubber stamp the policies, and he'll also be there to facilitate the claims. PRI will use the line-of-credit to pay out on the phony claims, which Gideon will be pocketing half of."

"I bet he lets PRI go bust to cover his trail even more; that would still leave him with a huge profit. What made you think of a wildfire?"

Autumn points to the top of the building. "The open windows and the newspapers. A wildfire with these winds is sending burning embers way ahead of it, and those windows are open to catch them and feed them to the newspapers."

"Even if conditions are perfect for them, they don't have a guarantee the fire will get close to this property. I bet they'll have someone here on the night to make sure this brush catches fire if the main fire is passing it by."

"I still want to look at those locations."

It takes no more than twenty minutes to drive to them all. We stop at the last one, a bend in a dead-end road that isn't overlooked by any homes or businesses. The brush on each side of the road is bending in the hot wind that's turning it into tinder. We get out of the car and I check the locations on Beau's phone again.

"What's up?" asks Autumn.

"They'll want to make the fire look natural. This spot is furthest from Blanco Canyon, but if you imagine a line following the direction of the Santa Ana winds from here, it roughly lines up with the other four locations and then Blanco Canyon. This will be the main ignition point, and the others will be lit in turn a few minutes later to make it look like the fire is jumping ahead in the wind. There could be more locations we don't know about; Beau was only one member of a team, and a back-up at that."

"When do they do it?"

"They're probably letting the weather decide for them. Some night when the winds are especially heavy would be perfect."

"So, any night in the next few weeks."

"That seems to be their schedule."

"Let's hope it's after Newcastle's party. He'll be harder to get money out of if it's already in his pocket."

"What's this party about?"

"You know who Gideon's son is?" says Autumn with disgust.

"Brooks Newcastle. He's going to run for the Senate next year, isn't he?

"The birthday party is an excuse for the large adult son to kiss the feet of assorted billionaires and have them write checks, so the whole of the Selous Group should be there. I think we know enough now to frighten them into writing a check for us as well. Pinder's an even weaker version of Enoch; if we put pressure on him, he'll go crying to Gideon."

"I worry Gideon might play dumb, try and deny everything, and then put the plan on hold. I mean, they can wait us out if they want, maybe work some more on making us disappear. There's no way to prove a conspiracy or a crime until the fires are actually lit, and there's no way to prove Gideon's attached to any of these properties or the contracts."

"The emails in Enoch's laptop."

"That's almost an ace card, but I can see a few ways Gideon could argue he wasn't the author of them. Anyway, it all comes back to proving he profits from the fires, which we can't."

"I'm not worried." Autumn says breezily. "He'll pay."

"Why?"

"We've got greed working for us. They're this close to their big score and they've all got well-thumbed brochures for superyachts or county-sized ranches in Montana in their back pockets. They see themselves as starving men, and we're threatening to snatch the food out of their mouths."

"It's all a bit of a tightrope walk, isn't it?"

Autumn puts her arms around me. "But where else do we find this kind of excitement?"

"This is probably our last chance to walk away. Let them have their greedy fun while we disappear."

"No, Tom," she says with a smile. "For better or worse, I want this to be the last act in my story. I don't want to slink away any more. I want to make someone else afraid. I want to fuck up these guys as casually as they do it to everything around them. You with me?"

"Yes."

For a moment I believe that we can scatter them like sheep, given a bit of luck. But I know the best I can do is act as a shield for Autumn. Gideon and his kind have organized the world to dance to their dreams and demands, so to stand in their way is to invite destruction. But we've set our course, and soon we'll see what the far shore holds for us.

We have lunch at Malibu pier, then drive back to the house. Some of Autumn's friends have left, new ones have arrived, and a competitive confusion of voices fills the house. I go upstairs to check the emails from Gideon on Enoch's laptop and get a clearer idea of what he told Enoch to do. The folder with the emails is gone. I'm not shocked. Lodestar undoubtedly has hackers who can remotely access the laptop and scrub it. Hessian does. In the end it doesn't matter; we have to convince the Selous Group, with or without the emails, that we know enough to put them in front of a judge.

I wake up on Friday morning to the distant sound of the TV in the kitchen. Autumn must be down there because I can hear the juicer going; she'll be making the horrible-looking drink she starts each day with. From the bed I have an uninterrupted view of the ocean through the picture windows. The sky is a sickly yellow, like a smoker's fingers. The TV weatherman is reminding us that high winds are forecast and the risk of wildfires is significant.

I come down to the kitchen in my running shorts. Autumn points to the TV.

"Check this out."

It's live footage of a wildfire that broke out last night up north to the east of Chico. A reporter is talking to camera while in the distant background a helicopter with a bucket dangling beneath it dumps its load of water into a cloud of smoke and flame. The reporter says that there are already reports of numerous fatalities.

"Coincidence?" Autumn asks.

"Tis the season."

"It would make sense to scatter their targets up and down the state. They wouldn't want to have one fire taking out all the phony businesses. Some sharp mind somewhere might notice an odd concentration of expensive claims in a small area."

"Gideon really should have included you in this scheme; I can definitely see you transitioning into a strategic planning position in the Selous Group, remuneration to be decided later."

She gives me the finger and asks if I want one of her liquid breakfast concoctions. I make a face and go for my run.

The wind is whipping down from the hills and blowing streamers of sand across the beach that slash at my legs as I run. The weather is keeping everyone at home except for determined dog walkers and runners like myself. Even the big houses lining the beach with their multiple decks and balconies seem deserted, the air crackling with the sounds of their awnings, canopies and flags snapping in the wind.

A woman standing near the surf line is staring down at something that might have washed ashore. It's Petty's Filipino caregiver. She's holding down her wide-brimmed straw hat with one hand and trying to control her floral skirt with the other. Petty is stretched out at her feet on his stomach, his face turned away from the water, and the metal detector lying neatly beside him as though he'd put it down carefully before collapsing. Her vacant look means she's in shock. I reach down and feel for a pulse in Petty's neck. Nothing. His eyes are open and some grains of sand are stuck to them. He's shit himself.

"How long since he collapsed?" I ask her.

She blinks a few times, which releases some tears, and tells me she doesn't know. It's probably only a few minutes, but it's of no importance; his death isn't growing in magnitude the longer it lasts. I ask her if she has a phone, and she takes one from a straw bag she has over her shoulder. I call 911.

"It's okay," I say, "an ambulance will be here soon. There's nothing you could have done. Is there someone at his home you can call?"

She shakes her head emphatically. "No. No one. It's just me and him and Octavio, the driver."

"I'll wait with you until the ambulance's here."

I turn my back to the wind and watch a kite surfer skipping over the waves. A man goes past walking his dog and both he and the dog make a deliberate effort not to look in our direction. Five minutes drag past before I hear a siren approaching. In the short time I've been waiting, blowing sand has piled up against Petty's body. His left hand is disappearing into the beach and a miniature dune hides half his face, leaving one dead eye to stare over a sandy waste.

The paramedics finally arrive and I jog back to the house.

Autumn looks up in surprise as I come in and says, "You weren't long."

"Too windy."

Around eight o'clock Autumn comes down to the living room. She's dressed for Gideon's party in a short black dress with golden threads woven through it that catch the light. Tamsin and Ashley try to guess which designer she's wearing and agree that it's Dolce & Gabbana. Autumn tells them it's Roseanna Ferrari. We take the Audi, and I tell her about the missing emails as I turn onto the highway.

"It doesn't matter now," she says. "We only have to let them know we've figured out their scam."

"Exactly. What's Gideon's house like? I want to say something cutting about his architect."

"Hey, it's my job to handle the snarky architectural comments. You can check the contents of his bookcase, if he has one, and make some scathing remarks about that. His house is in the style of John Lautner."

"Is that good?"

"Homes for American pharaohs," she says with distaste. "Not my style."

We drive up into the Hollywood Hills and Autumn points to a hilltop that wears a lavish crown of palm trees thrown into silhouette by the brilliantly-lit house hiding behind them.

"That's Gideon's,"

A valet takes our car at a gate halfway up the hill, while a young woman with a clipboard checks our names against a guest list and then waves us toward a waiting golf cart driven by another young woman. The driveway to the house hairpins up a steep slope, the native brush on either side giving way to a band of palm trees and flowering shrubs.

"Jasmine," Autumn tells me, just before I ask her what I'm smelling.

The driveway ends in a paved circle with a wedding cake fountain in the middle. The house is arched like a Quonset hut, but built of concrete and glass. A broad flight of steps leads up to a pair of dark, wooden doors set in a wall of frosted glass.

"It's not as big as I thought it would be."

Autumn grimaces. "Just wait, this is foreshadowing."

A man in a dark suit with a mic in his ear pulls the door open for us. He's got scar tissue over one eye and muscles fighting to get out of his clothes—Lodestar, no doubt. A long hallway flanked by closed doors and potted tropical plants leads us to the other end of the house, and I understand what Autumn meant. The entrance was merely an artist's rendering of this end of the house, which opens out onto the top of a wide staircase leading down to a massive area that's more hall than room, its arched roof pierced with star-shaped skylights. The far wall is all glass and has a view over the city that's probably worth more than seven figures by itself. There's a patio and pool outside, and terraced lawns that drop away towards the city like a giant's staircase. I can see at least a hundred people scattered inside and out, not counting the staff tending the bars and food tables.

"Impressive," I say. "Like someone upcycled an aircraft hangar."

"And furnished it like a Dubai hotel lobby. Fuck those skylights are tacky. You notice there isn't one personal touch or item in sight?"

"Maybe Gideon's got an office like Enoch's, full of baby pictures and taxidermy. Speaking of which, do you think Enoch's here?"

"It'll be fun if he is. There's Roger Pinder." She points to a man getting a drink at a bar in the living room. "Let's see if we can make his hair stand on end."

"You lead."

We step down into the vast room and a rush of adrenaline hits me as if I'm about to draw a gun. Pinder sees Autumn coming and almost drops both the drinks he's holding. He's in his fifties, and nondescript except for a chubbiness that's out of place in a room full of people whose spousal relationships probably aren't as long-lasting as the ones they have with their personal trainers. His string tie is the only distinctive thing about him.

"Long time no see, Roger. This is Tom," says Autumn, and takes my hand in hers.

"Hello, Autumn. Nice to meet you, Tom," squeaks Roger. Encumbered by his drinks, he makes a vague gesture with his right hand that substitutes for a handshake.

Autumn looks around and asks, "So where's your partner in crime?"

"Gideon?"

"No, I meant your wife. But Gideon counts too, I suppose."

"Outside."

"Who? Gideon or your wife?"

Pinder stammers and makes more clumsy gestures with his drink-filled hands before saying, "Both."

Autumn lowers her voice to a conspiratorial whisper and says, "You should congratulate us on joining the Selous Group. We're not into the assassinating African animals part, of course, only the swag side of things. We'll be taking the lion's share of what's coming to Enoch, if you'll forgive the pun."

"I see," Pinder utters feebly, his eyes darting around as though looking for rescue.

A young Chinese woman, tall, beautiful, and wearing a red silk sheath dress embroidered with flowers and butterflies on one shoulder, appears beside Pinder, slips her arm through his, takes one of his drinks, and smiles ingratiatingly at us. He stands straighter now that she's beside him.

"This is Mei," he says to me. "My wife."

She says hello, shakes my hand and begins asking Autumn about people in Palm Springs they both know. Something about Mei is darkening my mood; it might be the way she's taking quick glances at Pinder, as if gauging his mood or worrying about his desires. Or it might be because he's such an obviously empty man who's adorned himself with borrowed youth and beauty.

"A quick word with you, Roger," I say, and gently unmoor him from Mei's side—she looks nervously at us—and take him a few yards away. He looks at me with frightened eyes and licks his dry lips. "Are you ready to follow this all the way through, Roger?"

"What through?"

"The fires. I need to know that my partners are totally committed. I don't know if Gideon's kept you updated, but people have been killed keeping this a secret—Gantry can give you the details—and more might have to go. You have to stick with us when things get bumpy. I don't want to hear that anyone's backing out, because that's a person who might rat out the others. You've already a rich man, Roger, so this deal's just extra dessert for you, but I'm starting out and I'll put down anyone who fucks it up. But you're cool, aren't you? You wouldn't be here tonight if you weren't."

"Gideon told me everything's set," Pinder splutters. "No problems with me; I'm here right to the end."

"Good man, Roger."

I pat him on the back, which makes him flinch, and he hurries outside, not even glancing back at his wife as he leaves. I join Autumn and Mei, who looks confused by Pinder's hasty departure.

Autumn says, "Mei's been telling me that she and Roger have been looking at condos in New York. She wants to be beside the High Line, he wants a park view near the Guggenheim."

"Why not both?"

Mei finds this funny, or pretends to, and then excuses herself to go after Pinder.

Autumn arches an eyebrow. "Guess which iteration of wife Mei is?"

"2.0?"

"3.0. Roger's weak and not overly bright, but don't think he can't be vicious. He probably murdered 2.0. She had a drinking problem, and one morning Roger found her face down in their pool. Apparently, he'd forgotten to set the alarms the night before so he wouldn't have heard when she left the house and fell in the pool blind drunk. He didn't have a pre-nup with her, and Mei had just started articling in his lawyer's office. Timing is everything."

"He admitted to being in on the scheme."

"That was quick. How did you scare him?"

"I imagined what a tough guy in a movie would say to a weasel like Pinder and adlibbed from there."

"Yes, that's exactly what would work with him; it's why Gideon sent Mei over here."

"Did he?"

"She was outside with Gideon and he told her that her husband needed rescuing. She told me she couldn't understand what he meant by that. Mei's a nice girl, she might even like Roger, but she's realizing she's waded into a tar pit."

We're interrupted by Autumn's phone ringing. It's Rachel the property lawyer. Autumn talks with her while I scan the crowd. I've worked security and surveillance at parties like this in the recent past, although this is easily the most moneyed one. Mei was the first non-white guest I've seen. Even the staffers are white, which means the catering company was explicitly told this was a "high-end" affair: code for no blacks or Latinos. The rich think it makes them look richer to be served by whites.

Autumn ends her call. "Well, well. Rachel tells me that the company that owns Blanco Canyon also has another holding in California. Guess where."

"Near Chico?"

"That's right."

"You see? If you'd been in charge they wouldn't have made a mistake like having one fake company own multiple properties. Very sloppy."

"Should we keep shit-disturbing?"

"Yes. Only you should do it solo. I don't know these people, you do. Talk up how members of the Selous Group are working together on some deal; tell people to ask Gideon or Pinder or Cordell about it. Let that percolate through the party and then we'll pair up on Gideon."

"So, I'm organizing the beaters and we'll bag the tiger together?"

"Exactly."

"What are you going to do?"

"Drift around, maybe talk to Cassidy over there," I say, and point to a corner of the room where I've spotted Cassidy trying to look like a guest, squeezed into a poorly-cut brown suit and keeping us in the periphery of his vision.

"What's he doing here?"

"A job I've done before: keeping an eye out for guests who might be problematic. When I used to do it, I was looking for known drug dealers or people who were getting too high or too drunk. I think we're Cassidy's sole focus. I was wondering how Mei was alerted so quickly that Pinder was in trouble."

Autumn gives me a kiss and wanders off to a clutch of men and women talking about a wine auction. Cassidy can wait. I wander outside through glass doors that pivot like vertical louvers and almost reach the ceiling. The view is even better out here. To the left a fountain of light rises from the Hollywood Bowl, and distant bands of red and white lights mark out traffic on the I-10. The surrounding slopes and valleys are splashed and speckled with the lights of homes enjoying views not quite as good as this one. The people in them will be looking up at this blaze and dreaming of finding a way to buy their own eyrie.

Gideon's guests make me feel claustrophobic. The men are almost all older than me, some far older. They have wide, confident smiles that reveal snowy, showroom teeth set in tanned faces, and their laughter sounds like boasts. I recognize some of them: state politicians, an ex-LAPD Police Chief, businessmen who make noise on TV, a televangelist, the braying owner of an NFL team, and a sprinkling of older actors, some of whom I thought were dead. The wealthiest men are probably the ones I don't recognize. Everyone's rich, but I can tell from overheard snatches of conversation that their success has to be measured in this public forum. They coolly mention new acquisitions of property or rights or key alliances or the favor of those higher than them or, in lower voices, women, and then they try and read the degree of envy or respect they see in the faces around them.

The women have mostly coalesced into their own small groups and appear, on average, to be half the age of the men. Some look like teenagers dressing up as adults. They have the staged, gleaming perfection of luxury goods in a magazine advertisement.

Cassidy has followed me outside at a discreet distance. He's still pretending to look elsewhere, so I go over to him.

"Hotter or colder?" I ask.

"What?"

"Am I getting closer or farther away from Gideon?"

He snorts dismissively.

"I'd have thought you were too senior to pull a lame ass, party security job like this, Cassidy. But then you've had staffing shortages at Lodestar recently, haven't you? I hear they were fired without warning."

"Payback will be a bitch, Bridger."

"How about that: a sentimental assassin. You think Gideon or Gantry ever puts a dollar value on emotion? They wouldn't be where they are today if they did. You should learn from them; anyway, your cut of this should dry your tears. What is your cut, by the way?" He looks away with a sour expression. "You could take half of Gantry's share, you know. It'd be easy: you've got way more on him than we've got on Gideon. You know the fire plan in detail."

"I don't know anything."

"Fuck, man, you telling me it makes you happy to see these old, skinny-assed men hog it all? They look at us and can tell just from our suits that we don't belong. In their eyes we're no different than the people handing out drinks and picking up the dirty plates. You've even got numbers on your side; it's you and your men that make the company, not Gantry. Take it all from him, if you want. We could share information, make this our big payday, not theirs."

He hesitates before saying, "This is all bullshit you're spewing."

"You know it's not, Cassidy. You wouldn't have been ordered after us if we weren't doing what you could be doing too. This isn't about being brave or ballsy, this is about being bold. Figure out the difference and you'll be rich."

There's some doubt in Cassidy's eyes as he mutters, "Anyhow, it's too late now."

"Do what you have to do, man, but ask yourself if Gantry would do the same for you for what you're getting paid."

I walk away and get a vodka tonic from one of the outside bars. The wind is gusting hard and the tops of the palm trees are dancing to its erratic tune. I nurse my drink and scan the crowd looking for Gideon. On the lowest terrace is a wrought iron gazebo, and I can see a small group, including Pinder and Mei, facing a man leaning against one of the gazebo's supports. His back is to me, but the body language of the people in front of him indicates that he's commanding their attention. This must be Gideon, and I hope these people have filtered over to him to ask about the deal they've heard he's got going with some of his buddies.

I'm about to go down for a closer look when a man brushes against me on his way to the bar. It's Jasper Cordell. He's in his sixties, but he wears those years effortlessly thanks to a slim, athletic body and cosmetic surgery that's given him the expression of a surprised cat. He places a complicated order with the bartender for a drink of his own devising and then takes a bottle of Evian mineral water spray out of his pocket and spritzes his face. After a sigh of pleasure, he catches sight of me and frowns as much as his renovated face will allow.

"It's important to moisturise," I say approvingly. "These Santa Ana winds are bad for the skin."

"Tom, isn't it? I hear you gave poor Roger a violent case of goosebumps."

"That was quick. Word must have traveled like wildfire."

"How very—"

"Apposite."

"Exactly. But I don't get the shivers as easily as Roger."

I point to the gazebo and ask, "Is he down there trying to return his Selous Group membership card?"

"No," laughs Cordell, "Gideon's putting Roger's spine back together. So, you and Autumn want to move up in the world?"

The bartender interrupts us to hand Cordell a tall glass filled with mint leaves and a pale yellow liquid. It looks like it was siphoned out of a ditch.

"Move up? Is that how you see it? I'm only interested in moving away before your kind burn everything down."

Cordell rolls his eyes. "Spoken like someone who's only ever had a worm's eye view of the world—escape rather than achievement."

"What do you need so badly, Jasper, that you're willing to risk everything?"

"I don't *need* anything, but I can always find something new that I want. This is a case of a phenomenal return on minimal investment. I can't turn that down; my business reflexes simply won't allow it."

"Your jaws automatically snap shut when something brushes against them, is that it?"

"Something like that. And there's the risk, of course. That's what hunting's really about, after all."

"Fuck off, Jasper. The only thing you ever risked on those safaris was your face drying out in the heat and flaking off."

He sips his drink and says primly, "I learned long ago that personal insults are the death rattle of the weak."

He turns his back on me and walks away in the direction of the gazebo. I'm annoyed. I was enjoying myself. I hunt down some food at a serving station near the pool and see Cassidy sitting on a chair at the far end of the terrace, a plate of food balanced on one knee. He's turned the chair to face away from the crowd and is, apparently, looking at the view rather than myself or Autumn. After eating, I do a slow walk around the grounds. More people have arrived, and some of the earlier arrivals are getting louder and more animated. I hear snatches of conversation about a show at the Getty, a new farm-to-table restaurant in Missouri that's worth the flight, a property that's coming on the market in Watch Hill, a book club's unanimous disappointment with *My Brilliant Friend*, the best countries to get rescue dogs from, and Taylor's investment in an organic tea plantation on Maui.

A knot of men is gathered around a tall man in his thirties. It's Brooks Newcastle. His face is vaguely familiar to me from hits on cable news shows in which he rails against people and things outside his bubble. His brow is furrowed in a caricature of intellectual *gravitas* as he speaks loudly and makes chopping motions with his right hand as if conducting a deficient high school orchestra. I can't make out what he's saying, but I'm more interested in who's behind him. It's Cotton Pearsall. He's put on some weight since I last saw him in Hexum, but he has the same lazy, bemused smile on his face. He catches my eye and walks over to me.

"We're both thinking," says Cotton in his soft Southern accent, "how did that guy end up here?"

"Not so much, Cotton. Doesn't it seem to you that Grange County was just a farm team for where we are right now? You here with Brooks?"

"I help manage his political action committee."

"Really? And will you be as loyal to him as you were to Jubal?"

Cotton covers his grin with one hand like a shy debutante. "I don't know who you mean, but those were happy times, weren't they? Enjoy the evening."

He returns to Brooks' side and apes his master's stern demeanor as Brooks continues haranguing his audience. Now I have another reason to hate the Newcastles.

I find Autumn by herself at the top of some steps that lead down to the terrace where Gideon is holding court.

"Did you talk with Cassidy?" she asks.

"I gave him a workers-of-the-world unite speech and advised him to help himself to what Gantry is taking. I wanted to mess with him. Shall we go down there and separate the dragon from some of his treasure?"

"Let's."

We walk to the gazebo, where Pinder and Gantry are talking to Gideon, who turns around to face us in reaction to Pinder looking fearfully in our direction. Gideon hasn't aged well. In the hunting picture I saw he was at least ten years younger. Unlike Cordell, he's let time take its course and his naturally bird-like face has become reptilian. His slightly protuberant eyes are like marbles set in a piece of distressed leather, and his astonishingly long, white hair is tied in a ponytail that hangs down his back all the way to his waist. More startling is the belted, aqua-colored jumpsuit he's wearing; it's like looking at a member of a '90s boy band suffering from Methuselah Syndrome. He obviously doesn't give a fuck about how odd he looks because it's never stopped him getting what he desires—the gravity well of his billions assures him of that.

As if to underline my thoughts, he looks at Autumn with an obvious hunger, as though she was a rare dish being delivered to his table.

"The guest of honor!" says Gideon, glances at me, and adds, "And her consort."

Pinder laughs faithfully at Gideon's witlessness and looks towards Gantry for support. Gantry is staring coldly at me.

"I don't see Enoch. Is he late or just afraid of fire?" asks Autumn.

Gideon grins and shakes a finger at Autumn as though she were a naughty child. "You know very well he's indisposed. He had a fall that broke his heart."

"We're here for Enoch's share" Autumn says decisively. "Or Roger's; he appears to be regretting his decision."

"Share of what?" asks Gideon over a background of Pinder making sounds of protest.

"Really?" I say. "You're going to play pretend?"

Gideon fixes me with a look he probably reserves for assistants who bring him the wrong file.

"I've had you looked into, Bridger," he snaps. "You're just a dirty, backwoods cop with a vicious streak."

"Actually, I'm so much worse than that."

He's truly disgusted with me, and it's because I have the prize he wanted: Autumn. I put my arm around her waist and watch his jawline tighten.

"Oh, God," sighs Autumn, "let's not play insult tennis, Gideon. We're only here to agree on an amount that you and the other great white hunters can see as a reasonable alternative to prison."

"Why are you trying to extort us? What is this about?" barks Gantry, doing his best impression of a wronged and confused man.

"Are you wearing a wire, Gantry?" I ask. "Because you sound like a rookie undercover cop."

Gantry's face reddens, showing off the scar that runs from his neck down to his chest to better effect.

"And why would you say 'us', Gantry?" mentions Autumn. "We were talking to Gideon. You're including yourself in a group that you're probably about to deny exists."

Gideon says, "You were always wasted on Enoch, Autumn. You have twice his brains. You could do better in so many ways."

"Enough, Gideon; your compliments always make me feel like you've flashed me."

"Very well," he says neutrally. "What brings you here?"

"Blanco Canyon Road," answers Autumn, and then chimes off the names of the companies supposedly based in the derelict building as well the company that owns the building.

I say, "I filmed the inside of the building, which should be interesting for investigators down the road. I don't think anyone could look at the video and think that those were legit businesses. I also got some shots of Cassidy and his men leaving the building. That draws a connection to you, Gantry."

Gantry doesn't react, but Pinder is practically jumping out of his skin.

"For God's sake do something, Gideon," pleads Pinder.

"Take Roger elsewhere, Preston," snaps Gideon. "I need to talk to these two."

Gantry leads Pinder away to the far side of the terrace and puts a calming hand on his shoulder. It doesn't seem to help.

"I expected better from Roger and Enoch," sighs Gideon.

"Yes," I agree, "you'd think killing large animals would be an indicator of strong character."

Gideon ignores my comment. "I only brought them in as a kindness. I like doing nice things for my peers. We've always looked out for each other over the years."

"No, Gideon," says Autumn. "You needed them for the contracts with the companies that are due to burn. You needed legit businesses to sign those contracts in case someone at PRI took a second look at the policies. PRI couldn't be seen to be handling policies with companies you own. The other members of the Selous Group are a convenient smokescreen and a further layer of protection for you."

"I can pay you two something to go away," Gideon says sharply, "but don't think you can soak me."

"Fifty million," says Autumn.

"Ridiculous," answers Gideon angrily.

"It's Enoch's share. Leave him out in the cold; he started all this. Or take it out of yours. You'll still be making more than anyone else."

"I won't be giving up anything."

"I notice you didn't say anything about Enoch," I say.

"Why not call it all off?" says Autumn "Your plan is springing leaks all over the place. Too many people know about it."

Gideon tilts his head to one side and looks at Autumn in the manner of a Victorian gentleman staring in bemusement at something unlikely brought back by an explorer.

"Because I can do it, Autumn. Because it's possible. Because it's *my* plan. And mostly because even if you shout everything you know from the rooftops, there's no way I can be connected to anything. You don't really understand, do you? You're like animals that have wandered out of their proper environment; fish pulled up by a net from the bottom of the ocean. This is my world you're in. It's made by and works for me and Preston and Roger and Jasper. Nothing you can do can cause me trouble—that would be like expecting the sun to stop in its course. If it pleases me, I can make decisions and do things that change your world, but it can never work the other way around. I'm what history is: men who bend and break the world and make it into something different."

"And yet here you are," I say, "wasting time talking with fish."

"It amuses me. And the more I think about it, the more I feel perhaps Enoch shouldn't have a seat at the dinner table."

"We need your answer tonight, Gideon," says Autumn.

Gideon's smile isn't attached to any pleasant emotions as he replies, "Only because I want to stay on your very good side, Autumn. Yes to fifty. You and I will be much closer in spirit after this, and perhaps we'll eventually come to an accommodation of some kind."

"Tomorrow," says Autumn, "I'll phone you with my banking details and I'll expect the fifty by midnight Monday at the latest."

Gideon bows with mock gallantry. "Agreed. I look forward to any and all calls from you, Autumn. And now I have other guests to be charmed by."

He crosses the terrace and starts talking with Gantry and Pinder. The former reacts with anger, the latter with relief, to what Gideon is saying. A hot gust of wind lifts Gideon's white ponytail and sets it in motion flicking at imaginary flies.

"Man, he really hates you," says Autumn.

"How can you tell?"

"He went out of his way to not make eye contact with you. I've only seen him do that with mistresses who spoke out of turn."

"I'm honored. Shall we go?"

We start walking back up to the house. Autumn stops and points at a woman sitting with Mei on a bench that faces away from the house. She's in her sixties, and that makes her somewhat out of place here. Her clothes are expensive, her jewelry bright and plentiful, and her face a mask of boredom with a touch of drunkenness. Mei is trying to make conversation with her.

"That's Candy, Gideon's wife. And you see those three over there?" Autumn gestures towards a group of three young women standing on the edge of the terrace thirty feet away. "Those are Gideon's current girlfriends. He insists they show up at any big function that Candy's also at. She knows about them, of course."

Two of the women are white, with Slavic features, and look like predatory Instagram models. The third stands out as much as Candy.

She's as overtly sexy as the other two, but she's black, and looks uncomfortable, either because she's so close to Candy or because she's a statuesque island in a sea of white people.

"Why does he do it?" I ask.

"To humiliate her. Candy's an old school Hollywood Catholic. She won't divorce, and Gideon won't either because he'll lose half of everything. I think his plan is make her die of despair and alcohol."

"Fuck."

"Don't feel too sorry for her; she's a sharp-tongued racist from way back, and that's why Gideon added the black girl to the team."

I'm about to say something when I notice that Cassidy is moving quickly through the crowd towards Gantry. He has his phone out and shows something on it to Gantry, who responds with a short, sharp remark. Cassidy almost runs back up to the house. I take out my phone and check for news alerts.

"It's happening right now," I say. "A fire outside Thousand Oaks."

"They started it?"

"I don't think so—Cassidy looked too surprised—but they're going to take advantage of it, that's why he's sprinting out of here. So, do we try and stop them? I mean, it looks like the money's going to be ours, and we can still rat them out after we get it."

"I don't think we'll see a penny of it," Autumn says without emotion. "Gideon's ego is monstrous enough that he'd see it as total defeat if we got a dollar. This is his evil baby and he's very, very proud and protective of it. What do you think?"

"This evening has put me in a mood where I'd be happy to see this hilltop napalmed down to the bedrock right this minute, so, yeah, I'd love to stomp on Gideon's fantasy world, but that might kill our deal."

Autumn surveys the terraces, the house, then looks back at Mei and Candy and the three mistresses standing in a loose circle looking bored.

"I don't think I care all that much about the money anymore. I just want things to end." She takes my hands in hers. "I'm afraid my poor impulse control is taking over again: let's fuck them up."

"Can you get yourself back to Malibu? I don't think you're dressed for the occasion."

"What are you going to do?"

"I've got a gun, a shiny new Audi, and I'm wearing my best suit. I don't think I can do much, but I'll look great doing it."

"Get back in one piece. I'll still need your help with killing some billionaires."

Embers

I was driving my bike flat out, its engine making angry noises I'd never heard before, and as I leaned over to take the turn onto the road to the Settlement, I smelled smoke. A dancing glow was lighting up the sky ahead, and when I topped the last rise before the Settlement, I could see that the church was on fire, daggers of flame stabbing out from its open doors and windows. Smoke poured out of the open doors of the dining hall and the barn. The workshop and house were closed up and apparently unharmed.

I rode to the front of the house, jumped off the bike and let it crash to the ground as I removed my backpack and took out the Walther. The bike's engine died and I could hear Malachi's voice shouting something. He was on his knees facing the church, his arms wrapped tightly around his chest as though the fire was making him cold. My heart nearly stopped as I wondered if Rebecca and the others were in the church.

"No, no, no," howled Malachi.

I ran to him and yanked him around to face me. The flames from the church were reflected in his terrified eyes.

"Where's Rebecca? Where are the others?" I yelled.

"It's my fault," he blubbered. "I've been judged and ruin has come to us all."

"Fuck off!" I snarled and jabbed the butt of my gun into his ear. "Where are they!"

Malachi screeched like a cat at the blow and pointed to the house. "Caleb took them in there, all of them."

"What's he doing? What happened?"

"I don't know exactly. It was about an hour ago, maybe more, I was sleeping, and I heard Caleb bellowing, so I got out of my hut and saw him running towards the road and at the same time I heard a car door slam and a pickup went down the road with its headlights off. Then he just stood in the road and...roared. He made animal sounds for the longest time. He saw me looking at him from my hut and came at me like he was going to rip me in half, so I ran away into the woods until he stopped following. I came back and hid and saw him go into the house and then the light came on in his office. Nothing happened for a while, then he came to the window and I think I saw him drinking from a bottle. He came back out of the house, got a can of gas from the workshop and started this," sobbed Malachi.

"Then what?" I shouted. "Why did you say you thought he was going to kill everyone?"

"He went in the house and I heard horrible noises. Things smashing, and his terrible voice mixed up with screams and crying. It's my fault. Mine, mine, mine," cried Malachi, and began repeatedly striking his forehead against the ground.

I ran to the house and tried the door handle. Locked. I began kicking the door and screaming Caleb's name, then paused to listen and heard a panicky girl's voice and heavy steps that must belong to Caleb.

Caleb's voice boomed from the other side of the door: "What do you want, imp?"

"Let them out! The other buildings are on fire and it's gonna spread to this one!"

"You want them, monster? Just wait."

I heard him move away, followed by silence, and then screams accompanied by thumping noises like a post being driven into the ground. I threw my shoulder into the door, but it didn't budge, so I started towards the workshop to get the ladder. A shout from behind stopped me in my tracks.

Caleb was standing in the doorway, stark naked, one side of his body spattered with blood. The thick hair on his chest was matted down with sweat and blood, and he was breathing heavily. In his left hand was a near-empty bottle of Dewar's. Hanging from his right hand was what I thought, for a brief moment, was a large piece of cloth stained with blood.

He raised the object in his hand and said, "Is this who you were looking for? I have others."

It was Daniel, as naked as his father. Caleb was holding him up by one foot and gave his son a little shake as though trying to stir him into movement. The boy's head was split open, the pink and gray of his brain hanging out of a smile-shaped crack in his skull. Malachi was making gagging noises somewhere behind me. A monster's cough sounded from the dining hall and flames burst out of its doors, bathing us all in a quivering, yellow light. I remembered the gun in my hand and aimed it at Caleb.

"Let them out!" I shouted.

He threw his son's body at me as though it weighed nothing. I fired a single shot that splintered the doorframe as Daniel's corpse bounced on the ground and landed at my feet. Caleb ducked inside and slammed the door as I ran up onto the porch and threw myself against it again. He must have fumbled setting the lock because the door smashed open and caught him in the chest, knocking him off balance and making him slip in a pool of blood. He staggered back and collapsed against his bed. Sarah's naked, pregnant body was curled on top of the bed. Her throat was purple and black with bruises, and she stared at the ceiling without blinking. I moved closer to Caleb, leveled the Walther directly at his chest and yelled Rebecca's name. I heard a cry from the other room and a moment later Linda appeared in the doorway clutching a blanket to hide her nakedness. She was breathing like she'd run a marathon and shaking uncontrollably.

"Where's the others?" I yelled at her.

Linda stared at me as though I'd pronounced a death sentence on her and then ran out of the house. I edged to the doorway, keeping one eye on Caleb, and glanced into the other room. Abby was spread-eagled on the floor, her head horribly bruised and misshapen. The other children were on the floor near her, all of them killed like Daniel. Rebecca was lying on her back on the bottom of one of the bunk beds. Caleb had ripped her throat out with a dull knife or his bare hands. Her body, the bed and the floor were a field of blood. All of the dead were naked.

"I fucked them all before I killed them," said Caleb with drunken glee. "I even took a double dose of Viagra so I could do the job right. Look!" He pointed down to his erect cock. "Still ready for action! I was just going to do Monday when you showed up, you fucking thief."

"I didn't take anything."

"You took everything from me. You're a worm and a locust. Now I have nothing, no future, and these creatures," he slapped one hand on Sarah's rounded stomach, "must go into the darkness ahead of me. Why should anything I've enjoyed have enjoyment without me? Now put that gun down—I don't surrender to children."

I tightened my grip on the automatic and steadied my aim. Caleb must have had some mad, drunken idea that he could walk out of the house and give himself up to the police or run away, or perhaps he thought my weapon was only a bluff, because he was startled when he saw the look in my eyes. And scared. For a second I thought of the other man I had killed and how sick and empty his death had made me feel, and then, just as quickly, I realized I could live with that; I'd managed it before. I fired three times. As each shot struck his chest, Caleb grunted as though absorbing a tackle.

He looked in surprise at the dark blood streaming from his wounds and said, "You hurt me...It hurts."

I wanted to throw up but forced myself to go in the other room and see if Abby and the babies were actually dead. They were. I looked at Rebecca and tried to remember what the touch of her hands and lips had felt like. I closed her blue eyes and clumsily moved a blanket over her body. In the other room Caleb was making coughing noises. There was a red plastic gas container beside a bunk bed and I carried it into Caleb's room. He was spitting blood and using the bed frame to try and lever himself to his feet as I tipped the jug over and let its contents glug out onto the floor. Caleb took a lurching step forward and I shot him in the belly. He fell backwards onto the bed with a scream and clawed at his chest and stomach.

I came out of the house into a night filled with flocks of brilliant golden embers moving as one as they weaved and dipped through the air. The other buildings had become pillars of thrumming flames and above their noise I could hear sirens. Linda had wrapped the blanket around herself and was kneeling beside Daniel's body, one hand resting protectively on his shoulder. Malachi was behind her, mouthing words that I couldn't hear. He'd pissed himself.

I stepped off the porch and looked around for a piece of burning debris to throw in the house, but a wave of exhaustion hit me. I went over to Linda and stood beside her, my gun at the ready in case Caleb appeared at the door. A small squadron of embers gusted through the door and the house took a sharp breath as the gasoline ignited. There was no noise from Caleb, and I assumed he was dead until he crawled into the doorway on his stomach. The room behind him blazed with firelight and black smoke rushed out at the top of the door. He waved his hands beckoningly in our direction and tried to speak. Malachi took a few steps forward and then with a sharp cry turned his back on the scene and ran away.

Caleb raised himself up and in a wet, shrieking voice said, "Damn you, Malachi."

He collapsed with his body halfway out the door. His mouth was hanging open, and I heard, or imagined that I heard, a long whispering groan come from him. He must have died at that moment because some embers settled on his body and he didn't react. I became aware of Linda sobbing and the sound of sirens close at hand. Two fire engines and Reinhart's cruiser pulled onto the property. I pocketed my gun, helped Linda to her feet, then took her away from the burning buildings and sat her down on a stump.

Firemen swarmed into the light dragging hoses and shouting questions at me that I couldn't understand. Linda must have said something because they concentrated their hoses on the house. Reinhart was suddenly at my side looking astonished.

"What's that fat fool gone and done?" he barked.

"He set fire to the place and killed them all. Except Malachi and this one," I said and pointed to Linda, who had her eyes closed and might have been praying.

"Damn."

"I think he started this after someone took his money."

Reinhart gave a low whistle, took his cowboy hat off, and rubbed his head viciously. "Well, that's what I call intemperate. Any normal person would have called the police first thing. He was a crazy man."

"I got here after he'd done all this and shot him. He's lying in the doorway there."

"That's him? He's cooking up pretty good. Good work, Tom. And who's this?" said Reinhart, and pointed to Daniel's body, which was being covered in a thin layer of ash.

"Daniel, one of his sons."

"The man wanted to eat his own young, didn't he? Don't worry about anything, Tom; one way or another you're not going to be involved in this. Wait for me in the cruiser, and take this little girl with you and put her in the back. Run the engine and get warm."

I took Linda by the hand and lead her away. I'd forgotten that she was barefoot until she yelped and grabbed at one foot. I carried her the rest of the way and put her in the back of the cruiser. The keys were in the ignition and I turned the engine and heater on. The wind was sending ghostly streamers of gray smoke down the road.

"Where am I going to go?" moaned Linda.

"I don't know. Hospital first, probably."

I shut her door and stood in the road watching the fires. The firemen had their hoses aimed at the house, but it wasn't having much effect. One by one, the other buildings collapsed, sending geysers of sparks into the air. The house burned fiercely and I walked along the road trying not to think about what I'd seen and the part I'd played in creating it. The workshop was ahead of me, its big doors slightly open, light coming from the inside. I was sure it had been closed and dark when I arrived, but it was possible Caleb had set a fire there that had gone unnoticed. I went to the doors and saw that it was only the overhead lights that were burning.

"Malachi?" I called out.

There was no answer, but it was possible that he was hiding in terror, so I started looking under the workbenches. It was when I got to the far end of the shop and turned around that I saw him. The inside of the tall exterior doors had horizontal slats across their width, and he'd climbed to the top, maybe fifteen feet, and fastened a length of electrical cord to the top slat, then noosed the other end around his neck. He must have really wanted to die, because there was nothing to stop him from grabbing the slats for support once he felt the wire tighten around his neck. I picked up a hammer and threw it at him. It struck the metal door with an outrageous sound, a few inches below his dangling feet.

"You dumb motherfucker," I yelled, and hurried to the open door. I paused before I left the workshop and whispered, "Sorry, Malachi."

When I returned to the cruiser, Linda was lying across the back seat. She looked drowsy. The house was burning less intensely, and the other buildings were piles of rubble and low flames. The firemen had turned off their hoses and were standing in a group chatting. A little distance away, Reinhart was having an intense conversation with a fireman who looked like he was in charge. I leaned against the hood of the car and wondered if I'd be able to recover my bike. Some time later, Reinhart came up from the Settlement, his normally immaculate uniform spotted with dirt and ash.

He shook his head as he approached me and said, "Well, this has been some kind of Chinese fire drill. I had a feeling that that lard ass was going to cause me trouble."

"Malachi's in the workshop. He's hung himself."

"Better and better," laughed Reinhart. "Don't let this get you down, Tom. There was nothing you could have done. Now, just give me a quick blow-by-blow of what went on here tonight."

I told him what had happened, leaving out nothing, and let him digest my story for a minute before asking, "It was you who took his gold and stuff earlier tonight, right?"

He grunted in agreement. "I had Spence drive me out here and wait up on the road. Everything was dark and quiet; I even waited a while to make sure Gaunt wasn't moving around outside on the property. I was leaving with the box when I heard a shout. Maybe he'd been looking out his window without the light on. Anyway, I ran like a rabbit. I don't think he ever got a good look at me. I was going to bring it back tomorrow afternoon, but I guess impatience can be added to Caleb's other sins. Here."

Reinhart led me to the back of his SUV, lifted the hatch, and opened a storage panel on the interior wall to reveal the money box. He opened it and I saw that two rolls of cash were missing.

"Spencer already took his cut," he said, as though reading my thoughts. "This is yours." He handed me one of the rolls. "I'm not sure of the best way to get rid of the gold and those certificate things, but when I get it sorted, I'll put some aside for you. I know you were close to Malachi, and that's truly sad, but if you concentrate on the silver lining we've got here, it should help you out. I've always found that when bad things happen to good people, they've usually left something good behind, so it's not all a tragedy. Right?"

"Sure. I'll take that girl's passport as well. I promised it to her."

Reinhart gave me a big smile. "You are a man of your word, Tom Bridger. By God, you belong in one of my Zane Greys, you really do."

He handed me the passport, and I told him that I needed to go and see if my bike was toast or not.

The bike was covered with mud and ash, and it ran rough once I got it going, but it carried me up to the road where I saw that Reinhart was now in the back of the cruiser talking to Linda. She looked towards me and I could see that she was crying. I thought about stopping to ask Reinhart what was going to happen to her, but exhaustion was overtaking me, and the smell of the fire was turning my stomach.

I went to bed immediately when I got home, hoping to go to sleep in an instant, but lay awake until the sun came up, alternately blaming and exonerating myself for everything that had happened since I'd first met Malachi. Before falling asleep I wondered if he hadn't done the right thing when he hung himself.

It was around noon when I woke up, feeling more tired than when I'd gone to bed. I wandered around the house trying to find something to fix my attention on, but everything—books, TV, food—either irritated or bored me. I went outside and cleaned and fixed my bike as slowly and methodically as I could. The sun was out, and for a few minutes at a time I managed to detach my mind from combing over the previous night and exist in a state of dazed numbness. After finishing with the bike, I went to the kitchen, turned the radio on for the weather report and made a sandwich. The radio news report described "last night's tragic fire" as, according to the Sheriff's Office, a murder-suicide perpetrated by Malachi Gaunt, who had shot his father to death and then set fire to the family's compound. There was no mention of survivors.

I turned the radio off, then drove to the brothel. It wasn't open for business yet, and every window had drawn curtains. Winnie was standing on the front porch in her wolf-emblazoned fleece jacket smoking a cigarette. She looked at me with apprehension, as though I was an official there to condemn the building or herself, as I came up the steps and went through the door. Mona was in her room, curled up on the bed and weeping quietly into a wad of tissues.

"Is he really dead?" she asked as I came through her door.

"Yes, but there's this."

I gave her the passport and the wad of money Reinhart had given me the night before, about nine thousand dollars. She stared uncomprehendingly at the cash and the passport, fingering them carefully as though expecting them to crumble into dust.

"I can go now?"

"Yeah. Any time. You could take a bus this afternoon to San Francisco."

Mona dragged a small suitcase out from under the bed and began filling it with clothes. She worked quickly but took time to carefully fold each item even though her hands were shaking.

"Can you take me to the bus? I don't know where it is," she asked nervously.

"Sure. It's only a few blocks from here."

Winnie was still on the porch when we got downstairs, her expression at seeing us a mixture of shame and sadness. She said something quietly in Chinese to Mona, who flinched, and when we reached the sidewalk, Mona turned around and screamed a reply in Chinese. Winnie hurried into the house and slammed the door.

"What did you say to her?"

Mona got her breathing under control and explained, "I told her: how dare you say sorry."

We walked in silence to Main St. and sat on a bench in front of the bus station. The San Francisco bus wasn't due for forty-five minutes, and Mona stared at the ground almost the entire time, sometimes smiling, once or twice crying. The only time she spoke was to ask me again if Caleb was truly dead. The bus finally appeared and she boarded it without a glance back. As it rumbled away, I tried to imagine what it would feel like to get on one of those buses myself.

For the next week I kept a low profile, only going into town to get groceries. There were too many places that reminded me of Caleb and Malachi, and I couldn't shake the fear that people would be staring at me and blaming me for what happened. I was convinced rumors would have circulated thanks to the firemen. But I'd forgotten how easily Hexum turned its attention away from people like me. I began going into town more frequently and didn't notice anyone looking at me differently, although I sensed that some made a point of *not* looking at me. The only mention I heard of the fire was when I went to the book store and Latimer said he was sorry that my friend had died. He meant it and I thanked him.

The local newspaper and radio had nothing more to say about the deaths after the first reports, and as the days passed, I began to worry that there was something wrong or suspicious about the silence. I was also curious about Linda, so one Sunday I drove over to Reinhart's house. I could see him through the front window as I came up to the door. He was in his recliner, in uniform, watching a football game and eating from a box of Ritz crackers. With his armchair marooned in the middle of the barren living room he looked an exhibit in a museum. I knocked on the door.

"Haven't seen you around much, stranger," said Reinhart warmly, and waved me inside. "You follow football much? This time of year I like to see how the playoff games end. Some folks in Hexum can flare up a bit if the wrong team wins or doesn't cover the spread, so I like to be prepared. Forewarned is forearmed, as they say. What brings you over?"

"Uh, I was wondering if everything was okay after that thing at Gaunt's? Is Linda alright?"

"Nothing to worry about, Tom; the fire crew each got one of those gold wafers, so they're thrilled to bits. Anyway, everybody knew it was a bunch of kooks living out there—things were bound to end in craziness."

"And Linda?"

Reinhart rolled his eyes. "Well, that was a bit of a pain—took a lot of calls before I tracked down her family. I had to let her live in the jail for a week before one of her people came and took her back."

"She could've stayed with me."

"Oh, damn, I almost forgot: she left a letter for you."

"A letter?"

"I think I have it somewhere in the cruiser; I was going to drop it off at your place. Just wait."

Reinhart went out to his vehicle and I wandered over to the wall unit to look at his strange collection of trophies. I spotted one with a tiny figure skater on top that I was sure hadn't been there on my previous visit. On the piece of tape stuck to the bottom was written GAUNT'S PLACE JAN 1/00. Reinhart must have chosen this bizarre method to commemorate memorable moments in his law enforcement career, and as I looked over the dozens of trophies I tried to imagine how much bloodshed they represented.

Waving an envelope in one hand, Reinhart hurried back into the house.

"Found it," he said triumphantly, and handed it to me.

My name was written on the outside of the unsealed envelope. I thanked Josh for remembering the letter and left.

I was in a mad rush to read it but decided to wait until I was sitting down somewhere. The day was warmer than it should have been and it put me in lighter mood, so I went out to the Denny's at Mission Commons.

The waitress slapped a menu down on my table and said, "Didn't you used to come in here with your dad?"

I didn't recognize her, but Levi always flirted with waitresses so I didn't doubt she remembered me.

"I did," I responded tersely and gave her my order.

Linda's handwriting was legible but looked as though it was written by someone much younger. It began:

Dear Tom, I am writing to you from the jail, but I am not a criminal. Ha ha. Sheriff Reinhart is helping me write this because I need help with my spelling. I have been treated well here. I want to tell you that Rebecca really liked you. She talked about you a lot. If not for the terrible thing Malachi did I'm sure she would have gone to live with you. She said she would if it came to that. My brother Amos arrived this morning to take me back to Colorado. It's been so long since I've seen him I don't remember him, but he says he's Amos so he must be. Maybe one day you can do for me what you wanted to do for Rebecca. I will pray for that. I hope this letter finds you well. Fond Regards, Linda.

Reinhart had obviously dictated part of the letter so that her story lined up with his, but I wondered about Linda's uncertainty over Amos, and what sounded like her asking me to find her or rescue her. I tamped my worries down and concentrated on what she said about Rebecca. Was it true, or only a fabrication by Reinhart to make me feel better? I decided to believe what she'd written, which only made me sadder. I'd intervened in her life and Malachi's, and that act had set the dominoes tipping into oblivion.

As I drove home, I toyed with the idea of finding some way to leave Hexum, maybe go back east to New London. Even as I thought about what it would take to do that, I knew I was indulging in something weaker than a daydream.

The long driveway into my house was muddy from some rain the night before and I could see a fresh set of tire tracks going up to the house but not returning. Reinhart sometimes came out to see me, but we'd already met today. I worried that it might be Spencer or Jubal, one or both of them at the house to give me grief about returning Mona's passport, so I pulled off the driveway, parked my bike, and walked quietly up to the house through the brush. As I approached the house, I could smell weed burning, and my heart started to race.

Levi's truck was parked in its usual spot and I heard him shout from inside the house, "Amy, make a grocery list; the kid's got nothing but crap in the fridge."

"Yeah, when I finish this," answered a tired female voice.

I went back to my bike and sat on it without moving. I had told myself a hundred times that I wanted Levi back, or at least know where he was, and now that he had returned, I felt ill. I started the bike and went the rest of the way to the house. Levi came out of the front door as I got off my bike and stood on the front step staring at me with a blank expression, his hands on his hips and his legs spread apart as if blocking me from my home.

"You're back," I croaked.

"No kidding."

Like me, he didn't know how to handle this situation. There was a trace of fear in his eyes, as though he'd been dreading this moment. Levi held the door open and gave me a half-hearted pat on the back as I went into the house. The smell of grass was intense inside, and the source was a blonde woman in her twenties watching TV from the couch in the living room. She had a blunt in one hand and the remote in the other, and was flicking through channels like she was in a race.

"Amy, this is Tommy, my kid."

Amy looked over her shoulder, waved her joint in greeting, said, "Hiya," then turned back to the television.

Levi sat at the kitchen table and waved me over to sit down with him.

"I hear you did alright on your own."

I shrugged. "Where were you?"

"Jubal's got competitors. They grabbed me near Bakersfield. I was like a prisoner of war," he said with an exaggerated look of pain on his face.

"So they just let you go?"

"Yeah."

"Why didn't you let me know what had happened to you?"

"How could I? Anyhow, I'm back now, so it doesn't matter. Amy's going to be living with us. She's my girlfriend."

"I thought you were a prisoner or something. How did you meet her?"

"I got out about two weeks ago, and I had to do some stuff for Jubal down in San Diego. That's where I met her. You'll like her. She's cool."

I had immediately learned two things from this brief conversation: that Levi was lying, and that something about him had changed profoundly. If anything like this had actually happened to him, he would have talked about it for hours, each key facet of the story getting bigger and bolder. But his voice was subdued and impatient, like someone trying to get through a difficult interview, and he couldn't stop one leg from bouncing up and down. Levi had always been at his most relaxed and confident around me, and now he was acting like he was expecting me to slap a pair of handcuffs on him. I could see he'd lost weight, but I guessed it had more to do with drugs than any kind of prison experience.

"Has anybody come asking for me? I mean, other than Spencer and guys like that?" Levi asked quietly.

"No. Nobody's come around."

"Okay...Good...Good."

Amy turned off the TV and came into the kitchen. She was a bit plump, had long blonde hair and a round face that framed a child's simple smile. Her jeans were decorated with patches and beads, and she wore a peasant blouse that needed constant adjustment. She sat at the table and picked some bits of weed off her tongue before smiling placidly at both of us. Levi's agitated leg became worse.

"So," purred Amy, "you're Tom. You're even nicer-looking than your dad."

I didn't answer. She was wasted.

"Amy's gonna start a business here," said Levi encouragingly. "Horses."

"I'm great with horses," Amy said with passion. "You like riding, Tom?"

"I've never done it."

"I'll teach you! This is great riding country. Me and your dad are going to start a stable; take people for trail rides, maybe even overnight trips. Cool, huh?"

I couldn't believe anyone from Hexum would want to trek out into the chaparral on horseback, and I could imagine what would happen if people on horses ran into a guarded weed patch.

"And tell him your other idea, Amy: the rodeo."

Amy hugged herself, leaned forward with a dopey, excited look on her face and said, "This is a million-dollar idea, Tom, tell me if it isn't: you know what the problem is with rodeos? They're a hundred years old and they look a hundred years old. I want to make the Cirque du Soleil of rodeos. You ever seen those Cirque shows in Vegas? I love them, but it's all just old-timey circus stuff dressed up with music and costumes and shit, so why not do the same thing with rodeos? I've got a whole journal full of ideas for how to do it, but I don't have a name for it yet; something Spanish might be nice. Good idea, huh?"

"Sure," I replied. "So, you're going to, what, start a rodeo?"

"Nah. I'm going write up the idea for it, like a business plan, and sell it to someone. But I want a name for it first so I can trademark it." Amy suddenly made an irritated noise and looked reproachfully at Levi. "Baby, are we going to eat soon or what?"

Levi snapped to attention and said, "Yeah, let's go eat somewhere, make it like a celebration since we're all together now. We can grab groceries on the way back."

We went to an Outback restaurant at Mission Commons where I quietly ate my dinner while studying Amy and Levi. They didn't want or need me around; they batted ideas back and forth about Amy's rodeo, whether they should get one or ten horses to begin with, how long it would take to build a stable, and for good measure Levi dredged up his old plan for an exotic game farm. They bathed in each other's fantasies, especially Levi, who encouraged Amy in everything she proposed with an enthusiasm I'd never seen before. I looked at him closely as he drank in whatever Amy was saying and saw that he was getting old. His hair was grayer and his face had lines that weren't there before. He was probably twenty years older than Amy, and I could see he was desperate to keep this young woman. Fueling her dreams was how he was planning to do it. My memories of my mother were growing vague by this time, but I was certain I'd never witnessed this kind of relationship between them.

We stopped at the Safeway on the way back home, and Levi and I stayed in the truck while Amy went in to get groceries.

"It's going to be nice having a woman in the house, isn't it?" said Levi innocently as he fiddled with the radio.

I felt a lightning rush of anger and heard myself saying, "If you ever beat on me again, I'll fucking kill you. Ask Reinhart if you don't think I won't."

Levi sat silently, staring straight ahead. Several times I thought he was going to speak, but then he'd pretend to look at something in the parking lot or glance at his watch. After a few minutes he cleared his throat and said, "Amy's taking her time."

Nothing made clearer the change in Levi than the fact that he didn't react to what I'd said. He found a radio station he liked and we sat without speaking until Amy returned with a cartful of groceries. I didn't think what she'd got was any better than what I'd been supplying myself with. As we drove home, she and Levi started up with more chatter about horses and rodeos and assorted bullshit, while I sat thinking I should have gotten on the same bus as Mona.

Over the next month, Levi built a small stable and paddock on a half-acre of ground he cleared. Occasionally, and reluctantly, he'd ask me for help. I didn't mind helping—it took my mind off recent horrors— but he'd inevitably become annoyed at my silence towards him and dismiss me after a half hour or so. He worked hard but intermittently, motivated by his fear of Amy's disappointment if he didn't complete the prologue to her dream.

I lived as separate a life as possible. When I was at home I usually stayed in my room, but most of the time I was in town or out on the land. I could tolerate hanging out in Hexum's library, a big Carnegie building that smelled of floor cleaner and old books, unless kids my own age were there. They would stare at me from a distance and make hushed comments. Rumors had spread about me, I learned later, and I was now a local urban legend. I also spent time at Latimer's, sitting on a stool and reading while he did the same behind the counter.

When Amy wasn't stoned, and Levi was gone, I enjoyed her company. She didn't tire me with talk about horses and rodeos, instead, she told me long, interesting tales about growing up in beach towns up and down the west coast, pulled along by what she called "super-hippie" parents who divided their time between surfing and dealing dope. She could make me laugh with descriptions of her parents' wastrel friends, and she'd laugh as much as me at these memories. Every couple of weeks, however, she'd retreat to her bed and stay there for a few days, barely eating, almost never speaking. I'd look in on her during these episodes and she'd be sleeping or flipping through celebrity magazines she'd already read a dozen times. Levi called them her "blue" moods and didn't offer any other explanation.

When all of us were in the house I couldn't help but overhear their quiet, often stoned, conversations in the living room, and that's how I eventually, in dribs and drabs, learned that Levi had never been a prisoner of anything except his own fear. After I'd killed Mickey, Levi had been terrified that retribution would be coming for him from Mickey's associates. Jubal stashed him in San Diego where he had him work as a driver hauling vans full of illegals from the border to farms and businesses all over southern California. I was kept in the dark by Levi in case someone came around the house asking about him. Once, Amy asked Levi why he hadn't brought me along to San Diego. His answer was that he hated the idea of his land being abandoned. So, I had been left behind to act as something between a NO TRESPASSING sign and a friendly guard dog. These revelations didn't make me particularly sad or angry; by then I'd resigned myself to expecting nothing from Levi except weakness and poorly thought-out lies.

In early March I came home to find two horses in the paddock and Amy excitedly arranging all kinds of tack in the stable. Levi was leaning against the paddock fence and studying the horses—one black, one roan—as though he'd never seen their like before.

He gestured towards the animals as I came near and said, "How do you like that? I told Amy I'd get her some horses. They're from a trail riding outfit up in the mountains that went tits up. Amy says they're perfect."

"You going to go riding with her?"

"No. I've never seen the point of riding horses. You can fall off a horse, you know, really fuck yourself up, but you'll never fall off a pickup."

Levi wasn't making a joke, and he'd pitched his voice low so Amy wouldn't hear him. It struck me then that although Levi owned hundreds of acres of the surrounding land, he'd never really set foot in it. He'd driven up the few dirt tracks that veined our property when we'd first arrived, but only to get a sense of the scale of his domain. I knew every ridge and wash and hollow of our land, and dozens of square miles of the surrounding country. And then I recalled that it was a very long time since I'd heard him talk with passion about the chaparral and *his* land, as though the trees, bushes and soil were his soul made manifest. I supposed that now he saw the chaparral as nothing other than his workplace—an open-air factory where he feared and loathed his bosses.

Early the next morning, while Levi was still sleeping, I went outside and watched Amy saddle the black horse, who she called Turk. She was nervous, but sure in her movements as she put the bit in the horse's mouth, then led it out of the paddock and mounted it. The horse shook his head violently as though limbering up while Amy stroked his neck and made encouraging noises. She took him for a slow, circular walk in front of the house. The horse seemed pleased to amble pointlessly in a circle. Amy let him do two circuits before stopping in front of me.

"You going to be gone long?" I asked, assuming she was heading out for a ride.

"Oh, not too long."

"Have fun."

She smiled uncertainly but didn't urge the horse forward.

"Tom," she said hesitantly, "I don't know where to go."

I suggested some routes and told her about various landmarks, but in the end she convinced me to be her guide. She was worried about getting lost. I walked ahead of her and we went east, into the foothills. I hadn't gone for a hike this early in ages, and I'd forgotten how mornings, especially in the spring, were so loud with birdsong. There had been rain overnight, and the brush was generously decorated with teardrop diamonds of water. Amy let her horse trot or canter when we came to open areas, while being careful to always keep me in sight. We only talked when I pointed out the distinctive ridges, tracks or abandoned buildings she could use to orientate herself when she came out on her own. I didn't think she'd be riding by herself too often; when she flushed out a covey of quail she screamed and reacted almost as loudly when some deer and rabbits bounced away from us. Turk only snorted at these distractions. Amy was confident in her horsemanship, but not where it took her.

That first outing took two hours, and the next day she went on her own after I ignored her gentle hints that I should come along as well. She returned in less than half an hour, and I don't suppose she'd gone more than a few hundred yards from the house. The emptiness and sudden animal noises of the chaparral did, indeed, make Amy nervous, but what I eventually learned was that she had a horror of being alone. If Levi was away, which was often, she'd beg me not to go into town, and unless Levi was on a job for Jubal or Spencer, she accompanied him everywhere. It wasn't my companionship she needed; when we were alone in the house she'd watch TV, read magazines and self-help books, and sit at the kitchen table writing plans in her journal for the rodeo of the future. She didn't go out of her way to speak with me, but she drew comfort from having another person close at hand.

Eventually Amy persuaded me to try riding. Like Levi, I wasn't a fan of horses, but she was a good teacher, and Toby, the roan horse, was a placid animal who had an engaging habit of sighing like a bored old man. Our trips got longer and longer, sometimes lasting a whole day if Amy knew Levi wasn't going to be home. Those trips were pleasant, although she sometimes tired me with lengthy descriptions of whatever self-help book she'd just read. I was more interested in what she had to say about her upbringing or Levi. Having a woman living in the house had made me start thinking about my mother again, and led me to speculate on where she was and how I could find her. Talking with Amy about Levi was a way of reverse engineering an understanding of why my mother and Levi had got together, and why, possibly, she had left him.

During our long rides I would try, in a cautious and roundabout way, to draw her out about why she and Levi were a couple. The answer always amounted to the same thing: they could listen with delight to each other's plans and fantasies for hours. Over the last couple of years, Levi's appetite for grandiose schemes had dwindled, but now, with Amy, he was back to building cities in the clouds, and she could match him, daydream for daydream. None of this lined up with what I could remember of how Anne and Levi had been together; the frayed, inexact memories I had of their conversations revolved around work and money and chores. Perhaps there wasn't anything extraordinary or cruel about Anne abandoning us; she and Levi, I concluded, hadn't got along and the lure of a new boyfriend must have been stronger than whatever appeal a son had. Everything I'd seen from people since coming to Hexum told me that it was commonplace to use and discard people.

On the first really warm day in March, Amy and I went riding high in the foothills. The sky was cloudless, the palest blue, and peppered with scores of hawks, vultures and eagles migrating north. Amy usually didn't remark on the wildlife we saw on our rides, but I noticed her looking up at the birds passing over our heads and smiling. We hadn't followed any particular route, but then a zigzagging trail that ran up a steep slope caught my eye; we were close to the plateau where I'd burnt my clothes months ago. I headed us up the trail and, as I'd hoped, Amy whooped with delight as we reached the top and she saw the unending view to the west. She slipped off her horse and stood on the edge of the plateau.

"This is unreal. Do you think we can see the ocean?"

"No," I laughed. "That's way over a hundred miles away. You can just make out the curvature of the Earth, though."

"Holy shit, you're right."

"Go smell the trunk of one of those trees," I said, pointing to the nearest Jeffrey pine.

"Is this a trick?"

"No. You'll see."

She gave me a suspicious look but took a tentative sniff of the coppery bark. Her face broke into a smile.

"It smells like butterscotch!"

"Neat, huh?"

Turk stamped a forefoot and wandered off to nibble at some tall grass as Amy returned to soaking in the view.

"Do you like it here in Hexum?" I asked. "Don't you miss the ocean? It's where you grew up."

"Sometimes, but I didn't have much choice about where I grew up, did I? My folks liked it. Or maybe they just liked that there were lots of people like them who lived there. They both surfed, but they weren't what you'd call real surfers. I mean, you could call them beachers, I guess, if there's such a word. Chris and Marion liked the ocean and being on the sand and not doing anything in particular except get high and bullshit with their friends; they were even half-assed about selling dope. Just sell enough to get by and the cops won't bother you, was their motto. Levi left you alone here, didn't he?"

"Yeah. Almost half a year."

"Been there, done that. Not for that long all at once. When I was nine, we lived in a van for most of a year. We'd spend the day at the beach, anywhere from Venice up to Santa Barbara, and park overnight at a mall or the driveway of someone my parents knew. One night we were parked at a mall near Agoura, and they told me they had to go out to do some business and they'd be back in a couple of hours. So, they got in this car driven by another couple and I didn't see them for three days."

"What did you do?"

"Cried at night and ate at Taco Bell during the day. I had ten dollars of my own that lasted me for food—that's a lot of bean burritos. And I played in the toy section of Target. So, on the afternoon of the third day they showed up looking all scared and saying sorry, but they also had a big bag of cash that they were pretty excited about. I never found out what happened, or how they earned it or stole it. We stopped living in the van after that and moved into a house near Venice Beach that we shared with…everyone, really. They took off on their own more often once they had the house; I guess they figured I was safer in a house with people around. It wasn't true, but I never told them."

"Where are they now?"

"Costa Rica, I think. Your mother walked out on you and Levi, right?"

"Uh huh."

"Weird way to do it."

"Weird? What did Levi say about it?"

"He said when you guys were driving here from the east, she got in an argument with him and said that she wanted to go back to Connecticut. You don't remember?"

"What else did he say?"

"She left you guys at, like, a service area in Nebraska or Kansas, someplace like that. She got a lift from a trucker and headed back east."

"From a trucker?"

Amy looked at me in surprise. "You really don't remember? You must have blocked it out. I wish I could block out stuff."

There was nothing to block out. The night Levi took me from my bedroom in New London was still vivid in my memory, as were the occasions on the trip west when he told me that Anne had left us for a boyfriend. Levi had lied to Amy, and I couldn't conceive what led him to invent this story for her.

We stood there staring out to the west like a pair of explorers contemplating the hazy new world before them. A golden eagle skimmed directly overhead and chided us with its harsh cry. I thought some more about Levi and his lying and fantasizing and cowardice, and knew beyond a doubt that Anne had never abandoned me.

Fuel

It feels like it takes forever for the car jockey to find and retrieve the Audi. As I pull away from the gate, I turn on the radio and reach under my seat to see if the gun is still there or if someone's done a search and removed it. It's there, and the news is already suggesting that a blown transformer started the fire near Thousand Oaks. Cassidy has a head start on me; he and his men will probably be going to their targeted location closest to the actual fire and then move towards Blanco Canyon, firing up the brush as they go.

As I pass Woodland Hills on the Ventura Freeway, I smell smoke and, simultaneously, I see the lights of fire trucks in my mirror. Lots of them. They must be seriously worried about this fire spreading if they're already calling in units from elsewhere. A gust of wind makes the car shudder and I take the next exit in case the police have blocked the Thousand Oaks exits to non-emergency vehicles. I take a road that parallels Ventura and watch a dozen or more emergency vehicles barrel north on the freeway, lights strobing and sirens howling. Lots of people are outside their houses looking to the north, others are already jumping in their cars and leaving.

The homes give way to brush-covered hills and fields, and as I crest a rise, I look up at what I briefly think are the lights of distant planes in the sky. They're burning embers, dozens and dozens of them, hundreds of feet in the air and racing to the west like a flying circus of shooting stars. Some of the stars are curving down to the ground. The Lodestar location closest to Thousand Oaks is a trailhead, but there's no one there.

I stop and get out of the car. The sky is filling with more embers and a stronger smell of smoke. Cassidy must have judged that this blaze is going to be big so there'll be no need to light a chain of fires; he'll have gone straight to the location closest to Blanco Canyon. On the drive there I pass hilltops beaconed with fire; a barn near the road burns as two figures silhouetted by flames try to rescue some horses; and a young couple stand beside a car that's gone into a ditch and frantically try and wave me down. I turn down a dead-end road to reach the last spot on the chain that leads to Blanco Canyon. The top quarter of a grassy hillside to my right is carpeted with flames that the wind is bending almost parallel to the ground. At the end of the road a pickup parked with its lights on is facing in my direction. The man standing beside it is looking up at the sky, which is a blizzard of burning material. He's one of the men I saw unloading boxes at the building on Blanco Canyon.

I pull the Audi over and get out with my gun pointing at him and shout, "Where's Cassidy?"

He looks frightened, but not because of me. "I don't know."

I fire a shot over his head.

"Fuck, man, I can't reach him! I keep phoning but he doesn't answer. He's supposed to be back here by now."

A low roaring sound that was in the background has suddenly become much louder, and I yell, "Did he go to the building on Blanco Canyon?"

"He went down there to check if it was already burning so we wouldn't have to do anything here."

A popping sound erupts behind me and I glance back to see that the hillside fire has jumped the road and ignited a stand of trees. Burning leaves whip past my face.

"Shoot if you want, but I'm the fuck out of here."

He hops in his truck and roars past as I get in the Audi. I have to make a three-point turn, which only takes moments, but in that time a burning branch has fallen on the road and bullwhips of flame are scything across the asphalt. Even with the windows up and the air con blasting, the heat is baking me. I gun the engine and drive over the branch, exploding it into a cloud of sparks. As I race down the road, coils of golden flame reach out to caress the car. It takes only a few seconds to drive out of the flames, but my hands are shaking as I reach the intersection. A hundred yards down the main road I stop and check for burning debris caught under the car; there's nothing, but the air is choking me with its heat and smell. Three cars charge past heading south towards the ocean, the drivers and passengers looking terrified; a few of them have soot on their faces. A white horse bursts out of the brush and stands in the middle of the road, its sides heaving, foam dripping from its mouth and blood running from long, thin gashes along its flanks. It prances nervously until the sound of a giant bell being cracked makes me flinch and sends the horse screaming back into the brush. It's probably a propane tank exploding, and it could be a mile or a hundred yards away.

It's all over. The land is going to burn no matter what Cassidy does, but I decide to go past Blanco Canyon on my way back to Malibu to confirm that the Selous Group will soon be putting in their orders for his and her Gulfstream jets. It's only a mile away, and as I approach the turn off, a pair of cars, their sides scorched and tires smoking, screech out of Blanco Canyon and roar away. I turn onto the road and I'm met with giant tumbleweeds of dirty smoke that funnel down the road towards me. The smoke clears and I move forward cautiously until I come around a sharp bend and stop. The road ahead is a black, smoking ribbon through a tunnel of flame, and well past the end of the tunnel is Cassidy's Mustang, it's rear end fully ablaze, and beyond that a wall of smoke that spits out tongues of orange fire. Cassidy, his face contorted in pain, is crouched in front of his car. Ash and cinders rain down on my windshield, and when I use the wiper fluid it steams away in a second. The fiery walls of the tunnel twist and bend with the winds, and for brief moments they die down to almost nothing. I put the car in gear and weigh the odds of making it through to Cassidy and back again, but he doesn't leave me time to decide. When the flames suddenly subside again, he sprints towards me along the road. I think he's going to make it until he clutches at his throat and staggers; the superheated air is depleted of oxygen and scorching his lungs, and after a few more jerky steps he goes down on all fours. The wind and the fire roar as the flames rise up again and dart forward to consume this new piece of fuel sprawled on the road. I reverse back to the main road faster than I should.

The road down to the Pacific Coast Highway is frantic with cars and trucks fleeing the wildfire and emergency vehicles moving towards it. Helicopters thud overhead recording and observing. When I reach the beach house and turn the engine off, I notice that I'm panting. I stay in the car until my breathing's normal before going inside. The house is silent, but all the lights are on and my shouts go unanswered. I go out on the deck and see Autumn and her friends down by the water looking to the east. They don't notice me coming down to the beach; they're transfixed by the orange monster that's devouring the top of a faraway mountain. The firefly lights of planes and choppers dart around the beast and fill the air with a distant buzz.

Autumn sees me and cries, "Oh my God, what happened to you?"

The others join in her amazement, and I notice my clothes are full of small burn marks and my hands are streaked with soot and ash.

"Are you okay?" asks Autumn as she puts her hand on my cheek.

"I bring you greetings from Pompeii."

I give her friends a story about helping someone with a flat tire near the fire, and then Autumn and I go up to our room where I take a long shower to wash away the smell of smoke. When I come out of the bathroom Autumn's standing by a window watching the progress of the blaze.

"What happened up there?"

"Nothing good. Cassidy's dead and the Selous Group will be filing their insurance claims tomorrow. They didn't even have to strike a match. Cassidy went to check if the building was already on fire and got caught behind the flames."

"You saw him?"

"Yeah. He made a run for it, but..."

"Fuck. No one should go that way."

"Did I miss anything at the party?"

Autumn laughs coldly. "About a half hour after you left you could see and hear people taking frantic calls about their ranches and homes getting torched. The place emptied out like they were expecting an invading army to sweep through—some of them actually ran. Brooks' speech was canceled and he was so pissed he flipped over a drinks table. Carmen, his wife, tried to calm him down and he slapped her right off her feet."

"How did Gideon take all this?"

"He laughed till he cried. Seriously."

"You think he's going to come through with the money?"

She throws herself down on the bed and doesn't answer me. I lie beside her and almost drift off to sleep before she answers.

"What should we do if he does?" she asks.

"Leave. Move to some country that doesn't remind me of this one."

"That'd be hard. We'd have to have a boat and sail from place to place as soon as we heard certain accents or smelled the wrong food. You sticking with me if we get the money?"

"Like a burr."

"You didn't ask if I'd stay with you; I could trade you in for something younger with fewer scars that knows the difference between the Brutalist and Prairie schools of architecture."

"But would he be as easily led astray as I am?"

"That's true. Speaking of which, are you still on board with harming Enoch and Gideon?"

I'd been prepared to argue Autumn out of doing anything if we got the money, but after seeing Gideon and his partners in the flesh, hearing their lazy, brutal confidence, and then witnessing the fire and Cassidy's death, I find myself fantasizing about bringing pain and despair to the Selous Group. But I still have to offer Autumn an alternative; our chances of outrunning and outgunning these people are small—prey animals can only fight back for so long.

"I am," I tell her. "But we could leave this minute, before they have a chance to hurt us. We won't ever have to think about them again. I've got money stashed that could get us started somewhere else; more than a million. With or without Gideon's money, our odds aren't good the longer we stay; we're a loose end that needs fixing. But I'll roll the dice if you want to."

Autumn thinks about what I've said while I get up and look out the window. Traffic is heavy for this time of night and most of it is rolling south, away from the fire.

"A million?" says Autumn.

"More. And you wouldn't believe where it's hidden."

"Why haven't you used it before?"

"It's dirty money. So dirty I'd prefer never to see it again."

She joins me at the window. "It's not all about the money. I don't want them to win every time. Anyway, I've got my own running away money, almost three million. I've been taking kickbacks on every piece of art or furniture I've bought since we were married. I thought you wanted to take this as far as we can. Having second thoughts now?"

"Second thoughts are what I'm best at. I agree with you; I don't think we'll get a dime from Gideon. His kind don't share things they believe are theirs by right of conquest."

"Didn't I just say it's not all about the money?" Autumn says angrily. "That's a bonus, if it ever happens. I want Gideon and Enoch dead. I want their last thoughts to be that all their power, all the privilege they take for granted is ending at my hands. I've only ever told you a fraction of what men like Gideon and Enoch have done to me over the years. Some things I would never tell you because it would give them another victory over me. I need to see the look on their faces when they realize that their lifelong winning streak is ending for good."

I understand what she's saying because I've seen that look on men's faces in Hexum, except that when I killed them it didn't give me the peace or sense of justice that I think Autumn is expecting or hoping for. But I can't tell her that. She won't believe me now, at this late stage, and she'll do something dangerous or futile on her own if I don't act the intrepid knight and aid in her quest.

"Fair enough," I say. "Let's see if Gideon comes through and go from there."

"Good. Now let's go downstairs and make our last rites loud and happy and drunk."

I wake up in the morning with a dull headache. From where I'm lying in bed, I can see that a quarter of the cloudless sky is filled with smoke. Autumn is in the shower, so I go out on the deck off the master bedroom to check on the fire, which is closer and bigger. The scene reminds me of pictures Levi took of burning oil fields in Kuwait. The flames are just as intense, and although the smoke isn't as black, it rises to an unbelievable height, like the stalk of a monstrous plant reaching for the sun.

We spend the early afternoon walking along the beach, diving into the surf whenever the heat gets too intense. An air armada of choppers and water bombers is constantly over our heads, and people we pass on the beach talk of nothing but the wildfire. They seem giddy about it, rather than alarmed. When we get back to the house Autumn's phone rings. It's Gideon. She sits on the deck and listens intently, only uttering the occasional "Alright" or "Okay."

"Well?" I say anxiously.

"We're invited on a sunset cruise tonight aboard Gideon's yacht to watch the wildfire from the ocean. He says he'll transfer the money then and there."

"You're joking."

"He said Brooks is still upset that he didn't get to deliver his speech, so Gideon's invited some of the key people from last night's party to come out on the boat, ogle the fire, and listen to Brooks."

"I was going to say it sounded like a trap, but if he does have all these people coming along...How big is this boat?"

"It's too-much-money big."

"We should check it out, make sure he's telling the truth about all these people joining the fun. In fact, I'm going to go there right now and see if any Lodestar guys are swabbing the decks. Where is this yacht?"

"Marina Del Rey in basin A. That's where the big boys dock, but you'll need to know its name."

"Okay, I'll bite: what nautical pun did he use?"

"No pun. It's called *The Trickle Down.*"

I can't help laughing. "Jesus, Gideon really has no shame, does he?"

"You haven't seen anything yet, Tom," says Autumn, but she isn't amused.

The Audi's looking the worse for wear, so I take a blue BMW from the garage after I transfer my gun and a pair of binoculars from the other car. This evening's excursion is going to be casual, so I don't need to worry that my suit is, almost literally, toast. Traffic is stop and go almost all the way, and I don't get to Marina Del Rey until three o'clock. The roads around the marina are named after South Seas destinations, and the U-shape of Basin A is bracketed by Tahiti Way and Bora Bora Way. The parking is only for residents of the condos that encircle the basins, so I'll have to do a quick drive-by. *The Trickle Down* is most of a football field long and is docked at the far end of Bora Bora Way. Two vans from a catering company are parked near it, and some of the staff from last night's party are moving containers from the vans to the ship. There are no Lodestar faces around, but I only have time for a quick glance.

I drive around to the public parking lot on the other side of the marina, directly across the main channel from *The Trickle Down.* The place is busy with weekenders coming and going on fishing charters, people out for a walk, and others trying to get into overcrowded waterside restaurants. Seagulls scream overhead telling everyone to go home.

I find a spot at a railing overlooking the channel and study Gideon's vessel through my binoculars. It has three decks and looks more like an expensive condominium than a ship; lots of chrome and tinted glass, several different shades of highly-polished hardwood, and gleaming white surfaces. The crew, uniformed in navy-blue shorts and scarlet golf shirts, are as attractive and perfectly-formed as their ship.

A curving balcony juts out of the side of the ship, just above the main deck. A charcoal glass door leading onto the balcony slides open and Gideon, shirtless, his ivory hair unloosed, steps out. He leans on the balcony railing and stares down into the water, spits, and then speaks to someone in the room behind him. A moment later a face peeks around the edge of the door. It's Gideon's black girlfriend, and she tries to hand out a bottle of water to him. He impatiently beckons her to come over, apparently annoyed that she wants him to move away from the railing. She hesitates before dashing out to hand him the bottle and then darting back. She's naked. Gideon laughs and says something else. One of his Slavic girlfriends, also naked, comes to the door and answers him. Gideon chugs his water and then goes back inside, the door closing behind him smoothly and slowly—I imagine it making the squeaking noise of an airlock on a spacecraft.

After another hour of watching the ship I haven't seen any sign of Lodestar people. I drive back to Malibu and kill time reading on the deck while Autumn goes out shopping with two of her friends. I'm relaxed, even though I'm certain Gideon will be plotting against us. He didn't get that yacht by being forgiving or generous, but there's nothing more I can do to alter the course of events; anyway, I don't have a good track record when I try and do that sort of thing.

I don't bother bringing a gun when we leave for Marina Del Rey. The occasion is, after all, a kind of armistice signing, even though I'm sure it's really only a ceasefire. We arrive at the dock and find an area has been set aside for guest parking instead of the usual valet service. About a dozen guests are standing on the main deck near the prow, attended to by a waiter serving drinks.

Gideon is at the top of the ship's gangplank, but he only gives us a quick nod as we come aboard; he's deep in conversation with a fit, wiry, bald man in his sixties who looks familiar.

"Is that..?" I ask.

"Yes," says Autumn. "Brian Willett."

I remember him as the smirking star of thrillers and cop movies from thirty years ago that I used to watch on DVD when I was a kid. We pass through a smoked glass door into a salon that's nearly half the length of the ship. Like Gideon's house, it has the look of an expensive hotel lobby: broad, overstuffed chairs and sofas, glass coffee tables and a long bar against one wall. There's a couple of dozen guests milling around, including Gideon's wife and Mei. As we pass through the crowd to get to the front of the ship, I hear several of them chattering excitedly about seeing the wildfire from the ocean. One voice says, "If I'm lucky, I'll get to see the Prentice's house burn. He and his wife wouldn't grant us an easement for an access road for our place in Telluride, so, karma, baby."

The crowd at the front of the ship includes Cordell, Pinder, Gantry, and Brooks Newcastle and his wife, who clings to his arm and wears enormous sunglasses. Cotton isn't anywhere in sight; I might have spooked him. He can't have been pleased to see someone from Hexum.

Brooks shields his eyes against the sun and nods wisely as he's lectured by a pallid young man wearing an odd combination of yellow Bermuda shorts paired with a pink dress jacket, white shirt and green bow tie. And then I remember that he's the host on a news network and the goofy attire is his gimmick. Brooks is fit and trim like a recently retired athlete.

Autumn sighs. "Well, this bunch is the absolute fucking distillate of all the dullest people from last night's party."

"How can you say that? That man has a green bow tie."

"Oh, God, that asshole. I'm going back inside to talk to Mei. I don't suppose Gideon's going to seal our deal until later. Are you okay on your own, honeybunch?"

"Don't leave me too long, darling. I'll get lonely."

Autumn sticks her tongue out and then retreats to the interior of the ship. I get a drink and sit on a sofa well away from anyone else. For no particular reason a tendril of optimism creeps into my thoughts, but I know well enough to devalue this pleasant sensation. I'm getting some chilly side-eye from Gantry and Jasper, and blank looks from others who don't recognize me as part of their crowd or are puzzled by my jeans and less than pristine sneakers. I'm distracted by a long V of pelicans that wheel low overhead like an aerobatics team before kissing down onto the water, and when I look back Carmen is making a beeline for me. She's carrying a very full drink, a mojito, by the look of it, and as she sits near me on the sofa, she makes an inaccurate attempt to sip from it and spills a few drops onto her knee.

With the measured determination of the self-conscious drunk she says, "Hello, I'm Carmen."

Despite the sunglasses, I can see that one of her eyes is puffy and half-closed. She's younger than Brooks, blonde, is wearing a short, tight white dress, and has the polished, generic good looks of a beauty pageant contestant.

"I'm Tom."

Carmen nods slowly, takes a sip, and says quietly in a delicate Southern accent, "Nice to meet you, Tom. Jesus is my saviour. I tell that to every new person I meet. It's how I spread the word of the Lord. You see, I used to party a lot in college, and Jesus saved me."

"From what?"

"Partying."

"That's bad?"

"I *really* liked to party. It's what I was best at; all weekend, all summer, all year. Party. There were videos of me partying on YouTube."

"Did you meet Brooks when you were partying?"

She looks towards her husband, who's talking to Brian Willett and grinning like a fanboy. "No. After. He was looking for a Christian wife and found me."

She doesn't sound happy that Brooks found her.

A vibration runs through the ship and we begin to pull away from the dock. Carmen bites her lip and looks anxiously at the receding dock.

"You okay?" I ask.

"I hate being on this boat." She breathes deeply, and then says apologetically, "I mean; I don't like boats very much."

Gideon comes out from the salon, catches sight of us, and ambles over, a smile on his face for Carmen, but nothing for me. Carmen looks down at the deck.

"Lovely as always, Carmen. Brooks will be proud to have you by his side for his speech. Your beauty is a perfect frame for his ambition."

Carmen makes an inarticulate sound and takes a long drink.

"Wow," I say. "I'm sure you stole that line from an old movie, Gideon; say it again in a louche French accent and it might come back to me."

He pretends not to have heard my comment, but there's anger in his eyes, and in a tense voice he tells Carmen: "We'll see each other later."

Gideon pivots away and joins Brooks, gripping him by an elbow and whispering in his ear. Brooks gives Carmen a stern look, as though she was a badly-behaved pet. She jumps up with a gasp and goes inside the ship.

As we leave the marina and turn north, the setting sun is bronzing the water. There are no waves, just a slight swell that makes the ocean appear to breathe, and in the distance the smoke from the wildfire is drawing a dark curtain across the sky. I close my eyes and concentrate on the cries of the gulls following the ship; the human voices around me make less sense.

"See, I told you these were the dullest of the dull; they've put you to sleep," Autumn says as she sits beside me. "I saw Carmen with you. How is she?"

"Apparently, she doesn't party anymore, but she's a bit drunk and afraid of Brooks. He was expecting a sober beauty queen beside him for his speech, so she got a dirty look from him that sent her running."

"Was she going on about her partying? She mentions it obsessively because she wants to go back to those days. It's actually Gideon that she's terrified of."

"How so?"

"Little things I've noticed since I've known her; like she only drinks when he's around."

"She said something about hating this boat."

"Well," she says drily, "that would explain things."

"How?"

"I've heard stories about Gideon and his pleasure ship."

"Such as?"

"Women who come aboard expecting to find other guests discover that they're the solo attraction on a trip to international waters where the laws against administering roofies are lightly enforced, especially on a ship registered in Liberia."

"And Gideon would take his daughter-in-law one of these trips?"

"It would be irresistible to him. He can, and has, paid for all kinds of women; his concubines, for example. What Gideon wants most of all is what his money can't buy him, but blackmail, coercion and drugs can. Me, for example. It's all rape in the end, but he sees it, and enjoys it, as proof of his genius, just like the insurance scam. Gideon doesn't regard it as rape, he thinks he's won a battle of wits with his victim. He's one of those men, the ones who are gargoyles inside and out, who think their looks and their character can be transformed by money and the cunning of a pimp."

"He'll be gone soon."

"I've been thinking about that. You know how we can really screw the great white hunters? Kill Gideon tonight."

"Tonight?"

"People fall overboard. We only need to be alone with him for a few seconds. If he dies right now, the whole deal falls apart. All the insurance payouts go to shell companies he controls, so if he's dead, there's no way for the others to get their money."

"If he's dead it's possible the insurance claims don't even go forward. Interesting, but I'm not sure dropping him over the side is going to be that easy. Look." I point to the small, black dome of a surveillance camera mounted on the face of deck above us. "Those are all over the ship; I saw them when I was watching it this afternoon."

"Damn."

"It's possible there's a blind spot somewhere, but there's still the problem of forty or fifty pairs of eyes on board. I'll take a walk and check. Did you talk with Gideon again about transferring the money tonight?"

"I did, right after I left you out here. He was cool about it, and that makes me suspicious. To do the transfer he wants really specific information—bank transit numbers, and so on. He also said the money will come in a series of transfers from different banks and companies; four million tonight, and larger amounts over the next forty-eight hours. If he wasn't so eager to do this, I'd be fine with it, but something doesn't feel right about his attitude."

"Yes, he's was happy to have us killed, and now he wants to shower us with riches. Let me think about it while I look around the ship."

We take a slow walk all around the main deck. There isn't single inch of the ship that isn't in view of a camera. We finish up at the stern and watch the ship's creamy wake dissipate in the distance.

Autumn points at a section of the stern that looks like it's folded into the rest of the ship, and asks, "If that was deployed, do you think it could be seen by a camera?"

"First of all, what is it?"

"A water sports deck. It swings down and floats off the back of the ship so you can swim from it, dock ski-jets, that sort of thing."

"If you were in the water near the deck you'd be out of sight; get farther out and the cameras will see you. But how do we get Gideon to lower it and use it?"

Autumn uses her most seductive smile. "Do you honestly think he could turn down skinny dipping with me?"

"Really? And how about all the people watching?"

"What people? After the speech they're premiering Brian Willet's latest movie in the theater on the deck below this one. Gideon's one of the producers."

"I thought the idea was to dump him over the side while the ship's underway."

"I have another idea. And if it doesn't work, I'll have had a lovely swim. Any thoughts on the money?"

"The initial four million sounds like bait. It's big enough that we believe he's serious, but it's small enough that he doesn't mind not getting it back. There are two possibilities: he's delaying on more payments while he makes sure the links between himself and the insurance claims are invisible so he can stiff us on the rest of the money, or he's giving time to Lodestar to regroup and eliminate us. I favor the latter."

"So what you're saying is that's it's wiser to kill him rather than take a penny of his money."

"Uh huh."

"If I refuse to take his money tonight, he's going to think something's up."

"Tell him you're having second thoughts about where you want the money to go; say that you want to organize a more secure offshore account first. Or just make sure your plan works and we get to raise a toast to Gideon in a few days when he washes up in front of the beach house."

"Ooh, you've sold me on that image alone. Fuck all this talk about money; that's their language, and I don't want to use it anymore. Let's go hear what Gideon's idiot son has to say and have a good laugh. And, if I have to, I'll throw Gideon off the ship right in front of the cameras and say he was trying to rape me."

January 14, 1986

I didn't say a word on our ride back to the house. Amy made a few attempts to talk, but quickly sensed I was not in the mood. My thoughts were entirely taken up with the lie Levi had told her about my mother abandoning us halfway to California. When we got back home, Levi was mooching around the house and whining that he'd wanted to go out and eat, but we'd taken too long and now he wasn't hungry. He'd been drinking, which meant his workday had been unpleasant, and I knew that if Amy wasn't with us, I would've been in line for a beating. He had that angry, self-pitying look that was often the preface to violence, and as I watched him curse under his breath and stalk around as though looking for something hidden, I felt more detached from him than ever; he had lied about Anne twice, his second fabrication probably coming from forgetfulness and a weak attempt to gain Amy's sympathy. but I was also queasily wondering if he was doing it to cover his tracks in some way. It was then that I decided to move out of the house.

Amy got him calmed down and they went out to eat after I told them I wanted to stay at home. Levi seemed happy with my decision. The minute they left, I got on my bike and drove straight to Reinhart's house. He wasn't at home, so I cruised around town looking for him.

There appeared to be more blingy pickups and SUVs on the streets than ever before, and the brothel on Lincoln was as busy as Christmas Day; a group of men standing on the lawn were shouting up at two women on a third-floor balcony, begging them with comical piteousness to show their tits. I parked on Main St. and waited for Reinhart to make an appearance—he was bound to drive up or down it at some point.

It was about an hour before sundown and most of the people on the sidewalks were hurrying to get their errands done and get home. The ones who weren't hurrying, all men, leaned against their big vehicles and shouted to each other or nodded along to the heavy beats coming out of their stereos. Hexum's civilians didn't want to be on Main after dark when the men who lounged around got angry or excited. They were like Transylvanian villagers hurrying to get behind locked doors before loud, rowdy vampires came alive.

Reinhart appeared just as it began to get dark. The lights on his cruiser were flashing as he pulled over a dark blue Buick sedan that glowed it was so polished. The car turned into a side street opposite me and pulled to the curb with Reinhart right on its bumper. I crossed the street as Reinhart, his gun drawn, got out of the cruiser and quietly told the driver to get out. The man who emerged from the car was fortyish, dressed in black jeans and T-shirt, bearded, and had tattoos covering both heavily-muscled arms. He looked amused and held his hands out, palms facing Reinhart, as though he was about to perform a magic trick and wanted to prove he wasn't hiding coins or cards.

"Can I help you, sir?" asked the man in a mocking tone, and took the cigarette he had in the corner of his mouth and flicked it away.

Reinhart was standing about ten feet from him at this point and said calmly, "You're not allowed in Hexum, you know that."

"What?"

"No Dogs, ever."

"I'm just passing through town, man, not wearing a patch or anything; saw a friend, now I'm leaving."

"Black Dogs don't have friends in Hexum, or Grange County, for that matter." Reinhart noticed me approaching. "Hey, Tom," he said cheerfully, "do me a favor and cuff this tourist."

He passed me his handcuffs and told the man to turn around, put his hands behind his back and rest his chin on the roof of his car. The bearded man looked at me with surprise but did as he was told. I put the cuffs on his thick wrists after some instruction from Reinhart, who went to his cruiser and spoke on the radio briefly.

"You can't afford real cops anymore?" shouted the man at Reinhart.

Reinhart came over and put a friendly hand on the man's shoulder and said. "Tom, here, is worth two of your kind. You just relax and stay as you are for a while."

We backed off to the cruiser, and I asked Reinhart in a low voice, "Who's he?"

"Cody Grau. He's a biker, member of the Black Dogs out of Portland. They've got chapters in Sacramento and Oakland, as well. Bikers aren't allowed in Grange County, and they all know it. We do business with them, but they've got to stay on the outside, like camp followers. Grange County is kind of like a national park or nature preserve; we have very strict rules to protect the inhabitants. If the bikers got a toe in, well..." He threw his hands up violently to indicate disruption or destruction.

Another police cruiser pulled up beside us and two deputies got out. I'd seen them around town dozens of times, spoken to them once or twice, but now Reinhart introduced them to me: Vin Creasy was a beanpole of a man in his twenties with a perpetual look of surprise on his face and a voice that rarely rose above a whisper. His partner, John Stockman, was pushing forty and all muscle, his uniform clearly, and purposely, a size too small to show off his work in the gym. He had a habit of looking worriedly into the distance when speaking, as if on alert for enemies approaching over the horizon.

"Hiya, Sheriff," said Stockman.

"Did you bring them?" asked Reinhart.

Creasy reached into his cruiser and pulled out a pair of bolt cutters. The three of them went over to the biker, who's mouth went quickly from a grin to hanging open.

"What the fuck?" said the biker.

"Every tourist," said Reinhart, "needs a souvenir to remember a place by. We're all out of Hexum snow globes, so we're going to give you something else."

"What the fuck?" said the biker again, only now he started backing away.

Stockman moved forward and punched Grau in the stomach. He fell to his knees gasping for air as Creasy moved behind him, kicked him in the back to knock him to the ground facedown, and then knelt on him.

"Right or left?" whispered Creasy to no one in particular.

Grau got his breath back and cried out, "What? Why?"

"Left," chirped Reinhart.

Creasy wrenched Grau's left hand up and in one smooth movement brought the bolt cutter into position and snipped off the pinky finger. Grau let out a deep, vibrating groan. Creasy pulled him to his feet while Reinhart picked the finger up and held it delicately in front of the biker's face.

Reinhart waited until Grau had stopped making noises and said, "Something to remind you of your day in Hexum. Now, when your friends suggest a trip to Grange County, you show them your souvenir and tell them that they'll get one of these too if they come for a visit."

Reinhart carefully placed the finger in the biker's front pocket, took the cuffs off him, and opened the Buick's door like an attentive car jockey. Creasy gave the man a shove towards the car and he stumbled his way behind the wheel, curses replacing his pained cries. He tucked his maimed hand under his right armpit, started the car, and did a slow U-turn back to Main St.

"He didn't even thank me," said Reinhart in a hurt voice, "for not clipping his right hand. No one's going to miss the pinky on their left hand."

Creasy looked sadly at his pants, which were covered in blood. "Can I go home and change, Sheriff? My legs feel sticky."

"Certainly, Vin. And don't forget to save the cleaning bill; that's line of duty damage, so it's not coming out of your pocket."

"Thanks, Sheriff."

Creasy and Stockman got in their cruiser and left.

Reinhart looked down at the blood spatters on the asphalt and shook his head. "This doesn't look good." He went to the back of his cruiser and took out a sealed, white plastic bucket, brought it over to the bloodstains, took the lid off, and scattered what looked like cat litter on the blood. "That's better. It's just like graffiti, Tom; if you don't clean it up right away it encourages other people to make a mess. So, what brings you out tonight?"

"I was hoping you could help me find a place to live. I want to move out, live on my own. I can pay rent; I've got lots saved."

Reinhart said nothing at first. He put the bucket back in the car, then leaned against the front bumper, took his hat off and ran his fingers through his hair as he always did when serious thinking was called for.

"Is this about that girl Amy he's got now?"

"No. This is about Levi."

"So, what were you planning to do living on your own?"

"I want to go to school, get my high school diploma. And do some work for you, part-time, errands and stuff, if you need that kind of thing. Just for money to live on; I don't need a lot."

Reinhart looked at me intently and asked, "And after this high school diploma? What then?"

I knew the answer he wanted and I gave it to him: "Be a deputy here. I'd have to go to police college or something, wouldn't I? And I'd need at least a diploma for that, right?"

He put his hat back on and said slowly, "You sign on with me, Tom, and it's a big commitment. I'm not saying I'd need help from you often, but when I do, you'd have to come running, school or no school. And you might see and hear some things that aren't too pretty, like tonight, but that's the price for keeping Hexum orderly and free of the wrong kind of people. This is one of the last true American towns, Tom. We have some bad folks, sure, and our ways of doing things don't always accord with what you'd call proper civic etiquette, but that's what makes us special: we have the spirit that built this country. Lots of it. So, if you ever wonder why I'm asking you to do something difficult, keep in mind that you're working to a higher purpose. Can you live with that?"

"Yes, I can," I said firmly.

Reinhart grinned and shook my hand. "Don't worry about anything, Tom. I'm sure Levi will understand that you're of a pioneering disposition. Plenty of boys of your age in history struck out on their own and did great things: settled land, found gold, fought Indians. You've accomplished so much already, and one day I would be proud to see you in this uniform. I'll let you know when I find a place for you to bunk."

After he'd driven away, I went and sat on my bike. The men who had been loafing by their big vehicles were leaving their roosts, peeling away from the curb with shrieks of rubber and window-rattling bass growls. I'd lied to Reinhart. I figured to stay in Hexum only until I had a diploma and then move to L.A. or San Francisco, or maybe go back east and look for Anne. I'd considered leaving Hexum right away—a fantasy, really—but realized immediately that as a fourteen-year-old I'd have no place to live. Levi's feelings, or what he might do when he found out I was leaving, didn't worry me much; he'd only ever needed me as an uncritical audience for his boasts and fruitless plans, or as a punching bag for his bouts of self-loathing. He had Amy now, and she took the edge off his anger, if not his grandiose visions. I wondered, with a sickening sense of guilt, why he didn't beat her. Why was I, his only child, the one that had been thrashed and not a stranger? I had some worry that Levi would turn on Amy once I left, but I stuffed that thought away with other things I couldn't bear to think about.

Four days later, Reinhart came to the house early in the morning. Levi was away overnight somewhere, and I was helping Amy saddle the horses as he drove into the yard. He left his cruiser and came over to the paddock, leaning his elbows on the top rail of the fence and greeting both of us.

Turk ambled over to the newcomer with a friendly snort, but Reinhart backed away from the fence and asked, "Does he bite? I got bitten by a horse once and it hurt some."

"No, never," said Amy.

"Tom," said Reinhart with stiff formality, "I've found you a home."

"Oh," was my weak response. Although Reinhart had always come through for me, I hadn't expected this moment to arrive so quickly.

"What home?" asked Amy with alarm.

In a hollow voice I said, "I'm moving out."

She dropped Toby's reins. "But why?"

I didn't know what to say, and I discovered that I felt worse about leaving her behind than I did Levi.

"You and Levi will have the place to yourselves. Anyway, I'll come back and visit; we can still go riding."

"You don't have to go, Tom," she begged. "I know you don't get along great with your dad, but I can work on him, get him to..." Her voice trailed off as she tried, and failed, to find some link that could be repaired between Levi and myself.

"We can go right now, Tom," Reinhart said brightly. "You can't have much to take."

I didn't. My clothes went in two garbage bags, the books in a couple of cardboard boxes, and I filled another box with odds and ends—pictures, CDs, posters and my Walther. Amy stayed in the paddock and groomed Toby in a mechanical way as I brought my stuff out to the cruiser. After I'd loaded everything, I remembered a fat manila envelope Levi kept on a shelf in the living room in which he kept what he considered important documents. I went back inside and rummaged through bills and warranties until I found my birth certificate. I'd seen him take it out of the envelope about a year ago and look at it with curiosity.

I told Reinhart I'd follow him on my bike, but before we left, I went over to Amy, who was taking Toby's saddle and reins off.

"Just call me if you want to go riding,"

"Sure," she said, her expression more scared than sad. As I started my bike she shouted, "What shall I tell Levi?"

"Nothing. Same as he told me."

I hadn't asked Reinhart what he'd found for me or where it was. I'd assumed it would be some poky place above a store, or a spot in one of the big old houses that had been chopped up into apartments. He led me all the way to the north edge of town, where the houses gave way to an undulating prairie of sagebrush spiked with the occasional, lonely cottonwood tree. The last street on this side of Hexum was Cypress Ave, and the house at the end of it, sitting far from its nearest neighbours, was what Reinhart had chosen for me. It was like an outpost overseeing the prairie; a small, stucco bungalow faded to the palest shade of yellow. The sidewalk in front of it, like most in Hexum, was a cracked, weedy mess, but the front yard was tidy, and a young willow tree threw shade over half the house. There was even a short driveway to one side and a detached, clapboard garage.

Reinhart pulled into the driveway, bounced out of the cruiser and said, "I can't believe I didn't think of this place sooner."

I hopped off my bike, hoping the house was mine, but thinking I'd be sharing it with someone. Reinhart opened the front door with a key and ushered me inside.

The house had two bedrooms, an L-shaped living room, a narrow bathroom, and a galley kitchen. It was completely furnished with pieces that looked like they might come from an old motel. Gaudy oil paintings of mountain landscapes and ocean sunsets cluttered the walls. The air in the house was stale and had a dusty, vegetable smell, but everything was clean and orderly, and the kitchen cupboards were full of canned goods, mostly soups and baked beans. A picture window in the living room looked out over the sea of silvery green sagebrush that, to the east, lapped up against the foothills. The backyard was a rectangle of grass that was surrendering to the brush.

"Whose place is this?" I asked.

"Somebody who's not coming back. He had a hunting accident."

"What do I pay for it?"

"Nothing. The guy who lived here had a bank account that everything was paid out of automatically. He didn't have a mortgage, so it's just utilities. I think there's still lots left in his account. Anyway, enough to last you for a good long while."

I knew better than to ask the man's name or the nature of his hunting accident.

Reinhart left after helping me move my stuff out of his cruiser and bag up the men's clothes we found in a dresser and wardrobe in one of the bedrooms. In the unlikely event anyone came asking for the former resident, Reinhart advised me, I should refer them to him. Immediately.

After he'd gone, I sat in the backyard on a lawn chair I'd found stacked with three others against the back wall of the house. A breeze twitched the brush into life, and my mind wandered as I tried to come to grips with my new situation. I felt I should be happy about my independence, my freedom from Levi, but I knew that I now belonged to Reinhart, and I worried that the debts I owed him would eventually become a burden. I'd seen the awful things he could do when he wasn't angry, and I found myself imagining what he'd do if betrayed.

I didn't see Levi again until a week later. I was at Mission Commons, about to go into an electronics store to buy my first computer, when his pickup, the voice of Howard Stern blaring from it, jerked to a stop across the width of three parking spaces outside the store. He turned off the engine and leaned out his window like he was going to give an order at a drive-thru.

"You don't stick around to say goodbye?"

His face was slack, eyes unfocused, and I couldn't tell if he was drunk or stoned or a combination of both. It was an unpleasant look for him.

"You don't bother to come see me until you run across me here?" I said.

He had to think about that for a while.

"Why?" he finally asked.

I considered saying something about his beatings or Amy, or simply that I could only tolerate my own company, but they would all be full or partial lies, and I didn't care about lying to him any longer.

"You told Amy some bullshit about Anne leaving us at a truck stop. She never ran away with a guy, you just took me."

His fried mind was fumbling for a response, and in the meantime his face skipped through different expressions like a ventriloquist's dummy in the hands of an amateur.

"I just wanted to tell Amy something...really sad. So she'd feel sorry for you. So she'd like you." He searched his mind some more. "Your mom went off with a guy—really."

"Who?"

"I don't know. Some guy who'd just got out of prison. A loser. You mark my fucking words; she'll have come to a bad end with him."

Until that moment the worst I'd thought about Levi was that he'd stolen me away from my mother from some pathetic desire to raise his only son, the inheritor of the Bridger name. But I knew the way he exaggerated and lied too well by then, and when he used the words "a bad end," sounding like something out of an old movie or novel, I knew the truth was something darker.

"Is Anne dead?"

"No," Levi said quickly, and then, "I don't know. Probably not. If she's still with that guy, who knows? She did come with us halfway here, you've just forgotten; you were too young. If she didn't leave us, she'd be here now, right?"

His lies were a building collapsing floor by floor. He couldn't decide which of them worked best, and he knocked everything down looking for the right one. I felt sick, and almost certain that my mother wasn't alive. If she was living, she would have tried to find me and would have succeeded by now. A thin vein of hope still ran through me; I wanted to believe that she had left us if only so she'd still be out there somewhere.

"We don't need to see each other anymore, Levi," I said coldly, then walked into the store. I turned and watched Levi through the store's tinted windows. He stared at the door I'd just come through, and then after a minute he made a dismissive gesture, said something to himself, and drove away.

The next day, after I'd got the computer up and running, I typed my mother's name into a search engine. Nothing came up that I could make any sense of, and I instantly regretted having done it. I didn't know what I was more terrified of: seeing some evidence that she was dead or of finding her alive, contacting her, and then having her say that she wanted nothing to do with me. I doubted the latter would happen if she was alive, but the mere chance that it *could* stopped me from exploring further on the internet. I was confident that Levi was lying, but his words had poisoned me, and I put off any more searches into an undefined future.

The pleasure of living on my own soon drove away gloomy thoughts about Anne. I had new territory to explore, on foot and by bike, and the computer became a friend and a hobby. The first few weeks in the house I indulged myself in all-night sessions watching movies or playing on the computer, but then I began to think about going to school in the fall and how that would be my means of escape from Hexum, and I worried that my vampire hours might become a habit I couldn't break come September. I adopted a more regular routine, forcing myself to rise early and study Spanish and math before going out to do errands or roam towards the horizon. Sometimes, in the evenings, just before it became too dark to see well, I'd sit in the backyard and watch coyotes patrolling the brush, hunting out the plentiful rabbits. Later, a great horned owl that lived in a tree at the edge of my property would call out the arrival of night and glide away like a small, dark cloud. After a couple of months, I lost the nagging feeling that I was trespassing in the house. It was mine now, and I thought of it as a fort I'd earned, if not built.

Reinhart put me to work soon enough. I had two main jobs: driving and counting. The drug business in Grange County involved a lot of vehicles carrying men and equipment from the town to plots and labs in the wilderness and vice versa, and still more vehicles carrying the finished products out of the county. I drove empty vehicles, usually older, full-size vans, from place to place, leaving them where they'd be used later for various deliveries. Reinhart explained that using his own men or Jubal's for these jobs would be a waste of specialist resources. Besides, he told me, he didn't like seeing his men behind the wheel of crappy vehicles while in uniform. Similarly, the counting job was important, but not one he wanted uniforms doing. Reinhart needed to know how much product was moving out of the fields and labs. It was my job to count the bales and bricks and boxes being put in the vans that then fanned out to every corner of the state, and over the mountains to Nevada and Utah. The count was necessary, explained Reinhart, so that the correct amount of "city tax" could be paid. This wasn't a full-time job; I was filling in for others who did the work or helping out when things got busy. I drove or counted about three or four times a week, always alone, and Reinhart would slip me five hundred dollars for this work each week, sometimes more.

The labs were mostly in town, inside disused buildings that were formerly garages or small factories. Others were out in the hills, concealed in old mine workings that dated back to the nineteenth century. The copper mine that took over Caleb's property was the last working mine in the area, but at one time more than two dozen gold and silver mines had gnawed into the land. Now the tunnels held men, usually Asian, cooking up meth, while just outside the tunnel entrances generators ran night and day to give the labs power and light.

The weed farms were tucked away in valley bottoms or on steep, south-facing hillsides. The biggest operations were worked by Latino laborers. They lived in tents on-site or biked out from the big dorm houses in Hexum to the farms nearest town. I practiced my Spanish with them, and by the end of the summer I could manage halting conversations. There were also smaller plots that were run by the men—always white—who owned them. These guys invariably bitched and argued about the count and would not-so-jokingly try and sneak bales into the vans.

Two of the worst were the McSweeney brothers, Dale and Henry. Their half-acre plot was in a clearing beside a clear, cold creek no wider than a long stride that burst from a spring at the bottom of a cliff face. Reinhart said that the McSweeneys would probably make more money bottling the water and selling it in San Francisco than they got from their dope. The brothers were from some godforsaken west Texas town near Fort Stockton, and when they weren't complaining about my count or what they had to pay to Reinhart, they'd argue with each other about all things football—as it related to Texas—in twangy accents that I found hard to understand. The pair were notorious for going into Hexum and starting fights in bars, restaurants, stores, and brothels. Most of these fights began when one or both of them would declare that their status as "sovereign citizens" meant that they didn't have to follow this or that rule, such as paying the sales tax on a restaurant bill.

The McSweeneys bitterly, and loudly, resented that "a small boy" was in charge of the count. I laughed out loud the first time they said this because I was nearly six feet tall by then and they were easily a few inches below me. Both were in their early thirties and had deep-set eyes that were permanently and deeply suspicious of the world—they even looked askance at clouds drifting overhead. They had pot bellies, but skinny arms and legs which made them look like a pair of dusty, angry spiders. Based on the cellophane wrappers and sun-faded soda cans their land was awash in, they were living on nothing but Coke and Little Debbie cakes.

The fourth time I went out to the Sweeneys place Reinhart came with me; the pair had been getting more evasive with the count and needed a word from him. Dale was the yappier of the two, and as soon as he saw Reinhart, I could tell he was going to act up.

Dale put down the bale of grass he was carrying and hollered, "Your fuckin' kid is rippin' me off, Sheriff. He counts extra so he gets paid extra, I know it."

"He's not my kid, Dale, and if I trust him, you have to trust him; it's as simple as that. Try doing a better job of growing your crop instead of bitching. Any competent grower would have twice as much product if they had your soil and water."

"Me 'n Henry know what we're doing," hissed Dale, "and maybe we don't want to grow more'n we do now; anyway, we don't have a bunch of fuckin' greasers workin' for us like those assholes drivin' around town all day in their big, candy ass trucks. This is a proper American operation."

"Whatever, Dale, just don't argue about the count in future or someone who can make this land pay better might take your place."

Dale was bubbling with rage, but he could see that Reinhart was in one of his rare bad moods, so he stuck to muttering. Henry appeared, sipping a Coke, and the arrival of his brother gave Dale a small dose of courage, but only enough to confront me, not Reinhart.

He put his shoulders back and got right up in my face and said, "Listen, pretty boy, you just do your job right and me 'n Henry won't have to get tough on your ass."

Dale wanted to have the last word on someone, so he'd picked me. Reinhart didn't say anything, and I sensed that this moment had become a test.

"I don't know, Dale," I said agreeably, "the only thing I've ever seen you be tough on is a box of doughnuts."

He sucked in his breath and I knew there was only a split second before he reacted physically. I head-butted him so hard I saw stars. Dale fell onto his back, blood spurting from his flattened nose. Henry reached for the knife he kept on his belt and Reinhart had his gun out before Henry could even get his fingers on his weapon. Dale writhed in the dirt and made choking noises as blood poured down into his mouth.

"You hurt Dale," said Henry in a slow, amazed voice, and then took his hand away from his knife.

"He surely did," laughed Reinhart. "Now pick your brother up and earn a living instead of fooling around. And if either of you think about bothering Tom, just know it'll be the last thing you do."

I never went out to the McSweeneys again. Reinhart told me he approved of what I'd done, but it wasn't worth the risk to have me doing their count. In any case, the brothers disappeared from their land later that summer after they went to Redding and got thrown in jail for beating up a mall security guard.

Inevitably, I ran into Levi from time to time when I was working. We didn't avoid each other, but if we spoke it was only about some business at hand. Amy would call me if Levi was out of town and I'd go over and ride with her, and every now and then she'd show up unannounced at my house in the evening to watch TV. She told me that she liked a change of scenery and a different cable package. I enjoyed her company but couldn't stand her favorite shows—*Friends* and *ER*—and usually went on the computer while she watched them. After her shows were over, we'd talk about other TV programs or movies, her horses, and the ever-evolving plans for the Cirque du Rodeo. The day after her visits I'd be looking forward to the next one.

In late July I was worrying about the process of enrolling in high school. I was tempted to turn to Reinhart for help but decided this was something I wanted to do myself—there were only so many things I wanted to be indebted to him for. I went to Latimer and asked him how enrollment would work.

"Enrollment?" he said with surprise. "No more home schooling for you?"

"Different home, different rules."

"I see. Well, this being Hexum, things operate in a more informal way. Why don't you talk to the principal and see what can be arranged? There's always an arrangement to be made in Hexum."

"What's his name?"

"Parker Henshaw. I think he lives on Washington Ave."

Henshaw's house was in what passed for the better part of town. In style it was a smaller version of the brothel on Lincoln and was painted white with green window frames. Henshaw was in the front yard coiling up a garden hose when I came by. I was expecting someone older. He was in his thirties, heavily built with a flat top crewcut, and even though it was a hot day, and this was his summer vacation, he was wearing a white shirt and black tie. He looked at me with friendly curiosity as I came across the lawn towards him, probably thinking I was a student he didn't quite recognize.

"Can I help you?" he asked cheerily.

"Are you the high school principal? Parker Henshaw?"

"Yes."

"I need to go into high school this fall, but I've been home-schooled, so I don't have an academic record. Is there some kind of test I can take to get in?"

"Oh. There is, but there's a few other steps as well."

"I have my birth certificate."

"That's good," he said with a smile, "but why don't you introduce yourself first?"

"Tom Bridger."

Something in his eyes frosted over and his smile became a straight line. From inside the house I could hear children arguing over the rules of a game. I grew cold inside as I realized my name was a kind of dark spell.

He cleared his throat and said, "I…I suppose something could be done. Your parents—"

"I live by myself over on Cypress. I'll take a test anytime. I'm good at most things. How about here tomorrow?"

He looked nervously towards the house. "Uh, no. At the high school. I'll meet you at the main doors at twelve. Is that time alright for you? I can change it."

"Twelve's fine."

The high school was a long, one-storey cinder block building with narrow, rectangular windows near the roof line. It had once been painted white, but it was now flaking off in broad patches to reveal the gray of the bricks. As I walked up to its doors the next day, the place reminded me of a bigger version of some of the labs I visited.

Henshaw was already in the school and opened the door as soon as he saw me. We muttered "Hellos" to each other, and I went inside. The building was empty except for us, and the sound of our footsteps echoed sharply in the long hallways as I followed him to a classroom. A hazy light washed over the desks and chairs from grimy windows set high in the wall. The air was full of smells that were strange to me. Henshaw pointed to a desk on which there was a pen and a stack of papers. I sat down and looked through the papers. There were sheets with math problems, others with multiple choice questions about geography and history, and one with a single question at the top: *Name and describe your five favorite books and why you like them.* There were also some sheets of blank paper.

"You can start now, if you want," said Henshaw.

"Okay."

"And take your time, please."

He sat at the teacher's desk and started reading a copy of *Outdoor Life.*

I was done in just over an hour and had used all the blank sheets, front and back, to answer the books question. Henshaw took my work and started looking over it. After a few minutes he began throwing confused glances at me.

"Who home-schooled you?" he asked.

"Me."

"Oh."

He concentrated on my answers for a good fifteen minutes, looking up once to ask, "This book you like: *La Bête Humaine*? That's a French novel. You read French novels?"

"Yes. There's lots of action in it," I said defensively.

Henshaw riffled through the sheets a few times as though looking for something and then put them aside with a worried look on his face.

"Uh, I…What grade are you looking to go into?"

"Don't you decide that?"

"How old are you?"

"I was fourteen in January."

"I think maybe you could handle grade ten."

"There was no test on Spanish; isn't that a subject?"

Henshaw admitted that it was and tried speaking to me in it but gave up after I corrected his pronunciation twice. He sighed deeply and said that I would start in grade ten, and that I was to come to him if I had any academic problems. I followed him back to the entrance where he shook my hand and then let me outside.

Reinhart was parked directly in front of the school and gave me a wave as I came down the school's steps.

"How'd it go?" yelled Reinhart, leaning out of the driver's window.

"Good. I'm in grade ten. How did you know I was here?"

"Henshaw gave me a call yesterday, just to sniff out a bit about you, and I told him not to worry about all the paperwork. Go ahead and give him a test, I said, but I didn't tell him to make things easy for you. I told Henshaw he doesn't need to see a lot of documents or get a bunch of signatures. And he'll keep an eye out for you. He put you a grade ahead, did he? Probably so you'll be out of his school quicker."

This was the first time I was angry with Reinhart, but I didn't show it. I thanked him and he drove away. I'd wanted to settle the school issue myself, and, even though I suspected I would have had to contact him to smooth things over at some point, I hadn't wanted him in at the beginning.

A week before school began, I was out at a big growing operation on the eastern edge of Grange County, deep in the foothills. A team of Latinos were hauling bales up a long, dirt track to four waiting trucks, and I was chalking marks on each bale as it went by to let the loaders at the top of the slope know that it had been counted. The heat was infernal, flies were constantly in my face, there was no shade, and the men filing past sweating under their loads were rank. I had a headache and was thinking nervously about the start of school. Spencer was in charge of the trucks, and he came sliding and hopping down the slope towards me with a sour look on his face. He was wearing Utah Jazz shorts and T-shirt.

"Reinhart says you speak Mexican," Spencer snarled, "so tell these motherfuckers to sprint up the goddamn hill. It's too hot to wait around up there."

"I'm not in charge of this crew, you do it. Besides, it's no fucking picnic for them."

"You've grown into a big-headed, uppity little cunt, haven't you?"

"I'm too big for you now?" I said with mock astonishment. "Oh, that's right, you prefer toddler-size."

Spencer took a step forward and said, "You watch your mouth, shitbird."

"Or what? You won't buy me ice cream at the diner?" His hands tightened into fists. "Take another step and I'll kick your ass down this hill and bite your fucking throat out."

Spencer had height and weight on me, but he was soft. Levi had complained more than once that Spencer was "only tough with a crowd" and never got his hands dirty—one of the perks of being the boss's nephew. I stared back at him and hoped that he'd do something.

He pretended to be accidentally jostled by one of the men trudging up the trail, then turned around and shoved the man so violently he fell down, his bale splitting open when it hit the ground. Spencer charged back up the hill while the fallen man cried out in pain: his leg was bent under him at an odd angle. He was old, maybe in his sixties, and looked fearful as he tested his leg—if he couldn't walk, he couldn't work. I helped him up. His leg appeared to be okay, so he picked up the bale, thanked me and started limping up the track.

A minute later I heard shouting from the trucks. Spencer came into sight holding the old man by the collar and dragging him to the top of the hill. The man was still carrying the damaged bale, and Spencer was yelling at him to go back down and get it taped up. That was a twenty-minute round-trip for someone fit. The old guy stumbled a bit down the slope and screamed Spanish obscenities at Spencer that even he could understand. Spencer disappeared from view in the direction of the trucks while the man rubbed his knee and continued cursing at the top of his voice. A couple of laborers standing at the top of the hill jumped aside as Spencer came back holding a big automatic and one of them yelled, "¡Cuidado!"

The old man turned and cried out as Spencer started firing. He was a lousy shot; the first two bullets kicked high and went into the brush with a cracking sound, but he had a full clip, and I watched the rest of the rounds, seven or eight of them, tear through the old man's chest and neck. His body slid down the slope a good ten feet, his blood continuing for another twenty until the earth drank it all in.

Spencer pocketed the gun, gave me the finger, and went back to the trucks. The men carrying the bales started moving along the trail again, but no faster than before. A few of them crossed themselves as they stepped around the corpse. I marked the bales.

When school started, I immediately learned what my place was in Hexum among people who didn't move in the orbital field of Reinhart and Jubal: I was an invisible horror. No one looked at me or spoke with me, except teachers, and only when absolutely necessary. As I walked the hallways the other students edged out of my way and conversations died. Hexum was not a big place, and the things I'd done had been whispered about until rumors turned into grim myths. Also, working at the labs and farms meant that I was greeted and talked to on the streets by the men who owned the town after dark. Ordinary citizens saw this, and it marked me down as something to be avoided at all costs. In another age and place, a mob armed with torches and pitchforks would have been driven me outside the city gates.

I enjoyed the actual schoolwork, particularly math, which soothed me with its purity. English was torture because the pace of teaching was so slow. We were assigned *Oliver Twist* and told we'd be studying it for the entirety of the first term. I read it in two days and asked the teacher if I could go ahead and write whatever tests or essays she wanted done on the novel. The teacher, Mrs. Reynolds, clearly found it uncomfortable having me in her class, and she jumped at this opportunity, telling me that, if I wanted, I could just drop by to pick up or drop-off assignments—no need for me to attend class again. I could see the hopeful, pleading look in her eyes and agreed to her plan.

Reynolds must have mentioned her teaching plan for me to my other teachers, because within two weeks they had all suggested the same thing, one of them saying that I'd be a "remote" student, as though I was living in the Outback and getting my lessons by ham radio.

In early November I told Henshaw that I'd be on the "Reynolds" plan with all my teachers. He was as happy as a puppy. I'd been surprised, but not shocked, by my isolation from the other students; what made me decide to do school by correspondence course, as it were, was that my outlaw glamor had drawn a small group of boys to me. Some of them were wannabe gangsters and would misbehave in class with one eye on me as though seeking my encouragement or approval. Others were misfits or loners, and they thought an acquaintanceship with me would be the pixie dust that would charm away their freak status. In both groups I caught echoes of Caleb and Malachi, and that filled with me such intense dread it sickened me. I ignored their overtures of friendship, which only redoubled their desire to draw my attention. I daydreamed about being back in my house by myself, away from the neediness of these boys, and it was only a short step from there to leaving school.

A couple of girls took an interest in me. One, I found out later, wanted me to be her boyfriend so that she could convince me to beat up her father. The other was Jessica Munoz. She was a loner by virtue of her color. Hexum was a white town in practice, if not in fact. While there were plenty of Latino and Asian faces on the streets in certain parts of town, they were a cohort that was ignored and avoided, and had no children to send to school. Schools, businesses and the local government were all white. Jessica's parents were Puerto Rican and worked at the army base, and her chestnut skin was an unwanted reminder that Hexum's existence depended partly, maybe largely, on the workforce of its fearsome parallel world.

I'd been at school for a few weeks when Jessica, frowning with either anger or intense curiosity, stopped me in the hall and asked, "Did you put a kid on a bus for San Francisco about a year ago?"

I was so startled by this question I forgot to lie. "How did you hear about that?"

"My mother's friend Sylvia was on that bus. She said you scared the driver into taking the kid. Sylvia sat with the boy and he said you told him to go to the police and say he was lost."

"He *was* lost."

"Sylvia took him to a cop in the station and said she'd seen him wandering around. She knew better than to say he'd come from Hexum."

I didn't know what to say to that, and Jessica didn't wait until I'd thought of something. She hurried to her next class. The next time I met her was at Latimer's. She was standing in an alcove at the back where Latimer kept the science fiction and fantasy. We were equally surprised to see each other.

"I haven't seen you in here before," she said.

"I've been coming here for years. It's me who should be saying that."

"We moved to Hexum last September. I only found this place a few months ago."

"How do you like Hexum?"

"Not at all," she laughed drily. "Who could? I know you don't."

"How do you know that?"

"Your expression: you always look bored or suspicious or irritated."

I grinned as I considered that that was probably exactly how I looked most of the time, and said, "Maybe that's because of school."

"You're that way when I've seen you on the street, too."

"What are you getting?" I asked, pointing to the paperbacks she was holding.

She held up *Frankenstein* and *Renegades of Pern*. "You like sci-fi? Fantasy?"

"Mmm, not really."

"What do you read?"

"History. And novels set in other times and countries—places that don't remind me of here."

"You can't get further away from Hexum than outer space or Middle-earth."

"Hexum *is* in outer space, only the aliens look like me. You asked me one time about putting a kid on a bus: why?"

"It didn't agree with what people said about you. I wanted to check."

"Oh."

"See you."

She went to the front of the store and paid for her books. I followed a few minutes later.

Latimer put down his copy of *Heretics of Dune*, adjusted his nasty gray cardigan, and said, "She's tall."

"Uh huh."

"Nice looking."

"Yes."

"Good taste in books."

"No."

It was a few weeks later that I stopped going to school regularly. In that time Jessica and I would talk if we saw each other at school, often in Spanish once she knew I could manage the language. We'd mock our classmates and teachers or talk about things we'd seen or read. When I told her why I wouldn't be coming into classes anymore she shrugged and said, "I get it."

It was also about this time that I saw a change in Amy. Once school had started, I stopped going over for trail rides, and she wasn't dropping by in the evenings as frequently. In November, just after I'd quit school, I heard Levi was away for a few days and went to see her.

The first thing I noticed was that the horses weren't groomed to the usual high standard. They were cantering around in the paddock as though announcing they were ready for a ride. Amy was inside on the couch, half-passed out with the TV remote in one hand. A coffee stain ran down one leg of her sweatpants. There was no smell of weed in the house, so when she said hello as though trying to remember another language, I knew she was on something stronger.

"You okay, Amy?

"Fine," she said slowly.

"The horses look like they haven't been out for a while."

"I'm...fluish. Nothing serious, Tom. A little sad, maybe."

"Levi treating you alright?"

"He's away a lot. Too much."

I tried talking to her some more, but she was monosyllabic and seemed on the verge of nodding off. She came over to my place the next night and was more like herself, but from then on my contacts with her were less frequent. I would have missed her company, but Jessica more than took her place. One Saturday in December we met at Latimer's, which was becoming a regular thing, and she heard me talking to him about computers.

"You have a computer?" she asked with a gleam in her eye.

"Yeah, a Gateway."

She invited herself over to my place, and I spent the rest of the day teaching her how to use the computer. Her family couldn't afford or didn't want a computer, and she was mad to get her hands on one. It soon became a routine that she'd come over on the weekends, often all day, and play and work on the computer. She was also happy to get away from home. Her parents, Inez and Hector, fought a lot, largely over the issue of moving away from Hexum. Her father didn't want to go because of some promotion he thought he could get if he stayed.

It never crossed my mind that Jessica was my girlfriend or that we could have that kind of relationship. We felt more like a brother and sister. We'd fight over the computer, argue over what to watch on TV, and make fun of each other at every opportunity. But there was a comfort in having each other for company that we both needed desperately. She was an outcast at school, and I was an exile from the ordinary world. And we were united in two things: our loathing for Hexum and the imagined possibilities of a better life elsewhere.

The months ticked by and I began to feel that my life was now, for the first time, mostly pleasant. I'd numbed myself to the work I did for Reinhart and the things I saw and heard because of it, and I was saving money for the day when I could move away. School work remained a distraction, a kind of opiate, and something that I could hang my hopes on as part of my plan to leave Hexum.

Amy stopped coming over to my house when she learned about Jessica. I wasn't upset, although I told her it was okay if she kept visiting. She had become moody and quieter, and when she came over, I'd often notice her staring into space instead of watching her TV show. My trips to go riding with her became very infrequent, and she seemed to take part in them merely to please me. It didn't come as a total surprise when I went over one day and walked in to find her at the kitchen table about to inject herself. The house smelled of cigarettes and burnt food. Amy looked at me guiltily but continued methodically with the job. I sat down and let her finish.

"Heroin?"

She nodded. "Just a little something to take the spikiness out of the day. It's only when Levi's gone. I think too much when I'm alone."

"Why don't you go back to San Diego? You know lots of people there."

"I do, I do," she said, her eyelids lowering and an uncertain smile spreading across her face. She pointed to where she'd jabbed the needle. "But they like this shit, too. That's why I wanted to get away from there. Clean country living and all that."

"So when are you going to stop?"

She pulled herself up from the chair and said in a thick voice, "When I stop remembering this and that."

She moved slowly to the living room and flopped onto the couch. One of the unwritten rules of Hexum was that drugs could go out, but they couldn't come in. Heroin wasn't a made-in-Hexum product. I worried what would happen if Jubal or Reinhart found out about Amy's habit, or that Levi was probably supplying her. She was snoring gently as I left the house.

In April of 2001 I was riding with Reinhart in his cruiser when he got a call on the radio that there was piece of luggage that needed picking up. We were on our way to a lab on some errand, but Reinhart pulled over immediately and radioed back asking where it was. Behind the grain silos, was the answer.

"Damn," said Reinhart as he clicked off the radio. "Everybody off with the flu and now this." He looked over at me. "You're fifteen now, right?"

"Since January."

"And you've done every little thing I've asked of you and done it well. The day I get you in a uniform I won't have to worry or work half as much as I do now. But that's some ways off yet. We've got a little job to do that isn't so pleasant, but I think you're ready for it. It's only a bit of heavy lifting, really."

The two tall, wooden silos hadn't held grain in a very long time. They had become bleached sentinels guarding the western approaches to Hexum, their sagging roofs looking out over a prairie dotted with the ruins of other structures. The railway had once come here and carted away ore and cattle and grain. The buildings that had been part of that world had decayed into skeletal shapes poking out of the sagebrush like dangerous reefs in an ocean.

Reinhart and I walked in to the silos from the road along a low, narrow ridge that used to be the railway line. We found a man sitting on the ground, his back against the silo's ancient planks and his head slumped on his shoulder. He'd been shot through the left eye, and wore a yellow and black monocle of wasps that fed at the edges of the wound.

"Huh," said Reinhart. "I don't recognize him. You?"

"No."

The dead man was emaciated, white, maybe forty, with bad teeth and skin, and dressed in ragged clothes that were too large for him. Reinhart put on a pair of gloves and went through the man's pockets and pulled out a battered wallet that only held a driver's licence. Reinhart studied the picture on the licence.

"Damn. This says he's twenty-eight. He look twenty-eight to you?"

"He looks like an unwrapped mummy."

"I'll say. He's a tweaker, is what he is. This is what they end up looking like. I hope Jubal isn't behind this, because he knows he's got to clean up his own messes. Now, where to put him?"

"Doesn't he go to the morgue?"

"No. We like to keep our statistics simple in Grange County. You see, if we did the paperwork every time someone didn't die of natural causes, busybodies in Sacramento might start asking questions. People think a place this size should have a certain murder rate and we just fulfill their expectations. But then we have to get rid of the extras. You know, by my reckoning, killing someone is a piece of cake—it's getting rid of the body that's a pain in the ass. If you scamper back to the cruiser, you'll find a big old cardboard box in the back that's full of body bags; it'll be easier to drag him out if he's ziplocked."

We eventually got him in the back of the cruiser, and Reinhart drove towards the mountains and then down a rutted dirt road through a forest that had burnt in a wildfire the previous summer. Tufts of green new growth were appearing at the roots of the blackened and branchless pine trees. A few miles later, just past the burn, the road was blocked by a rockslide.

"That's us," said Reinhart, pointing at a pile of branches near the road.

We moved the branches away to reveal a round, stubby, brick chimney poking out of the ground that was exhaling a cool draft smelling of mold and water. I couldn't see to the bottom of it.

Reinhart pointed down into the darkness. "Know what this is? Ventilation shaft for one of the old mines. I've used this one before, but there's dozens of them around if you know where to look. Let's get our friend."

We left the one-eyed corpse in his black cocoon and tipped him down the chimney headfirst. His descent was almost noiseless and ended with a distant, thumping splash.

I got a hundred dollars for moving that piece of luggage, and others followed on an irregular basis. Reinhart had his own odd rationale for where he dumped bodies: the ones that had been murdered were fed down old mining shafts or dropped in inaccessible canyons and gullies that were often no more than slits in the ground. Overdoses were taken out to the remotest parts of the foothills and left in the open for scavengers to deal with. Reinhart told me that he didn't want to fill up his best hiding spots with degenerates. Every now and then a hunter would find remains in the wilderness, but if he was from Hexum he knew better than to say anything, and if anyone from the outside stumbled on bones, they were told it would be "investigated."

It was around this time that Jessica and I started sleeping together. She'd been on a three-week family visit to Puerto Rico and when she came through my door after getting back, we both found it wasn't enough just to say "Hi." The sex was something we'd both foreseen happening and thought about but had been hesitant to act on in case it freaked out the other person. We took precautions, but it was still a miracle that Jessica didn't get pregnant during that spring and summer.

Two months after 9/11, Jessica's father transferred to a combat unit and went to Afghanistan, and Jessica began staying at home more. Her mother was lonely and worried, and needed Jessica's company. And so, from spending almost all our time together, we went to seeing each other once or twice a week. Early in the following year, Reinhart started finding me new jobs. My Spanish was quite good by then, so I was sent out occasionally to talk to workers in the fields, telling them what to do and where to do it. He even brought me into the Sheriff's Office to translate during interrogations. There were also more delivery jobs—supplies for the mines and plots—but the most important job was the one I had in a small basement room in the Sheriff's Office.

Only Reinhart had a key to the room, which was bare except for a large metal table, a chair, and metal shelving covering one wall. Fluorescent lights were set in the ceiling and a vent high in one wall let in a whisper of air conditioning that kept the room too cold. The shelves, when I would be let into the room by Reinhart on the last Sunday of each month, were stacked high with money; some of it was in bricks held together with rubber bands, but most was loose in shoeboxes, grocery bags, and lots and lots of manila envelopes. Reinhart would give me a list of names with dollar amounts beside them. There were normally fifty or so names on the list, and my job was to sort through the money and apportion out the correct amount for each person, then stuff it in a new envelope and put the person's first name and initial on the outside. The amounts went from two thousand all the way up to fifteen and sometimes higher. Each deputy got 5k. The money was in all denominations except ones, so it usually took a couple of hours to sort out the correct payments. The highest paid people on the list were the mayor and some other town officials. There would still be lots of money left on the shelves when I finished. I never counted out the extra, but it probably varied from forty to seventy thousand a month. This was Reinhart's share. He'd come back when I'd done, give me two hundred dollars, and I'd be on my way.

My new jobs meant that I spent more time around the Sheriff's Office, something that Reinhart encouraged because, he told me, it would one day be my home away from home. I didn't mind hanging around. On the top floor was the 'rec room.' It was full of couches

deputies could flake out on, the biggest TV I'd ever seen, and a constant
supply of free food brought in from Hexum's restaurants. It was
entertaining listening to the deputies talk about the absurd or outrageous
things they'd seen and done on their shifts, but it didn't make me want to
stick around Hexum and join them when I was older.

The theme behind much of their banter was the pleasure they got
in being able to dominate others. Over time I also realized that, to a man,
they worshipped Reinhart, and it wasn't only because of the monthly
envelopes of cash. Most of them, at some early point in their lives, had
been aided or rescued by Reinhart. For some it involved being pulled
from a bad situation at home, for others it was a crime covered up, and
for a few it was something so dramatic they'd only talk about it in broad
hints. Others were naturally servile with a taste for violence, and
Reinhart could offer them a life that would otherwise only be available to
them in their fantasies. So he was a savior to all of us, me, perhaps, most
of all. But the idolatry of the deputies made me uneasy. When they spoke
admiringly of Reinhart I thought of his Spartan house, the closet stocked
with nothing but uniforms, the shelves filled with second-hand trophies,
and I felt sure that there was something in him I never wanted to know
the truth about.

The only exception among the deputies, and the youngest, was
Dexter Long. He didn't spend much time in the rec room, and when he
was there barely joined in the general bullshitting. He also didn't go out
of his way to praise Reinhart. His uniform was always untidy, which
irritated Reinhart, as did the permanently pained expression he wore on
his pudgy face. Reinhart would often look at him and say, "Is something
the matter, Long?" Dexter would shake his head and say, "No. Couldn't
be better." About a year after I'd become a semi-regular fixture at the
Sheriff's Office, Long heard me telling a deputy that I liked playing *The
Sims* computer game. Long's pained expression disappeared, and he
pinned me down for a long, detailed talk about *The Sims*, *Myst* and his
other favorite computer games. We started to hang out at his desk in the
office and talk computers rather than go upstairs. I asked him how he'd
come to be a deputy, and he told me that he had an older brother who
was in Folsom on a manslaughter charge. Reinhart had fixed the
evidence so that he didn't get a murder one rap, and now Dexter was a
deputy rather than the computer programmer he wanted to be.

In January of 2002, just after my sixteenth birthday, Amy called me to come out for a ride. I hadn't heard from her in months. She had been yo-yoing between using and being clean, so I didn't know what to expect when I got there. It was a clear, cold day, and the chaparral surrounding the house and paddock was glazed with frost. The horses were in the paddock and trotted over to greet me, their snorting breaths filling the air with ephemeral clouds. Amy came out of the house looking better than I'd seen her in a long time. She'd lost weight, she was dressed neatly, and her eyes were clear and alert.

"Hi, Tom," she sang out, and gave me a hug. "I think you've grown some more."

"You're looking good."

"I know what you're getting at," she said with mock seriousness. "No, I haven't been using. I have something better now: Jesus."

"Oh, God."

"Yes, exactly. Don't worry, I'm not going to try and convert you—I have my hands full working on Levi. Let's ride."

We went along some familiar trails, sometimes letting the horses choose where to go. About a mile from the house I pointed out some mountain lion tracks in the snow and reminded Amy to keep the horses in the stable at night. She was in a fiercely happy mood that I was unfamiliar with, telling me how her days were now divided between Bible study, minding the horses and, a new hobby, learning how to cook Asian dishes.

"You see," she said. "I'm never alone now. If Levi's gone for an hour, a day or a week, I always have Jesus with me. I know he's not just watching over me, he's beside me, guiding my actions."

"So he's good with a wok?"

"Ha ha. He's guided me away from drugs, I know that."

"And how's Levi?"

I knew how Levi was when he was away from home; while working I'd sometimes be greeted by men with the laughingly-delivered question, "Did you hear what your old man did?" Levi now had a reputation for both ruthlessness and drug- and booze-fueled idiocy. He'd accept bets and dares to commit absurd acts of violence, vandalism, and theft, and generally be a fuckup. The McSweeneys had done these sorts of things out of a sense of demented entitlement. Levi did them to be called crazy and brave by men who thought he was a fool for doing them. Jubal gave him the jobs with the highest risk: moving drugs to places that were thick with police patrols, or to clients who might pay for their delivery with bullets. He also sent Levi to deliver beatings or death to debtors, cheats and people who'd crossed Jubal in a dozen different ways. Levi was valuable to Jubal because he was so expendable. His addictions made him sloppy, but as long as he was willing to go blindly and willingly into any danger, he had value as cannon fodder. And if he ended up becoming a piece of luggage in Hexum or elsewhere, it would be no great loss to Jubal.

"Levi is a troubled soul," said Amy.

"I hadn't noticed."

"Now, now, Tom, he is your father."

I bit my tongue.

"Levi," continued Amy, "is like me; he has wounds that won't heal. That's the devil that lashes him. I think it may be because your mother abandoned the two of you. When he's taken something that mellows him out, I try asking him about it, to understand his feelings, but when he talks about it his story keeps changing. It's like he has try out different stories to avoid the hard truth that he wasn't wanted, and that's why he and I are so right for each other; I wasn't wanted either, only it was parents in my case. If he comes to Jesus, his pain will lift. It did for me."

We didn't talk much for the rest of the ride.

The next time I saw Dexter I asked him if he could help me find my mother.

"Why?" he asked nervously.

"You must have, you know, police channels you can go through, special ways you can find people online."

"I don't know. Reinhart likes to do that sort of thing himself. I might get in trouble."

"Her name's Anne Charlebois. I remember it was just after July 4th when we left to come out here, so maybe find out about missing persons reports from around there at that time. Unidentified bodies."

"She's dead?" asked Dexter with alarm.

"I don't know. Could be. Or maybe her name turns up on a database and she's living somewhere else. I just want to know for sure. It shouldn't be hard; it's detective work on a computer."

A gleam came into Dexter's eyes and he said he'd give it a try, but he'd have to be cautious about it.

He must have been very cautious, because I didn't hear anything from him until February. I'd just finished the monthly money count and had gone up to the off-duty room to eat and watch the Super Bowl. Most of the deputies were there, and a few prisoners, manacled, who'd paid to be allowed upstairs to watch the game. Dexter, looking agitated, came into the room and beckoned me outside.

"Let's go down to my desk," he said in a conspiratorial whisper.

The main office was deserted, but Dexter still checked around a few doors before joining me at his desk.

"I've found out a few things, but I don't know if they'll help you. Even if they do, you have to keep this on the down low. I've been communicating with other police departments out east, and Reinhart does not, I repeat, does not like us talking to other cops. First off, I couldn't find any trace of Anne Charlebois anywhere that you couldn't easily look up online, but there was a missing person's report filed with the Connecticut State Police by Gail Charlebois in September of 1994."

"That's my aunt."

"Right. So, the investigators went to an address in New London and talked to the landlord, who told them that Levi had said that he and his family were moving to Florida."

"Florida?"

"Florida. He and Anne supposedly had jobs waiting for them at a resort, but they had to leave right away. The landlord said he thought Levi was bullshitting until he gave him two months' extra rent, in cash, because he was breaking the lease. He also asked him to clear out anything left in the house after you guys were gone."

"What was left?"

"Other than the furniture the place came with, there was only some stuff in the kitchen and women's clothing. Then they talked to the grocery store where your mother worked and were told she didn't show up for her shift and they never heard from her after that. That was the end of the investigation."

"They didn't think any of that seemed weird?"

"They checked a bit further and found that Levi and Anne had skipped out on landlords at least twice in the past three years, so their conclusion was that this disappearance was routine for them, and they probably were down in Florida."

"Except Levi gave his landlord two months' rent. That's not skipping out."

"True, but they had no reason to investigate further; there was no evidence of a crime."

"So that's it?"

Dexter swallowed hard and said, "There were three unidentified female bodies found in the summer and fall of that year. I have their physical details."

"Go on."

He took a small notebook out of his desk and flipped it open. My heart began to pound.

"One was found in the woods near Mohegan Sun, the casino. She was a suspected suicide. Five-foot-ten, in her twenties, probably weighed close to 200 pounds. No distinguishing features."

"Too big."

"Another was in a shallow grave, badly decomposed, but she had long black hair."

"No. She had really short hair."

"The other one was a drowning victim, accidental or otherwise, partially decomposed, and the only distinguishing feature was part of a tattoo on one arm. Did Anne have a tattoo?"

"When was she found?"

"Uh, July 17th."

"What was the tattoo?"

"A date. The first letters of the month were gone so it read as *ary*, like in Janu*ary* or Febru*ary*. The rest of the date was the 14th of whichever month, and the year was 1986."

I had my hands on my knees and looked down at them, surprised that they weren't shaking or sweating.

"Did Anne have a tattoo?" Dexter asked again.

"No, she didn't. Nothing at all like that."

"Well," said Dexter encouragingly, "that's some kind of good news."

"Yes."

"That's all I got for you. I wish there was more, but…"

"No problem. Thanks, Dexter."

He started talking about computer games, anxious to get back to a happier topic. I was deaf to his detailed descriptions of what he'd achieved in *RollerCoaster Tycoon*, but acted as if I was paying attention. After a few moments I even forgot he was nearby. I was visualizing my future as an arrow-straight road across a flat prairie. In the distance of this imagined landscape was a landmark without shape or form. It was a point at which, when I reached it, everything would change. I had no doubt of this. The landmark was the moment when I would kill Levi.

Venom

Two crew members put a small platform near the prow of the ship as Brooks stares impatiently at them. The ship is at anchor about a mile out from Malibu Pier. All the guests are on the front deck, their faces turned towards the land as they watch the wall of fire advancing down the mountains towards the ocean. Some of them "ooh" and "aah." The sun has gone down, and the blue and red lights of emergency vehicles flash in the darkness in front of the flames, heralding its triumphant progress.

"I bet," says Autumn, "that Brooks starts with a fire joke."

"I don't see him as the sort of guy who opens speeches with a gag."

"Calvin Mercer, the toad in the bow tie standing near him, will have written it. Brooks has an adversarial relationship with humor."

Brooks gets on the platform, puts his arms behind his back, narrows his eyes, and juts out his chin as though expecting his mere presence to bring silence. Mercer, standing to the side of the platform, claps his hands furiously to draw everyone's attention. People settle on chairs and couches, while others stand at the rail, one eye on Brooks, one on the blaze. Gideon is standing at the very back of the crowd right beside Carmen, who has both hands wrapped tightly around her drink and a mannequin's smile on her face. Gideon is grinning like he's won a prize.

In the silence that falls in the moments before Brooks speaks, I can hear the fire as a deep, humming noise, like a giant subwoofer in a distant car passing through the night.

"Welcome, ladies and gentleman," begins Brooks. "Well, I think I can guarantee you a fiery speech tonight."

A ripple of laughter runs through the crowd. The bow tie smirks at the response.

"Jesus fucking Christ, that was worse than I expected," groans Autumn.

"Maybe he'll finish with some prop comedy," I say.

Brooks waves a hand towards the fire. "Actually, I'm glad we can see this happening tonight. Our country, our way of life, is being consumed in exactly this way. When I look at all of you, I see people who worked hard all their lives to build greatness—not just wealth, but corporations and foundations and trusts that will endure for generations. Your very names are on mighty buildings and roads and rivers that go back to when this country was founded. There are people in Congress, people in the media, and a rabble of keyboard monkeys and talking heads who hate success. Your success. They think success is unfair, that it's not right, that your success should be taken from you and given piecemeal, like feed thrown for chickens, to people who *complain*, who have *grievances*, who think they're owed a *living*, who were born on the wrong side of a border, who think they've been *oppressed.* These people believe they're *special*, and, to be honest, they are...special needs." Another ripple of laughter. "We have to stop letting our rights as successful people, the most successful the world has ever known, be eroded, stolen and regulated by people who were left behind long ago by Nature and by their attachment to dead and dangerous political ideas. Make no mistake, like that fire, there is a destructive force at large that wants to deny the fact that this country was built by us. This is *our* country." The ship has slowly swung around and Brooks is now backdropped by the wildfire, its flames boiling up from the ground and bursting apart in yellow and white shards as it consumes propane and gas tanks. "Let me use a biblical analogy, something that I know will please my lovely wife Carmen, who brought some much-needed religion into my life." Heads turn and look back towards Carmen, who manages to beam ecstatically and look nauseous at the same time. Gideon, hard by her side, nods sagely. "As God created woman from a rib, we created America from our heritage, our ambition, our hunger for success. And how we choose to use what we've created is something that must be left to our pleasure. So, we need a fire of our own; a fire of will and purpose and direct action to consume those dead ideas and their purveyors, and tonight I'm here to announce that I will be bringing that fire by fighting for a seat in the U.S. Senate to represent the great state of Colorado, where Carmen and I have enjoyed many weekends at our place in Aspen." Some cheers and general applause. A few people look at their phones.

"I'm going for a walk," I say to Autumn. "I've heard this kind of talk before."

"I'll come; I need to find a bathroom."

"Of course," continues Brooks, "every fire needs fuel, and the fuel for my fire rests in your hands...and wallets."

The guests groan and laugh as Autumn and I make our way towards the inside of the ship. Brooks continues his speech with details about his PAC and campaign team. Autumn heads down a staircase and I pause by the door into the main salon. Gideon and Carmen are in front of me and to the right, shielded from general view by the edge of a couch. Her smile looks like it's been fixed on with spikes. Gideon, his white hair done in a tight, thick braid that reaches his waist, has his hand up the bottom of Carmen's dress. He sees me out of the corner of his eye and makes a comical face that's meant to suggest he's a naughty boy.

I go into the salon where food and drinks tables are being set up. The only person not working is Gantry, who stands at a window staring at the fire. He's wearing a white linen shirt with the top two buttons undone. He's probably chosen the color and left it open to billboard the pink burn scar on his neck that travels down to his chest—look at me, I'm a warrior.

"It's like Kuwait in '91," says Gantry soberly. "Beautiful, in its own way. The power, the uniqueness of the event."

"Oddly, those weren't Cassidy's dying words."

"Am I supposed to feel sorry? He was paid well."

"Minimum wage compared to your return on this deal. By the way, they've got a few dozen dead already up in Chico."

"Tell you what: I'll cry over them, you cry over those three men in the desert, one of whom hasn't even been found, and we'll call it even."

"It's all collateral damage, right? Start a fire, drop a drone on a market; it's so easy to do when you've got someone else doing the work."

"You seriously think the living matter? After your career? The things you've done? I've read files on you, Bridger. You and I know that the world is designed for those at the apex. Life flows up to sustain the top. Grass and zebras produce lions. Sunlight and plankton produce blue whales. Catholics and pedophiles produce a fucking pope."

"And enough dead bodies gets you a general."

"Exactly. Or a billionaire."

"Now, now; you aren't there yet, and you really can't include your wife's money. I hate having to remind people that you're not a gold digger."

"I won't be needing hers. Once that chickenhawk out there is elected my ticket is punched."

"So you'll be his military consultant?"

"After a sizable donation, yes."

"I didn't think senators needed military advisors."

"They do when they eventually run for president."

"You're counting on that tall pile of shit getting elected?"

Gantry points towards the burning land. "Have you seen what gets elected these days? Being a pile of shit makes him an odds-on favorite. Anyway, this whole Colorado thing is to increase his brand awareness. It would actually be better if he loses and avoids the taint of being a career politician. But it all depends on getting the money ball rolling with those people out there, which won't be easy; no one likes Brooks, and Gideon won't give him a dime outside of his trust fund. I may have to stick to squashing bugs like you. Oh, well; at least it's work I enjoy."

"Too bad you and your men aren't good at it."

Gantry moves closer to me and says, "You won't be saying that once you're the main focus of my attention, which you will be one of these days."

"There's no money in going after me."

"Can't I still hunt for pleasure?"

People start drifting in from the front of the ship, so presumably Brooks is finished, or he's losing their attention. A man comes over to talk to Gantry, and Carmen, looking distraught, hurries into the salon and goes down the same staircase Autumn used. I go to the ship's stern for a closer look at the water sports deck. It measures about 20 by 15 feet and is lowered into position with a hydraulic winch. A sign beside the winch controls has a long list of safety requirements including the need for a crew member to be present at all times when the deck is deployed. I go back into the salon to get something to drink and give Autumn the bad news. I'm beginning to wonder what's taking her so long when she comes back upstairs with Carmen, who looks drawn and pale.

Autumn leaves Carmen sitting on a chair and comes over to me. I tell her about a crew member having to be present while the deck is in use.

"Well, shit," she says.

"There was always a risk we wouldn't be alone with Gideon out there. That's if you can get him to swim in the first place."

"If there's just one member of the crew watching, could you distract them?"

"Probably, but if someone thinks there's something suspicious about Gideon drowning, they'll zero in on us pretty quick."

"What if Carmen was doing the distracting? You wouldn't even have to be around."

"Carmen? You think she would?"

"Yes. After what she told me downstairs."

"I can guess. I saw Gideon groping her while Brooks was speaking."

"Oh, there's much more than that. Let's go outside."

We go to the forward deck, which is empty except for a few people filming the fire or taking selfies with the flames as a backdrop. The sea is still calm, but it puckers gently in a thousand places as if from raindrops—it's ash falling from the sky.

"So," says Autumn, "I was about to leave the washroom when Carmen comes staggering in and throws up in the sink. I get her cleaned up and calmed down, and she starts talking. Remember what I said about Gideon and the rumors about his sea-going rape parties? He took Carmen out a month ago, spiked her drink, and took her into his special stateroom. Carmen had a hard time describing it, emotionally speaking. Gideon films everything that goes on in the room, and that includes the participation of a couple of crew members as *actors* in these films. Gideon doesn't film himself having sex, he's too careful for that, but he likes watching others fucking his women and watching it later for shits and giggles. And for blackmail. Tonight, for instance, Gideon told Carmen she has to come out on the ship next week; the guest of honor is Mei, and Gideon wants them co-starring. If she doesn't, images from her film will be circulated."

"Does Mei have any idea what's in store?"

"No. Roger's pimping her out. He got the same offer as Enoch: give me a taste of your wife if you want in on the deal."

"Gideon was more interested in you agreeing to being his mistress rather than abduction."

"True. But that's how his mind works; he's turned on by violation, by taking something innocent and turning it inside out. He figures I'm too jaded, too experienced, to be sufficiently humiliated by one of his porn shoots. Think about what he is: a billionaire who's never heard the word 'no' in his life and who can buy any pleasure he wants. But after a while, if you're as psychopathic as Gideon, buying fun isn't enough, it becomes routine, dull, and you have to stimulate yourself with things that are forbidden or beyond the reach of money."

"It's not only billionaires who think that way."

"I agree. I met lots back in the day, but this one still wants me so badly it hurts, and that's why he'll go swimming tonight."

"You'd better talk to him now before the screening starts. I'll see if I can get Carmen to help us."

I find Carmen on the rear deck sitting on a chaise longue. Her white dress is flecked with a few small stains, and she sits with her eyes closed, humming to herself. Her eyes slowly open as she hears me approach. She looks tired and defeated.

"Feeling better, Carmen?"

She nods.

I pull a chair over and sit down. "What were you humming? I almost recognized it."

"A Gwen Stefani song. It was my favorite when I was a kid."

"Which one?"

"'The Sweet Escape'. It centers me."

"Nice." I pause and think that maybe Autumn should have handled this. I can't imagine Carmen wants to talk to a man right now. "Carmen, how would you like to have Gideon out of your life forever?"

"Forever?"

"There's a chance of it. It's not a certainty, but if you could do something for Autumn and I tonight it would help a lot."

"Gideon hates you," she says in a monotone.

"How do you know that?"

"I overheard him talking to Preston Gantry at the party last night. Gideon was saying that Autumn was dirtying herself by being with you, and that a nobody shouldn't be causing him this much trouble. Gideon was really angry. Preston said you're more resourceful than he'd expected."

"Well, you can get compliments in the most unexpected places sometimes."

In the same flat voice, she asks, "What are you going to do to him?"

"It's best you don't know. Autumn and Gideon are going to go swimming while the movie is on. There'll be a member of the crew at the stern watching them, just over there by that winch. All you have to do is draw the crewmember's attention for a few minutes. That's it."

Carmen bites her lip. "What you're going to do isn't right, is it? I mean, it's a sin."

"Not for me, but for others, probably you, yes. Don't do it if you feel it's wrong."

"Gideon is wrong. He's the most wrong creature that's ever lived. If you get rid of him, you have to promise me you'll get into his room and destroy his DVDs. Tonight. He has things I want gone."

"I understand. And even if things don't work out, I'll try and do that. Where's his special room?"

"On the deck above this one, at the front of the ship on the right."

It's the room I saw him come out of earlier today when the ship was docked.

"He keeps everything on DVDs? Not on a computer?"

"No. He's afraid of being hacked. He keeps everything in that room. What do I have to do again?"

She's numb with booze and a sadness that refuses to come out in tears, and I have to explain her simple job twice more. I leave her on the chaise longue and go into the salon, which is emptying out as the guests go downstairs to the theater. Autumn and Gideon are together at the far end of the room, deep in conversation. Gideon's face is stupid with lust. They finish talking and Autumn strolls past me to the rear deck and gives me a wink. Gideon talks with a senior-looking member of the crew and points to the rear of the ship. He finishes issuing orders and comes over to me with a smirk on his face.

"Take a good look around," he says, "this is the last time you'll see the inside of this ship, unless you want a job crewing."

"That little show you put on earlier with Carmen? Was that for me or just to remind Carmen that she's owned body and soul by the Newcastles?"

"For me, of course. You have a really middle-class mind, don't you? You probably think my sexual behavior should have some kind of control or governor that makes it accord with my age and looks, which, I'll freely admit, are less than perfect. Awful, in fact. Why do I do it? I exhausted all legitimate pleasures long ago, and if the actuarial tables are to be believed, I only have ten or so years left. I intend to use them badly. As I've grown older, I've only become more terrifying to women. They never liked me much to begin with, but money fixed that with some of them. So now I embrace the terror I produce in them. I can taste it on their skin. It's delicious."

He gives me a playful tap on the shoulder and turns to go down a stairway. I fight an urge to grab his wrist and twist his arm off. I assume he'll be right back up after he's made a token appearance at the screening that's about to start. A noise from outside distracts me. One of the crew, a man my age, places towels on a deck chair and then begins operating the deck winch. Autumn stands near him, leaning casually against the rail. Carmen, in her white dress, is almost invisible curled up in the corner of a long, white couch that backs against the outside salon wall. I'm unsure if she'll actually be able to help us.

Gideon re-emerges from a different stairway on the rear deck and practically skips towards Autumn. I step outside as Gideon starts taking his clothes off, placing them haphazardly on the chair with the towels. He strips down completely, and I hear Carmen make a small noise of disgust. Gideon's fit for his age, surprisingly muscular, but with skin like a peeled apple that's sat out for a while. Autumn takes all her clothes off and puts them beside Gideon's. The winch operator is disinterested; it's likely he's seen a lot more than this if he's worked on Gideon's yacht for any length of time. Autumn goes down the steps built into the stern of the ship. Gideon glances back at me and makes his silly face again before going down to the deck. The winch operator stands at the top of the stairs and observes them. I move quietly to the two heaps of clothes, feel Gideon's pockets and find a small key ring that also holds a fob for an electronic lock. I pocket it and go up an outside stairway that leads to a balcony on the upper deck.

I have an unobstructed view from above as Autumn dives into the ocean. The fire is illuminating the water with shafts of light that reach down ten or more feet and turn Autumn into a golden mermaid as she swims slowly underwater. Gideon, still standing on the deck, is either transfixed or hesitant about jumping in the water. His right hand is busy playing with his semi-erect cock. Autumn surfaces and floats on her back close to the deck.

"So nice," she says invitingly.

Gideon makes an ungainly, feet-first jump into the water and comes up with a gasping yelp. He gets his breath back and begins swimming towards Autumn, who turns on her side and dives again. Gideon paddles on the surface, looking down at her naked body as she twists and turns directly beneath him, and laughs delightedly when she tugs at his foot. He dives down a few feet and reaches for Autumn, but she flashes away from him with a few elegant kicks and comes up for air. Gideon says something I can't hear as he slowly splashes towards her. Autumn swims slow circles around him, speaking quietly and moving ever so slightly away from the deck.

Carmen comes into view below and walks up to the crewman at the stairs.

"Excuse me, could you give me a hand over here?" she asks demurely.

"Uh, sure," he says hesitantly.

"I dropped my phone behind that couch and I can't reach it."

The man looks uncertainly towards the swimmers, but he's probably aware that Carmen is the boss's daughter-in-law, so her request carries weight.

"Yes, no problem," he says obediently, and follows Carmen.

As soon as they're out of my sight, I look at Autumn and see that she's registered the watcher's disappearance. She says something to Gideon and dives straight down, her legs arcing into the air before sliding silently underwater in a perfect vertical line. Gideon takes several deep breaths and follows her. He struggles to get down to where Autumn is suspended in the water as though lying on a bed, her hands and legs moving languidly, and her hair fanned out around her head as if on an invisible pillow. Gideon kicks his legs furiously and extends an arm to touch her golden skin. He almost makes it, but then turns to return to the surface. Autumn jackknifes forward to grab the end of his braid and pulls him deeper with several rapid kicks. Gideon's arms flail over his head as he's turned upside down; he pivots to face Autumn and she lets go of his hair as he reaches for her hand. He tries once more to swim up, but this time Autumn grabs him around an ankle and stops him with a jerk. Gideon reaches for her imprisoning hand, but panic makes him stop and try to force his way to the air above with manic strokes of his arms. Autumn's dead weight is too much for him. His left hand breaks the surface as his mouth opens in astonishment and lets in the ocean.

Autumn rises up beside him and gives his head a gentle push to send him deeper before pulling herself onto the deck.

From somewhere underneath me I hear Carmen say, "Maybe I dropped it at *this* end of the couch. Could it be under the cushions?"

Gideon, his white braid twisting and trailing behind him, sinks lower. His body tumbles slowly on an invisible axis and drifts away in the current like a space-walking astronaut who's had his lifeline cut. The wildfire suddenly grows more intense and light stabs down into the water to reveal a dark shape moving underneath Gideon and following him. In a few more seconds both shapes are lost in the darkness.

Autumn comes up the stairs to the deck and starts towelling herself. She looks around in confusion and says sharply, "Where's Gideon?"

The crewman hurries into sight and looks down at the water.

"Didn't he come up?" asks Autumn.

"No. Did you see him get out of the water?"

"Well, no, I just assumed he did while I was swimming on the other side of the deck."

"Mr. Newcastle!" shouts the crewman. He shouts twice more, swears, and picks up a phone mounted beside the winch mechanism. He mutters into it and then races down the stairs to the floating deck and shouts Newcastle's name again before diving into the water. An alarm starts pinging as Autumn dresses herself and more crew come spilling onto the deck. Carmen stands beside Autumn and whispers something to her, to which Autumn replies with a nod.

I duck into a passageway and follow it to where I think Gideon's special room should be. The door at the end of the passage has a small, rectangular black box on the wall beside it with a tiny red light in its center. I pass Gideon's fob over it and the door clicks open.

The room is dark and my hand finds a light switch on the wall as I close the door behind me. Pot lights in the ceiling reveal a large, square room with tinted windows along the wall facing the balcony that I saw Gideon standing on earlier today. A king-sized bed, covered in an eye-popping, tiger-striped bedspread, is a garish island in the center of the room. A few mirrors and some bland oil paintings of seascapes decorate the walls. Hanging from the ceiling over the bed is something that looks like a climbing harness done in leather. A camera tripod stands at the foot of the bed, and the video camera that goes with it sits on a shelf against one wall along with a laptop. A built-in bookcase beside a wall-mounted TV holds stacks of DVDs in plain cases. The air, smelling of air freshener and a lemony cleaning product, almost makes me gag.

I remove the memory card from the camera before looking quickly through every drawer and cupboard in the room. I don't find any other recording equipment or computers, just lots of women's lingerie in a rainbow of colors and styles, enough to open a store. The DVDs in the bookcase, several dozen in total, have hand-drawn labels on the front, each one bearing a different woman's name, sometimes several names. I go out on the balcony toss the memory card and laptop overboard. The sound of raised and excited voices drifts up from below. I go back inside and take the DVDs out of their cases, return to the balcony and Frisbee them away from the ship. I'm sure Carmen won't be the only person on the ship glad to learn that Gideon's films have disappeared.

I leave the room and take a stairwell that comes out in the main salon, which is filled with people who've abandoned the screening. They remind me of crowds I've seen at accidents and murders: many of them are excited that something unfamiliar is pumping adrenaline into their systems. Gideon's wife is sitting on a chair looking more perplexed than stricken. A female crewmember kneels beside her, speaking quietly and patting her hand.

The rear of the ship is busy with controlled panic. Crew are hurrying to put a pair of ski jets into the water as well as a launch. A searchlight scans the ocean, and the man I assume is the ship's captain is talking to Brooks, who's trying hard to look upset. Urgent voices spill from several walkie-talkies, one of them coming from a Coast Guard vessel on the way to the scene. Gideon's clothes are still sitting on the chair. I go over to them, wait until no one's looking, and put the key ring back in one of the pockets.

The captain turns his attention to Autumn. She's standing by the rail looking out at the water and doing a better job of appearing upset than Brooks. He asks her some questions, and she answers them without taking her eyes off the ocean. I look for Carmen and find her back where she was originally sitting, only now she has a plate of sandwiches in front of her and a tall glass of Coke. She's really enjoying her sandwiches.

As I sit beside her, and without looking at me, she says, "Well?"

"It's all gone overboard, everything that I could find in his room, anyway."

She doesn't react, but a moment later a giggling fit makes her choke slightly. She takes a sip of her drink and whispers, "I just thought something that's *so* stupid: I wished Gideon was alive so that he'd know he's dead. Stupid, huh?" Her laughter this time is tinged with hysteria.

"Careful you don't choke."

Autumn and the captain finish talking, and she walks over and sits with us, the concern in her face draining away in an instant.

"That went swimmingly," she says.

Carmen snorts.

I ask, "What was the captain questioning you about?"

"Where I last saw Gideon, his position relative to the deck, did he seem short of breath or ill? That sort of thing. Gideon didn't have much strength in him, really. I thought I'd have more of a struggle, but it was no worse than controlling a small dog at the end of a leash. If only I'd known years ago how easy it is to get rid of his kind."

"It's what comes next that's hard. The Selous Group, Gantry in particular, might get vengeful now that their scam's died with Gideon."

Autumn shrugs. "They'll soon find something else to focus their greed on."

Carmen looks at Autumn. "Can I come with you when the boat gets back? I don't want to go home with Brooks. He'll be in a bad mood."

"Don't you have any friends or relatives you could crash with?"

"No. At least, none that wouldn't be afraid of what Brooks might do if he found out they were helping me."

"In that case, stay with us and feel free to tell Brooks exactly where you are," says Autumn. "I'd love to show him off the property. We're at the Malibu house; you've been there before, haven't you?"

Carmen agrees that she has and starts laughing again. Her eyes are bright and she's breathing rapidly. Autumn recognizes that Carmen is losing it, so she moves closer to her, holds her hand and starts distracting her with gossip about people they both know. I hang around until I see that Carmen's calming down, then get up and watch the search effort.

The jet skis are moving slowly in circles a couple of hundred yards astern, while the launch patrols towards the shore. The captain is barely containing his temper while arguing with Brian Willet about which way the current might have taken Gideon, and a boat moving fast with its searchlight on—probably a Coast Guard vessel—is approaching from the south.

Surprisingly, the remaining members of the Selous Group aren't anywhere in sight. I hunt around and find them huddled together on the forward deck talking in low voices, like a trio of angry and baffled wizards arguing over why a spell's gone wrong. Pinder's normally soft features are rigid with tension, and Gantry looks like he wants to slap the other two. Cordell's surgically sculpted face only allows him to register mild irritation. He catches sight of me and clears his throat with a dramatic staginess that almost makes me laugh.

"If you're waiting for Macbeth," I say, "I don't think he's coming."

Cordell isn't amused. "Don't you dare make jokes, you little shit," he hisses. "That was a great man who died tonight. He taught me what it means to be a billionaire."

"And the world's poorer for his death, isn't it?" I say mournfully.

"You and Autumn arranged this, didn't you?" growls Gantry.

"Really? It's Gideon who was supposed to pay us for keeping your secret, and later tonight he was going to start transferring the funds. Gideon dead does nothing for us."

"We're all screwed," moans Pinder.

"No, no," I say. "His debt passes to you three. Fifty million."

Cordell laughs as much as his stiff face allows. "You really are a half-witted grifter, aren't you? We don't get anything either. Gideon had to initiate the insurance claims, not us. There's no money coming in. All those businesses in Malibu and Chico are ash and nothing but ash. The only silver lining to this is that your blackmail scam died with Gideon. We don't own any insured properties, we only have contracts with them, which are now useless."

I do my best to look confused. "But you have contracts with Gideon's phony companies."

Cordell rolls his eyes. "Our having links to fake companies isn't proof of anything if no one's being defrauded. You've got nothing on us."

"Yeah," Pinder chimes in, taking his courage from Cordell, "you've got nothing."

"But what about Brooks?" I say defensively. "Doesn't he take things over?"

They all chuckle over that.

"Brooks," says Cordell bitterly, "is more of an idiot than you. A disgrace to his father. Gideon wouldn't let him go anywhere near his businesses, and until the estate's sorted out all he has is his trust fund. But if you and Autumn want to pester Brooks for fifty million, be my guest; you might as well ask a jellyfish."

I try and look dumbfounded as Jasper stalks off angrily, trailed closely by Pinder.

Gantry stays behind for a moment, a shrewd look on his face, and says, "If I see you alive after tonight, you'll regret it, Bridger."

He follows the other two, and I wonder if he was buying my act.

Autumn and Carmen are where I left them. Carmen is calmer and excuses herself to go see Gideon's wife.

"What have you been up to?" asks Autumn.

"Laying down a smokescreen. Gantry immediately accused us of killing Gideon, so I tried to give he and Jasper and Roger the idea that we're as screwed by Gideon's death as they are."

"Did they buy it?"

"Jasper and Roger did, I think; I'm not so sure about Gantry."

"No matter. We'll be gone soon. It's almost time to leave the battlefield."

"And go where?"

"I think we should go to LAX, look at the departure board, and plan from there. I'm tired of it all. We have to leave before this country consumes us like Cassidy."

"So no more art, no more architecturally-significant homes?"

"None of it was ever really mine. I could never be truly attached to things bought with Enoch's money. A whore shouldn't take pride in how splendid the whorehouse is that she works in. Anyhow, I've got a good chunk of money to start over with, and then you've got your hidden treasure."

I wish I'd never mentioned it to her.

"You said it's *almost* time to leave the battlefield?"

Autumn looks at me says tensely, "Let's talk about it back at the house."

It's not like her to avoid a question, and it worries me.

It's near midnight when the captain announces over the PA system that we'll be returning to port and leaving the search to the Coast Guard. In some distant part of the ship a couple of people cheer. When we step off the ship in Marina Del Rey, Carmen sticks close to us. Brooks is still onboard talking to the Coast Guard and doesn't notice her getting into our car.

As we drive back to Malibu, we hear on the radio that an evacuation order for homes along the Pacific Coast Highway might be given in the next twelve hours. Carmen has fallen asleep, and I have to prop her up as we go into the house and take her to a bedroom. Two of Autumn's friends, Tyra and Mike, are in the kitchen making something in the food processor and bombard Autumn with stories about the fire and people they know who've had to flee or have even lost homes. I go out on the deck and find myself staring at the surf, half-expecting Gideon's body to flop onto the beach. The wind has changed direction, and the wildfire is now obscured by its own smoke that throbs with orange light. Autumn comes out on the deck and puts her arm around me.

"I went up and checked on Carmen; she was staring out the window and muttering about the end times. I gave her a sleeping pill."

"It's probably for the best she came here, otherwise she might have told Brooks everything."

"I'll get her calmed down tomorrow, take her shopping, maybe a spa. She can say what she wants to Brooks and the others after we're gone."

"What was it you didn't want to tell me on the ship?"

She fixes me with her green eyes and says, "We still have to kill Enoch. And Roger."

"Roger?" I say with surprise.

"I can't forgive him for what he was going to do to Mei."

"I can understand getting rid of Enoch, that's vengeance, but Roger? This is sounding like a guerilla war."

"Very apt. I was thinking more Bonnie and Clyde." Autumn separates herself from me and leans against the deck's railing. "When I held Gideon's ankle and felt his body relax into forever, it was as though I'd crested a mountain range and seen something astonishing on the other side. It was a feeling of grand achievement, the kind that makes you want to scream. You don't know how much self-control it took for me not to shout for joy when I got out of the water and saw that grub drifting away. It wasn't killing that moved me, it was taking everything away from a man like Gideon with so little effort. All his power and fearfulness gone in an instant. I want to taste that sensation again."

I don't know what to say to her. Something she said reminds me of Gideon and it makes me feel ill.

"We don't have much time if we want to leave the country soon. This kind of thing takes planning, and the longer we stay here the more likely we'll be in someone's crosshairs—the cops or Gantry."

Autumn waves a hand dismissively. "We're not in that much of a rush. Roger and the others are confused and scared, busy gnawing their own legs off in frustration at losing out on all that lovely insurance money."

I could tell her that in my experience each murder breeds other killings the way a corpse produces maggots, but she'd only argue that we'd gotten away with everything so far. I can only protect Autumn by agreeing to walk down a very dark road with her.

"Okay. One down, two to go. But there can't be any chance of a link between us and Roger's death. Being in the neighborhood when one billionaire dies is happenstance, but twice? That's a guaranteed visit from the cops. Let's talk about it more tomorrow."

We go to bed. Twice during the night Autumn wakes me by crying out in her sleep.

I come down in the morning to the sound of Carmen arguing with Brooks over the phone. A night's sleep away from him has fortified her. She's perched on a stool at the kitchen island calmly telling him that she's not coming home for a while, and he's bellowing about what this is going to look like to people when his father's dead. The news is on the TV in the living room and they're announcing that the Santa Monica fire is now partially contained, several people are confirmed dead, but the fire near Chico has worsened and the death toll might be huge. I leave the house's cocoon of air conditioning and go down to the water's edge where Mike is doing yoga with Tyra. They see me coming and point to the ocean. Autumn is swimming parallel to the shore about forty yards out, attacking the water as though she's in an Ironman competition. The air smells of burnt plastic and the sky is smeared with smoky clouds the color of a banana skin. I sit on the sand and wait for Autumn to finish her swim.

When she comes out of the water she's gasping for air.

"How long were you in?" I ask.

"An hour?" she pants. "My head needed clearing. Bad sleep."

She flops down beside me and leans her head against my shoulder while she gets her breath back.

"I've been thinking about Roger," she says. "If you don't believe we can do it safely, let's not. Enoch will be enough. But I definitely want to try."

"We will. I'll need to know where he lives and what his routines are, if he has any. Can you call Mei and get an idea of what his movements are going to be for the next few days?"

"No problem. She'll be dying to talk about what went on last night. They have a condo in Sierra Towers in West Hollywood, but I think they're staying at their ranch near Santa Clarita. He likes horses, and she pretends not to be bored living out there." She pauses and pushes sand around with her feet like a bored child. "Listen, I feel like I'm forcing you on this; if you don't want do this thing with Roger, I'm fine. I was amped up last night, and I guess I'm greedy, like them. Gideon and Enoch should be enough for me."

"Alright. I'll scout around, try and find a safe way to do it, but if not, we'll leave, right?"

"Right." She stands. "You coming up?"

"In a bit."

As she jogs to the house, a weight lifts off me. I don't want murder becoming comfortable for her. Oddly, I'm still okay with the idea of killing Roger. His palpable weakness and cowardice, his subordinate position in the Selous Group, even his doughy body has made me see him as inconsequential. But he's not. According to Autumn, he probably killed his previous wife, he was offering up Mei to Gideon like tribute to a liege lord, and now he's crying because he's not profiting the way he was hoping to from the immolation of people in Chico and Santa Monica. I've killed people for worse reasons, some for no reason at all, so why bother to spare Roger? He would have stood tall, in his own quiet way, in the pantheon of Hexum's monsters.

After she showers and dresses, Autumn gets on the phone to Mei. I can tell it's going to be a long conversation, so I go for a run along the highway. Traffic is light, but there seem to be fewer emergency vehicles. The air overhead, however, is still busy with helicopters and water bombers. When I get back, Autumn is finishing her call with Mei.

"Mei's staying in West Hollywood for the week to supervise some redecoration, and Roger's at the ranch playing cowboy."

"Good. So how does he spend the day there?"

"He goes for a ride in the morning before it gets too hot, and another in the evening. The rest of the day he does fuck all. If Mei's there she forces him to use the gym, or at least swim some laps in the pool. If she's staying in West Hollywood, he spends most of the day watching TV or fooling around on the computer, or so the housekeeper tells her. Occasionally he goes out to play golf, but most of the time he's just killing time. Oh, he likes to snack a lot."

"Sounds like heart disease might get him before we do. Is there more than a housekeeper there?"

"A handyman, ranch hand, whatever you want to call him, plus a maid and the housekeeper."

Autumn opens her laptop and shows me the ranch's location. Pinder's got a big spread that's made bigger by bordering a state park. I switch to satellite view to get a better idea of the land. It's corrugated with ridges and gullies that look as though they've been gashed into the earth with a knife and far enough away from the trails in the park that I shouldn't have to worry about bumping into stray hikers. I have the germ of an idea.

"So?" asks Autumn.

"I'll go have a look now. You?"

"Spending the day with Carmen. I figure the longer we keep her away from Brooks, the better for her and us. I'm going to try and convince her to dump his ass."

"That should be easy."

"You'd think so, but she's still got that dutiful, Christian wife exoskeleton that needs to be chipped away. She doesn't have any clear memory of who she is without Brooks and that Jesus guy, but I'll work on it."

Autumn and Carmen are gone by the time I come down from my shower. I hunt around for binoculars and a backpack, which I fill with bottles of Fiji Water from the fridge. It's going to be hot work hiking to Pinder's property. Autumn's taken the BMW, which leaves me a choice between a singed Audi and a Lexus. I take the Lexus.

I get to the park before noon, then start up a trail that'll take me within a mile of Pinder's ranch. Between the heat and the continued threat of fires, no one else appears to be in the park except the small lizards that dart across my path. I leave the trail after a half hour and climb in and out of gullies and push through some thick brush before making it to Pinder's land. I know Los Angeles isn't far away, but it feels like I've crossed into a wilder, separate world, especially after I find the remains of a deer that's been cached under dirt and leaves by a mountain lion. I check Google Maps and change direction towards an area on the other side of the ranch that, according to the satellite pictures, is even steeper. I've used up half my water by the time I get there and walk along a ridge flanked by several ravines.

Only one spot suits my purpose. It's steep, with sides that almost count as cliffs, but at the steepest point it's only about a thirty-foot drop to the bottom. Not perfect, but it will have to do. I rest in the shade of a desert willow and slowly drink another bottle of water. At least my backpack is lighter. My plan isn't looking good now, but as I think about where Autumn and I might disappear to, a solution to the problem of killing Pinder comes into view.

I take off my backpack, empty out the bottles, binoculars and gun, and quickly find a stick that should do the job. Afterwards, I cast around for a hiding place and find a crevice between two boulders that's shady. The backpack fits nicely in the space, and I add some branches on top, including the stick I used, to hide it completely. I chug the three remaining bottles of water and put all the empties, as well as the ones that were in the backpack, out of sight in another crevice. The gun is tucked in the back of my pants and I loop the binoculars around my neck.

It's a half hour later when I come to the top of a gentle slope and see the rear of Pinder's house a hundred and fifty yards below me. It's a long, two-storey, faux log cabin with a deep balcony running the length of the second floor. The central section is teepee-shaped and juts sharply up above the rest of the building to accommodate a great room with massive windows. In the center of the room is a stuffed grizzly bear rearing on its hind legs. The outside of the house is randomly decorated with wagon wheels, longhorn cattle skulls, elk antlers, and crossed Native American spears. It looks like someplace in the suburbs where you get meals with Wild West names and the servers come to your table in a gang to sing 'Happy Birthday' while wearing silly hats. No wonder Mei likes to spend time in the Sierra Towers. A rectangular pool is at one end of the house, and at the other is a barn with an attached paddock.

I sit cross-legged under the shade of a tree, a screen of tall grass shielding me from any casual glances from the house. There's no movement around the property; I might as well be watching an empty building, and I'm already regretting finishing those last bottles of water. The only excitement is when a hawk drops down near me and takes a gopher. Right at six o'clock a young man in shorts and sandals comes out of the house and goes into the barn. He's presumably the ranch hand, and ten minutes later Pinder crosses from the house to the paddock. I have to make a conscious effort not to laugh. He's in full cowboy gear: white shirt with embroidery on the shoulders, string tie, burgundy nosepicker cowboy boots, also embroidered, and a fawn cowboy hat with a raffish crow feather tucked in the hat band. It's more cosplay than cowboy, and he walks as though auditioning for the role of gunslinger in a theme park.

A door in the barn swings open, and the ranch hand leads out a gray and white horse. Unsurprisingly, the horse's saddle is a mess of silver trim and embroidery, and Pinder swings up onto it with a boost from his hired hand. I need to see what route he takes away from the barn so I can be in place to grab him during tomorrow evening's ride; if he comes in my direction right now, I'll have to let him go—I'm too tired to handle things tonight. Pinder canters away to my right along a well-worn trail that leads up a hill and disappears into the trees. I begin the long walk back to the car.

Autumn phones as I'm driving back to Malibu and asks me to meet she and Carmen for dinner at Fins, a seafood restaurant in Manhattan Beach.

"I'm a bit of a mess; is that okay?"

"How bad?"

"Disreputable would be an improvement."

"We'll order a more expensive bottle of wine to make them happy."

Fins is on Ocean Dr., done up like a landlocked version of Gideon's yacht, with views of the beach and pier and full of glossy people who are very happy to be where they are and to have lots of money. I walk into the place, attract a few stares, and do a double-take myself when I see Autumn sitting at a table and then realize it's Carmen. She's had her hair cut and colored to match Autumn's.

"Where's Autumn?" I ask as I sit down.

"Washroom. You look...dusty."

"And you look changed."

"I wanted something way different, something that Brooks would hate."

Autumn comes to the table and says, "Have you met my stunt double?"

"I noticed."

"Brooks hates red hair," Carmen mentions matter-of-factly. "He says, 'Why would a woman want to have hair that wasn't blonde?' I thought a tribute to Autumn would really piss him off."

"Carmen," says Autumn, "got another call from Brooks today and he told her that he hoped the reason she wasn't by his side at this difficult time was because she was mad about his father being, and I quote, a bit 'touchy-feely' with her. It showed, said Brooks, that he really liked her. So after we did some shopping she got her hair done."

I ask Carmen: "He knew what Gideon was doing?"

"Seems so. But they didn't see much of each other, so maybe he didn't know about everything."

"I take it you're not going to see him again?"

"Only in a lawyer's office. My pre-nup is brutal, but I figure if I tell Brooks I'll sue his father's estate for sexual harassment and exploitation, and him for being aware of it, I should get a serious slice of the pie."

"I don't doubt you will," agrees Autumn. "Senators-to-be don't like answering questions about pimping their wives."

"And no more talking up Jesus," Carmen says happily, and then laughs at our looks of amazement. "Brooks asked me to do that. It was part of what he called his 'narrative.' He used to be an absolute party monster in college, and that's saying something cuz he went to Tulane.

He knew voters would hear stuff about him in college, so he thought a story about being saved by me, brought to Christ, would be a moral insurance policy."

"Were you ever born again?" asks Autumn.

"In the last year of college. Me and Brooks met at Tulane in my final year. He was there for a bowl game. I'd had a bad experience at a party the previous year, and I thought maybe I should try another path. Brooks did a good job of pretending he was as Christian as me, then, after we were married, he dropped the whole church thing pretty quickly. He said it bored him, and not long after I realized that was the only thing he and I would ever agree about. Sometimes when I'm real stressed, I start believing God's got a plan, but then I think about Brooks and Gideon, and I think His only plan is to make things easy for pricks like them. Sorry for cussing. I have to admit it: I married for money, and the only cost to me was being raped by my father-in-law, so now I'll divorce for a lot more money and maybe trash Brooks' political life down the road when it suits me."

Carmen's gone from laughing to wiping away some tears. Autumn reaches out and takes her hand.

A server arrives at our table, introduces himself, fills our water glasses, and asks, "Are you interested in hearing about our catch of the day?"

Autumn answers, "As long as it's not Gideon, yes."

The server pretends not to be confused by the comment and discreetly joins in our laughter. He'll be used to playing along with entitled, smartass customers in a place like this. When we pay up, I tell Autumn to leave him an outrageous tip. As we leave, I pull her aside and tell her why it would be best if I dealt with Pinder by myself.

She thinks about it as we walk away from the restaurant, waits until Carmen is in the car, and says, "Alright. But don't do it if you think it's too risky."

"Like we said: one down, two to go."

She's relieved at not being involved, and it makes me happy that she's not as dead to violence as me—I'm already thinking about where I'll stop for an ice cream on the way back from killing Pinder.

I make it to the treeline above Pinder's house by four-thirty the next day. I settle in beside the trail he'll take for his evening ride and watch the house, hoping that he hasn't opted for golf and dinner out instead of a ride. As before, there are no signs of life around the property. A burgundy Mercedes that wasn't there yesterday is parked in front of the house. A bit after five, the front door of the house opens and Pinder comes out with a woman and escorts her to the Mercedes. I get my binoculars out. Pinder is in a bathrobe and shower sandals, the woman is wearing elaborately torn jeans and a white tube top that makes her inflated breasts look sculptural. I recognize the Slavic features; she's one of Gideon's now ex-girlfriends. They chat briefly, kiss, and she drives away in the Mercedes. Pinder hurries back into the house, looking very pleased to have been the first to scavenge something from Gideon.

Right on time the ranch hand comes out of the house and goes into the barn, and a few minutes later he's followed by Pinder, who's duded up in his souvenir shop western gear. I go down the trail and hide near the big, leafy branch I've put across it. A few minutes later Pinder comes along, keeping his horse at a trot. He stops at the branch, makes an annoyed sound, and swings down from the saddle. The horse sees me before Pinder does and snorts in alarm as I walk quickly towards him with my Walther out.

"Oh, shit," squeaks Pinder, and puts his hands up as though he's the craven banker being ambushed in a western, which, I suppose, he is.

I take the horse's reins. "You're not dying today, Roger. Clear that branch away and start walking up the trail. We're meeting someone who wants to ask you questions about Gideon's insurance scheme."

"Who?"

"Someone who wants to take over from him."

Pinder moves the branch and we continue along the trail, he in front getting his pristine wardrobe dusty, and me behind leading his horse. I have to keep Pinder reasonably calm for the time it's going to take to walk to the ravine, and the fiction I've told him should keep his mind busy—he's naturally inclined to imagine the world's well-stocked with people as avaricious as Gideon and himself.

"Who is it?" he asks after a while.

"It's someone who knows a good opportunity, like you did with Gideon's girlfriend."

"I...I," he stammers, and then gives up looking for an explanation. "Jasper took one of the other girls, the white one, and I was phoned by Marta. I didn't contact her, she reached out to me," he adds plaintively.

"You sound like you're on the stand at a war crimes trial."

We walk in silence until Pinder asks, "Why are we meeting way out here?"

"He doesn't want phone or computer records of communications, and he definitely doesn't want to be seen in public with you or other members of the Selous Group. If Enoch and Gideon had followed basic security protocols, I wouldn't have become involved."

"What do you get out of this?"

"A broker's fee. I need it after Gideon ruined everything by going for a swim."

Pinder's more relaxed now that he thinks I have a financial interest in this meeting; as long as people around him are motivated by the prospect of money, he feels he's on safe ground.

"I am sad about Gideon, you know," he says quietly. "He was a special man. I always said he was a billionaire's billionaire. He told me once that you have to be as aggressive in having fun as you are in business, and that was the key to being successful at both. He believed great achievements should be followed by great pleasure."

"Which makes it a tragedy he never got to enjoy Mei."

Pinder looks at me nervously. I shouldn't have said that, but his pathetic hero worship of Gideon makes me want to rush him to his death. I don't need him becoming suspicious and trying to run away or attack me; the wrong sorts of injuries on his body would raise questions.

"We turn off here, towards that ridge," I tell him, and he obediently follows my directions.

"My feet hurt," he grumbles.

He's only ever walked in those boots from the house to the barn and back again.

"Almost there," I say soothingly.

We scale the ridge and reach the edge of the ravine. There's nothing in sight except brush-covered land that has the topography of crumpled paper. The sound of a distant jet is the only reminder of the modern world.

"Stop here."

He's round-eyed with bewilderment, and it stops me from doing what I need to. He's a witless child playing dress-up, a chubby princeling who's measured out his life in toys and games, and it fills me with misplaced pity and hesitation.

"So where's this guy who's going to get me my money?" he asks innocently.

I point behind him and drop the horse's reins as he eagerly turns his back toward me, and then gasps when I grab his belt with both hands and practically lift him off his feet as I put a shoulder in his back and shove him forward and over the edge of the ravine. He doesn't have time to scream before he hits the bottom. I was hoping he'd go down headfirst, but he lands on his side with a thump that raises a cloud of dust. He's not moving, but I can hear him whimpering, so there's still work to be done.

I retrieve the backpack, making sure that the zip is still fully done up, and take along the stick I used before. At a spot fifty yards away, the ravine's slope is shallower, and it's there I climb down to check on Pinder. He's lying on his right side with his back to me, his breathing sounding raspy. His head must have smacked into a rock, because there's blood seeping from a teaspoon-sized depression in the back of his head. A few feet away a collared lizard sits under a creosote bush bobbing its head up and down in silent protest at this invasion of its turf.

Pinder's eyes flutter open and he asks weakly, "What happened?"

I'll have to hurry.

"Did I fall?...I don't think I can move... Are you there, Tom?"

I put the backpack down, unzip the main compartment a couple of inches and give the bag a gentle shake.

"I can't see out of one eye...My left eye. Is there something in my eye, Tom? Why can't I move?"

The rattler pokes its head out of the backpack and tests the air.

"I'm so clumsy sometimes and I do things like this...It hurts to breathe, too."

I pin the snake down with the edge of the stick and then grab it just behind the head with my right hand.

"Do I look okay? I wish I could see better...Are you still there, Tom?"

I draw the snake's body out of the backpack, grasping it near the tail with my other hand. Its intricately-patterned body, almost four-feet long, is a perfect match for Pinder's outfit, and it flexes to the sound of its rattle as I kneel behind Pinder's head.

"What's that noise? Am I bleeding anywhere?"

The snake's jaws hinge open when I put it against Pinder's neck, its fangs hanging down like a curved pair of pearl-colored stalactites. The rattler hesitates for a moment, gauging the heat coming from the creature in front of it and then daggers its fangs into the neck just below the ear.

"Ow," says Pinder with mild surprise.

The snake maintains its bite for a few seconds, gently flexing its jaws like a man savoring his first greedy bite of a rare delicacy. When it releases its grip—a teardrop of venom still hanging from one fang—I toss it away and watch it glide out of sight.

Pinder coughs wetly and moans, "Oh, my...oh, my...The pain's not going away...Is the horse okay? Is Mei coming to get me?"

Last of all, I check his pockets and take out his phone. It was shattered in the fall and isn't working, so that job's been done for me.

"Thirsty," says Pinder.

I sling the backpack on and go back the way I came, stopping to recover the empty water bottles from yesterday. The horse is standing at the edge of the ravine looking down at Pinder, its ears swiveling with curiosity as it listens to his disjointed words turn into choking sounds. I lead it a couple of hundred yards away before dropping the reins. It ambles off to nibble a bush. The horse won't find its way back to the barn before dark, which is less than an hour away, so even if the staff immediately raise an alarm, they won't find Pinder until morning.

There are about a dozen people at the house when I get back. One group is playing a board game, while others swap stories about the wildfire. Autumn is describing, probably for the umpteenth time, what happened on the yacht. Carmen is flirting with Jessie, an actor in a Netflix series. I go to the office and watch a baseball game. Autumn follows me up a few minutes later.

"Well?"

"The news will say he was thrown by his horse and had the unbelievably bad luck to land on a rattlesnake."

"Jesus," she says with emotion, then sits in a chair on the other side of the room.

"At least he didn't burn like those people up north."

"I know, I know." She pauses as she curls up in the chair, her arms clasped tightly around her knees. "It's just that...It's still a fucking horrible death, isn't it?"

I want to say I've seen worse, but I leave it at, "Yes, it is."

Autumn stares blankly at the floor. "That's enough. We'll leave Enoch alone."

"Why the change of plans?"

"It's making me ill. I was okay at first, but now I can't stop thinking about the two I've already killed; I mean, the actual physical act of it. The first man was going to kill me, the second ordered me killed, was a rape hobbyist, and burned people for profit. Both of them *should* be dead. Both of them *earned* their deaths. I tell myself that it was justified, that I was crazy with righteous goddamn fury, but I can't do it again. I took too much pleasure in the moment I killed them; it's the same thrill Gideon got each time he drugged a woman and knew he was minutes away from raping her. I don't want that warped sensation of power anymore. And now I've let you go and do my dirty work. I was going to tell you not to, but...I'm sorry."

"Don't be. I'm glad. This is how you leave their looking-glass world. Let's get out of here and talk about where to escape to."

"We'll go on Thursday."

"Thursday it is."

We take two bottles of wine down to the beach and argue the merits of Croatia, New Zealand, Costa Rica, and Sri Lanka until we get drunk and start speculating on what life would be like in Vatican City, an abandoned missile silo in South Dakota, a Chinese junk sailing the Andaman Sea, a falling-down castle in Spain, and a barge on the Canal du Midi. We end by making love in the sand, the clouds above us catching orange reflections of the fire still burning in the mountains. When we stumble up to the house much later, we find Carmen and Jessie lying together under a beach towel on the deck, both of them naked and asleep.

It takes them less than 24 hours to find Pinder. I'm driving to my apartment at about noon to pick up my passport when I hear on the radio that a helicopter spotted his body first thing in the morning and that he was positively identified an hour ago. Police sources are saying he apparently died in a fall from a ridge, possibly after being thrown by his horse. The coroner will find the snakebite wound, and the story will be a mild sensation for one news cycle.

By the time I return to Malibu, the number of guests has shrunk by half, and all of them are in or near the ocean, including Autumn and

Carmen, almost indistinguishable from each other when they're in the water with their matching hair. I stay on the deck by myself, luxuriating in the anticipation of being away and free in a few days. Autumn comes up to the deck when she sees me, a more relaxed smile on her face than I've seen in a long time.

She towels off and asks, "What are you going to miss most?"

"A Mexican place on Pico. You?"

"Some paintings. I'll have to start making my own."

"You'd be very attractive with smears of paint on your face and holding a palette."

"You think that's what an artist looks like?"

"Sexy ones, yes."

"Idiot. I was talking to Carmen and she wants to go to her house, pack a bag, and then to the airport. She's flying to Atlanta tonight to stay with Jessie while he shoots his series there. I volunteered you to drive her. I'd come, but there's some people coming over I want to say goodbye to before we leave."

"No problem. Where's she live?"

"Paradise Summit. It's a gated community up in the hills near Pacific Palisades. Gideon built it and gave Brooks one of the houses."

"I know it. Is Brooks going to be there? I'd enjoy restraining him if he gets difficult with Carmen."

"That would be fun, but he's gone to speak at a libertarian, incel, states' rights, bigfoot conference in Kansas."

"Before they've found his father? And with his mother still grieving? I'm dismayed at his lack of familial warmth."

"He'll be praised for showing fortitude and devotion to his cause in this time of tragedy. In their ecosystem the young happily eat the old, and the old feast on the young. The winner is the one who gets up from the dinner table last."

"Like Hexum, only with better zip codes."

Carmen says her goodbyes to Autumn just after dark, and we go to the garage and get in the Lexus. I mentally kick myself when I notice I've forgotten to take my backpack out of the back of the car. When I return to the house, I'll put the empty water bottles in the trash and pitch the gun into the ocean. The garage door swings up and I turn right onto the highway. Traffic is light, and the sound of a motorcycle trailing behind us makes me think of my dirt bike. I haven't ridden a bike in years, and I idly hope we end up in one of those countries where the main form of personal transportation is a scooter.

"Thanks for doing this," says Carmen apologetically.

"It's a pleasure. We owe you a lot."

"I could say the same. It's like you and Autumn lifted a curse that was on me."

I don't have any confidence that Brooks won't arrange for more curses to come her way.

A pair of headlights comes up fast behind us and passes the motorcycle so closely that the bike swerves to the right, its two riders giving the car the finger as it overtakes us in turn with a belching roar. It's a Ferrari convertible, and both Carmen and I say, "Was that…?" a few seconds after it's passed us. We spend the next few miles debating whether it was Robert Downey Jr. or not.

I turn left onto Sunset Blvd. and then another left on Paradise Summit Dr. The motorcycle and its helmeted passengers are still behind us. The figure on the rear of the bike swivels to look back down the road. No other vehicles are in sight. The passenger turns around and taps the driver on the shoulder twice. It's an all-clear signal. They're fifty yards behind us and the road ahead is winding, empty, and sheathed by scrubby hills.

"Carmen," I say sharply, "reach over and pass that backpack to me. Now."

She doesn't hesitate, but she's afraid.

I unzip the bag and pull the Walther out as the motorcycle begins to accelerate.

"Get as far down on the floor as you can."

She throws an agonized look at our pursuers before slipping out of her seat and crouching on the floor of the car.

The motorcycle has closed half the distance and is pulling out to pass me when the passenger reaches inside a pannier on the right side of the bike and brings out an ugly little Uzi.

Red River

The fact of Anne's death was precious; it granted me the freedom to become fully detached from Levi. I'd never stopped thinking that he had some kind of claim on me as my father. Now, I could look at him as just another one of Hexum's thuggish fuckups, no different from the McSweeneys, or the noxious jackals who loitered outside the brothel on Lincoln begging the guys going in for a loan of ten or twenty dollars so they could get laid as well. Levi had denied me the knowledge that my mother was dead; he'd let me dream and imagine for years that she was out there somewhere. While I was sure that Levi had been involved in her death, I stopped short of thinking he murdered her. Perhaps there'd been an accident he covered up? That would be his style. I didn't tell anyone Anne was dead, not even Jessica. It was a hoarded secret that I wanted to save for Levi's ears only.

My relationship with Jessica had cooled as I became more involved with Reinhart, doing more and more jobs for him to build a nest egg that would take me away from Hexum. When we were together, I'd tell her censored stories of what I'd done for Josh, or things I'd heard around the Sheriff's Office. I thought these tales were amusing or startling, but she wasn't entertained, and saw them as evidence of me falling under the spell of the men who, as she described it, had turned Hexum into a "zombie crackhead theme park." We fought a few times over that. She was also having to deal with social ostracism because of our relationship. She had told me that virtually no one at school would speak with her, but I only commented that that was no great loss considering what kids in Hexum were like. It was arrogant and insensitive of me, but I'd grown up without the friendship of others my own age, until Jessica came along, and I couldn't comprehend how this was a problem. I had her and that was enough; I didn't feel isolated, so how could she? I wasn't able to fully appreciate that I wasn't normal. Knowing that my mother was dead put yet another barrier between us. At times I wanted to tell her, but then I'd draw back from it. Somehow, I thought foolishly, it would make me even more of a damaged outsider in her eyes, and the oppressive knowledge that Anne was gone forever often sent me into cold, silent moods during which I bitterly retraced the jagged-edged timeline of my life.

In April of 2003 Jessica's father's unit was sent into Iraq a few weeks after the main invasion force. He was in supply and logistics, so it didn't seem as though he'd be in too much danger, but I could see that Jessica was living under a cloud of worry.

She and I were watching the progress of the war on CNN one night and I said optimistically, "This isn't a war, it's the military equivalent of kicking the drunks out of a bar at closing time. Your dad'll be home in two months."

"Drunks don't shoot back, asshole," she snapped at me, then left the house in a rage.

It was around this time that Reinhart began to loan me out to Jubal. He never said I had to do anything for Jubal, only that there was an opportunity to pick up extra money.

"I wouldn't ask you, Tom, but Jubal's got a bit of a manpower problem right now."

I warned Reinhart I wouldn't have anything to do with Levi or the house on Lincoln, and he was cool with that.

My first job was simple enough: I had to pick up Spencer, who'd injured himself and couldn't drive, at his house and take him around on various errands. I almost considered saying no—the prospect of being close to Spencer was nauseating—but it was an easy two hundred dollars.

I had never been to Spencer's place. It was in the foothills a few miles south of J.J.'s, at the end of a wide dirt road that had once led to a mine. I had my driver's licence by then—not that the local police cared—and also a green Nissan pickup that had been left behind by the victim of a hunting accident. When I rounded the final bend in the road and saw Spencer's home, I thought I'd come to the wrong place. The house was nothing special—a two-storey wood frame structure painted light blue—but the half-acre of yard in front of it was littered with toys and sports equipment. There were soccer balls, basketballs and footballs, lawn darts, a slide and swing set, a trampoline, and a couple of remote-controlled toy cars. A large, oval aboveground pool was beside the house. I expected a family to come out on the porch and look at me curiously, but Spencer, wearing New England Patriots gear, came out of his house slowly, his right foot in a walking cast. He limped over to my pickup, climbed in, and told me where to go without once looking at me.

Age was doing cruel things to Spencer. Or rather, he was doing horrible things to himself to deny aging. His hairline had retreated entirely, but he'd mounted a ferocious counterattack with a comb-over held in place with hair product that shone wetly and smelled of cucumber. He'd never given up his trademark look of team-branded clothes, but he was forty or fifty pounds heavier than when I'd first met him, and he was trying to squeeze it all into sizes he fit nearly a decade ago. A pale slice of stomach showed where his T-shirt didn't meet his shorts, which were straining against his fat ass. He looked like a buffoonish, mean-spirited cartoon character whose eternal fate it is to sit on tacks or get kicked in the butt by livestock.

I waved a hand at the yard before starting the Nissan and said, "Is it a sports-related injury or just gout?"

"Fuck off and drive."

I took him to various labs, a new Latino brothel, a couple of stores, and some homes. He was on the phone when he was in the truck, talking to Jubal or members of their crew. After a couple of hours, he told me to drop him off at J.J.'s.

It was early afternoon when we pulled into the parking lot.

"Go around the back," said Spencer.

The rear of J.J.'s was a parking area for the vans, trucks and cars Jubal used in his business. There were always a few guys back there tinkering with the vehicles, but today there was a small crowd grouped around Jubal, who was standing over a man kneeling on the ground, his hands zip-tied behind his back. We got out of the pickup and joined the crowd.

"You ain't never gonna have enough money to pay me back," Jubal yelled at the man.

The kneeling man was Adam, a member of Jubal's crew. He hadn't been around long, and I hadn't spoken to him more than a few times. He was tall and skinny, in his twenties, and had a diffident manner that didn't seem right for Jubal's bunch. I could see him as a preacher in a small church he'd built with his own hands.

"I've a house I can sell, Jubal," begged Adam in his high, flute-like voice.

"A house? You want me to be your fucking real estate agent? You owe that money now!"

Adam tried to stammer his way into another offer or explanation, but ended up whispering, "I'm sorry, Jubal."

Jubal answered that by kicking him in the shoulder and knocking him to the ground, then turned to a man near him and said, "Bring Woody out."

The man dashed into the back of the building and returned with a lidded, white plastic bucket. He was also carrying a thick pair of elbow-length gloves, the kind workers use on power lines. Jubal slipped the gloves on, opened the bucket, and pulled out a three-foot long rattlesnake that drew appreciative murmurs from the crowd as if he'd performed a magic trick. Adam kept chanting, "No, Jubal," in a low voice right up until Jubal let the snake bite him on the bicep. Some of the crowd swore. Adam began to cry.

To no one in particular Jubal said, "Toss him in one of the trucks and take him out of town and dump him. Adam, you probably got time to hitchhike to another town and go to hospital before you die or your arm falls off. But don't ever let me see you in Hexum again."

Adam was panting and sweating profusely as two men picked him up and dragged him to a mini-van.

Jubal dropped the snake to the ground and watched it coil into a ball. The crowd dispersed quickly.

"I should probably let Woody out of that bucket more often. It can't be good for him to be cooped up like that." He extended a gloved hand and the snake struck lethargically at it. "You see? It's like he's not even trying, the poor little guy."

"My two hundred," I said to Spencer.

Spencer reached into his pocket and pulled out two fifties.

"Reinhart said two hundred."

"Then get the other hundred from him, asshole."

He dropped the fifties on the ground and started limping away. I stepped around him and grabbed Woody just behind the head as he half-lunged for the second time at Jubal's outstretched hand. His body coiled weakly around my arm as I walked towards Spencer and said, "How much did you say?"

Spencer suppressed a cry of horror, reached into his pocket with a spastic gesture and yanked a hundred out and dropped it as he backed up into a truck. I returned Woody to the bucket, closed the lid, and picked my money off the ground. Jubal said nothing but gave me a friendly nod as he took the bucket and went inside. Spencer followed him, his face very red. The few men who were still hanging around grinned slyly at me.

As I drove away from J.J.'s I was feeling very pleased with myself; I'd put Spencer in his place and impressed Jubal and his cronies. If Jessica had witnessed my actions, she would have told me that I was an idiot for valuing the esteem of creatures like Jubal and those who grinned like dogs as they took his money. And she would be right, but I couldn't shake a guilty feeling of superiority and triumph.

In mid-June I heard that there had been some kind of accident out at Levi's place two days previously. Amy had been clean for a long stretch by then, but my immediate thought was an overdose. I drove out to Levi's in the early afternoon and found that a section of the paddock had been crudely repaired. Amy had acquired two more horses—Rex and Tilly— back in January to join Toby and Turk, but I could only see two in the paddock.

I found Amy at the kitchen table chewing a pencil and staring at a Sudoku book. She didn't look wasted, but she didn't seem right, either.

"Everything okay?" I asked.

"Mm-hmm. You?"

"I'm fine. What happened with the paddock?"

"Well," she said calmly after a long pause, "A few nights ago Levi came home and drove his truck into the paddock. He was drunk. Rex and Tilly got out. I was in town at the time. Anyway, they wandered down to the highway. A truck from the mine hit both of them, and I found them just after the accident when I was driving home. Rex was dead already, but I had to shoot Tilly. Her front leg was torn off. The driver was awfully upset; he said he has horses of his own. Now, before you say anything I'll let you know that I've already forgiven Levi. He's fighting demons, has been his whole life, and I've been helping him the best I can. He will come to Jesus one day, I'm sure.

"Amy, you can't fight demons when you choose to work for them, and Jesus is going to get fucking bored waiting for Levi to show up."

"I have to try, Tom."

"Where is he now?"

"Gone for a week on a job."

"He left you here alone after that?" I said angrily.

"I'm fine, Tom, I'm fine." She put her hand over mine. "I have strength I didn't have before. And spare a thought for Levi; think how he must feel about causing the accident."

"Why don't you go away for a while? A vacation."

She shook her head. "I have everything I need here. My horses, Levi...and you!"

I had a brief urge to argue the point with her, to warn her that life could only be worse the longer she stayed in Hexum and with Levi, but from experience I knew how little potency I had as a prophet.

"I'll check in on you, Amy. Call me if you want company or anything."

"I will, Tom."

She walked me out to my truck, asking on the way about Jessica and congratulating me on graduating high school. Her smile as I drove away was big and natural, but I didn't think it made it into her eyes.

Amy vanished from my mind the next day. I was at home, sitting in a lawn chair in the backyard reading *Rendezvous with Rama* when Jessica came around a corner of the house looking miserable. I jumped up, and as she took me in a ferocious hug, I knew there was bad news about her father.

"What's the matter?

She couldn't speak at first, her breathing was too rapid and shallow, like someone gearing up for a scream. "His Humvee hit a mine," she said finally. "They say he's badly injured and he'll be transferred to a military hospital in Germany as soon as his condition stabilizes."

"Shit."

"Mom's a wreck. I'm a wreck. Fuck this war, fuck everything."

I asked her a score of questions about what they'd heard from the army, but it amounted to nothing more than the savage news that the war had ended the wrong way for Hector. We sat together in the yard, her head on my shoulder, my hands in hers. When I ran out of comforting words and she exhausted her best-case scenarios, we sat in silence in the late day sun and watched the eccentric trajectories of swallows flying low over the sagebrush.

"They look like X-wing fighters, don't they?" said Jessica.

"Are you saying Hexum's the Death Star?"

We made some more stupid jokes about *Star Wars* and, bit by bit, her mood lifted fractionally; enough, at least, for her to agree to go out and eat before returning to her mother. We went to Denny's and quietly made fun of the food and the customers, and began to feel adjacent to normal.

"So," said Jessica, "we haven't talked about what's next."

"As in?"

"We've graduated. Are you going to leave Hexum? I hope so."

"I am," I said with false eagerness. "It's just that I thought I'd wait another year to go to college, save some more money. Don't forget, I'm a year younger than you. I don't want to be Doogie Howser at college."

"Don't worry, Tom; no one will ever think you're young. But you are leaving?"

Jessica looked doubtfully at me as I agreed that I was. I couldn't tell her I had unfinished business with Levi, and, what was worse, the idea of leaving Hexum was beginning to frighten me. I was growing comfortable in my life in Hexum. I knew the town was a freak show, but that made the idea of living somewhere normal unsettling. How could I live among ordinary people and not eventually be regarded, at best, as an oddity, or, at worst, as a danger? In Hexum I had respect and a place in the hierarchy; the outside world was offering none of that.

"How about you?" I asked.

"I don't know now. I wanted to take biology, but we'll have to see, I guess."

The rest of the meal was mostly eaten in silence, and when I dropped Jessica off at her home, her kiss was an afterthought.

For the next week I saw Jessica every day, sometimes for just a few minutes. The good news was that Hector was stabilized, but the authorities still hadn't revealed the nature of his wounds. The day that he was flown to Germany, Jessica came over to my place and we had a relatively normal evening together, including spending time in bed. She was cautiously optimistic that night because they'd received word that a date had been set for Hector to be flown to Walter Reed Army Medical Center in Washington, D.C. The next day Inez got a call from a doctor in Germany who explained that Hector's injuries were no longer immediately life-threatening, but they were "life-changing" and "disfiguring." It was a terse, bureaucratic way to describe a man who was now blind, missing his right arm and leg, probably brain-damaged, and had third-degree burns across half his face.

There was nothing I could say to assuage Jessica's pain. Her father was effectively dead, but she and Inez decided to move to Washington immediately to sit by the bedside of his ghost and, in Inez's case, pray for a miracle. In the only moment of lightness Jessica could muster before leaving Hexum, she said that she'd be praying for "Bones" McCoy to arrive from the future and make things right. Their departure was rushed and chaotic, and Jessica and I barely had a second together until the morning I met her outside their bungalow near the army base. Inez, looking brittle and haggard, sat behind the wheel of their over-packed car staring straight ahead. She and Hector had never acknowledged my existence, probably thinking it might bring them bad luck. I couldn't blame them.

"Let me know what the doctors say when he gets to Walter Reed. They probably have specialists there who can do more than whatever they've got in Germany," I said in my most encouraging tone.

"Sure. So, we'll talk, right?"

"We will. Let me know about anything and everything, and never, ever start rooting for the Capitals."

She laughed. "I don't even know what that is. Maybe you can come out sometime; not soon, but when, you know, things get more settled for us there. Plenty of colleges around Washington." Her look turned serious. "Even if you don't come see me, get yourself out of Hexum. A place this wrong is going to collapse in on itself one day."

"A year at most and I'm gone."

She put her arms around my neck. "You know, we've never said we love each other; is this a good time to do it?"

"It is. I'll go first: I love you."

"Me too."

Inez glared at me as I kissed Jessica. We said our goodbyes, and they began their drive to the other side of the country. Jessica phoned me briefly four days later to say that they had arrived safely and that her father was due to arrive in another week.

Until she was gone, I wasn't aware of what Jessica had meant to my sanity. I needed her perspective, her acid comments on the things I heard and saw at 'work,' to remind me that Hexum was an aberration, a sagebrush Bedlam, and that there was another way of living I could enjoy. I like to think that her presence would have changed what happened two weeks after she left.

Early on a Sunday morning the phone rang in my house, and I answered it thinking it would be Jessica with news about Hector. It was Levi. He had never phoned me before, and we barely spoke on the odd occasions we met in or out of town.

"Can you come over?" he slurred.

"Why?"

"I need help."

"With what?"

"It's Amy."

"What's happened? Is she okay?"

"It's Amy."

"I heard that, Levi!" I said furiously. "What the fuck's wrong with her?"

"Just come over. Be a pal," he mumbled before hanging up.

I drove recklessly to Levi's, suffocated with the same dread as the night I went to the Settlement for the last time. The horses were in the paddock when I got there, which I briefly took to be a good sign as I had thought Amy might have gone missing in the chaparral and Levi wanted me to search for her. I came through the door and Levi was leaning against the fridge, his eyes half-open. a cigarette that was mostly ash hanging from his lips. I could see into the living room where Amy, positioned with her back towards me, was sitting on the couch. She was watching a Pat Robertson sermon with the sound turned up loud.

"What the fuck, Levi? What's the problem?"

He pointed to the living room with a lazy, deeply stoned gesture as the ash from his cigarette crumbled into gray snow.

"Amy?" I called sharply.

There was no answer.

I hurried into the other room and found her looking half-asleep, staring at something unimaginably distant with unfocused eyes. Her skin was the waxy shade of white that death leaves behind. A ruby jot of blood marked the spot in the crook of her pale arm where the needle— still cupped in her right hand— had found a vein. I sat in front of her on the edge of the coffee table. A fleeting smile was fixed on her face for eternity. I carefully lifted the needle out of her hand and dropped it in an ashtray, noticing as I did so that her hand was calloused from handling tack and mucking out the stable. The chimp-faced preacher on TV was talking about Iraq until I vanished him with the remote. I rolled down the sleeve of her sweatshirt to cover the injection mark, then gently brushed her cheek with my hand.

Levi dragged himself to the doorway, bumping into a chair and a wall like a lethargic pinball.

"I found her like that when I got back a few hours ago," he said with annoyance, as though Amy had pulled a dirty trick on him. "She must have forgot to cut it. I told her to cut it. It must have been goddamn pure. I knew it was good stuff I bought. She's been real down since those damn horses got flattened, and I thought some of that might help her, get her chilled until, you know, she…" He trailed off.

"You brought her smack," I said softly.

"I figured she could use some," he whined. "I'm thoughtful that way."

He stumbled back to the kitchen table and sat down heavily.

"Why am I here?" I asked.

"Huh? Oh. I need to dump her somewhere—one of those shafts, maybe. Jubal and Reinhart would be really pissed if they found out about this. We can put her in the back of the truck and cover her with a tarp. I woulda done it myself, only I'm a little under the weather."

"You're fucking wasted."

"Yeah, well, this has been stressful."

"She's not being dumped. Go sleep it off and I'll take care of it."

Levi stared at me vacantly for a moment, waved his hand in a "whatever" gesture, then drifted into his bedroom.

I went to the paddock and saddled the two horses. They pranced and nuzzled me as I worked, happy that they were getting an outing. Levi was snoring when I went back into the house and began wrapping Amy in a striped, wool blanket, which I secured with some lengths of thin, cotton rope. I carried her over my shoulder to the paddock and laid her gently across Toby's saddle. He looked back with curiosity at this strange shape that smelled familiar. I lashed her to the saddle, tied a shovel and pickaxe to the back of Turk's saddle, and led the horses out of the paddock, a length of rope linking my saddle to Toby's bridle.

I swung up onto Turk, who sighed contentedly and set off without any urging. The day was hot and clear, although as I moved higher in the foothills, I could see fat, cauliflower-surfaced thunderhead clouds moving in from the west at a stately pace, like overstuffed dowagers out for a walk, their long skirts of rain trailing across a green lawn. There was no breeze, and the horses kept their tails busy chasing flies. I didn't push them hard because of the heat, stopping once to let them drink at a ribbon of creek that filled a small pool beside a sandy patch of ground covered in small, white butterflies waving their wings as though trying to fan themselves.

I reached the plateau after a couple of hours. It was unchanged since the first time I'd taken Amy there, except that one of the tall pines had been split and charred by a lightning strike. I removed the shovel and pickaxe from Turk, then carefully lowered Amy's body from Toby's saddle and laid it on the ground near the spot where she had marvelled at the view. The horses began to crop the grass and wildflowers. The soil was a mix of sand and small rocks, and I only had to use the pickaxe a few times. I made the hole deep and placed her in it with her head pointing towards the coast. I filled the grave in, heaped rocks on the disturbed earth, then added a pile of dry timber which I set alight—a layer of ash might frustrate the nose of any resident bear.

I got back at about three in the afternoon. Reinhart's cruiser was parked by the house, and he came out as I was unsaddling the horses. He stood on the other side of the fence keeping a wary eye on Toby and Turk.

"Someone said he saw you hauling ass through town out to here, so I thought I'd come around and see what the problem was. Levi told me Amy passed. He tried to lie about it at first, but your father is one terrible liar."

Not for the first time I was amazed at how quickly Reinhart was able to find out everything that went on in Hexum. I imagined him looking into a scrying mirror from *Harry Potter* hidden in a closet of his bleak home.

"It's a shame about the girl," continued Reinhart, "but that's what happens when you mix hard drugs with soft people. Did you put her down a shaft?"

I shook my head. "No. Amy didn't deserve that. I thought she should have one last ride on her horse, so I took her up into the mountains and buried her in a place that she liked—a flat clearing with tall pines and a big view. Amy thought she could see the ocean from there."

Reinhart slowly took his hat off and rubbed his head as he looked at me with a mix of surprise and embarrassment. His chin quivered, and he rubbed his scalp more furiously as tears started rolling down his cheeks.

"Tom," he choked out. "you are a hero. A man of fine feelings and iron...I can't say anymore except that you are a hero."

Reinhart wiped away his tears, reached across the fence to shake my hand, then walked over to his vehicle. I didn't know if I was touched or appalled by his reaction.

"Josh," I said as he opened the cruiser door, "can I borrow a pair of handcuffs?"

"What do you need them for?"

"To get answers to questions."

He hesitated, but then tossed me his handcuffs and the key before driving away.

I pocketed them and went into the house. Levi was in the living room watching a baseball game.

"Is Reinhart gone?" he asked nervously.

"Yeah."

Levi took a small vial from his pocket, opened it, tipped some yellow powder out of it onto the back of his hand and then snorted it.

"This is my own stuff. You can be damn sure I cut it proper. Reinhart and Jubal would be pissed if they knew I was using. Not that it's any of their business; they give me the shitty jobs and sometimes I gotta take the air out of the stress balloon with some medicine. Amy was just careless. What'd you do with her?"

I sat down across from him and watched the heroin take him over. He had immediately forgotten what he'd asked me and turned all of his attention to the game. I waited until a weak, silly smile appeared on his face that told me he was fully stoned. He was making this easy for me.

"Tell me about how Anne drowned."

"What?" he answered in a thick voice. "Anne?"

"The cops found her body in the water near Mystic about a week after we came out here. She never went with us. She never ran off with some boyfriend. They found her clothes in the house. And she didn't go swimming, because she couldn't swim, so you had to have dumped her body in the water. Was she alive when you put her in? Was it an accident? You can tell me if it was an accident, I won't be mad, I only want to know the truth for once. I want to stop thinking about her. You owe me for taking care of Amy. You owe me for abandoning me while you fucked off to San Diego."

The expression Levi habitually wore when he thought of a winning lie flashed across his face; it was a kind of startled joyousness, like someone bumping into an old, dear friend on the street.

He switched to a mournful look and said, "It *was* an accident. I'm sorry, Tom, but I couldn't tell the truth because the cops wouldn't have believed me. We went out crabbing at night, on a little road that passes over a channel. The tide was running out really fast, and I'd gone back to the car to get something and I heard her fall in. I ran back and she was gone. Just gone. It was so dark and, like you said, she couldn't swim and the water was racing, man, absolutely racing. I panicked; I mean, what would it look like? Me and her go out at night and only one comes back? And we were planning this new life out here together for you. I couldn't throw that away, could I, Tom?"

"This was the new life you got because of your inheritance, right?"

Levi paused before replying, "Yeah…My inheritance. It gave us a big opportunity. And it worked out, hasn't it? Look at what we've achieved by coming west." He swung his arm around as if inviting me to regard a vista. "I've got all this land, I'm sorta my own boss, and you've got…your own house. We're living the dream, buddy."

"I'm glad you told me, Levi. It's good to clear the air. I figured it must have been an accident. You want a drink? I'm getting a soda."

He giggled with relief. "Yeah, grab me anything. We'll watch the game together, right?"

"Sure."

I didn't have to look hard for a gun. Levi had acquired five or six of them over the years, and he left them all around the house. Amy had never liked seeing them and was always stuffing them in cupboards and drawers. I found a Browning Hi-Power, checked that it was loaded, and returned to the living room. Levi was berating a Red Sox player for hitting into a double play and didn't even look up at me as I stepped near him and smacked the gun hard into his temple. He keeled over with a groan, and I grabbed him by the collar and dragged him off the couch.

"Get up," I shouted, and stuck the gun barrel in his eye for emphasis.

He picked himself up with more moaning and one hand pressed to the side of his head.

I pushed him towards the front door and said, "Outside. Get in your truck."

He staggered out the door, threw up his arm to shield his eyes from the sun, and was turning around to say something when I fired a shot into the ground at his feet. He yelped and hurried to his truck.

"Get in the passenger side, Levi."

He opened the door and struggled to get his stoned and stunned body into the cab.

"What the hell, Tom? I told you it was an accident. You said it was okay!"

I tossed him the handcuffs. "Cuff your left wrist, pass the other cuff under the seat adjustment bar under your seat and then do your other wrist. Don't do it properly and I shoot you right now."

He was shaky and slow, so it took him two tries before he did what I asked. He was now doubled over in the seat, his hands shackled down near his feet.

"I'll give you a chance to tell me the truth, Levi. How did you drown her? Why did you do it?"

"It was an accident like I told you," he pleaded.

I shut the passenger door and went into the house and got a Dr. Pepper. When I came back out, Levi, only his head visible behind the door's window, looked at me in confusion as I drank the soda while leaning against my Nissan. It didn't take him long to react to what was happening.

"Hey…Hey! Open the door, Tom, it's getting too hot."

There wasn't a cloud in the sky, the temperature was in the eighties, and the windows in Levi's truck were all done up. The blood leaking from his temple was being washed away by his own sweat. He asked me twice more, each time in a more strained voice, to open the door. Between his calls I could hear the Red Sox game from inside the house. His cries to me became incoherent. I took my time, a long time, finishing the drink and then opened his door. His clothes were soaked and he gulped at the outside air.

"The truth, Levi," I said. "How and why did you kill her? Tell me and I'll take the cuffs off and you drive away from Hexum and never come back."

"An accident is what it was, Tom, I fucking swear it."

I closed the door and he screamed, "No! Alright, alright…It was like I said before, but…I pushed her."

I opened the door again and calmly asked, "Why?"

"She was going to leave me. Take you away. And she would've got half my inheritance. My money. Bridger money. It was like stealing my name. You and me, Tom, we're the last of the Bridgers, the last direct descendants. I'm not nobody. Our people started this country; Bridgers were governors and officers and…and…and guys who owned whole towns. You know we've got a whole island named after us? Bridger Island, near New London where we used to live. They gave it to one of us as a reward for clearing out the Indians back in the day. That's our heritage, Tom, and Anne was breaking the chain. She didn't see how important you were to me, that we needed to stay together so I could pass on the family history and help you be a part of it. I did it for both us, Tom. We're making a name for ourselves out here now; I mean, everyone who's important in Hexum already knows who you are, and you're only, what, seventeen? How successful is that? I couldn't let Anne take the money from me and risk losing this opportunity. Her people were nothing. Us, you and me, we're exceptional. And you're better than me, Tom, better than Jubal and Reinhart and all the rest, and that's because I brought you here. Hexum has been the making of you, Tom."

Levi was sobbing with emotion and nerves when he finished speaking, His breathing had become shallower and more rapid as he saw that the more he talked, the colder my expression had become.

"I'm still awfully hot out here, Tom. I'll leave town if that's what you want. I can go down to San Diego and start over. I don't get any respect around here, anyway. Take the cuffs off me and I'll go; I won't even pack, I'll just slide over behind the wheel and head on out. At least get me a drink, I'm really suffering here."

"So am I."

I slammed the door shut and retreated to the front steps of the house. It took a little over forty minutes. For the first five minutes or so he shouted and begged, thinking I was only tormenting him some more, then he tried banging his head against the window to break it, but he couldn't hit it at the right angle and only made himself bleed more. After he gave that up, he tried to pull the door handle with his mouth, which wasn't a bad idea, but he was very weak by then. The last thing I heard from him were hooting noises of pain as he cooked inside his shiny, blinged-out oven.

When I finally opened the door his body sagged out like a pile of wet laundry. I touched a finger to the damp, red skin on his neck and didn't find a pulse, so I took the cuffs off his wrists, dragged and wrestled his body onto the bed of my truck, and covered it with a tarp. I chose a ventilation shaft six miles away at the base of a hill. It sat in a pebbly clearing in the sagebrush and was framed in weathered wood and rose four feet out of the ground. When I removed the sheet of plywood that covered the top of the shaft a gust of air, like a giant's grateful sigh, escaped from the darkness below.

I dumped Levi's body out of the pickup and dragged it over to the shaft. Lifting him up to the lip of the opening wasn't the struggle it might once have been; the drugs had winnowed a quarter of the weight off his long frame. For a single, irrational moment I thought it would be cruel to dump him down headfirst, but then I realized he might become stuck if he went feet-first. Levering his body into the hole and feeling gravity taking over the job with kindly silence was the worst moment for me. I didn't regret killing him, but the realization that I would never see his face or hear his voice again hit me with a fierce intensity. I wanted him gone, and yet I felt something was ripped out of myself and the world with his death. His body scraped and rattled its way down the black tunnel like something scaly returning to its den. There was no thump or splash at the end, only a silence that I listened to for a minute.

I went back to the house on Cypress and sat in the backyard. The phone rang. It was probably Jessica—she usually phoned on Sundays—but I didn't answer. Later that day, towards sunset, I was sitting at my computer playing *Risk* and began to shake, first my hands and then my whole body. I'd been thinking about Dexter and the tips he'd given me for beating the game, and in thinking about him I'd remembered, word-for-word, how he'd told me about the tattoo that identified Anne. I could see her body rushing away in the dark water, the mad, gamboling tide pulling and tumbling her. And I saw Levi: a broken and discarded scarecrow lying on cold stone, a single star far above him showing the greatness of his fall. These vomitus images jostled for my attention like a pair of ghosts fighting for possession of a house they want to haunt.

The shaking continued, off and on, for what felt like hours until I had a short, sharp bout of crying that exhausted me so much I passed out on the couch. In the morning I felt hollowed-out and dehydrated. A thunderstorm rolled through in the early afternoon, and when the rain slackened, the smell of wet sagebrush filled the house and I found the will to leave and do groceries. I phoned Jessica when I got back and we had a flat, halting conversation about her father. She would have noticed something was wrong with me, but Hector had spent the last few days having seizures and that was, naturally enough, dominating her thoughts.

For the next few days, I was busy doing jobs in and out of town, but I found time each day to drop by and take care of the horses. A week after Levi's death, I ran into Reinhart at a lab inside a barn on an abandoned ranch east of town. I was yelling at the Asians sorting the meth into baggies to get a move on, when Reinhart walked in to collect an envelope from the guy who owned the lab.

After he got his envelope, Reinhart came over to me and asked, "You doing okay, Tom? That thing with Amy was tough, real tough."

"I'm fine, Josh."

"Say, I know you don't really talk with Levi, but have you run across him anywhere? He's kinda dropped out of sight."

I considered lying to him with an invented story about Levi being messed up and fleeing to one of the cities on the coast. If Levi never showed up again, Reinhart and Jubal would shrug and figure he OD'd somewhere or got himself shot. But Levi didn't deserve a lie. He used and enjoyed lies too much to benefit from one in death.

As if reminding Reinhart of something he already knew, I said, "He had a hunting accident, Josh."

His eyebrows shot up. "He had...?"

"Yeah."

"A hunting accident."

"That's right. Now I have to go kick some asses if this van's going to get loaded on time."

I worked steadily for Reinhart over the next few months, as well as doing jobs for Jubal. Neither questioned me about Levi, but their manner towards me changed. They treated me as an equal. Their silence about Levi was a way of acknowledging that I'd crossed a great gulf and joined them on the other side. I found a new home for Amy's horses, and Reinhart said he'd talk to Elmer Crippen about "finding" a will Levi had left with him that would name me as the sole beneficiary.

Jessica and I continued to stay in touch, but our conversations became more rote: updates on her father, how her mother was doing, what she'd read or seen. Because all her energy was taken up with caretaking her parents, she had decided to delay college. I could read between the lines that Hector wasn't expected to live out the year. I never told her that Levi was gone for good. When Jessica would ask what I was up to, I replied in generalities and pulled the conversation around to her again. She wouldn't have wanted to know what had become of me.

My imagination, like that of some brooding, wounded monster, was filled with a desire to see people suffer and to know that others were in pain. My soul couldn't hold all the anger and resentment and aching regret that was choking me, and I reasoned that my suffering would be eased if the world was filled to the brim with the excess. I fantasized about accidents and diseases and horrible crimes happening to people I knew only by sight: grocery store cashiers, waiters, clerical staff at the Sheriff's Office, and even random strangers. I reasoned that if anguish was all around me, if grief and rage were commonplace, my own agony would become banal and tolerable—merely another drop in an ocean of horror.

In October Jubal hired me to escort and supervise two truckloads of Mexicans being driven up to Las Vegas from Calexico, a border town in the Imperial Valley. My job was to collect payment from the *coyote* who'd brought them over the border and then drive ahead of the trucks and warn the drivers by walkie-talkie if I spotted Border Patrol agents or cops. The truck drivers were already in Calexico, and I drove down in a silver Camry that I'd be using as the escort car.

The rendezvous was on a hay farm two miles north of the border. I pulled into the farm's driveway at dusk and saw what I thought were several large, rectangular buildings silhouetted against the indigo sky near the farmhouse. The big structures were, in fact, stacked hay bales, and the farmhouse was actually a work-site trailer. The Camry's headlights washed across the trailer, and a stocky man in his sixties came outside and moved arthritically over to my car.

"Can I help you?" he asked with a smoker's raspy voice.

"Yeah. I'm Jubal's guy. Is Arturo here?"

The old man looked at me in surprise, realizing that I was in charge. "Uh, he is. I'm Mason. He's on the other side of stack three with the trucks."

"This your farm?"

He cracked a yellowy smile. "Mine? Nah, man, there's over ten thousand acres here! I'm the foreman. Newcastle Land Holdings owns it and leases it to an investment company called LRG in Boston; at least, that's what it says on the paperwork. I'll take you to Arturo."

We walked around the corner of the nearest ziggurat of hay and I saw the two trucks, both full-size rigs, standing near the furthest stack, their lights illuminating a high wall of enormous hay bales stacked three high that was as tall as the trucks. A red Jeep was also parked beside the stack. Sid and Mark, Jubal's drivers, were standing in front of the trucks and greeted me as I reached them. Bales had been removed from the bottom of the wall and light was coming out of the cave-like opening.

Mason pointed at the hole and said, "Arturo's in there. You can't miss him; he's a white Mex."

I walked through a tunnel three bales deep and came out into a quadrangle formed by the hay walls. A crowd of people was milling about, talking quietly in Spanish and gathering up backpacks and bags. A waning moon cast a cadaverous light on everyone. Two men with flashlights were telling the crowd in Spanish to get ready to go.

"Arturo?" I said loudly.

One of the men with a flashlight came up to me.

"Yes?"

"I'm Tom."

He was thirtyish, dressed in an expensive pair of jeans and a turquoise dress shirt that looked like they'd been bought an hour ago. The pinched expression on his face was saying that the smell of the crowd was bothering him. His companion with the other flashlight was wearing a shiny black San Antonio Spurs jacket and matching track pants. He had the size and build of a jockey, and darting, predatory eyes that immediately put me on edge.

"You're Tom?" asked Arturo in unaccented English.

"That's right. So let's do a head count and you can pay up and we'll get going."

In Spanish, his sidekick said, "This is a fucking kid. He sent a kid. Play him, Arturo."

I didn't react to what the jockey said, letting them think I didn't understand Spanish.

Arturo smiled broadly. "Of course. I'm sure you don't want to hang around this cattle pen any longer than I do."

He told the crowd to file out slowly and board the trucks. They obediently began shuffling out, an equal mix of men and women, most of them young, some in their early teens. They were all exhausted; a few even walked with their eyes closed. All of them carried water containers of some variety. There were 106 of them, and I was supposed to collect two hundred a head, paid out of the two thousand Arturo's bosses had already charged them to get to the farm.

"I make it $21,200, Arturo."

"Fuck this faggot, man; you can screw him around and we can keep most of it," said the jockey, adding a shit-eating grin to make me think everything was cool.

"What's your little buddy saying?" I asked innocently.

"Nothing. He's just anxious to go," Arturo said off-handedly. "I think there's some confusion over the price, friend; it's one hundred each. It's, like, a bulk discount. I've never shipped this many before. It's a great deal for Jubal."

"It's two, Arturo. That's what Jubal told me."

The jockey said, "This punk'll fold; keep at him."

"I'll tell you what, Tom. I'll give you one hundred a head now, and when you get back to Jubal, if he says that's not cool, then on your next trip I'll make it right. That's fair, isn't it? Anyway, I only brought enough cash to cover at a hundred a head."

I pretended to think over the offer.

"You've got the gutless cunt, Arturo, he's gonna fold. I can see it in his eyes."

"Okay," I said. "I'll let Jubal sort it out. Where's the money?"

"In my Jeep. Let's go."

I let Arturo and the jockey go ahead of me through the tunnel. As soon as we were outside, I put a hand on the jockey's shoulder, spun him around and punched him hard in the throat. He fell to his knees choking and gasping.

"Hold that fucker," I snapped at Sid and Mark as I pointed to Arturo, who was rooted to the spot.

They grabbed Arturo, and I stood in front of the jockey looking into his bulging, desperate eyes for a moment before kicking him in the balls. He collapsed onto his side and I turned to Arturo.

In Spanish I said, "You must be this dwarf's girlfriend, Arturo, because he treats you like his bitch. If I tell Jubal what you tried to do, he'll tell your people south of here and your head and your body will end up on different sides of the border. Is that what you want?"

"No," squeaked Arturo.

"You got a knife, Sid? Mark?"

Sid took a folding jackknife from his belt and tossed it to me. Arturo was sweating profusely in the cool night air. Mason was lurking in the background and enjoying the show, an unlit cigarette hanging from his smiling mouth. I bent over the jockey, who was wheezing with pain, and grabbed his left ankle. He tried to pull his foot away, but I knelt down on his leg, flipped the knife open and sliced through his Achilles tendon. His screams sounded like paper tearing. Arturo began swearing quietly in Spanish. I walked over to him and savored the fear that was consuming him like a flame.

"Where's the money, Arturo?"

"Glove compartment," he said weakly.

There were thick rolls of hundreds in the Jeep's glove compartment. I counted out the amount owed to Jubal, bound them up in two rolls with elastic bands, and left the rest behind. The jockey was still crying out. I showed Arturo what I'd taken.

"I'd be in my rights to take everything you've got, Arturo, or to hurt you like I hurt this *pendejo*, but we're going to do business again, and I'll allow you this one mistake. But don't you or your people ever disrespect me or Jubal's business again. Right?"

He nodded vigorously.

"And I'll never see this fucking creature again, right?"

Arturo nodded and I told Sid and Mark to let him go. He dragged his wounded companion into the back of the Jeep and took off without saying another word. I'd considered harming him, but I didn't know how his higher-ups would react to that.

The trip north took eight hours along secondary roads that gleamed softly in the moonlight, like a shiny thread coming off a distant spool, as they unwound across vast and stony deserts. The trucks were miles behind me, and for most of the drive I might as well have been a solo explorer on a lifeless planet. I replayed what I'd done to Arturo's man and thought of different ways I could have handled the situation that didn't end with me crippling him. But the alternatives didn't take away the satisfaction I got from knowing that I'd sent his life into a decaying orbit.

We got to Las Vegas as the sun was pinking the horizon. The drop-off was in a subdivision under development on the edge of Henderson that was nothing but dirt roads and staked-out building lots. A security guard at the entrance to the site took three hundred dollars from me and went back into his trailer. Eleven vans of various sizes were waiting for us, and as the people hopped and stumbled from the trucks, they looked stunned to have reached the end of the line. The men driving the vans, mostly Latinos, were telling everyone to hurry into their vehicles, but I noticed one driver pulling aside teenage girls and directing them into a white, windowless Ford Econoline that had no seats. The girls were confused but followed his friendly instructions and sat cross-legged on the floor. The driver slid the door shut, then got behind the wheel and moved off slowly, saying something to the other drivers from his window that made them laugh. I knew what was going to happen to them and considered pulling my Walther out and greeting the dawn with a couple of shots aimed at the Econoline's tires. But I didn't. The van, pregnant with misery, rolled past me.

I paid the truck drivers their fee of two thousand each before they left. They lived in Vegas and would be returning to Calexico in a week for another load. Jubal had booked a room for me in a motel far from the Strip. I slept for five or six hours, showered, then drove back to Hexum. The next day I met Jubal at the Hexum Diner and gave him his money, minus my three thousand for the job.

"Everything go okay?" he asked.

"No trouble at all."

He looked at me appraisingly and said, "Mason tells me you don't take shit from anyone."

"I don't like people jerking me around, but who does?"

"That's true. No one does. It's human nature."

Jubal counted off a thousand from one of the rolls I'd handed him and passed it to me. "That's for protecting my business. My business is me. You've learned that faster than most of the abortions I've got working for me. Good work."

I did four more runs to Calexico before the end of the year and never saw Arturo or his friend again.

Jessica phoned me on January 7th to tell me that Hector had died the previous day at Walter Reed. Her voice was hoarse, and exhaustion made her almost inarticulate. She promised to phone me back on my birthday.

She sounded better when she called a week later and wished me a happy birthday. "You have any plans? You know what: you should drive down to L.A. instead of hanging around Mordor—spend some of that dirty money on good, clean fun."

"By myself? I'd feel weird, and I don't think they rent hotel rooms to eighteen-year-olds."

"How about coming to Washington? Not now, this month, but in the spring?"

I was on the cusp of saying yes, of telling her that I would abandon Hexum and move east, but I had a haunting certainty that Hexum would come with me, that what I'd become wouldn't wick away no matter how many thousands of miles I travelled, and I'd bring destruction to Jessica. I told her the truth:

"Uh...I'm going to go to a police academy in February. I'm going to be a cop here in Hexum."

"What the fuck?...Are you kidding?"

"No. But I'll just do it for a year or two. It's something to keep me busy until I figure things out. I thought about college, I really did, but I don't know what it is that I want to do."

She didn't speak for half a minute and then said slowly, "So what you want to do is help make that hellhole more of a wasteland than it already is."

"No, it's not like that. I'm just going to do basic cop work, keep my nose clean, until I figure out what's next; a year or two, tops."

"It's Reinhart, isn't it? He's got in your head. You never talked about him the way you did all those others, how they were losers and assholes and head cases."

I actually meant what I'd said about only putting in a couple of years as a cop, but she was right about Reinhart. Becoming a deputy was something I owed him, like a knight answering a call to bear arms for his lord, and I dreaded what he might do if I tried to escape from his lands. The idea of being "clean" was a lie and a humorous fantasy. Serving Reinhart was, by definition, very unclean.

We argued some more, and the conversation ended with her saying bitterly, "Don't call me again unless you've left Hexum for good."

I phoned her a couple of times in the next week, but she always hung up on me. I nursed my sadness at losing her by imagining a future day when I'd show up at her door like a soldier returning at the end of a campaign, triumphantly announcing that I'd abandoned Reinhart and Hexum. It was a daydream that faded quickly.

I went to a police academy in San Jose. It was thirteen weeks of being surrounded by people who wouldn't have lasted a month in Hexum. They talked about serving the community, representing their people, giving something back, patriotism, and justice. I thought about the counting room and ancient mines filled with the newly dead, and I finished the course not having exchanged a social word with any of them.

May 20, 2004 was my first day at work. There was no ceremony or swearing-in; I put on my virgin uniform and went to the Sheriff's Office as I had a hundred times before, but instead of heading to the counting or rec room, I was met by Dexter, who walked and talked me though some administrative detail before showing me my desk, right next to his. Reinhart came in later and wished me luck, but he seemed tired and distracted, qualities I'd never seen in him before. I found out why in the following weeks.

In the months that I'd been away, the level and variety of crime in Hexum had begun to spike upward. Reinhart and Jubal were becoming victims of their own success. Word had spread that ours was a land of opportunity, a new world where a man could stake a claim in the wilderness or an abandoned building and create a chemical empire without any worries about the law. It was a meth gold rush. Grange County was spread over a thousand square miles of sagebrush prairie, jagged foothills, and forested mountain slopes, and Reinhart had to try and find all the new operators to collect the taxes. Not all of them wanted to be found or agreed with Hexum's tax laws. Jubal had to maintain his monopoly on deliveries out of Grange County and explain to independently-minded drug lords that he was their only option for getting their product to market. The new empire-builders brought along workers and muscle, and these excited monsters piled into Hexum on their off-hours to drink, fuck, fight, and give us work.

There was also the civilian problem. While some of the locals were getting rich selling supplies, everything from cars to generators to groceries, others were beginning to grumble, and a few were complaining to people in Sacramento about random gunfire at night and dead bodies on streets and lawns in the morning. Hexum's citizens had known better than to open their mouths, but desperation and fear were emboldening them.

My transition from civilian to deputy was effortless. I already knew where almost all the labs and farms were. I'd collected taxes, and I'd dealt with angry or crazed men all over Grange County for years. Actual police work, like attending car crashes or investigating assaults and murders—the ones that weren't ignored or permitted—was more challenging, but those cases were usually left to Dexter and two other deputies, Emmett Swallow and Clint Pascoe. Myself and twenty other deputies spent our time settling beefs, breaking up fights, busting heads when the fights didn't stop, and, of course, ensuring the smooth running of the drug business that paid our monthly bonuses. By the end of my first week I'd pistol-whipped a man, beaten another unconscious with a pool cue, fired warning shots multiple times, vandalized a car to punish a driver for doing doughnuts on Main, dumped a body, and shaken down a score of men for a crime we called "being stupid in public," which meant anything that seriously annoyed us or the civilians. Arrests were rare; Reinhart wanted to keep our crime stats low and our shakedown profits high. All this money went into the counting room in the basement, and there was never any skimming; after all, why would we cheat Reinhart? He was making us rich. Our regular pay was nearly 60k, and the money from the basement was now up to 8k a month.

By December the money was coming in even faster, but we were getting burned out. Every workday was a soup of adrenaline and violence as we tried to control the ever-expanding guerilla army camped within and without Hexum. It was difficult to calm down after shifts, and time off was often interrupted by urgent calls to come to the aid of other deputies caught up in bar brawls or needing help shifting bodies. On my days off I'd sometimes make the drive to Reno with Dexter and John Stockman to play poker. It was a good way to blow off steam and avoid being called for help. The casinos didn't care about my age as long as I flashed my badge. Reinhart could have alleviated the problem by hiring more deputies, but that pipeline was empty for the moment.

A week before Christmas, Reinhart called twelve of us in for a special meeting. We crowded into the rec room where Reinhart and Jubal were huddled together staring out a window at the rain-washed parking lot and muttering quietly to each other. Reinhart had been uncharacteristically snappish lately, and there was speculation that bad news was coming from Sacramento.

Reinhart turned from the window once we'd settled and said gravely, "Boys, we are dealing with a plague of lawlessness in this town like I've never seen. I do not understand why people think they can come here and carry on like damn savages, but that's the hand we've been dealt. It stops, starting today. If we don't get a lid on this situation, outsiders, people with fat asses from sitting on office chairs all day, are going to be coming here to fix things, and you all know what that means. The problem is that we've been too nice. A simple, old-fashioned beating, like the kind your daddy gave you, doesn't breed respect anymore. Yesterday I had a civilian, a church-going fellow, say to my face that he didn't think I was doing a good job. Can you believe it? That's how topsy-turvy things have gotten. I blame the internet, but that's neither here nor there. Hexum has heard our bark, but now we're going to pacify it with our bite. I only have one guideline for you: when you get into a situation with one of our local miscreants, think about what you would have done to him before today, and then do something far, far worse. And if that means filling up every ventilation shaft in the county to overflowing, then so be it. Now, you're probably asking yourselves why I'm meeting with you guys and not the rest. That's because you twelve are my 7th Cavalry. You are the best. I'll be giving you men the hardest patrols because I know that there's none tougher. Hexum will be proud of you. You will make the law rule." Reinhart paused for a drink from his coffee mug. "Jubal, here, is going to give us some auxiliary support, kind of like an irregular militia, for those of you who've read a bit of history. We won't have time to be picking up luggage anymore, so you contact him and give him the location and his guys will do the rest. Also, if there's someone you can't find who needs to become luggage, call me, I'll approve it, and Jubal will take care of it if he can."

"Are Jubal's crew off-limits, or do we apply the same guideline to them?" asked Stockman. "I mean, his guys are part of the problem half the time."

"Not anymore," growled Jubal. "I've warned them that this is coming. Treat them the same as everyone else. If they're stupid enough to get in trouble, then I don't want them."

"And Jubal's going to be our scout—kind of a Kit Carson. Tell them what you told me, Jubal."

Jubal put on a grim expression and said, "I've heard that cartel men have been sniffing around the county, as well as Crips. And I've had two loads hijacked by guys who were probably Black Dogs. What's more, those bastards have opened a clubhouse ten miles north of the county line near Sparta."

"That's right," barked Reinhart, "we've got those damn bikers camped on our borders now. They think they smell weakness. So, we gotta be alert to all these people. If you see a Mexican dressed good or driving a better car than he should, pull him over. That goes double for blacks; there shouldn't be any of those in Grange County except the ones that work at the base, and we know them by sight. Obviously, it's hard to spot Dogs, but Jubal tells me a lot of them favor driving BMWs. Can you believe it? American bikers driving German cars. That's how low these Dogs are. I'm surprised they don't drive Vespas instead of Harleys. We're going to start bringing law back to Hexum right this damn minute. Me and Tom and Vin are going to go over to the house on Lincoln and get rid of those deadbeats who hang around outside. As for the rest of you, I'll be sorely disappointed if at least one of you hasn't unholstered on someone in the next 24 hours."

Vin and I followed Reinhart in our squad car for the short drive over to Lincoln. It was a little after opening time for the brothel and cold, squally rain showers were making its customers run from their cars to the front door. The house's windows were steamed up, and I caught myself wondering what kind of life Mona had found back in Indonesia. Two men were standing on the sidewalk greeting the men going to the house with quick words and begging gestures. They were both white, in their forties, and wore jeans and coats that had probably seen a few different owners before dressing them. Their faces looked like they'd gone through several lives as well.

Reinhart told us to cuff them as we got out of our car. The men looked at us with the blank, accepting gaze of cattle and put their hands behind their backs with the calmness and efficiency that comes from muscle memory.

"Now lay them down on their backs in the road with their feet up on the curb," said Reinhart with unusual ferocity.

The men look alarmed, but didn't speak; they knew from experience not to question an angry cop.

Reinhart stood over them. "Does one of you have a car? Do you drive?"

"Me," whispered one of them. "We live in it."

Reinhart raised his foot and stomped viciously on the left knee of the one who spoke, then did the same to his companion. Both made remarkably little noise, considering how much pain they were in. They were used to assaults. Neither of them would walk properly again.

"Get in your car and drive until you run out of gas," said Reinhart. "If you come back, I use my gun instead of my boot."

We took their cuffs off, and the pair leaned on each other as they hobbled down the street in their ragged, soaking wet clothes, like characters in the last scene of a silent movie before the screen irises to black.

This brand of curb-stomping became our starter model punishment, and in the months and years to come, men who suffered it counted themselves lucky they left Hexum with only a ruined knee. The next evening, Vin became the first of us to scale up the punishment. He and I were called to one of the new bars that had sprung up on the road out of town that led to the army base, the mine, and the property that had once been the Settlement. The bar was called Hijinks and had been built inside the abandoned motel that I'd once hidden at while waiting for Caleb to drive past.

We pulled into the parking lot and found a crowd watching a tall white guy methodically kicking another man who was curled into a ball protecting his head. The man on the ground had a cut on his forehead that was bleeding heavily and grunted quietly as each kick landed. The kicks weren't that strong, more like attempts to humiliate than injure. The crowd was mildly amused by the scene, and when they saw us arrive, started drifting back into the bar. The man doing the kicking noted our arrival but didn't stop his assault. I recognized him as a middle management figure in Hexum's drug trade.

Vin got out of the car first and said in his slow, flat voice, "Step away from him, sir."

The kicking man shook his head. "Nope. I ain't finished yet."

"Yes you are. Get back."

"He was staring at my girl like she was for hire."

A woman stepped forward and shouted, "It's true. He even changed where he was sitting in the bar so he could look at me better."

She was good-looking, not wearing much of anything, and it took me a few moments to realize she was the girl who'd wanted to hook up with me in high school so I could beat up her father. I couldn't remember her name.

"Last warning, partner," said Vin.

"Mind your own business, you turkey-necked piece of shit."

His girlfriend laughed.

Vin frowned as if carefully considering the depth of this insult, then smiled as he pulled out his Glock. He looked across at me and said, "This is going to be great."

Vin fired twice, the first shot hitting the man high in the shoulder and knocking him down, the second going through his forehead and sending a plume of brain, scalp, and skull across the parking lot. The dead man's girlfriend made a gagging noise and ran into the bar. The man on the ground kept himself rolled into a ball.

Vin holstered his gun and said, "Tom, radio in and tell them Jubal's guys need to do a pickup here. We'll wait."

This is going to be great.

I debated whether Vin's statement had meant he was looking forward to shooting a man dead, or that life under Reinhart's new guideline was going to be wonderful. It was probably both.

And life did become wonderful for Vin. By May of the next year he'd gunned down seven more men and one woman. There may have been others he never told us about. Except for myself and Stockman, all the other members of the 7th Cavalry had at least two bodies to their credit. Stockman preferred handing out ferocious beatings. I stuck with curb-stompings. Reinhart was disappointed in me, but he didn't say anything about my relative leniency. As vicious and ruthless as we were, it didn't stem the tide of violence or the inflow of people trying to earn a quick fortune. Those we wanted to terrify became more evasive, and even civilians became afraid to call us for help except in the direst emergencies. Jubal and his men disappeared three or four people a month, including a reporter for the local paper.

I kept telling myself I was only a year away from leaving Hexum, but the years added up and the money I was supposed to be saving for my escape vanished in trips to Reno and Las Vegas. I tried to find a buyer for Levi's property, but without success; it didn't have any buildings to put a lab in, there wasn't enough water to supply a weed plantation, and civilians were leaving Grange County, not flocking in. Levi's chaparral kingdom became a one-house ghost town. Thieves would have stripped everything valuable out of the home, but it was known that I owned it, and no one wanted a Hexum cop looking for them. Idle curiosity made me check on the place every few months, and my visits became a kind of time-lapse photography as I watched the chaparral advance and embrace the house. I didn't regret seeing it vanish.

I numbed my emotions at work to such a degree that it began to affect my memory. Someone would remind me of an incident that had taken place days or weeks previously and they'd have to go over it in detail until I could remember my part in it. Inevitably, I did more than curb-stomp.

I shot three men in the winter and spring of 2006, and by the fall of that year I couldn't recall the shootings without intense concentration. The first man I killed had fired at me as I came up to his house to tell him to turn off his stereo. He'd put his speakers in the front windows to annoy a neighbor. He came running out the front door, firing wildly as he ran towards his car, the shots zipping past my head until his pistol jammed. I put three shots in his back as he pulled open his car door. He dropped to the earth with a long, tired sigh. He'd probably been terrified at the thought of what I was going to do to him and wagered that killing me and fleeing town was his best option. My second victim was standing over the body of his wife in an empty house they were squatting in. He was explaining to me why he'd beaten her to death when I ended his rambling justifications with a single bullet. The third man was high on something and smashing up parked cars with a baseball bat. I didn't even bother getting out of the squad car to gun him down when he started staggering towards me, his face rigid with drug-fueled rage,

When my shifts ended, I'd return to my house on Cypress, change into running gear, and go for long cross-country runs. It helped me sleep without having to take a drink or two. Watching anything on TV other than sports became impossible; the lives of fictional people and their tailor-made problems and resolutions repelled me. Reading, however, was still a reliable way to lose myself for a few hours, and my small house began to look like an annex to Latimer's store. There was a succession of girlfriends in those years, all of whom lived in Reno or Las Vegas. They knew me as a small-town cop who liked to visit on weekends and spend money in clubs and at the tables and on expensive presents. Occasionally I'd take one of them for a week to Cabo San Lucas or Los Angeles. As generous as I was, they all tired of me after a few months; my forced pleasantness would suddenly break apart and they'd see nothing but sadness and self-pity.

Late one night in April of 2007 I returned to my desk at the Sheriff's Office after a tiresome shift and began writing up reports. Dexter was the only other person in the office and sat at the next desk doing the endless paperwork that was dumped on him so that the rest of us could spend time on patrol. He stared at me sadly as I half-heartedly filled out forms.

"What's up, Dexter? You look like you've got regrets about something you ate."

"How do you stand doing it every day?"

"What?"

"Hurting people. I don't mean you shouldn't," he added hastily and apologetically, "I mean…How do you get used to it?"

"What makes you think I'm used to it?"

He gave a feeble shrug and answered, "I don't know."

"I stopped worrying about hurting people long ago. I get through each shift by thinking that the next one can't possibly be as bad, and I try not to hurt them as much as the next guy—Vin, for example. Besides, the world's a hurt machine, Dex, and we all play our part in keeping it in good working order."

"You really think that?" said Dexter, his eyes wide with disappointment.

"Seems reasonable to me."

"Josh wants me to go out on more patrols. He says I need to be blooded."

"We are short this month."

"I don't want to go out—I want to quit," he said in a shaky voice.

"What about that brother you've got in Folsom? Didn't Reinhart get his charge dropped down to manslaughter?"

"He assaulted a guard so he's getting another five years on top. Am I supposed to stay in this shitty job forever because Drew's a retard? Why don't you quit with me? We could spend a year going to poker tournaments all over the world. I got lots saved."

For a moment I tried to visualize a life away from Hexum. Nothing came to me. Where my imagination should have been there was only a carnival of rancid memories that bound me to the town like a witch's curse. My ruination fit comfortably in Hexum; there was no reason to take it into the outside world.

"We'll leave one day," I said soothingly. "You think this can go on forever?"

"Oh, shit," gasped Dexter.

"What?"

He pointed at my chest. "There's a bloody tooth stuck to your breast pocket."

"Damn. So there is. I thought all his teeth landed on the floor."

I used a tissue to pluck the tooth off my shirt and drop it into a waste basket. Dexter hurried to the washroom.

Dexter did have to go out on patrol more often, but he was in a constant state of terror that made his partners nervous, and the worst punishment he inflicted was looking disappointed in people. He was calmer when he rode with me, chattering about poker and video games and his favorite horror movies, but Reinhart pulled him off patrols permanently in July of that year. He would have been with me on the afternoon of July 12, and, immediately after the fact, I was glad he wasn't. In the end, however, it didn't really matter.

It was past noon and I was in Latimer's arguing with him that *The Left Hand of Darkness* was miles better than *A Canticle for Leibowitz*. The heat and the hour of the day meant things were quiet in Hexum, and I didn't want to exchange the dim, musty coolness of the book store for my cruiser parked outside, with its smells of stale food and hints of Stockman's Axe body spray leftover from last night's shift.

I exited the store holding a novel called *Spider World: The Delta* that Latimer had convinced me to buy. My cruiser was parked in some shade on the other side of Main, and I moved slowly across the wide street reading the blurb on the back of the book. There was no traffic, not a moving car in sight, and when I looked up as I was halfway across, the only people in view were an older couple standing on the sidewalk. They were staring at something behind me that was filling their faces with alarm. The woman brought her hand up in front of her mouth as if to suppress a scream and the man started pushing her behind a mailbox. As I threw myself down on the asphalt and drew my gun, I thought, briefly, that I was going to look incredibly foolish if there was nothing behind me but an empty sidewalk.

Two pistol shots cracked over my head and ricocheting pellets hit me in the calf from a shotgun blast that furrowed the road. I sprayed rounds at the three men standing on the sidewalk, one holding an outsized revolver, another with an automatic pistol, and the third with a pump shotgun. They dove for cover behind a red pickup. I got to my feet and fired steadily at the truck to keep their heads down as I ran backwards to the cruiser. The man with the shotgun tried a shot from under the pickup that blew apart the cruiser's grill and headlights. I wanted to radio for backup, but I couldn't open the cruiser's doors without leaving myself in the open, so I went around to the back and popped the trunk to get at my shotgun. A bullet smacked into the trunk lid and I got down low as I pulled out my weapon.

"You dumb motherfuckers!" I hollered. "No one shoots at a cop in Hexum and lives."

"You'll be dead first, pretty boy!" came an answering shout.

I'd only gotten a glimpse at the trio but the voice left me in no doubt: it was the McSweeneys, Dale and Henry. I knew they'd come back into the county months ago and had started up a small lab run by themselves and their uncle Cyrus. I hadn't had any dealings with them beyond noticing the dirty looks they gave me whenever I ran across them. It was also obvious that they were using their own product. Cyrus was the brains of their little operation, but that wasn't saying much. He looked the same age as his nephews, had a hawkish face perched on a spindly frame, and was now running in a crouch across the street to my right firing his shotgun from the hip, one of his shots blowing out the glass door of the shop behind me. I fired back twice with my Glock but missed and out of the corner of my eye I caught a glimpse of Dale on the left sprinting to my side of the street. Both were now out of my sight behind parked cars. From across the street, Henry kept firing with his cannon of a revolver to keep me pinned down behind the cruiser. They had me bracketed and in the open behind my vehicle, so I fired quickly to the right and left with the shotgun at the cars I guessed Cyrus and Dale were crouched behind, then scrabbled backwards into the store through its now-empty door frame, keeping low enough so that there was a chance they'd missed my escape. It was a picture framing business and I ran through to the back where the rear door was swinging open thanks to the frantic exit of the staff. An alley ran behind the store and I sprinted to the left, yanked open the back door of the third business along, pushed through piles of empty boxes, and came out into a shoe store. A man was hunkered down behind the sales desk and screamed when he saw me. Through the store's window I saw Cyrus reloading his weapon and sneaking looks towards my former location behind the cruiser. I moved slowly around the desk, brought the shotgun up to my shoulder and edged closer to the window. Cyrus must have seen some movement and without hesitation fired in my direction. The window shattered and collapsed as the man behind the desk screamed again and I fired back. My shell exploded the car tire next to Cyrus and put a hole in his arm as he threw himself to one side and fired another wild shot that tore up the store's ceiling. He was half-standing, racking his weapon and swinging it towards me, when my second blast cut away almost all of his throat. Cyrus stayed on his feet for a moment, blood spraying from the void under his jaw, before his unsupported head bowed down as if in prayer and he fell limply across the hood of a car and slid to the ground.

From across the street Henry yelled, "Where is he? Cyrus? You okay, Cyrus? Where you at, Dale?"

Dale didn't answer. I crept to the empty space where the window had been. The man behind me was sobbing uncontrollably. Without stepping out of the store, I swung my gun to the left and aimed down the sidewalk. Dale was hiding in the entranceway of the Subway about sixty feet away, his pistol aimed in my direction. He was expecting me to come out of the store and started firing before I did, his first shot catching my shotgun in the stock and ripping it out of my hands and onto the sidewalk. I jumped back as he stupidly emptied his clip at nothing, and when I heard him curse to himself, I jumped out of the store window, scooped up my shotgun and fired. I only managed to destroy the Subway's windows, but some flying glass must have caught him because he screamed with pain. I stepped over Cyrus' body and got between the parked cars.

Henry called out plaintively, "I can't see you, Dale. You see Cyrus?"

Dale should have answered, because Henry broke cover and stepped uncertainly into the street from behind the red pickup, looking nervously in all directions and waving his revolver around like it was a flashlight. I didn't want to spray shotgun pellets into stores on the other side of Main, so I put down my shotgun, drew my Glock and put two rounds into Henry's chest. He staggered back against the tailgate of the pickup and sat down hard, his head flopping forward onto his chest.

Dale bellowed with rage and I heard him running towards me along the sidewalk. I spun around and aimed over the hood of the car I was leaning against and pulled the trigger. It jammed. Dale fired and I took a hammer blow to the side of my head that knocked me down and unfocused my eyes. He skidded to a stop in front of me and I was dimly aware of a torrent of curses and spit coming from his mouth as he aimed at my face. A booming rifle shot sounded behind me and Dale flew back onto a bed of broken glass with a hole in his forehead and most of his brains all over the storefront.

Blood started running past my ear as I turned clumsily towards the sound of the shot and fumbled for the shotgun. It was Latimer. He was standing in the middle of the street holding the old hunting rifle he kept behind the counter. I remember thinking I had rarely seen him outside of his store, and that it was too hot for him to be wearing that ugly gray cardigan. There was a small movement behind Latimer and he fell violently forward at the sound of Henry's revolver firing. I got to my feet like a drunk and saw Henry lying on his side ready to fire at Latimer again, but he changed his aim when he spotted me. My first shot went wide and mangled his legs, but the second pulped his head and ended his howl of agony.

Latimer was on his back and losing consciousness when I got to him, a snake of blood moving hastily away from his body along the asphalt. He lips tried to form words, and his eyes looked towards me, but then he shifted his gaze to the sky and was content to stare at that forever.

At the hospital they said I'd taken a ricochet above the ear that sliced my scalp, but nothing worse. They tweezered the pellets out of my leg, stitched up my head and sent me home with some painkillers. Reinhart insisted I take a week off, and excitedly declared that something in the town should be named after me. Dexter came over to my place and played computer games with me whenever he could, and from him I learned why the brothers had come after me.

"Vin was telling me," said Dexter, "that the McSweeneys were leaving the county to go back to Texas. They got pushed out of their business, and before they left, they told people they wanted to settle a score with you."

"What score?"

"Dale said you suckered him once a few years ago and that started their run of bad luck."

"Being born started their run of bad luck."

Latimer had no relatives that could be found, and when I searched his apartment over the book store the only really personal item I found was a journal he kept listing and critiquing each book he'd read over the last fifteen years. Some of the entries had notes pencilled beside them reminding him to recommend the book to different customers. Jessica's name came up often in the later years, mine less so. I had his body cremated and scattered the ashes in the sagebrush behind my house. The landlord wanted to clear out the store, but I told him I wasn't in favor of the idea and he handed me the keys. The store became my personal library and a hiding hole when I didn't want to be found.

I couldn't shake thinking about Latimer's death. What tormented me was the realization that my actions had set in motion a chain of events that led to Henry putting a bullet in his back. If I hadn't head-butted Dale, if I'd let him walk away after insulting me, or if my reaction had been less humiliating for him, Latimer would be alive. I brooded on this over weeks and months and added up the other instances in which I had paved the way for another's death. I divined that killing Mickey had sent Levi on the path to meeting Amy, and my confrontation with Spencer had led him to shoot the man carrying the weed bale, and, worst of all, my meddling in the lives of Rebecca and Malachi had resulted in mass slaughter. I even wondered if Hector had signed up for active duty in order to use the bonuses and higher pay to get Jessica out of Hexum and away from me. I obsessively mapped out schematics of my life that showed how the reverberations of my tiniest actions had afflicted people around me. Dexter listened politely, almost fearfully, to me when I explained how I was a landlocked Jonah, an algorithm for creating bloody chaos.

I remained as ruthless as ever in my job, although my memory of that period is weak; my newfound obsession with proving myself to be an agent for grief consumed my thoughts. I continued to hand out pain and death while wearing a uniform, at times, it seemed to me later, with the goal of proving my own hypothesis. Leaving Hexum never appealed as an option; I reasoned that it would be cruel to release myself on the wider world, especially since I wouldn't be able to resist contacting Jessica.

Things came back into sharp focus for me in September of 2008. I was alone in the rec room sipping rum and Coke from a Big Gulp cup while watching someone on CNN talking about the Lehmann Brothers bank collapsing. Clint Pascoe came into the room, scooped up the remote and turned off the TV.

"What the hell?" I said.

Clint couldn't speak for a moment, gagging on his words as though they were large and jagged. "Dexter's dead."

"Fuck off. He's not on patrol, he's in Reno this weekend with Emmett—they're playing in a tournament."

"Emmett just phoned from there. Dex and him were jumped going back to their motel last night. Emmett got beat up pretty good and woke up in hospital. The police told him that they found Dex's body outside the city. Emmett says it was Cody Grau and some other Black Dogs that did it."

Two days later we got all the details: Dex and Emmett had seen some Black Dogs in the casino but thought nothing of it—Reno was neutral territory. Grau and four or five Dogs had grabbed them outside their motel room, beat Emmett senseless, and taken Dex away in a car. They took him north of the city to an isolated, dead end road near Spanish Springs, cut all his fingers off, then chained him to the back of a car and drove through the desert until Dex was broken, skinned and dead. Emmett hadn't told the Reno cops about Grau and the Black Dogs; he knew Reinhart would want to deal with this his own way. Grau had finally taken his revenge for losing a finger.

Two weeks after Dexter's death, Reinhart assembled his 7th Cavalry on a sagebrush-covered plateau well north of Hexum, just inside the county line. As soon as we arrived, it dawned on me that Reinhart had chosen this location for its sweeping views north into Fremont County where the Black Dogs had their clubhouse. Reinhart paced in front of us, his face furrowed with anger. I was sufficiently enraged by the loss of Dexter to forgive Reinhart his display of cheap theatrics in dragging us to this location and then stalking around like Patton's understudy.

"Boys," he began, "tomorrow at dawn we are going to teach those savages in Fremont County a lesson in how men who are loyal and true respond to barbarism. They took one of our own, and we will take all of them. We are going to ambush those bastards in their clubhouse while they sleep and shoot them down before they have time to pull their pants on. Whoever kills Cody Grau gets whatever valuables we find in their clubhouse and a month's vacation starting the moment that animal stops breathing."

Reinhart brought out maps and satellite photos and gave us the plan. The clubhouse was formerly a ranch building and sat in a steep, narrow valley in the foothills. A little-used gravel road ran in front of it, and behind was a few hundred yards of brush-choked land that ended at the Wintu River. Jubal, Reinhart told us, had reliable information that the Black Dogs were using an old mine on the site to house a lab. Ten to fifteen Dogs were probably at the clubhouse. The plan of battle was that Reinhart, Stockman and four other deputies, along with ten of Jubal's men, would come along the road at dawn and open fire on the clubhouse. Some of the guns would be firing tracers to set the place ablaze. Reinhart figured that with the road denied to them, any Dogs trying to escape would run out the back of the clubhouse and head to the river thinking they could follow it to a road a few miles away. Myself and the other deputies, and a dozen of Jubal's men, would be waiting on the far side of the river to cut them down. I was in charge of this group.

The temperature dropped overnight, and when I led my troop in the pre-dawn darkness along the bank of the Wintu, the river had a coiling doppelgänger of mist floating above it. We reached the area for our ambush and I spaced the men about fifteen yards apart, with myself in the middle of the line and Vin on my right. As we waited and the night began to weaken, the striking beauty of the place was revealed: the opposite bank of the river was grassy and bordered with a wall of trees and shrubs medallioned with dewy spider webs that shivered in a slight breeze. Birds vocalized absent-mindedly. Narrow game trails led out of the brush and down to the river, which formed a gleaming path up to the mountains, the tops of which were being forged into gold by the rising sun. I thought of Amy and wished that we had ridden through this land together.

The pop and boom of gunfire began to the north, a few tracer rounds shooting up into the sky like manic fireflies. I tightened my grip on my shotgun. Less than a minute after the shooting started, a clap of thunder sounded and a fireball flared up into view.

"Jesus," said Vin, "they set off the propane tank. I saw it on the satellite picture but didn't think anything of it; it's right beside the building."

"Quiet," I said.

The gunfire continued as a thick column of smoke rose into the air, and I was beginning to think no one would make it to us when a figure ran out of the brush on the other side of the river far to my left. Three shots rang out and the man collapsed on the riverbank. More shots sounded to my right and a Black Dog jumped into the open nearly in front of me. I noticed he was barefoot in the moment before Vin put a round from his AR-15 through his head. The Dogs broke cover in ones and twos, some of them armed and firing wildly. A man charged out of the bushes directly across from me carrying a sawed-off shotgun and we both fired at the same time. His shot lacerated the tree branches over my head and mine sent him tumbling to the ground, his body coming to rest by the water. Shots continued to ripple along the river and I realized there must have been more bikers in the clubhouse than we'd been led to believe. A man wearing a leather vest and blue sweatpants staggered out of the brush in front of Vin as though he'd been pushed. He had a long salt and pepper beard and was breathing heavily. Vin shot him as he waved a small pistol around uncertainly, and a split second later two figures burst into view behind him, the one in front armed with an automatic in each hand and pouring fire towards Vin's position as he ran directly into the river. Vin yelled out in pain as I snapped off a shot that churned the water and folded the gunman in half, then another aimed at his companion, a small man in a jean jacket and baseball cap who was standing stock still on the riverbank with his hands over his face. He went down with a scream. The man in the river tried to keep going through the waist-deep water with one hand clutched to his bleeding side, and even fired blindly in my direction until I put a full load through his chest. He went under slowly, like a reluctant swimmer entering cold water. The current spun his body downstream, a comet's tail of blood fouling the river behind him, and grounded him gently on a pebbly beach.

The sound of firing had stopped from the direction of the clubhouse, and no more Black Dogs appeared at the river. I checked on Vin and found that a round had creased the length of his left forearm, leaving him blood-soaked but intact. Our men were coming out of cover and adding up the dead, and Reinhart radioed me to ask how we'd done. I told him no one had got past us as far as I knew. Before wading across the river, I waited for the body of a fat man floating on his back to go past. He was shirtless, and his domed island of flesh was puckered with three bullet holes that added thin, red rivulets to the pinkish water that lapped around him. The dead man on the beach was missing a pinky finger. It was Cody Grau. The body of the man who'd followed him out of the brush was thirty feet away and partially obscured, but I could make out a spill of long, blonde hair against the green grass. I got closer and saw that it was a woman—the one whose boyfriend Vin had shot outside Hijinks. The girl who had wanted me to beat up her father in high school.

It suddenly came to me: Monica. I had finally remembered her name.

The Desert at Night

The motorcycle screams closer and I twist around to reach out the window with my gun hand and fire backwards as I brake hard. My shots miss, but the driver goes into a severe speed wobble reacting to the gunfire and my flaring brake lights. The passenger drops the Uzi as panic makes him clutch at his partner for support, which then throws the driver off-balance. They hit the deck as they pass us, the bike howling off the road and somersaulting along the ditch, while the men bounce and cartwheel down the road in front of us. I stop the car.

"It's going to be okay, Carmen, but stay down."

Our attackers are conscious but barely moving. I check the rear-view mirror. There's no one coming, but I can't count on having enough time to get out of the car and do anything to the men, so I drive over the outstretched arm of the passenger. He screams, and his partner frantically tries to drag himself off the road but doesn't make it before the tires go over his legs.

I continue up the road and tell Carmen she can get back in her seat.

She fights back tears and asks, "Are we safe now? Who were they?"

"You're safe. It was your hair. They were staked out near the Malibu house, and when we left, they thought you were Autumn."

I follow Carmen into her house and wait while she packs. It's a cool box of metal and glass walls filled with just enough furniture to make it look occupied. The view over Los Angeles and the ocean from the back of the house would be splendid if it wasn't a sight I never want to see again. Carmen's done in no time, and we drive to the airport in silence.

She gets out of the car at Terminal 5 and says, "I hope you and Autumn find refuge somewhere." She pauses. "I don't think it counts for much, but God be with you."

I phone Autumn as I drive back and tell her what happened.

"I thought those bastards were done with us," she says furiously.

"This is Gantry's doing. I don't think he ever bought Gideon's death as an accident. Roger's death on top of Gideon's is too much coincidence for him, and he figures other members of the Selous Group might be next, including himself. That was his pre-emptive strike."

"What do we do now?"

"Leave right now. Tonight. There's no guarantee he won't try again in the next 24 hours."

"Alright. I'll pack our stuff."

After Autumn hangs up, I think about the foolishness of killing Pinder. I should have learned by now that my violent actions almost invariably have an equally violent echo. It's my own personal law of physics.

Autumn comes into the garage as I park. Something's wrong.

"You're not going to believe this," she says as I get out of the Lexus. "My fucking passport's in Rancho Vista. I thought it was here, but then I remembered I took it to Rancho Vista."

"Okay. Not the end of the world. We drive there, pick it up, and go on to Las Vegas and catch a flight. We'll be in Vegas first thing in the morning."

"Why not come back to L.A.? It's quicker."

"By the time we drive back, LAX will be closed till the morning, and I don't want to hang around the city any more than we have to. Also, all these cars might have trackers on them by now, only this time they'll have put them where I can't find them easily."

"They'll know we're going to Rancho Vista."

"We'll go to LAX first, drop the Lexus, and get a rental car. If the Lexus is tagged, they'll think we're flying out from there."

"I guess that's it then. I haven't told anyone here we're leaving; I thought if the house is occupied it would make Lodestar think you and I are still around."

"How long do you think it'll take your friends to realize you're gone for good?"

"They could go on enjoying themselves for months or years without noticing. They'll assume I've gone to Europe or Taos or Rancho Vista and that the open house is indefinite. The maids will keep coming in to clean, the maintenance man has his routine, and the housekeeper has a credit card she uses to keep the house stocked. They're all paid regular as clockwork by one of Enoch's companies, and unless he drops by, the fun could be eternal, or until he runs out of money, which is almost the same thing. You need to grab anything before we go?"

"Yeah."

Autumn puts our bags in the car while I go up to the office and open Enoch's gun cabinet. I don't want to be caught with only my Walther and its half-empty clip if Lodestar tries again. Enoch has a pair of assault rifles in the cabinet—a Mossberg MMR and a Savage MSR— each with three full clips. The weapons are in their cases and look like they went straight from the store and into the cabinet. He probably bought them on impulse after he'd seen them looking fierce in a heist movie. I only want more ammo and another pistol, but it would be nice to have Lodestar outgunned if we meet again. I take the rifles and magazines, and a box of shells for the Walther.

Autumn raises an eyebrow as I load the rifle cases in the trunk of the car. "Enoch owned those?"

"He was taking the threat of a North Korean invasion very seriously."

"And who are *we* invading?"

"I know, I know, but I don't want to be caught short if things go wrong, and we have to plan as though things *will* go off the rails. The minute we go into the house to get your passport, either Enoch or the security system is going to let Gantry know where we are."

"I doubt Enoch's back at the house without people to tend to him, but it's possible. You think Lodestar's still monitoring the security cameras?"

"We have to assume so. Even if there's only a one per cent chance of them figuring out we're going on to Vegas, let's be prepared. All those open desert roads make me less nervous with some long-range weaponry at hand."

Autumn gets behind the wheel as I load the Walther.

She eyes me loading the gun and asks, "You think Gantry would try again so soon?"

"It's not likely, but I don't trust him to do the sensible thing and give up. Getting to Pinder was one thing, but the chances of us killing Gantry would be on a far different order of magnitude, and he must know that. Plus, he risks exposing himself to the police every time he tries something. It's deranged."

"We made him crazy," Autumn says confidently. "He could see himself crossing the finish line and joining the big dogs in the billionaires' club. You've no idea what that means to people like him. They need that fantasy benchmark to tell them they've won, that they're not falling behind. And you know what drives him even more insane? He was stymied by a softcore porn actor and a cop from the sticks. People like us should be his employees or mistresses or victims, but it's against nature for them to impede his plans or be more able than him."

"Yes. We're an insurgency that frustrates and enrages. If we were a small country we'd be taking drone strikes right about now."

I resist telling Autumn my other reason for wanting to go to Las Vegas; we only have to make a small detour to retrieve a treasure I never wanted to see again. But now, with the fact and dream of escape so close at hand, I'm thinking some more money could pay for ironclad anonymity in a new country and put us even further out of reach. Gantry's ferocity and determination has me worried. But the thought of going down into that valley again is chilling.

We park in the long-term lot at LAX, and Autumn goes to pick up a rental car. If there is a tracker on the Lexus it will be blocked by the mass of the parking structure. She returns with a Toyota RAV4 and we transfer our gear to the new vehicle and leave.

It's after midnight when we get on the I-105. Traffic's moving well and I'd like to put my foot down and race to Rancho Vista, but I can't take a chance of getting pulled over.

When we get past Corona, Autumn asks, "What do we do if Enoch's there?"

"If we leave him there, he'll contact Gantry. He won't know where we're going but if they have someone nearby, they might try and intercept us."

"How about we tell him half the truth; that I'm getting my passport and we're heading back to LAX? Think that will throw them off the trail?"

"That could work. Or we could kill him."

I can still shock myself by how easily the idea of killing comes to me.

Autumn stares out the window at the dark, empty desert and says, "Part of me wants to kill him, but I've run out of hate. I thought it was an infinite resource, but it turns out it's not. I don't want another death if I can help it."

"So, what do we do with Enoch? Give him a severe talking-to?"

She grins. "I can go as far as scaring the crap out of him. That might be fun."

It's after two o'clock when we get in view of the guardhouse at Bighorn's gated entrance. I stop the car.

"I'm going to hop out here. You drive through and I'll see if the guard makes a phone call immediately after you pass him. He may have been told or paid to alert someone if you come back. Stop the car about a hundred yards up the road and I'll meet you there."

Autumn takes the wheel and drives forward slowly. The car shields me from view as I walk along the far side of the road and then crouch down in a ditch as she turns into the entranceway. The guardhouse is a neon island in the darkness, and the elderly white guy manning it in his faux cop uniform appears pleased that a car has rolled up to break the tedium. He recognizes Autumn and raises the gate after exchanging a few friendly words. She drives up the road, and the guard takes out a crossword puzzle magazine.

I catch up with Autumn after making a wide detour through the rocks and scrub.

"Well?" she asks.

"Everything's good."

"Enoch's home. I asked the guard if there were any other guests up there and he said not as far as he knows. It crossed my mind that Gantry might have put some men in the house."

Enoch's house comes into view and Autumn puts on the brakes.

"Why should check things out first," says Autumn nervously. "That guard may not have been on duty when Lodestar guys came through."

"If they're there, then we've already been spotted, but let's be ready in case they're just sitting around the kitchen or asleep. Park here and we'll go on foot the rest of the way."

We arm ourselves with pistols and begin a slow walk up the driveway. The rooms overlooking the driveway are dark or dimly-lit, but Enoch's office window is flickering with light from his television; I assume he's fallen asleep there, or a Lodestar man is spending the night shift watching TV. The door leading into the garage has a numeric entry pad, and after Autumn enters the code, I push the door open with my foot. The Yukon and Maserati are the only vehicles in the garage. That's good; a Lodestar team would have left their vehicle out of sight in the garage. I go up the stairs to the house while Autumn waits at the bottom. The door at the top of the stairs is ajar, and I can hear the TV from Enoch's office. It's ESPN. I move into the hallway and creep forward to the office door and look in. Enoch is asleep on the couch. He's wearing a white polo shirt that's flecked with food stains, and pale green golf shorts. The TV provides the only light and it gives the mounted heads on the walls dramatic shadows that makes them seem ready to spring to ghostly life. It's colder than ever in the house. I go back to the stairs and tell Autumn it's safe to come up.

"Where is he?" she asks.

"Asleep in his office."

"Back in a second."

She goes to her bedroom and comes back a moment later waving her passport.

"Let's go," I say, exhilarated at the thought that we're only a four-hour drive from Vegas and a flight to the other side of the world.

Autumn hesitates at the top of the stairs to the garage and whispers, "I want to see him one last time."

Before I can argue she goes past me and steps just inside the office. She stares at him as if he were something in a store window she was thinking of buying and stays like this for a minute or more.

She snaps out of her trance with a deep sigh and says, "All those years. What a goddamn waste."

Enoch's whistling snore changes pitch and he opens his eyes. Autumn's demeanour doesn't alter but her hand tightens on her gun.

"Autumn?" rasps Enoch.

"It's me," she answers without emotion.

He struggles to get into a sitting position and his tired, confused eyes wander from Autumn to me and back again to Autumn.

"Why are you here?" he asks in a baffled tone.

"My passport, Enoch, just the passport. We're going back to L.A. so we can fly out first thing in the morning."

His eyes dart down to the weapon in her hands.

"No, I'm not interested in shooting you. You're not worth the bad dreams, but now that you're awake you can sit here quietly while I say goodbye to my paintings."

"I need to take my pills and they're in the kitchen," he says petulantly. "I forgot to take them earlier."

Autumn shrugs and looks at me. "Do you want to mind him?"

"Sure."

We go to the kitchen where Enoch opens the fridge to get a bottle of water. The fridge's light makes him look pale and insubstantial, like a vague memory come to life. At the kitchen island he fumbles open a pill box with compartments for each day of the week. A half-dozen pills, as brightly colored as jewels, spill out. He makes fussing noises as he picks each pill off the counter and swallows it with a tiny swig of water. Autumn looks at him with disgust, then walks into the living room. She turns on some lights and walks around the vast space with her gun held loosely at her side.

"I'll be selling that stuff she's looking at," mutters Enoch.

"Is spiteful the best you can do, Enoch?"

"It's just a fact," he grumbles.

A pirate's crew of black thoughts fills Enoch's eyes as he looks at her and then me.

"Why don't you two leave? Get her out of here. She's only doing this to torture me. I don't want to see her again."

"You think she came here to waste time hurting your feelings? You're lucky she didn't wake you up with a bullet to the brain."

"Autumn has no cause to be this angry; she's had a sweet ride with me. Even you know that."

"Loaning her out to Gideon was part of the sweet ride?"

Enoch shifts in his seat and avoids my eyes like a poker player who's had his stone cold bluff called. "You wouldn't understand. It wasn't anything serious; it would only have been like the acting she did in those films of hers. Anyway, you didn't know Gideon; he got possessed when he wanted a particular girl. It was a compulsion with him, but it's that kind of drive that made him what he became. He was a hundred per cent in everything he did."

"In one shape or another, I've known Gideon for a very long time. If you'd like to repeat what you've just said to Autumn, I can guarantee you'll find her aim much improved."

Autumn calls from the living room: "Tom, bring Enoch in here."

I wave Enoch towards the other room. He goes ahead of me, his face stiff with resentment. Autumn is sitting on a chair in the middle of the room, her attention entirely on the giant *Standard Station* painting. She motions Enoch to sit in a chair near her. He sits and stares at his feet. He's shivering.

"I want you to take great care of this painting, Enoch," says Autumn. "I assume you'll sell it, but I don't want it going to some hedge fund manager or a Gulf prince. If I ever come back to this country, I want to know there's a place where I can go and see it."

Enoch shrugs like a punished child being asked if he'll be good the next time.

"The rest you can sell wherever. If you had any sense, you'd keep them to surround yourself with some life." Autumn sits silently for a moment. "Did you ever spend a minute looking at this painting, Enoch?"

"It's a gas station," he says petulantly.

"It's a portrait of you and your kind, if you knew how to look: straight lines and brutal, geometric servings of a few simple colors trapped in a black void."

"Then why do you like it?"

"It shrinks and tames you. It traps you in that frame for eternity, like a wicked genie."

"You're crazy."

"My crazy doesn't go beyond seeing what I want to see in a painting; yours is believing that your greed gives you meaning." Autumn gets quickly to her feet and Enoch flinches as though expecting a blow. "We're going now. One other thing: in case you forget to do it, which I doubt, please make sure I don't benefit financially on the day you die."

Enoch's look of anger is the purest, truest expression I've ever seen on his face.

"That won't be fucking long," he roars.

"What?" says Autumn.

"Heart disease, that's what. I was diagnosed over a year ago and they said I could expect another three years, four at the most."

Autumn looks baffled at what he's said, and in a tightly-controlled voice she says, "Do you expect me to be sorry for you?"

Enoch fidgets and gives another of his child-like shrugs.

"You knew," continues Autumn in a rising tone, "that you were dying and you still went ahead with Gideon's ridiculous fucking scheme? What were you expecting to do with that superyacht you were going to buy? Turn it into history's grandest Viking funeral ship? Why do any of it, Enoch, when it wouldn't buy you a single extra day of life?"

Enoch's face fills with confusion and he looks around as if expecting Gideon's ghost to waft into sight and provide Autumn with a snappy answer. "It was an opportunity...It was foolproof...Why should I stop making money? It's what I do. Saying no would have been stressful for me, and my specialist told me to try and lead a calm life filled with as much joy as possible. He said that might even extend my life a little."

"How's that worked out for you, Enoch?" I ask.

"You two are just bullies," he whines. "I'd like to see you talk to Preston like that."

There's something worrying about the way he's mentioned Gantry. Autumn's focused on Enoch and her gun hand is tightening.

"What about Gantry, Enoch?" I ask sharply.

"Nothing."

"You're lying, and your heart won't be what ends your life if you don't tell me the truth."

It takes him no time to do the smart thing: "Preston's coming here this morning. He told me we have to talk about what to do next."

"There is no 'next,' as far as Gideon's plan goes, so what do you two have to talk about?"

"I don't know," says Enoch. "He insisted we meet here instead of Royal Palms. He said we shouldn't be seen in public after everything that's happened. I wanted to stay at the casita. I don't want to be here anymore; there's no one to look after me and it's got nothing but bad memories."

Autumn slowly brings her gun up and takes dead aim at Enoch. "Here's your cure for bad memories."

As much as his bad knees allow him, Enoch leaps to his feet and backs across the room.

"Don't, Autumn," I say warningly.

"Every fucking breath he takes is an assault and an insult."

Enoch's gone all the way across the room and backed himself against the window that makes up the entirety of the wall. Behind him the pool's blue water glows promisingly, like a portal to another dimension, and in the blackness beyond, a thick web of orange and white stars marks out the sprawl of Palm Springs.

I whisper to Autumn: "You don't need to do this. It's going to be done for you very shortly."

She hasn't really heard me. Her eyes are moist and her trigger finger is tightening.

"Don't," I say again.

"Why the fuck not?" she snarls.

"Because at this range," I say urgently, "the bullet will pass right through him, shatter the window, and we'll be sucked out into space."

She lowers the weapon and looks at me with bewilderment.

"It's true," I say calmly, "the icy embrace of deep space awaits."

Autumn slowly smiles and chokes back a laugh that turns into a snort.

"You stupid bastard," she laughs, "now I need a tissue." She lowers the gun. "Die in your own good time, Enoch."

She goes to the kitchen as Enoch slides down the glass and lands on his ass with a small thump. His face is sad and pale, and he places one hand gently over his heart. He could be dying right this moment, or he might linger on for a few more years, but he has that look of awful clarity I saw so many times in Hexum; death as an imminent, irrevocable fact has come violently into his view; it's a landmark that approaches far faster than he thought possible and grows swiftly on the horizon, blotting out the sun and casting its long shadow towards him.

I leave him frozen under the spell of his own death and go to the kitchen. Autumn is eating a banana and drinking some water.

"We have to go right now," I say.

"You worried about Gantry? He won't be here for hours."

"His scorched earth policy doesn't only apply to us; I think he's coming to kill Enoch. Gantry doesn't need to see Enoch, he wants a meeting here because it's isolated, and he and his men will come before dawn to do the job. They'll make it look natural, possibly suicide, or they might even try and lay it our feet, but I'm sure they're coming. And they could be here any minute."

"Why kill Enoch?"

"Gantry's being military and tidy. No loose threads, no one who might talk under pressure, no one left alive that he can't trust. When I killed Pinder I was undoubtedly doing Gantry's job for him. He was the weakest of the bunch and was probably number one on the hit list."

"What about Jasper?"

"He and Gantry seemed tight, but don't be surprised if he has a fatal accident in the near future."

"Enoch's going to phone Gantry as soon as we're gone. Is that a problem?"

"I not sure he's going to be doing anything for a while."

She steps into the living room and looks at Enoch, who hasn't moved and doesn't register her presence. He picks fretfully at his shirt with the hand that covers his heart as he stares at his truncated future.

"Let's go," says Autumn

We grab some food and bottled water and return to the garage.

I point to Enoch's Yukon. "We'll take that, instead."

"How come?"

"We'll need something with more clearance to get that treasure I told you about."

"Where is it?"

"Off highway 95, south of Vegas."

"Do we really need to? Is it enough money to make it worthwhile?"

"We can't guess how hard Gantry will come after us. The money could buy us new names and passports in the right country."

"This isn't about wanting to make things even between us, is it? I don't care if you don't have a dime. Don't be one of those guys who gets pissy because a woman's footing the bill."

"No. The money's just a weapon, and we need to be well-armed."

We move our stuff to the Yukon from the RAV4 and leave. The guard at the gatehouse barely looks up as we drive past, and we're heading east on the I-10 in no time. Autumn is driving and has the radio tuned to a station playing EDM, but the volume is so low it's like listening to interference. A freight train paces us a few hundred yards to the north, its cyclopean headlight illuminating destitute plains of creosote bushes, and I take a hypnotic interest in watching it slowly fall behind us. I wake up maybe an hour later when Autumn gives me a tap on the shoulder. We've turned north onto 95 and the radio's off.

"What?" I yawn.

"I switched to a news station and one of the first stories was that the LAPD is *seeking* Preston Gantry for help with one of their investigations."

"Huh. That guy I found in my apartment must have rolled over, plus too many Lodestar-connected bodies have been turning up. Gantry's in full panic mode. He probably figures he can distance himself from what his foot soldiers have been up to, commanders always can, but now he's worried the cops might get to Enoch."

"This can only be good news for us."

"It feels like it, doesn't it?"

We stop at Vidal Junction for gas, and I take my turn behind the wheel. Autumn goes to sleep almost as soon as we pull away from the gas station's comforting island of light. The road north to Vegas is quiet at the best of times, but at night cars appear as rarely and startlingly as comets in the night sky, and I speculate that the people driving them will all have desperate stories or lies to tell once they reach their destinations.

I have a rising sense of hope that we'll make it to McCarran Airport, but my imagination for what might come next is hobbled by the awareness that we're retracing the route I used to take from Calexico up to Vegas. I remember the face of the man I cut at the hay farm, and the confused looks of the girls being put in the white van. The road dips into the great, shallow bowl of the Mojave Valley, and the moon, hanging low in the western sky, turns it into a limitless and empty amphitheatre that's lit solely for the pleasure of the Dead Mountains squatting to the east. I have a stupid urge to cry, and I stop by reminding myself that tearful regret from me would only be an insult to a legion of victims.

I slow down as we pass through the town of Searchlight and Autumn wakes up.

"How far?" she asks sleepily.

"Those are the lights of Vegas up ahead, maybe sixty miles."

"Good."

"We turn off in about twenty miles and it shouldn't take more than an hour to get in and out."

Autumn looks at me appraisingly. "You really don't want to go to this place, do you?"

"No, I'd rather not."

"Even though it's some fabled land of riches. Or is it just an X marks the spot kind of thing by the side of the road?"

"Neither."

"So, you've left this money out here for, what, years?"

"Years."

"It must be very dirty money."

I don't have the words to answer her, and she doesn't press me for an explanation.

The sky is beginning to lighten as we pass Nevada Solar One, its hundreds of acres of mirrors turned to greet the sun. I turn off the highway onto a paved road that leads east to the Colorado River.

"What are we looking for?" asks Autumn.

"The entrance to a track on the left. It's marked by a pair of stone pillars."

"Will they still be standing?"

"It would be a hell of a job to take them down."

As I say this, I see them up ahead, a pair of rough-hewn granite pillars nearly twenty-feet tall that glow with a ruddy warmth in the pale light.

"Jesus," says Autumn, "when you said pillars, I was thinking something more architectural; those are like…I don't know."

"I think they were meant to look like menhirs."

"Yes. I've heard that word before."

"Think Druids."

"Druids?"

"It makes sense when you see the rest."

The sandy track between the standing stones is barely visible, and as I turn between them, I notice that there are no recent tire tracks. The stones, however, have been tagged from top to bottom, and numerous chips and gouges testify that they've been used for target practice. The track is in decent condition, but as it winds into some hills it begins to deteriorate; the runoff from once-a-year rainstorms has carved narrow trenches into our path. The driving is slow and it takes nearly a half hour to cover four miles.

"Is it near?" Autumn says anxiously.

"We're there."

The road rises sharply to seemingly end on a ridge that's at right angles to us, and I stop on top of it. The track continues down into the valley that I last saw ten years ago, and the sight of it makes me feel nauseous. The sun has come up over the horizon and sends a long, haunted shadow out from the perverse building sitting a quarter mile away at the far end of the narrow, almost perfectly rectangular valley. The double row of palm trees, at least several hundred, still flank the track as it runs straight and true along the valley floor right up to the building's entrance.

"What the hell," Autumn says with awe, "am I looking at?"

"Welcome to Palmyra."

Palmyra

I stayed by Monica's body while the dead were counted. She was on her side, one outstretched hand resting on the Yankees cap that her long blonde hair had been hiding under. The oversized jean jacket and baggy black pants she was wearing looked like choices made in a panic as the clubhouse was being shot apart. I hadn't spent more than fifteen minutes talking to her in my life, most of it terse responses to her flirtatiousness. I wondered if she wouldn't be lying at my feet, her pretty face disfigured by my ruthlessness, if I'd taken up her offer in high school.

Stockman splashed across the river to me, shouting, "Including the one beside you, twenty-three Black Dogs dead and Vin's the only one on our side who got nicked."

"Twenty-two. The girl doesn't count."

"Girl?" He got closer. "Oh, shit, you're right. Collateral damage really is a bitch, isn't it?"

Josh radioed and asked how we'd done and let out a long whistle after I told him the number. "Hoo-ee, that's a lot of meat to move. We've got nine Black Dogs ourselves. They musta been having some kind of special meeting or party here. I'll send some ATVs down to you and we can take the bodies over to the mine entrance. It's at the foot of that hill to your right."

It took until noon to shift the bodies to the mine's mouth and then drag them fifty yards inside the tunnel. While we were doing this, I realized that I hadn't seen Spencer all day, or for the past week. He was usually a keen observer of scenes like this, but when I asked Jubal about Spencer all I got was a vague answer about another job going on somewhere. A hard, steady rain fell as we began our mortuary detail, dousing the burning clubhouse and filling the valley with a smoky fog that irritated the eyes. The tunnel leading into the hill had a downward slope and was lined with ancient and rotted railway ties. The Black Dogs had put in new roof supports, lights, and a ventilation hose that ran all the way to the lab, which was in a broad, low-roofed chamber a good two hundred yards inside the hill. Three other tunnels ran off this room, but they were dark and unimproved.

Myself, Josh and Jubal looked around the lab after the last of the bodies had been brought in and laid along the sides of the tunnel. Jubal collected a few baggies of meth and moaned that we'd probably missed a big shipment.

"Don't whine, Jubal," said Reinhart, "we got what we wanted: we culled the herd good and proper."

"Did you hear that?" said Jubal suddenly.

"What?" asked Reinhart.

"Listen."

At first all I could hear was the erratic splash of water dripping from the low, rocky roof. Then I heard it: a sound like the wind that carried with it whispers and trills and moans. Jubal moved stealthily over to the nearest of the darkened tunnels, listened intently, then beckoned us over. The sound was definitely coming from the tunnel, but it was no clearer, and I got the impression it was coming from a great distance.

"What is it?" said Reinhart in a hushed voice.

I said, "Might be anything—running water, wind moving through the tunnels."

"The kid's right," agreed Jubal. "These tunnels can go for miles, up, down and around. We could be hearing echoes from something on the other side of the mountain or a mile under our feet."

"You don't think it's people?" whispered Reinhart.

We listened some more. The sounds didn't resemble speech in any way, except if you wanted to believe they were the distant, hysterical ravings of something mad.

"No way," said Jubal. "No one would go down those tunnels; they're a cough and a bump away from collapsing all to shit."

The three of us kept listening to the noises until Reinhart, sweat beading on his brow, said in a shaky, barely audible voice: "There's ghosts in some of these mines, you know. From the old days. I've read stories."

Jubal and I glanced at each other. Both of us were trying to keep a straight face. I pictured Josh at night in his empty house, sitting in his marooned armchair reading a Zane Gray story about a haunted mine.

"Why don't we go, Josh?" I said briskly.

Once we were all outside again—Reinhart speed-walked out—Jubal went to his truck and returned with ten sticks of dynamite. He wired the explosives fifteen yards inside the mine and set them off after we'd backed away a couple of hundred feet. The tunnel barked out a cloud of dust and dirt, and the entrance vanished as the land immediately around it collapsed. If the mine wasn't haunted before, it was now.

Whatever 'valuables' had been in the clubhouse were destroyed in the fire, but I did get a month off for killing Grau, and Reinhart gave each of us in the 7th Cavalry a bonus of 5k. I did some checking on Monica and learned that her parents had left Hexum a few years previously. She had stayed on when they departed, playing girlfriend to a succession of local hard cases, all of whom were now dead or in prison. She'd left the county after Vin had shot her boyfriend in the parking lot and had taken a casino job in Reno, which is where she met Grau. I imagined her urging Cody to take revenge on a Hexum cop as recompense for that shooting. Even if she did, she hadn't earned what I did to her—I was far more deserving of lying under that hill.

I had a month off, but the massacre at the Wintu River had flattened me. I made half-assed plans to go to Vegas or L.A., I even thought excitedly for a day or two about going to Japan or Europe—any place that wouldn't offer me reminders of Hexum. But I stayed in my house reading, watching hockey, and spending long hours on the computer for no particular reason. I couldn't even be bothered to go out for a run. After two weeks of this I woke up one morning determined to go somewhere. I loaded up a bag and drove west to San Francisco with a vague idea of continuing up the coast to Canada and then who knows where. At the back of my mind was the idea of never returning.

It was dark when I got to San Francisco, and I used my bonus on an expensive hotel downtown, intending to only stay for four nights before moving north. The next day I set to work on being a tourist, visiting Fisherman's Wharf and the San Francisco Museum of Modern Art. I ate Thai food for the first time. I saw a San Jose Sharks game. I checked out clubs, book stores, bars, and went to a Coldplay concert. I spent a night with a woman who said my smile was charming once I got it going, but that it appeared I was injuring muscles to produce it. I decided to stay longer. After six days I was feeling unsettled, but not in any way that I could put my finger on.

It came to me on my seventh day as I was sitting in a restaurant staring at a view of the harbor through rain-soaked windows: I was anonymous. People's eyes passed over me here, but not in the wary, or quick and fearful manner, that I was used to in Hexum. In this city I was a tourist, a customer, a face among many thousands with no history or threat attached to it. I was seized with a lightness of spirit that I hadn't felt since I'd had Jessica in my life, and at that instant I committed myself to leaving Hexum. I became lightheaded with a euphoric feeling of impending freedom, but also apprehensive at the thought of fleeing Reinhart and Jubal's kingdom. There was the thorny fact that no one who owed fealty to either of the pair had ever left Hexum easily or freely. But I also knew that I was done with being part of crimes like Wintu River; Monica's ravaged face was in no hurry to leave my dreams, and Hexum was engineered to produce a reliable flow of nightmares.

Two days later I was walking along Market St., enjoying a walk without purpose on a sunny day, when I stopped to go into a Starbucks. I opened the door and saw that the seats were all taken, there was a long lineup at the counter, and Spencer was sitting at a table with two men. He was facing away from me and hadn't seen me step inside, so I ducked back out and watched him from behind cover across the street.

The guys he was talking to weren't known to me and didn't look like the types Jubal and Spencer did business with. They were white, in their forties, and wore bland, dark suits that were more like uniforms than something the men had chosen for themselves. Shockingly, Spencer wasn't in his usual athletic gear. He was wearing tan chinos, a pale blue and white checked dress shirt, and had a dark blue suit jacket draped over the back of his chair. A rolled-up tie was stuck in the breast pocket of the jacket.

Spencer looked deeply worried. I'd seem Spencer scared and angry, but this unfamiliar expression alarmed me. The three left the Starbucks together, Spencer doing up his tie as he came through the door. I was worried they were going to hop in a car, but they started walking up Larkin St., and I followed them for four blocks to Golden Gate Ave. where they crossed a plaza to enter an office building. I'd let them get farther ahead as they crossed the bare plaza, and as I hurried to follow them through the entrance, I saw that it was a federal government building. On the other side of the glass doors the dark-suited men were flashing their badges as they led Spencer through security.

I was astonished, but I must have looked confused because a woman coming out of the building asked me if I needed help finding my way.

"Is this the police station?" I asked, knowing full well that it wasn't.

"No, but the F.B.I. offices are in there. Is that what you were looking for?"

I told her I'd been misdirected and walked away.

Spencer had flipped, there was no doubt of that. If he was under arrest he would have been in handcuffs, not having a serious talk over coffee with F.B.I. agents. Or he might have been discussing the parameters of a deal before being walked into their offices to be charged. The fact that it was the F.B.I. had me even more worried; they wouldn't be interested in Spencer alone, he had to be part of a broader investigation.

I took a cab back to my hotel, checked out, drove back to Hexum and went past Reinhart's house to see if he was home. As usual, the curtains weren't drawn on his windows. He was sitting in his armchair under the standing lamp, a paperback held close to his face, so I continued on to the Sheriff's Office. I didn't want to be doing a search on the computer while Reinhart was around. It was about ten o'clock so, fortunately, the office was deserted—on-duty deputies were on patrol or in the rec room. I logged on to my computer and searched for any arrest records for Spencer. The only hit I got was for a traffic stop three weeks previously in Oakland. He'd been pulled over past midnight for driving erratically and given a ticket. Spencer claimed that the ten-year-old boy who was in the car with him was his nephew. This was probably what the F.B.I. was squeezing him on. The feds must have had their eye on Jubal and Spencer's operation for a while and he conveniently delivered himself to them by getting pinched with a minor. It was equally possible Spencer had initiated contact with the F.B.I. in order to save himself from going down for a long stretch.

My first inclination was to run. Spencer was weak, so it was almost certain that in addition to giving up his uncle, he'd also spill everything he knew about Reinhart's empire. The problem with running was that, when and if arrest warrants went out, I had nowhere to hide. There was also the question of Jubal. He'd been evasive about Spencer when I'd asked his whereabouts at Wintu River, which made me wonder if he didn't know what was going on and was preparing his own plea deal or hasty exit from Grange County.

The temptation to tell Reinhart what was happening was strong; I knew he had influence outside of the county, but I didn't think that applied to the F.B.I. There was yet another option available to me, and when I woke up the next morning, I knew that it was the only realistic one: I had to kill Spencer. His death might not end the investigation, but it would slow it down enough to give me time to plan a final escape from Hexum.

When I went back to work, I let it be known, as quietly as possible, that I needed to be told when Spencer came back to town. For three days there was no word of him, and I worried that the only time I'd hear about him again was when F.B.I. agents swept us up. Just after Christmas Pascoe informed me that he'd seen Spencer driving through town. The only sure way to kill him without the risk of being seen was to ambush him at his home, but I decided to wait. Pascoe might get suspicious if Spencer was killed immediately after giving me news of his arrival.

The following night I was on patrol with Stockman when we were sent over to the brothel on Lincoln to check on a report of trouble. Snow had been falling and clothed the dark house in a clean mantle of white that almost made it look cheery. A man, crying out in pain and swearing, was on his knees in the front yard, blood pouring from his face. A speckled trail of blood marked his path from the porch to the spot where he was kneeling. We got out of the patrol car and Stockman pulled on the black leather gloves he favored if he thought there was a chance of giving someone a beating.

The man looked up as we approached and shrieked, "See what they did to me!"

His face was a piece of steak that's been driven over.

"Who?" asked Stockman.

"Those fucking army bastards! I paid for my woman and then they came in and said they got first choice on everything. I told them to fuck off and then they jumped me."

"Fuck," I said to Stockman, "it's Zach."

"Shit, so it is."

Zach had once owned one of the bigger weed farms in the county until he started putting his profits up his nose. His coke addiction lost him the farm, and ever since he was just another itinerant laborer working at other people's plots and labs. But mostly he drank, snorted when he could afford it, and spent whatever was left in the brothels. He was now the base metal coinage of Hexum's economy.

"You wanna check inside?" asked Stockman. "See if they'll give Zach some compensation?"

"Sure,"

"They gotta give me something, man," moaned Zach. "I'm hurt bad."

A year previously the army had ended vehicle testing at the base and turned it into a conference center for high-ranking officers. From what we heard this meant they spent most of their time hunting—illegally—on the base's 50,000 acres and fishing in a couple of first-rate trout streams on the property. Reinhart had passed the word that staff from the base were to be handled with care; he didn't want us damaging someone who could make noise in D.C.

I went into the house while Stockman tried to calm down Zach. Winnie, wearing one of her awful fleece jackets, this one illustrated with a moose, was in the hallway directing an older Asian woman to clean up the blood that was splashed on the floor and walls. From upstairs came the sound of roaring laughter and the voices of several men singing 'YMCA'.

"Winnie," I barked, "get one of those assholes down here. Now."

She looked daggers at me but trudged up the stairs. A minute later, a man in an officer's uniform with a narrow, stupid face came staggering into view and stopped halfway down the staircase. He was drunk, red-faced, and leaning on Winnie for support. He didn't look much older than me, so I figured they'd sent down the most junior among them to deal with the bothersome local cops.

"What?" he slurred out.

"Someone got really fucked up tonight. How about you and your friends see what's in your wallets so the guy can go home happy?"

The officer laughed and went back up the stairs. Winnie stayed on the staircase. The laughter upstairs died down for a moment and then rose up again like a hysterical cheer.

"How many are up there, Winnie?"

"Too many."

The same officer came back down with a big, silly grin on his face and I knew something stupid was going to follow.

He started giggling as he pulled a small foil packet out of a pocket and said, "The general says your friend can have this."

He threw it towards me. It was a condom.

"Tell him we're sorry," the officer continued, "but he could've had this hot mama instead." And to illustrate his point he stuck his hand between Winnie's legs and gave her a violent squeeze.

I had my gun out and pointing at his head as she was still crying out in pain and clawing his hand away. He hiccupped in fear and tried to run up the stairs, but missed a step in his panic and crashed down, his chin striking one of the steps and knocking him out. He slid down the stairs like a broken Slinky. Winnie burst into tears and ran to the kitchen. I thought about going upstairs and silencing the laughter but holstered my gun and went outside.

Zach was taking up handfuls of snow and using them to wipe the blood off his face. Stockman had retreated to the patrol car to keep warm.

"Sorry, Zach, I got nothing for you. They're being total pricks. Maybe I can squeeze something out of them later."

Zach looked up at me with the big, disappointed eyes of a child. Tears washed down the swollen contours of his face, turning pink with blood before falling and darkening the snow around him even more. He tried to say something but could only manage a choking sound of rage. I joined Stockman in the car and we left.

Two hours later we got a frantic call from the dispatcher telling us to return to Lincoln Ave. While we were still blocks away from the brothel we could see a yellow glow illuminating the tree tops. When we pulled up in front of the house a sheet of flame was holding the door open and each ground-floor window revealed more flames busy with destruction. Women and men were crowded onto balconies and leaned out of windows on the upper floors screaming and calling for help.

Stockman was yelling into the radio asking where the fire department was as I got out of the car and ran around to the back of the house where I thought I'd once seen an outside staircase. The staircase was there, but none of the doors that led onto it were open, and I remembered that they were kept locked so the girls couldn't sneak out. People were pounding on the doors from the inside. A shed was sitting near the house and I pulled open its doors hoping to find an axe. The space was full of old, disused gardening equipment, but also a dusty crowbar. I heard a scream behind me and turned to see that two women had jumped from a balcony and were lying motionless at the side of the house. As I ran up the staircase to the first landing a man was trying to climb down a drainpipe from the third floor. He lost his grip and dropped with a moan—I heard his legs breaking as he landed. I jammed the end of the crowbar into the gap between the lock and door frame and yanked. With a dramatic cracking sound, and helped by the weight of the people pushing against it from the other side, the door burst open. A stream of soot-smeared young girls, women and men staggered out of a smoky hallway and onto the stairs as I raced up to the next landing. There was no one pounding on the third-floor door and I was about to go back when I heard a cough from behind it. I cracked it open with the crowbar and a cloud of black smoke barreled out. Two women and a man were lying on the floor. They were still breathing, but unconscious, and I dragged them out onto the narrow landing. Sirens howled in the background as I fireman-carried the women down first and then went back up for the man. His army uniform was badly singed, and he had a burn that ran across his neck and down onto his chest. As I was bringing him down, Reinhart and some firemen appeared at the back of the house and I let them take the man the rest of the way down. I was exhausted.

I staggered to the front of the house and saw that others had leapt from the house. They were shattered but alive. Remarkably, the firemen managed to knock down the fire before it consumed the whole building. I watched the whole thing from my cruiser as I nursed a rum and Coke that Stockman had thoughtfully got for me. The snow was pelting down harder and enveloped the charred brothel in an infernal cloud of steam and smoke. Reinhart was deep in conversation with the man I'd pulled from the house, who was sitting on the back bumper of an ambulance with an oxygen mask pressed to his face. Three bodies were laid out on the front yard, which was still stained with Zach's blood. Two more were added to the collection before I finished my drink. All of them were women, and the last to be laid down was Winnie. I recognized her fleece jacket.

Reinhart came over to the car and tapped on my window. I lowered it a few inches.

"What's up, Josh?"

"See that fellow I was talking to? The one you pulled out?"

"Uh huh."

"That's a general," said Reinhart gleefully. "He and his platoon of brass hats were blowing off some steam tonight."

"I expect generals like to get fucked same as everyone else."

"That's so, but they don't like the world to know about it, especially when the whorehouse they were in burns down around their ears. He'd like us to keep this quiet, and I said that was fine if we can count on him as a friend. You did some good work tonight, Tom."

"It's always a good night when you can make a new friend."

Reinhart hooted with laughter. "Ain't that a fact!"

"Any word on how it started?"

"No one told you? It was Zachary Nugent; he used to run a plot on Copper Creek. The way I heard it, he got kicked out of here earlier tonight and came back with a can of gas, walked right in the front door, splashed it around, lit it and ran."

"Where is he now?"

"We got him a half hour ago. Our new friend doesn't want a trial, so Vin is going to find a nice, warm shaft for Zach. That was my plan all along, but the general doesn't need to know that, does he?"

Reinhart laughed again and returned to organizing the clean up.

I got home near dawn and immediately went to the bathroom to throw up. I told myself it was the booze on an empty stomach, but it was because I'd always have the smell of the burning Settlement in my memory.

I phoned the office later that day and told them I'd be taking time off sick. It was time to deal with Spencer. The destruction of the brothel made me feel things were coming apart in a hurry. The tricky part was how to do it. His movements were too unpredictable to ambush him anywhere but his home.

I spent two days watching Spencer's house from a nearby hilltop, but the only consistency to his movements was the inconsistency. He came and went on no schedule and would be away anywhere from fifteen minutes to five hours. There was, however, one thing he did with regularity: tucked into the end of a shallow box canyon a few hundred yards from his house was the entrance to an abandoned mine. The door guarding it was modern, made of steel, padlocked shut, and hidden behind a screen of bushes. He visited it each day that I watched, always carrying a sack with him and staying inside for no more than twenty or thirty minutes at a time. When he left, the sack was empty.

Now I knew how to stage his death. It would be a robbery. The mine was undoubtedly where he was storing his earnings, and although Reinhart and Jubal would be shocked that someone would rob and kill as high profile a figure as Spencer, it wasn't beyond the bounds of possibility; Hexum was awash in desperation, and they might even think it was retaliation from what was left of the Black Dogs. I only had to wait until Spencer opened the mine door, shoot him, and leave with his money. I could see it appealing to Reinhart's Old West sensibility and imagined him calling Spencer's killer a "bushwhacker."

Spencer hadn't gone go to the mine before two o'clock, so I got myself in position near the entrance at noon the next day and waited. It was approaching five and I was growing concerned that he wasn't going to show when I heard his heavy footsteps coming up the trail. I was behind a tree near the mine door, and when I heard him stop, I looked out and drew the Browning Hi-Power I'd kept from Levi's collection of guns. The red, bull's head logo of the Chicago Bulls on the back of his jacket was staring straight at me as he twirled the knob on the combination lock that secured the door. I considered firing the moment he popped the door open, but I didn't want shots echoing around the hills and alerting anyone. I'd have to do it inside the mine. He got the lock open, stuck it in his jacket pocket, grabbed the sack that was at his feet, pulled the door back and stepped inside. I got a glimpse of a dimly-lit tunnel before he swung the door shut.

I moved to the door and listened carefully. There was a rattling sound of something metallic being moved around. All I had to do was throw open the door and start blasting; Spencer couldn't have moved more than thirty feet down the tunnel, and there was every chance his treasure box was only a few feet away. I heaved on the door and stepped inside with my gun hand raised. The space was empty. My eyes adjusted to the gloom and I saw that the tunnel ended only ten feet away at a brick wall, but there was a square hole in the floor at the base of the wall from which the top few feet of an aluminum ladder was protruding. I went quietly to the hole and saw that the ladder went down to another tunnel ten feet below. The sound of Spencer's footsteps was fading quickly in the distance. I could have waited there for Spencer to return, but I wanted to find where he kept his loot, so I went down the ladder with agonizing slowness to minimize its rattles and squeaks.

The lower tunnel, lit by a string of lights hanging from the ceiling, stretched far ahead of me, the lights disappearing as they made a sharp right turn into yet another tunnel. The sound of running water, like a badly-leaking faucet, was coming from somewhere, and also music. I crept up to the corner of the tunnel the lights went into and saw that they ended a hundred feet away in a rectangular chamber. Spencer had his back to me and was sitting at a card table to one side of the room. A boom box hanging from the wall was playing 'Jolene'. I moved slowly up the tunnel, the music covering the sound of my feet on the gritty floor. Someone was sitting across from Spencer. The figure was male and had his head down as he gobbled food off a plate. Spencer was eating from a bag of Oreos. I froze, wondering how this person entered a tunnel locked from the outside. I instantly thought it might be Jubal, and that he had access to this room via another route. If it was Jubal, I'd have to kill the pair of them. I moved faster as I closed the distance and got ready to fire. Spencer's friend looked up from his plate, letting out a high-pitched scream as he locked eyes with me. It was a teenage boy.

Spencer leaped up and looked at me with utter horror, his right hand moving quickly to his jacket pocket.

"Freeze, Spence!"

"What the fuck are you doing here?" he stammered.

"Who's the kid?"

As I spoke, the boy darted across the room and climbed on to the lower half of one of two bunk beds set against the wall. There was a sleeping bag on the bed which he crawled under slowly as if hoping I wouldn't notice him disappearing.

"Spence, turn around, spread your legs and put your hands on the wall." He did as he was told. "Who is that?"

Spencer had to lick his lips before he could speak. "It's someone I'm looking after."

"Try again, motherfucker," I said, and punched him viciously in the kidney with my free hand.

Spencer gasped with pain and sank to his knees. The boy wailed as though he was the victim of the blow.

"What's his name? Where's he from?"

Spencer thought about answering, but then shook his head.

I aimed carefully and put a round into his right hand as it was pressed against the wall. The echoes of the shot mingled with Spencer's cries and the wailing of the boy.

"He's just a kid I've been keeping!" howled Spencer. "He's called Jimmy."

"How long's he been here?"

"A while," he hissed through clenched teeth.

"The next one goes in your gut if you don't get more talkative."

Spencer, still on his knees, turned and faced me, his left hand cradling the bleeding wreckage of his other hand. "It doesn't matter how long. He was alone. No one was taking care of him. He was free for the taking. Worse things coulda happened to him, you know. He's had an easy life here—food, TV, no school. It's kinda like heaven for a kid."

"Why's one kid need two bunk beds?"

"Well…" he said, then left his mouth hanging open as he waited for a lie to come to him.

I kicked him in the chest and felt his ribs crack.

"Oh, God," moaned Spencer.

"What have you been telling the F.B.I.?"

He recoiled as though I'd hit him again.

"I saw you in San Francisco, Spence. I followed you and those two agents from the Starbucks all the way to the federal building. You weren't wearing team colors that day; couldn't you find a team with a rat logo?"

He bowed his head down. "They want me to wear a wire, but I haven't done anything for them yet. I got a lawyer working out a deal."

"Horseshit. You've told them something, given them a general idea of how things work in Hexum. They wouldn't let you go without a deal in place."

"I'm just a small part of it, man," he cried out in frustration. "The feds got their noses pointed towards here because of Jubal."

"What did you say about Reinhart and the Sheriff's Office?"

"I said he's on the take. They didn't ask about the deputies. They're interested in Jubal because of the Calexico pipeline and some other stuff."

"You must have talked a lot more than you're saying. They don't take people into the F.B.I. offices for a quick chat."

"No, no, no," he pleaded. "They didn't have much to use against me at first, but then they…"

"What?"

He looked off to the side. "They found out other things."

"Yes?"

"Kid stuff. On a laptop I had in the truck."

I was about to put a bullet into his head when the boy jumped on my back, wrapped his arms around my neck and yelled, "Don't hurt him!" over and over. Spencer got to his feet and tried to take a revolver out of his jacket pocket, but it fell out of his shattered hand. I fired at him but missed thanks to the boy interfering with my aim, and Spencer darted across the chamber and down a darkened tunnel as I threw the kid off my back. I got to the tunnel mouth and heard Spencer's rapid footsteps receding in the distance. I squeezed off two shots, the muzzle flashes giving me a brief glimpse of the red bull's head retreating into the darkness. His footsteps continued out of earshot, so I assumed I'd missed. I considered following him, but decided he'd have the advantage of me in the dark.

The boy was squatting on the floor crying softly. I turned off the boom box and sat on a chair by the card table. The sack Spencer had brought with him sat open on the table; it held Tupperware containers of food, cans of pop, and some coloring books and cartoon DVDs. The boy was dressed in stained L.A. Clippers gear that was too large for his pale, skinny body. His eyes were large and blue, and set in a pinched face that was sad and feverish. He threw uncertain glances at me and began rubbing the poorly-cut stubble on his head with a rhythmic violence that made me think of a long-caged animal acting out its madness. The smell in the chamber was zoo-like as well.

"So your name's Jimmy?" I asked quietly.

He shook his head. "I'm Boo-Boo."

"Spencer said you're Jimmy."

The boy thought about this as he wiped at his runny nose. "He only calls me Boo-Boo. I'm Boo-Boo and he's Yogi. That's our names. He gave us those names. I'm only supposed to call him Yogi."

"I think your name's Jimmy, and that's what I'm going to call you, okay?"

"What's happened to Yogi?"

"He's run away. For good. Is there another way out through the tunnel Spencer went down?"

"No…You were hurting him."

"Because he was hurting you, keeping you down here like a prisoner."

"Oh, no," said Jimmy excitedly. "He's protecting me. Bad guys want to kill my mom and dad and my sister. And me too. Yogi says that when the bad guys aren't around anymore, I can leave and he'll help me find them. They're all hiding, too."

"What are their names? Your parents, I mean."

He shook his head. "I don't remember. Just mom and dad."

"What's your last name?"

Jimmy stopped rubbing his head for a moment as he concentrated and then said, "I…I don't know. I can't remember." He started sniffling again and tears came back to his eyes. "Can I find them if I don't know their names?"

"I'm sure we can. I'll help you. Do you remember your sister's name?"

He brightened a little and said, "Crystal. She's older than me."

I should have been hurrying out of that dungeon, but I was transfixed by what the boy was telling me, while also trying to decide what to do with him once we got out. I wasn't worried about Spencer coming back; he was unarmed and wounded.

"How long have you been in here, Jimmy?"

"I just had my fifteenth birthday, so since I was five."

"Fuck…What happened before Spencer brought you down here? Where were you living?"

"Near here, I think." He began to look panicked. "Are you going to take me out of here without Yogi? The bad guys will get me; Yogi says they're everywhere around here, always watching cuz they think Yogi's helping me."

"The bad guys are gone, Jimmy. I promise. Now tell me what happened."

"Some men came one night and took mom and dad away from the house. They had guns. Then, later, a man with a funny-looking face took Crystal away, and Yogi came and got me."

"Funny-looking how?"

"He had a face like this," he said, and made a V-shape with his hands.

"Okay," I said as I felt something pull at my memory. "Does Spencer ever take you out of here?"

"At night. To the house. Sometimes during the day. If he has to go away for a long time, he leaves me down here with lots of food and things to watch." He pointed in the direction of the bunk beds. In addition to the beds there was also a TV sitting on a low table, a DVD player, more chairs, and a bookcase crowded with DVDs and comic books, and a variety of canned foods. "A while ago he was gone for a whole week. I think it was a week."

"Who sleeps in the other beds? Does Spencer bring other boys down here?"

Jimmy lowered his head. "Yes. There used to be three of us, but Spencer said they got sick and he had to take them to the hospital."

"Did they come back?"

"No. I miss them."

"Does he have boys up at the house?"

"Only for visits. I have to show them how to do what makes Yogi happy."

"That's enough, Jimmy. We'll go now."

His eyes widened in alarm. "The bad guys!"

"Gone. I guarantee it."

"What about Yogi?"

"I'll come back later and find him, and in the meantime, we'll look for your family."

Jimmy smiled uncertainly and got to his feet. I put a hand on his shoulder and steered him back down the tunnel. We were near the intersection with the main tunnel when I heard a sound behind me and realized how stupid I'd been to leave Spencer's gun behind. I spun around and drew my Browning. Spencer was standing by the card table and emptied his revolver at me, two bullets throwing sparks off the ceiling, the others singing past me, before I returned fire and knocked him down with a shot that caught his calf. He screeched with pain and kept pulling the trigger on his empty weapon. I walked back to him and saw that I'd been lucky: he'd been shooting with his wrong hand and had started firing from too far away.

I stepped down hard on his bleeding hand and said over his howls of pain, "This is your home now, motherfucker. Lights out for good in two minutes."

I reached into his pocket and took out the combination lock and the keys to his pickup, then went back through the tunnel and found Jimmy curled in a fetal position on the ground. One of Spencer's slugs had caught him in the temple. I didn't bother checking his pulse; his brain was visible through a hole above his ear. I kept walking.

When I went back up the ladder, I could hear Spencer limping along the tunnel after me. He made a feeble effort to grab the ladder as I pulled it up after me.

"Don't, don't, don't," he begged. "You can have the money in the house, Tom, all of it."

I laid the ladder down and looked at the yellow electrical wire that ran out of the hole, went along the wall, and ended at a junction box near the door. A black wire ran down to the floor from the box and into a piece of gray, plastic tubing, which presumably ran underground from that point all the way to the house.

Spencer's voice sounded very far away as he cried out, "Don't do this, Tom. I can make you so fucking rich. I know where Jubal's money is; it's all yours."

I looked through the opening in the floor. Spencer was on his knees, breathing rapidly, his bleeding hand held in front of him as though asking for alms.

"Don't worry, Spence," I said soothingly, "I'll be coming back." He laughed with relief. "In about a year. The smell should be gone by then."

The bellowing noise he made was charged with all his pain and fear, and he kept it up as I pushed open the door to let in the sunlight, then took out my gun and blasted the junction box off the wall. The torn, dangling wires sparked briefly and the light coming up from the lower tunnel winked out. I stepped outside, closed the door with a pleasing crash, locked it, and headed to Spencer's house.

My plan had gone to hell. I'd wanted Spencer found full of bullets and his money missing to create an easy-to-digest story of robbery and murder. The desire to punish Spencer, to send him to a slow, dark death, had overruled my common sense. And, of course, my life and career in Hexum had given me a refined sense of cruelty.

If Spencer was going to vanish, his truck had to as well. It was too risky to be seen driving it through the county, so I drove it into the brush as far I could, about a half mile, and squeezed it into a grove of oak trees. From there I hiked back to where I'd hidden my Nissan over a mile away.

Spencer's disappearance didn't go unnoticed for long. Two days later I heard that Jubal was looking for him all over town, and the day after that, Reinhart asked all the deputies to find out where Spencer had got to. A week afterwards I got a call from Reinhart to come out to Spencer's place.

"Did you find him?" I asked.

"No, but I'd like you to look around his house with me. I don't mind admitting you've got a sharper mind than mine for this kind of detective work, so I thought you should give it a once over. Could be there's a clue staring me in the face."

"No problem. See you soon."

My first thought was that Reinhart had figured out I was behind Spencer's disappearance, and that I'd be walking into a trap. But Reinhart could ambush me anywhere if he was convinced I was guilty; he didn't need me to go out there. Also, I had to believe I'd built up enough credit with Reinhart that he'd ask my reasons for killing Spencer before doing anything. If I'd had any kind of plan for leaving, I would have done so right then, but instead I drove to Spencer's place.

I turned the last corner on the road in to Spencer's and saw Reinhart standing by his cruiser in front of the house. Jubal was with him.

"How's it going, guys?" I said amiably as I got out of my vehicle.

"Just fine, except I hate having a mystery on my hands," said Reinhart.

"You got any ideas, Jubal?" I asked.

He shook his head and I thought about Jimmy's description of the man who took his sister.

"Let's go," I said, and waved them towards the house.

We went inside and I tried to look attentive as I moved from room to room. Jubal seemed unusually quiet.

"Jubal," I asked in my best detective voice, "is the first time you've been in here since Spencer's been gone?"

"Yeah, today."

"How come you didn't check in here before? You were asking about Spencer a week ago."

Jubal shrugged. "I came past once, saw his truck was gone, and left. I figured if his truck wasn't here, he wasn't gonna be either. I was phoning him all the time."

"Does anything look out of place, Jubal? Something missing? I mean, it all seems normal to me."

I didn't mention the toys scattered throughout the house.

Jubal threw up his hands and said, "I don't get it. Spencer always tells me if he's going out of town. Most of the time, anyway."

"What about the Black Dogs?"

"No way," protested Reinhart. "They're scattered to hell."

"Well," I said, "if there *are* any left who wanted payback, it'd be Spencer they'd snatch."

Jubal narrowed his eyes and said, "How come?"

"He lives out here by himself. You live in your club; Josh and I are in town. They could come in here at night and no one would see them."

"Why take his pickup?" asked Jubal suspiciously. "Why not just shoot him here?"

"That truck's new, isn't it? It's gotta be worth, what, 30k? That's worth stealing. And consider what they did to Dexter and what we did to them—they might want to play with Spencer for a while. Maybe they want to find out where his money is, or yours, Jubal. Does Spencer know anything that'd be worth kidnapping him for?"

Jubal swore under his breath.

Reinhart made an exasperated noise and said, "Well that's that, then. We'll wait and see if he shows up somewhere."

Jubal nodded in agreement and we went outside to our vehicles where he was quick to get in his pickup and wheel away. After Reinhart drove away, I let out a sigh of relief. But there was still the problem of Spencer's truck. It would eventually be discovered, and that would raise questions.

It wasn't until a week later that I thought of a way to remove the truck safely. I should have thought of it earlier, but I was distracted with worry about what Spencer had revealed, and whether Jubal was involved as well. And, too often, my off-duty hours that should have been devoted to thinking of a solution were lost to drinking. The main problem was that the truck, an F-150, was bright yellow, had a bull bar on the front, a light bar on the roof, and heavily tinted windows. All this made it instantly identifiable to everyone in Hexum County. I planned to hike to the car with some tools and spray paint, give it a quick and dirty makeover, and drive it out at night when I'd have a better chance of passing undetected. After that I'd take it to a wrecker's yard in Redding that disposed of any vehicle for a fee, no questions asked.

Reinhart had asked us to visit Spencer's house occasionally to make sure it wasn't being broken into, so the day before I was going to take care of the truck, I went out to check on things. A plain, black pickup was in front of the house that I didn't recognize, but the two men knocking at the front door of Spencer's house were the F.B.I. agents I'd seen him with in San Francisco. No ill-fitting suits for the agents on this day; they were wearing jeans, work boots and winter jackets. I drew my gun as I got out of the cruiser.

"Come towards me slowly with your hands on your heads," I said loudly in my sternest cop voice.

Their ingratiating smiles disappeared instantly and they did exactly as they were told. If they'd talked with Spencer for any length of time, they knew how dangerous it was to see a deputy in Hexum with his gun drawn.

"Now on your knees with your hands behind your heads."

They did it perfectly.

"Officer," said the taller of the two, "we only wanted to interview the homeowner. He doesn't seem to be at home, though."

"Interview? What's that supposed to mean?"

"We rep a company that does exploratory drilling. Destry Oil and Gas. We're interested in gas deposits in this region. We're looking for permission from landowners to do some drilling."

"Uh huh. How about you take your wallets out and toss them to me."

They did it just the way they knew a cop likes to see it done: slow and deliberate. I picked up the wallets and moved behind them. Their names were Reuben Oates and Travis Bochner, and their driver's licences showed San Francisco addresses. They had business cards for Destry, one of which I kept. I looked carefully for anything that would identify them as F.B.I., but they were clean. There was, however, a receipt for a Holiday Inn in Swan Valley, a town forty miles to the east and outside Grange County, that showed tomorrow as a check-out date. I tossed their wallets back to them and said that the homeowner was away, and because of a rash of break-ins in the area we were being thorough with anyone who looked out of place. I kept things cordial and professional, and warned them that this part of the country wasn't a good place to trespass. They thanked me profusely, apologized for causing me trouble, and left with many waves and smiles.

I got in my cruiser, wrote down their names, and ran a licence plate check. It came back as a Hertz vehicle out of San Francisco. The Bureau couldn't be faulted for the cover story they gave the pair; masquerading as the front men for an exploration company gave them a ready excuse for wandering all over Grange County. Depending on what Spencer told them, they might be exploring the county's wealth of ventilation shafts. Clearly, however, they were concerned enough about Spencer's disappearance that they went right up to his door, which probably wasn't the normal protocol for handling snitches. But it had given me a way to avoid the risk of exposing myself by moving Spencer's truck.

The next day was my day off. I got up early, drove to Swan Valley and found the Destry car outside the Holiday Inn. I parked a good distance away from it and got my camera out. An hour later, the agents left the hotel with their bags in hand and I began snapping. They took the interstate to San Francisco and I waited until their view of me was blocked by a truck before passing them. It was a weekday, and I was hoping they'd go into work before going home. I got to the federal building on Golden Gate Ave before noon and parked on Larkin St. directly across from the underground parking entrance for the building. After a half hour I was thinking they'd taken the day off, but their pickup soon turned the corner and I got two clear shots of them as they turned to go down the ramp.

It was getting dark when I returned to Hexum, and I immediately went looking for Reinhart. I found his car parked at the Maxi Donuts out at Mission Commons—his usual spot at this time of day. The shop was surrounded by shining, corpulent SUVs and tricked-out pickups, which meant Reinhart would be inside receiving thick envelopes and the fawning attention of the men who needed his protection. He waved me over to his booth as I came in and I made a signal that I wanted to talk outside.

We met inside my truck.

"What's up, Tom?"

"I found two men at Spencer's house yesterday. They claimed they were with an exploration company scouting for drill sites." I handed him the Destry business card. "But their vibe was all wrong. I smelled cops, and their vehicle was a rental. They said they were staying at the Holiday Inn in Swan Valley, so I went there this morning, saw them leaving, and followed them to San Francisco." I showed him the pictures of the pair in the Holiday Inn parking lot and driving into the federal building. "This is them in Swan Valley and then going into F.B.I. headquarters in San Francisco."

Reinhart didn't say anything. He took his hat off, gave his ivory-white hair a rub and stared out the window. I studied his face for a reaction, but it was a bare stage, and it occurred to me that his default emotional setting was cheeriness. I'd seen him angry at times, but in the normal course of things he papered over every event, no matter how monstrous, with a smile. He was Hexum's lord of misrule, yet he fervently believed, or hoped, that all it took was his ready grin to silence the anguished cries caused by his reign. But deep underneath the easy smile was, I was sure, a twisted, damaged personality that had partly revealed itself in his tearful reaction to my burial of Amy, and in his sweaty horror at the sound of ghostly noises in the mine. In the dim light his tanned face was dark and furrowed with age, like a grim, crudely-carved wooden idol found deep in a silent forest. The prospect of betrayal had frozen him in place.

It didn't look as though he was going to come out of his trance, so I said, "And there's a chance that the feds have their hooks in Jubal as well. After that business in Fremont County I asked him where Spencer was and he was evasive as hell. Remember? And then Spencer wasn't to be found after that and Jubal didn't say a thing. Now we've got the magically vanished Spencer and there isn't a single goddamn clue. If Spencer's alive, he's talking. The question is, is he ratting on his uncle or all of us? Maybe the F.B.I. already has Jubal in their pocket and they're leaving him out here as a plant. He could be wired up every time he meets us."

In a flat voice Reinhart asked, "So why did Jubal start worrying about Spencer now?"

"I don't know. Maybe he's pulled a fast one on Jubal; told him that nothing's going to happen, but now he's gone into witness protection because the ax is about to fall."

Reinhart put his hat back on. "Okay. I'm going to look into this. Not a word to anyone." He looked down at his feet and in a hushed voice said, "Tom, whatever you think you've owed me for stuff I've done for you over the years has now been repaid in full, and then some. We're not a father and son, but by God this confirms for me that we should have been." He shook my hand and stepped out of the truck, stopping before closing the door to say, "You know, I figured things were going to go upside down and sideways as soon as that Kenyan was elected."

I fought back feelings of pity and tenderness for Reinhart and hated myself for having them.

Back at home I poured a drink and toasted my success in muddying the waters. It didn't matter now if Spencer's car or body was found; any questions raised would be seen by Reinhart through the prism of Spencer's treason. He would undoubtedly do the same checks on Spencer that I had and put two and two together when he saw that traffic stop in Oakland. More importantly, I'd bought time to organize an escape from Hexum. From what Spencer had told me, the F.B.I. was in the preliminary stages of their investigation, and now, with him gone, they'd have to reboot, and I was hoping that would take months. In the meantime, I could build up a cash reserve and then leave.

I saw little of Reinhart for the next week. He spent a lot of time in his office with the door closed, which was startling to all of us who were used to him being constantly out on patrol. When he did leave, he wouldn't say where he was going, but on one occasion a deputy spotted him driving his personal car, a white Chrysler 300, towards Sacramento. I knew what had caused this shift in his habits, but I still found this behavior unsettling. His erratic schedule and appearances continued for most of a month, and during that time I twice spotted pickups with professional-looking DESTRY EXPLORATION signs on their sides driving around the county. The F.B.I. was ramping up their scouting of our territory.

One evening in late March I was at home watching TV when I heard a car stop in front of the house. My first thought was that it was the F.B.I., and I almost reached into the drawer that held my Walther. A second later I heard Reinhart's cheerful whistle outside and I opened the door to find him beaming at me.

"Tom," he said excitedly, "justice is ours."

He bounced into the room like a child hyped-up from a day out at a theme park who's bursting to talk about his adventures. But first he dove into my fridge and got himself a Pepsi, then began pacing around the living room smiling to himself.

"What, Josh?"

"As of today, the feds are officially off our case."

"How?"

"Oh, it took some doing, but it came down to reminding certain folks in Sacramento and elsewhere about the happy and profitable times they've spent in Grange County, even if they were only passing through. Of course, I had to help them remember the good times, and find people around here who'd swear out affidavits on the subject. Once they recalled how happy we've made them over the years, they got on the phone to Washington and told the right people how fine and temperate a place Hexum is and there was no need to waste valuable F.B.I. resources here when our beloved country is facing so many real enemies. But you know what the clincher was? Our friend the general. Took a while to get a hold of him—he's in Iraq playing whack-a-mole with camel jockeys—but once he heard about our problem, he said it would be his pleasure to help the Bureau see Grange County in a more rational light." He paused for a drink and sighed contentedly after a long burp. "Pardon. That was last week. And today I got a call to say that the F.B.I. has closed the investigation. Life can return to normal, Tom—the county's saved."

"That's some spectacular work, Josh."

"I have to protect my men, Tom, that's what being a leader means. Anyway, what right do outsiders have to come around and tell us how to do things? You know what really peeved me about this? It was called Operation Destry. They named it after *Destry Rides Again*, one of my most favorite western movies! How am I supposed to watch it now and not remember all this tomfoolery?"

"So, we're all cool? No more agents cruising around?"

"That's right; we're living on open range again. Now, there's a few kinks I got to work out, but nothing at all for you to worry about."

"Did you hear anything about Jubal? Was he part of their team?"

"No, he was a target, not an ally. But I think he knew Spencer was in trouble and didn't tell us. I thought Jubal was more of a straight shooter than that."

"What about Spencer? They have any ideas what happened to him?"

"Nope. No one knows what's become of that freaky fool. Could be dead, could be gone; Jubal told me he used to talk about moving to Vietnam or Cambodia, or someplace like that. He never had much grit, so maybe he felt the heat and lit out."

Reinhart left a few minutes later, over the moon at the prospect of being able to go back to patrolling Hexum as much as he wanted. I'd done my best to look happy at his news, and part of me certainly was—I had no desire to be perp-walked into a federal courthouse—but as he revealed that his version of a peace accord had been signed, a feeling of depression grew in me. My motivation to leave Hexum had weakened. There was nothing truly stopping me from putting the town behind me forever except my own moral laziness. It was so easy and so tempting to stay and feast on the big money and soothe myself by pretending that my brand of violence was less cruel, less profligate than that of my fellow deputies. Without the fear of prison driving me, I doubted I had the strength to abandon Reinhart and Hexum. But on the nights when I didn't drink enough, the dreams I had about Wintu River were sufficient to remind me of why I still wanted to flee.

The disaster that had nearly engulfed us energized Reinhart. He pushed us harder to whip the town into shape, and he led the charge by spending almost every waking hour in the saddle. Jubal's men were kept so busy picking up after him that Jubal complained to Reinhart that he was hurting his business. I did my part, too, and counted myself a fine fellow for only crippling men instead of killing them. By July, Hexum was as quiet—a very relative term—as I could remember it, and the money was rolling in even faster. People were eager to pay their taxes, every penny of them, and much of that flowed into the frequent bonuses that Reinhart flung to us with calculated abandon.

It was around this time that I answered a call to go out to the old grain elevators on the east side of town. One of them had collapsed during a storm the previous winter and its stumpy remnants sat like a sacked castle surrounded by a moat of shattered planks. Someone had phoned in about a horrible smell coming from the ruins and I was expecting to find a body stuffed in the wreckage. I poked around the hillock of wooden debris and found nothing worse than a dead dog.

Several hundred feet away was the skeleton of a barn. Reinhart's SUV was parked behind it and he was outside the vehicle talking with another man. He was taller than Reinhart, practically looming over him, and was wearing a sleeveless, black T-shirt and a straw planter's hat. It was Cotton Pearsall, Jubal's new number two man after the disappearance of Spencer. Cotton had joined Jubal's crew more than a year ago, and, unlike most of Jubal's men, he was quiet, never swore, and unusually competent. I'd dealt with him a half-dozen times and always got the jarring feeling that I was dealing with an area manager for a chain of stores rather than one of the maniacs Jubal habitually employed. He spoke with a Southern accent that was never raised in anger or excitement.

The two were deep in conversation, and Reinhart wasn't his usual smiling self. It made me uneasy that they were talking in this out of the way spot, and I left before they caught sight of me.

I saw Cotton again at the weed farm the McSweeney's had once owned. I was picking up a tax payment from the new owner, and he was supervising four weary Latinos loading the trucks. He waited until I returned to my cruiser carrying a bundle of cash in a grocery bag and then approached me with a broad, car salesman's smile.

"How's it going, Tom?'

"Just fine, Cotton. You?"

"Hot, tired, and busy, but that's how I like it. Work is good for me, keeps me from fretting."

"Fretting? And why do you *fret*, Cotton?"

"I worry myself unnecessarily about the smooth running of Grange County."

I couldn't get a read on him; his round, pink face and bland smile was a Kabuki mask of benign inoffensiveness.

"And what exactly makes you worry unnecessarily?"

He shook his head ruefully, as though embarrassed to have brought up the matter. "The way I see it, Jubal and Sheriff Reinhart have created a model for how an enterprise like Grange County should function. The county is a business built on the stewardship of two men who've turned the raw material of this land into something unique." He paused, apparently waiting for me to fill the gap with fulsome agreement.

I stared at him steadily, resisting an urge to roll my eyes. "So I sometimes worry—"

"Fret," I said casually.

"Yes, fret," he agreed, a slight breeze of annoyance ruffling the placidity of his expression. "I worry that so much relies on their skill and energy holding everything together. But then I think that they've got perfectly capable men behind them, particularly Sheriff Reinhart, so the continuity of this great enterprise is assured."

"Continuity. For the seismic day when one or both of them retires?"

"Exactly. I hope when that day arrives the county can go on to greater strengths, perhaps plant its foundations more firmly here and elsewhere; join with similarly ambitious and effective groups. Organize. Consolidate."

"I see. And capable men will be required for that."

"Exactly. After all, without men like you and I to handle a period of transition, things would deteriorate, the county could lose its essential character, and I'm sure you wouldn't want to see that." He pointed at the men loading the truck. "Those people would be more than happy to pour into Grange County and run it right into the ground. Everything we've built, gone in a moment."

"Well, Cotton, it's nice to hear that you're concerned with the future, but in my experience, Hexum gave up the hope of a planned, organized future long ago in favor of nasty, fucking surprises, one after another."

"That's still a kind of future, Tom; one that we could manage."

I said something about being late for my next tax collection and left. Cotton was delusional, but I was sure that his allusive musings were somehow related to his meeting with Reinhart. And it was screamingly obvious that he was sounding me out for some theoretical future in which power would pass to us.

Reinhart almost never socialized. When he wasn't at work, which was most of the time, he was at home reading his westerns or watching TV. In early August he insisted I meet him at J.J.'s for "home movie night," explaining that we had a special job to go to afterwards and I should come armed. Jubal put on these events about twice a year, but I had never attended one, and I wasn't sure if Reinhart went to them or not. The less I heard about them, the better.

Jubal's "home movies" came in two flavors: DVDs he got from Mexico which showed the cartels torturing and killing their enemies, and DVDs from his brothels recording the rapes of women and girls when they were first brought to Hexum. Jubal's men and any deputies could go to home movie night for free; civilians had to pay two grand to watch the fun. I'd been told Jubal could make up to 50k at one screening.

Showtime at J.J.'s was supposed to be at nine in the evening, so I showed up after ten hoping that it would be over, or, better yet, that Reinhart would have gone off without me. I didn't want any part of special jobs which required that I be armed. I wasn't in uniform, but I did wear my gun. Jubal had a large, boxy room at the back of his complex where he hosted his home movie nights, and I parked near it amongst a crowd of Hexum's most expensive vehicles. One of Jubal's men was standing outside the back door and opened it for me as I walked up to reveal a darkened room filled with the upturned faces of men grinning at a screen I couldn't see. A gust of raucous laughter came out of the room and, almost obliterated by this noise, the thin screams of a woman. I told the doorman I'd wait outside. He shrugged and closed the door.

Twenty minutes later men started exiting the building. I leaned against my truck and nodded in reply to their greetings. Engines and stereos were fired up, and a roaring, rumbling caravan left Jubal's oasis and struck out through the night for Hexum. Reinhart, Jubal and Cotton came out of the door followed by a group of Jubal's men and a few deputies, none of them in uniform or armed. I was beginning to wonder why Reinhart had wanted me out there until he pulled out his gun and shot Jubal in the back of the head. A chorus of astonished curses and shouts filled the air as Jubal hit the ground like an abandoned marionette. Reinhart turned to face Jubal's men with his weapon at the ready. I had my Glock out and stepped forward to Reinhart's side. Cotton was at the edge of the crowd holding an automatic down at his side. He was looking at Jubal's men, not Reinhart.

"Now, now, now," said Reinhart, waving one hand in a 'calm down' gesture. "Let's not get all riled up. We don't want to spoil a fun evening by bringing more bullets into it." The crowd grew quiet. "You're all wondering why Jubal isn't with us anymore. Well, the short answer is that Jubal might have had divided loyalties, and we'll say no more about it. The long answer is that Grange County needs a fresh, new approach to how we do business. Operations need to be streamlined and put under one roof. You know how organized the people outside the county are, so it follows that we have to get with the times if we don't want to be behind the times. Starting now, Cotton Pearsall will be taking Jubal's place, administratively-speaking. He will report to me. We will work as one unit. If any of you can't live in this new system, you have five minutes to get to your car and leave the county." No one moved. No one breathed. "Good. Now, I'd like us all to bow our heads and share a moment of silence for Jubal. He will always remain in our memories as one of the founders of what Grange County has become."

Most of the crowd bowed their heads, while myself and a few others stood with our mouths hanging open. Cotton's head was down and his lips moved in a faintly audible prayer. Jubal looked the most astonished: the explosive pressure of the bullet's impact in the back of his head had popped his eyes almost entirely out of their sockets.

"That'll do," said Reinhart after a silence that felt like an eternity. "Cotton, I'll leave you to lay Jubal to rest."

Reinhart indicated I should follow him, and we walked quickly to the back of the parking lot where his cruiser was parked.

"Tom, I'd hoped you'd have been here earlier. I could've filled you in; I didn't want this to be a shock for you."

"So, Jubal was that kink that needed to be worked out."

He laughed. "Can't slide anything past you, can I? The only condition for putting the F.B.I. back in their box was putting Jubal in one, so to speak. I thought about it some, and I began thinking, why am I sharing the county with Jubal? It's the way of the world for big fish to swallow little ones, and it'll be more efficient if everything goes through me."

"Consolidation."

"Exactly."

"How did you come to choose Cotton?"

"Jubal had been telling me what an asset he was after Spencer was gone, so I got to know him a little. He's sharp like you, sees through situations in a snap, gets things done and isn't certifiable like most of Jubal's crew. You got any opinion of him?"

"Ambitious."

"Only natural in one his age."

A pickup rumbled past carrying Jubal's body under a tarp on the truck bed.

Josh sighed. "I will miss Jubal, but I'm sure he understands I had to do what I had to do."

He got in his cruiser and left, and by the time I got behind the wheel of my truck, the only person still in the parking lot was a man hosing down the spot where Jubal had lain.

I don't remember much of the rest of the month. One day I'd be feverishly planning my exit from Hexum and the next I'd sit like a zombie in my house, an unopened book on my lap and a drink in my hand. On one of my zombie days I was sitting in the backyard staring at the horizon and working on my fourth vodka cooler when Cotton came around the corner of the house. He'd come to tell me something about deliveries or taxes, but I barely listened to him. His accented voice was flat and rhythmic, like a minister reading a dull sermon to a bored congregation. It struck me that in the times I'd been around him he'd never given a hint as to why this life appealed to him. Jubal's men, the deputies, and all the others who ran the county's drug trade talked incessantly about the pleasures their trade earned them: women, money, booze, cars, trips, and the freedom to dominate and kill. Cotton, as far as I'd ever seen, was all business.

I interrupted his flow of organizational chatter and asked, "Why are you doing this job, Cotton? I mean, what are you getting out of working for Josh? It feels like you haven't connected to the soul of Hexum."

"And what kind of soul is that?" he said with amusement.

"You saw it in all its three-dimensional glory on home movie night. It's a compound of suffering, death, and profit—the three main active ingredients in Hexum. And, of course, the pleasure that produces for the survivors and winners. You see, it's hard to trust someone in this business who isn't in it for the right reasons. Was it the home movies that stirred you? Go ahead and tell me; I want to know you're one of us."

He pursed his lips disapprovingly and said, "I have no fondness for that sort of thing, Tom—it strikes me as tawdry— but as a reward for employees whose tastes run that way, it's an effective tool in team-building and creating loyalty. And, yes, it is enriching for the business in a way that's more cost-effective than most."

"Fuck me; you consciously chose and strung those words together in that order, didn't you? But answer my question: why join our merry band? What itch are you scratching?"

He glanced at the empty bottles beside my chair and smiled. "I'm not a complicated man; I like to find a challenging job and do it better than anyone else. God gave me a keen mind, self-discipline, and energy; so much so, in fact, that I'm sure He doesn't want me using His gifts in any common way. I honor God with my work."

I clapped my hands slowly. "You get better and better, Cotton, but you forgot to mention vaulting ambition."

"Vaulting?"

"Never mind."

"Aren't we much alike, Tom? Sheriff Reinhart says you're the best he has."

"The best? I count myself a lazy coward, which shows what passes for the best in this county."

"He thinks you'll be in his place one day."

"Did he say when that day would be?"

"On the day he dies, I expect."

"I don't think that's happening soon. There'll be portents to warn us of that—comets blazing across the sky, earthquakes, red rain, a fall in the price of SUVs."

"You're drunk, Tom," Cotton said kindly.

"Mission accomplished. You have any more news for me?"

"I've removed two of Jubal's men: Luke and Andy."

"Removed them where?"

"They weren't happy with Sheriff Reinhart's new chain of command. In relation to that, I've asked the Sheriff if he'd reconsider his policy of hiding bodies away all over the county. It seems unnecessarily risky. I've told him I can get access to an industrial incinerator, the sort of thing they use to get rid of dead livestock and pets. Perhaps you could support my initiative."

"Josh thinks it adds a romantic, Old West touch to the disposal process. You have to learn to appreciate his aesthetic."

He sounded sad as he said goodbye and went back to his car.

Cotton's visit had turned my stomach, and instead of finishing my drink, I poured it out and went for a wobbly run that left me dehydrated, headachy, but sober. After a shower I did a count of what I had saved and got a total of just over 200k. It was enough to make a fresh start elsewhere, but the weaker part of me was waiting for a perfect moment to leave. I wanted a portent.

One night in early September, I was coming back into Hexum along a back road after a patrol when I saw Reinhart's SUV, its lights flashing, parked on the side of the road ahead of me. It was a remote spot beside the blackened ruins of Fuller's Mill, the county's oldest building until it had been consumed in a wildfire a month previously. Reinhart had pulled over a green Elantra and was standing at the driver's window. He would expect me stop and offer assistance, but I really didn't want to; a thunderstorm was coming up quickly from the south and I didn't feel like getting soaked. I parked behind his cruiser and got out of my vehicle as the sky was pierced with forked lightning that illuminated a vast and muscular storm cloud. The sound of a giant's footfalls followed a few seconds later.

Reinhart wasn't pleased to see me. His smile was in place, but his eyes were cold and resentful. The driver of the Elantra was a black woman in her thirties, and she looked at me with such terror that it almost startled me into taking a step back. She was wearing a white blouse and a navy-blue blazer and skirt. My first thought was that she was a real estate agent or hotel receptionist. Her hands had a fierce grip on the steering wheel

"Hey, Josh, what's up?"

"Everything's okey-dokey, Tom. This lady isn't where she should be."

The woman looked at me and said, "Please, sir. I'm just lost. I was telling the sheriff I'm on my way from Reno to Oakland and I got lost when I left the interstate to get something to eat."

"You're well and truly lost, ma'am," said Reinhart. "You sure you didn't mean to come to this spot? You meeting someone here?"

"No, sir. Not at all, sir. Like I've been telling you, sir, I read the map wrong. I thought I could take a shortcut back to the interstate."

She was close to tears and Reinhart was looking at her with an intensity I'd never seen in him before.

"She could follow one of us back to the highway, Josh," I suggested.

Her face lit up with a smile. "Oh, yes, sir! That would be terrific. Thank you so much, sir."

The emphatic, pleading way she kept saying "sir" was making the hairs on the back of my neck stand up.

"That's a good idea, Tom," said Reinhart. "Why don't you go back to the office and I'll get the lady headed to Oakland after I've finished questioning her."

There was a steeliness towards me that I'd never experienced from Reinhart before, and I mumbled something about the approaching storm before going back to my car. As I passed him, he was leaning into the driver's window and the woman was responding with a wide, helpless grin that was hiding a scream.

I'd only driven a few dozen yards when gunshots of rain struck the car and a crooked white finger struck the ground with an electric crash a hundred yards to my right. The rear-view mirror reflected a swirling watercolor of red, blue and white from the lights of the two parked cars, and I drove another couple of hundred yards before checking the mirror again. The road was totally dark and flashes of lightning barely revealed the outlines of the two cars through shifting walls of rain. I turned the cruiser around, killed the headlights, and drove back slowly, unsure of what I might find. When I was thirty feet from the other cars I stopped and tried to make out any signs of movement. Both appeared to be empty. I let a few minutes pass and was about to get out of the car when I spotted movement from the back seat of Reinhart's cruiser. The rear driver's side door opened and Reinhart backed out into the sheeting rain. As he did so, two items slid out of the car and onto the road, one dark, one white, both limp. He picked them up and beckoned impatiently to someone in the car. The woman exited the cruiser slowly. Her blouse was open, her bra dislodged, and, except for her shoes, she was naked from the waist down. Reinhart handed her the navy-blue skirt and a white pair of panties and said something that I couldn't hear over the downpour. Slowly, mechanically, she began to dress. Her hands weren't cooperating and she kept stopping to wipe rain from her face. Reinhart turned away in annoyance and saw me. I was expecting anger from him, but what I got was a blank look that changed in an instant to a foolish smile and a wave, as if I'd caught him doing something clumsily.

The woman finished dressing and then limped back to her car, with Reinhart one step behind. I didn't want to look at her face but found myself studying it, trying to gauge the degree of her pain. She had a twisted smile on her face as if she was about to laugh at how completely and outrageously horrible life can get in the blink of an eye. Reinhart opened her car door, said something as she got inside. and then closed it gently.

She started her car as Reinhart came over to mine. I lowered the window.

"If I was any wetter than this, Tom," he chuckled, "I'd be underwater,"

"I came back because your lights went off. I thought there might be trouble."

"Well, thanks for your alertness. I was okay, but you never know, do you? Now, would you mind leading this young lady back to the highway? I've got work back at the office and I shouldn't be wasting my time on silly traffic stops."

"Sure."

My hand slipped down to my holster, and I visualized putting round after round into Reinhart's back as he returned to his car. Killing him was an idea that had been at the edge of my thoughts ever since Wintu River, but each time the temptation arose I pushed it away, frightened that I could even think of something that blasphemous. I wanted to flee Reinhart, not curse myself with his murder.

I U-turned and shouted to the woman that she should follow me. A sudden brilliance of lightning revealed her empty, harrowed expression. I recognized it as Hexum's resting face.

By the time I got back to the office, Reinhart had changed into a dry uniform and was behind his desk drinking coffee and nibbling a doughnut. His hair was standing up in damp little peaks, like the top of a meringue, and he hummed to himself. He noticed me enter, waved me into his office and closed the door.

"I'd like to apologize to you, Tom," he said, as a barely tamped-down smile tugged at the corners of his mouth. "I regret you saw me like that. It was embarrassing for you and for me. I'll have to admit I let myself go a little bit tonight, but there it is. I do have my moments of high-spiritedness, but, in my own defense, the many hours I spend in this job mean my opportunities for fun and games are very limited. I should probably take more time off." He nodded in agreement with himself, and then his sunny grin broke cover as he added, "Damn it, there's just something about a frightened woman that makes me want to plunge right into her."

He laughed to himself and looked down at his hands and flexed them a few times, as if recalling what he'd done with them barely an hour ago.

"Forget it, Josh," I said, each of the three words scalding me in turn as I uttered them. "We're all in the same boat."

"That's right, Tom, and thank you for saying it. It's good to keep things in perspective." He suddenly leaned forward and whispered, "I've got a secret, you know, and I'm only going to share it with you."

I dreaded what he was about unveil.

"I won't tell you now because all the details haven't been worked out, but you'll be the first to see it. It's a humdinger. It's…" He looked around as though expecting to find the appropriate word dancing in the air like a butterfly. "It's everything I've ever wanted, only I didn't know I wanted it. And I'd say you're the only man in Hexum who can understand it. I'll not say anything else until the time comes."

Reinhart said no more about his secret for the next few weeks, and his usual good mood became elevated into something akin to a child counting down the days until Christmas. He laughed even more easily and was very forgiving when on the job; on two occasions, men he would normally have shot dead were, instead, left with shattered limbs. The deputies speculated that he was either planning to get married or that some financial windfall was about to drop that would make Reinhart set for life. I doubted either scenario. I'd seen how he related to women, and money, except as a tally of how total his control of the county was, held no interest for him—his house was little more than a sleeping shelter, and his infrequent vacations were spent with an invalid brother in St. Louis once a year, or in quick trips in Las Vegas to see performers like Rich Little and Don Rickles. Reinhart didn't even gamble.

In the first week of October I was in Vegas when I got a call from Reinhart.

"I'm in Las Vegas, Tom. You free tomorrow?" he asked excitedly.

I was shocked that he'd contacted me. We'd been in Vegas at the same time before, but he had never made any attempt to reach out to me.

"Sure, I guess. What's up?"

"You'll see it tomorrow; what I was telling you about—you know, the secret."

"Okay. Where do I go?"

"You drove down in your truck, right? Pick me up at ten outside my motel."

He gave me the address of a place three blocks off the Strip and said he'd be waiting on the sidewalk. I wondered if he'd bought himself a place in the city and wanted to show it off, but his frugality, as evidenced by his choosing a motel that probably didn't cost fifty bucks a night, made that idea seem unlikely.

His motel, when I saw it the next morning, was a tired-looking, two-storey structure with rusty balconies and a rectangular pool in the forecourt in which a newspaper was floating. I almost didn't recognize Reinhart. I'd never seen him out of uniform, and there he was on the sidewalk minus his cowboy hat and wearing New Balance sneakers, white shorts that were too short, and a riotously red, yellow and green Hawaiian shirt. He was also holding a small briefcase. I pulled next to the curb and opened the door for him.

"This is a big day, Tom, a big day."

"Where are we going?"

"South along highway 95 about thirty miles and I'll show you where to turn when we get there. But not another word until then."

We'd only gone a few blocks when he noticed a souvenir shop on a corner and told me to pull over. He hurried into the store and came out with something in a plastic bag.

"I forgot to get one of these in all the excitement," he said, and took a small, golden trophy out of the bag. It was a cheap piece of crap, maybe ten inches tall, inscribed with the words, *World's Greatest Beer Drinker*. "You have any tape I can use?"

I pointed to the glove compartment where I had a roll of duct tape. He tore off a small piece, stuck it to the bottom of his trophy, wrote on it with a pen he found on the dashboard, then put his prize back in the bag and sighed with contentment as if he'd finally completed an important task.

As I drove, he chattered about how hot the weather was for October, his favorite gags from the Tom Dreesen show he'd seen the night before, and the bumpy flight he'd had from Sacramento down to Vegas. He wanted to tell me his secret so badly it was hurting him, but he didn't want to spoil the big reveal. I was only half-listening to him; our route was retracing the final stage of the Calexico run, and my memory had its claws in me.

Nevada Solar One appeared on our right, its fields of mirrors a shining black lake in the middle of a dusty plain, and Reinhart said, "Turn at that road up ahead."

We turned left onto a paved road that went east towards the Colorado River.

"What am I looking for?" I asked.

"Turn again at a pair of stone pillars. You can't miss them."

His smile was fierce with anticipation, and when the pillars came into view he actually giggled and clapped his hands. The pinkish granite columns were improbably tall, nearly twenty feet, and looked as though they'd been shaped with crude tools. They were intended to evoke some idea of primitive splendor, but all I could think was that they looked like the entrance to a theme park ride.

The pillars were flanking a smooth, sandy road that had been recently graded, and when I turned the Nissan onto it, Reinhart said breathlessly, "Not far now."

The road wound between scorched hills and then rose sharply, ending on a ridge that was at right angles to us. I stopped at the top of the ridge and found a long, steep-sided, rectangular valley in front of the me. The track went down into the valley and ran between two rows of palm trees, several hundred at least, before arriving at a large building about a quarter mile away.

"What the hell is this, Josh?"

"It's mine, Tom. I'm buying it. It's called Palmyra."

"You own it?"

"I pay them tomorrow. When I was running around trying to sort out that F.B.I. thing, a lawyer told me about this place, said it was for sale cheap, showed me pictures."

"Who built it?"

"No one knows. The lawyer thought it was someone from the Middle East. But he also heard it was supposed to be one of those retreat places for a tech guy from Seattle. Another fellow said it belonged to a Russian who wanted someplace special to stay when he came to Vegas. Anyway, everybody says whoever built it lost everything in this whole financial meltdown thing that they won't stop yakking about on TV, and the outfit that bought the debt from the bank wants to get what they can. The one thing everyone agrees on is that it's called Palmyra."

"What are you paying?"

"Two million," he said proudly.

"Holy shit."

"Putting those palm trees in the ground cost more than that."

"Why do you want it?"

"Wait'll you see the rest. Now drive down slowly, real slow, all the way to the house."

The road down into the valley was steep and I had to put the Nissan in first gear as it slid slightly on the loose surface.

Reinhart pointed ahead and said, "Now the best part begins."

I moved slowly along the path and its improbable procession of palm trees, their fronds moving slightly as if sensitive to our arrival. The trees were standing at precisely the same distance from each other, both in their rows and in relation to their mates on the other side of the road. They were fully grown, and I didn't doubt that it had cost millions to put them in place.

In a hushed voice Reinhart said, "Look."

He was pointing at a human figure leaning out from behind one of the palm trees, staring at us. I swore and hit the brakes.

Reinhart laughed delightedly. "Check it out."

It was a statue. I got out of the truck and went for a closer look. It was my height, its base buried in the sand, and was made of polished cement. The figure was male, with a boyish face and a head of intricate curls from which a pair of goat horns emerged. Its chest was bare, the legs furred and ending in hooves, and between its legs was an enormous, erect cock. The hands were grasping a pan flute and pressing them to its obscenely smiling and puckered lips.

From behind me Reinhart said, "I bet you know who that is."

"It's Pan."

"I knew it! I knew you were the right person to bring here. No one else in all of Grange County can appreciate this place except you and me—you even more than me."

I returned to the truck and we started down the road again. There were dozens more statues on each side of the road. Some stood proudly in the open between the palms, others lurked behind the trees looking coy or menacing, depending on the nature of their godliness. All the Greek gods appeared to be present, the female ones depicted in the nude with bodies apparently based on Playboy centerfolds. When the sculptor ran out of Greek deities he had moved on to the Egyptians, and we passed jackals, crocodiles and falcons standing on human legs. The last section of road was watched over by winged lions with the heads of men. I guessed they were Babylonian. None of it made sense unless we were arriving by chariot.

Reinhart had been talking the whole way, announcing the names of the few gods he recognized, admiring the symmetry of the palms, and repeatedly mentioning what a great deal he'd struck. I was acutely conscious in a way I hadn't experienced before of how utterly mad he was. His bizarrely austere life in Hexum was now, unaccountably, reversing polarity into princely extravagance in this abandoned desert kingdom.

"I forgot to tell you about the water!" he blurted out. "There's an aquifer under this land, something left behind by the Colorado a million years ago. It's what waters the palms, and they say it should last a thousand years. I could turn this whole valley into a garden if I wanted. Imagine that."

The palm-shadowed driveway ended at a square, stone building nearly a hundred feet wide and maybe thirty high with a domed roof. The palm trees continued on in a perfect circle around the perimeter of the structure. We got out of the truck and tried to take in what I was seeing. A wide staircase made of green-veined white marble took up nearly half the frontage and led to a deep portico supported by a dozen Doric columns. The front of the stone building was pierced with tall, square windows, each bracketed by niches holding busts of scowling men. Birds of prey done in iron, and in a variety of dramatic poses, perched along the roofline. It was impossible to say what it was trying to look like—an ancient Roman temple, a Deep South mansion, a Gothic crypt—but it was stupid and bloated and hideous; a berserk expression of wealth and power filtered through a despotic, syphilitic imagination.

"Ain't this a wonderment, Tom?" said Reinhart.

His face was filled with childish awe, and he was clutching his briefcase and the bag with the trophy to his chest as if they were holy objects.

"Let's go inside," he urged me.

He hurried up the steps to a pair of monumental wooden doors that belonged on a Transylvanian castle and pushed them open, waving me inside as he did so. The interior was completely empty. The light from the windows fell in solid shafts into a giant, hollow box of a building. There was no second storey, no decorations, nothing but walls towering over drifts of dust and grit, and small, long-tailed lizards that skittered away into the darkest corners of the room.

"I know, I know," said Reinhart pre-emptively, "it's unfinished. But what do I care? I only need a bit of electricity for lights and a fridge. Feel how cool it is? Pipes from the aquifer run under the floor. I don't even need air conditioning! I guess I'll have to put in some kind of bathroom."

He ran to the center of the room and said, "I can have my chair here, a big TV over there, and that's pretty much it. Oh, I almost forgot: look up."

In the middle of the roof was a small circular hole that revealed an unblinking blue eye of sky.

"It lets the hot air out. It's got mesh over it so bugs and birds don't get in." He pointed to a small drain cover in the middle of a slight depression in the floor. "And here's a drain directly under it for the once or twice a year it rains. Know what it's called?"

"An oculus."

"Damn, you're good, Tom."

I pictured Reinhart reclining in his chair in this domed space, a standing lamp beside him creating an atoll of light in a sea of dusty darkness as he read about honest, plain-talking lawmen defending towns and settlers. The image was so magnificently demented I wanted to laugh.

"Why this place, Josh? Are you retiring here or something?"

"Why? I need this to keep me going. It gives me a greater purpose. I told you before; I didn't know I needed this place until I saw it. This is bigger than me, and I need to finish it, get it set to rights. Did I tell you there's a pool out back that's almost done? I kid you not, it's shaped like an octopus." He paused and reached up for where his hat should have been and then rubbed his head instead. "I don't think I've shown it, but I've been feeling tired and dull lately. Sometimes I get the sensation that I'm…unraveling like an old sweater. I'm no spring chicken, Tom, and as rewarding as it's been to serve the people of Grange County, I need something to leave behind, something that says I was here, that I made a difference. Does that sound too proud, Tom? Too foolish?"

He desperately wanted my approval, so much so that I thought he might cry if I said the wrong thing, and so my final act of cowardice was to say, "No, Josh. You should do it. This place fits you like a glove."

"Thanks, Tom. I needed to hear that from you." He smiled mischievously. "I guess I can start decorating now."

He moved to the windowless back wall where, hidden in the shade, was a preposterously deep and wide fireplace. Reinhart took the trophy out of the bag and placed it in the middle of the mantelpiece.

"What's in the briefcase?" I asked.

He patted it and said proudly, "The reason I got a great deal on Palmyra. Remember? those gold certificates of Caleb's? I kept them for a rainy day. It wouldn't be smart to leave them in my motel room. They're payable to the bearer, and that hooked the company selling Palmyra; they can slip these overseas, cash 'em, and report a loss on my purchase price so they get a tax break. Clever, huh?"

Reinhart had once promised me a share of Caleb's gold—not that I cared—but his forgetfulness about the certificates, and his lunatic desire to complete this sterile edifice, cemented my determination to leave Hexum as soon as possible. He was becoming unhinged, and it was imperative to get away before he moved on to human sacrifices.

I was smiling to myself at the idea of Reinhart leading reluctant deputies in a pagan blood ceremony as I idly picked the trophy off the mantelpiece and looked at the tape on the bottom. Reinhart had written FULLER'S MILL, SEP 8/09. I did the math and remembered the half-naked woman staggering out of Reinhart's cruiser by the side of the road, then recalled Elmer Crippen referring to Reinhart's "situational" interest in women. I thought of his other trophies back in Hexum, and especially the one that had CALEB'S PLACE written on it along with the date on which the Settlement had burned. Linda. I'd left her wearing nothing but a blanket in the back of Reinhart's cruiser that night. She had been crying as I left, and Reinhart was getting in the back of the car to question her.

Reinhart was standing with his hands on his hips as he slowly surveyed his cavern with a look of intense satisfaction. "I'll come down every month, at first; more often when things are finished. First thing is to hire a security company to keep an eye on everything, not that people would have any reason to come out here. Well, I guess we'd better get back."

I waited on the top of the steps outside as Reinhart closed the ridiculous doors. He seemed to appreciate the echoing sound they made inside the house and patted them approvingly as if they were obedient dogs.

"It's stupid hot," said Reinhart as he passed me on the steps. "Silly of us not to bring something to drink."

"Josh," I said quietly.

He stopped and faced me. I was on a step above him so my punch felt more forceful as I drove it down into the side of his jaw. His relaxed, unconscious body collapsed and spread-eagled itself across the steps. I moved a few feet away, sat down on the top step of the staircase and rubbed my sore right fist.

The avenue of palm trees stretched out in front of me to a hazy vanishing point, and I sensed what the man who dreamed this place into existence had wanted. He would have stood where I was—in his dreams—watching people approach along the length of his roofless colonnade, and joy would come to him from knowing that their astonishment and envy was increasing with every yard they traveled. His happiness would be complete when they arrived in front of him and he could see those petty emotions in their faces, and those who were arriving would know in that same instant that their small, covetous souls had been laid bare before him and thereby rendered them weak and subservient—that would be the crowning glory for Palmyra's creator.

I felt sick and exhausted, even as a cold fury, one even more intense than when Levi had confessed to killing Anne, began to fill me. I let the rage fire my imagination.

Reinhart twitched and I went to the cargo box in my truck and retrieved some zip ties and a knife. Sprawled as he was on the broad steps of that hollow palace, Reinhart looked like a body cast out after a violent coup. I flipped him on his stomach, zipped both his wrists and ankles together, then lifted him onto the bed of the truck. Last of all, I picked his briefcase off the ground and tossed it onto the passenger seat.

I drove around to the back of the building to see if the structure got any madder and to add fuel to my anger. More palms were planted around a series of ragged trenches clawed out of the ground, which were presumably the beginnings of the octopus swimming pool. The valley wall facing the rear of the property was at a shallower angle and covered with tire tracks from large vehicles. This must have been the route construction vehicles used to get in and out. The other road was too steep for loaded trucks, not to mention that they would chew up the surface of what was intended to be Palmyra's Appian Way. I followed the tracks out of the valley and stopped at the top. The tire marks swung off to the right along a beaten-down route that undoubtedly joined up with the paved road. If Palmyra had ever been completed, this would have been the route for staff and delivery trucks. Directly ahead of me lay a flat wasteland ending in some rounded hills devoid of even a hint of vegetation. I headed straight for them.

It took twenty minutes to get in amongst the hills. Reinhart hadn't stirred, but he was still breathing. I drove through one shallow valley after another, none of them marked with tire tracks—not even dirt bikers ventured out here. I stopped after maneuvering the pickup through a cleft that took me into a circular valley sitting between three hills. Reinhart's ragged breathing might have been the loudest living noise to echo against those hills. When I dropped the tailgate, his unfocused eyes opened and he tried to sit up. I grabbed his ankles, slid him towards me and took out my knife.

"What's happening?" he asked in a drunken voice.

I moved him into a sitting position on the tailgate with his legs dangling off the back.

"Why did you hit me, Tom? What's this about?"

I started cutting away his clothes, starting with his shirt.

"Good God, Tom, you gone crazy?"

He kept asking me variations of the same questions as I sliced away his shorts and underpants and pulled his shoes and socks off. I said nothing. He was so astonished he didn't even attempt to resist. I pulled him off the tailgate and the tatters of his clothes fell to the ground.

"Are you stealing from me, Tom?" he asked furiously. "You can't be doing that, you just can't. And what's this foolishness with my clothes?"

He was a ludicrous sight with his darkly-tanned arms and head set off against the white of his torso and legs, like something that's been pulled out of its shell. He returned my look and must have seen his death in my eyes because he began to cry.

"Don't do it, Tom. We can work something out. I don't know what I've done to make you turn like this, but it can be fixed—fixed any way you like it."

I took him gently in my arms and laid him down on the stony ground.

"Oh, sweet Jesus, don't cut me, Tom, don't cut me. Tell me what to do, tell me how to make things right. Forgive me, Tom. Forgive me for whatever I've done and take me away from this awful place."

I almost spoke, but it was better that he should die without knowing the reason. Ignorance and mystery would salt his wounds.

He groaned deeply and lost the power of speech as I raised the knife and cradled his head in one arm to hold it steady. It was a beautiful old hunting knife with a bone handle that I'd found in the garage of my place on Cypress Ave. I'd have to throw it away after soiling it on Reinhart. I put it down and picked up a narrow, jagged rock that fit perfectly in my hand and would do the job just as well.

The last thing that came into Reinhart's eyes was a hopeful glint when he saw me put aside the knife. Two quick stabbing blows with the rock was all it took to crush the vision and hope out of those eyes. He screamed, and I stepped away as he began thrashing himself bloody on the ground like a fish dragged onto land. I cut the zip ties binding his hands and feet with my knife and he reached up to his face to feel the wet ruins of his eyes coursing down his cheeks. I picked up the remnants of his clothes, the zip ties, closed the tailgate, and got behind the wheel.

Reinhart was shouting my name over and over as I drove away. I stopped at the cleft and looked back. He had struggled to his feet and was sweeping his arms around as though hoping to touch me; his terror was so great he hadn't heard the sound of the pickup moving away. The sun was at its zenith, and his howling, bloody body was a gnomon in the middle of that scorching sundial of a valley, and his meager shadow the only shade for miles. The heat burned like an infection, and I doubted Reinhart would last out the day. But I hoped he would; that he would be mocked by the cool of the night before the sun came up the next morning to flay his life away. He took an uncertain step before falling to his knees, his mouth hanging open in a continuous howl.

I returned to Palmyra by the same route, parked behind Reinhart's almost-home and took the briefcase out of the pickup. The wealth it contained was tainted beyond measure, and I considered destroying the certificates or giving them to someone, but the only person who came to mind was Jessica, and I knew that she wouldn't want any part of them. One of the palm trees at the back of the house had

been poorly planted, leaving its roots partly exposed. The briefcase fit
neatly between the roots and it only took a few minutes to cover it and
the roots with sand and stones. I swore to myself that I would only return
for the certificates in the direst of circumstances.

On the drive back along Palmyra's grand boulevard I imagined a
horror movie in which the ranks of statues would come to vengeful life
because I had killed their master. The only movement was from the
lizards.

Back in the city, I put Reinhart's torn clothes in a charity clothing
drop box, then, later that night, tossed his wallet, minus the cash and
credit cards, which I'd cut up and thrown out, in an abandoned and
foreclosed housing development northeast of the city. If the wallet was
ever found the cops would think he'd been abducted and robbed.

I stayed in Vegas for the next two days, as I'd been intending,
and when I returned to Hexum, deputies were already beginning to
wonder where Reinhart was. After a week panic began to grip them. I
almost left town then and there, but it was known that I'd been in Vegas
the same time as Reinhart, so suspicion would have fallen on me
immediately. On the ninth day the Vegas police informed us that his
wallet had been discovered, and his car and possessions were still at the
motel. No one needed to be told that Reinhart was dead, and a meeting
was called in the rec room to address the situation.

All eyes turned to me. Everyone knew that I was closest to
Reinhart, and he'd never been shy about extolling what he considered
my virtues. This was an opportunity to ease my own departure from
Hexum, so I told them about Spencer's involvement with the F.B.I.; how
Reinhart had saved the day by calling in favors; and that Jubal had died
because Reinhart had had doubts about his loyalty. The deputies were
dumbfounded and alarmed that the county and their lives had come close
to destruction without them being aware of it. That's when I told them
that with Reinhart dead—I pinned the blame on Black Dogs, who now
functioned effectively as the boogeymen of Grange County—it was
likely the feds would come charging back. The meeting broke up in
stunned silence, with nothing decided or planned.

Vin Creasy was the first to go; the next day, in fact. He must have
thought that he'd be a prize catch if the F.B.I. rode into town, so he left a
badly-typed resignation letter on my desk that said he was moving to
Florida to be with his ailing mother. Three more deputies left before the

end of the week. None of them bothered with letters. My warning about the F.B.I. had worked—not that there wasn't some truth to it—and now my own departure would look unexceptional.

Early on October 15, a Thursday, I loaded the Nissan with a suitcase holding my clothes and a few books, and a satchel with roughly 200k in cash. I drove down to Vegas and deposited 175k in a front-money account at the Bellagio. The next morning, I converted most of the rest of my cash into traveller's checks. That afternoon I got on the first of two flights that took me to Panama.

It was a ramshackle escape. I planned on monitoring the situation in Grange County from afar, seeing if the F.B.I. really would start taking down people. If it looked like they were getting serious, a Panamanian passport would be easy to get, and with that I could fly back to Vegas, retrieve my money, and go from there. If I'd managed things better, I would have got my money out of the country sooner, because if the F.B.I. was determined enough they'd have no trouble figuring out that I'd gone to Panama.

In the end, I spent less than three months in Panama. The F.B.I. did come into Grange County, but only to dismantle Jubal's operation. I read news reports of what was happening on the internet and phoned a couple of deputies who fleshed out the details. It was apparent that Reinhart's string-pulling was still being felt, and that the feds were limiting their interest to drugs and people-smuggling. John Stockman was arrested, but only because he was caught driving a load of weed. A few more deputies quit and the state attorney general ordered the California Highway Patrol to manage law enforcement duties in the county on a temporary basis. No one knew what had happened to Cotton Pearsall.

Reinhart and Jubal's empire dissolved with an almighty whimper. The labs and pot fields were busted or abandoned, the operators who escaped the dragnet moved on to other counties or states, the laborers and sex workers scattered to the cities or were deported, the deputies who remained went back to living on their salaries, and no one higher up the food chain, in Sacramento or D.C., lost any sleep. The skeletons lying in crevasses, forests and mines were left undisturbed and only ever remembered in nightmares.

I returned to Las Vegas and bought a house for 15k from a bank that held the underwater mortgage. It was in a subdivision on the edge of the city that was just a few years old but was mostly empty. It suited me living in a modern ghost town. The curving suburban streets had drifts of sand in them, and I saw coyotes wandering the area more often than people. I tried to make a living playing poker, and did so for most of a year, but eventually too many of the dead-eyed, money-obsessed players around the tables were reminding me of people, living and dead, I'd known in Hexum, and I became a stupidly aggressive player, as if hoping my crazy betting would drive them out of my sight.

My resources were dwindling when I heard about Hessian Security from another player at a poker table. He told me that they were based in L.A., paid well, and only employed a certain kind of ex-cop. I contacted Hessian, and when I told them I used to work in Grange County, I was offered a job immediately. I sold the house in Vegas for what I paid for it, moved to Los Angeles and rented an apartment near Pico Blvd.

For the right fee, Hessian would bust a union, finger thieving employees, chase down debtors and embezzlers, make nuisance lawsuits go away, and discourage witnesses. And it would be done as roughly or as illegally as a client was willing to pay for. The "operatives", as we were called, were ex-cops, almost all of whom had become unemployable in law enforcement. I actually liked my work, at first. It was all so benign after what I'd been doing. What was slapping a warehouse worker around or blackmailing a union organizer compared to killing and maiming? I was practically a saint. Occasionally I even let myself think I was doing a public service; a few times a year Hessian would get a contract to deal with an abusive father, husband or boyfriend, and I'd feel good about putting the offender in a wheelchair.

After a few years, however, the work became dispiriting. Hessian specialized in what it called "clearances," which involved operatives going undercover in businesses to find cheats and thieves. I'd be sent in undercover for a few days or weeks at everything from car dealerships to hotels. Because I was fluent in Spanish, I was often placed in firms that suspected their Latino workers. I'd make a big deal about not knowing Spanish and then eavesdrop and do a bit of basic investigation. It became a tedious routine of overhearing conversations about stealing cleaning supplies or giving relatives unauthorized discounts or fiddling the petty cash. The losses to the businesses were often laughable, but the owners and managers liked keeping their employees fearful and intimidated.

In 2018 Hessian got a contract to do clearances for MRG, the Marsden Restaurant Group. It was a chain of semi-fancy restaurants that appeared independent but were all under one corporate roof. The restaurants were themed French, Italian, Mexican, or Asian, and all carried different names and interior designs. There were more than 100 of them scattered across California, Nevada and Arizona. I was assigned exclusively to the MRG contract. It was a clearance job like any other, but the restaurants were elegant, the food was excellent, and they were located in the better zip codes.

The charm of the restaurants wore off when a hostess I got fired for taking tips to let people jump the reservation queue crashed her car into a tree and died. Some said she was too upset to be driving; her closest friend at the restaurant thought it was suicide, since a single, 44-year-old woman with no job skills except looking good in a short, tight black dress—the required attire for women at MRG—might not view her firing as "an opportunity for reflection" as the manager had put it when he canned her.

My next MRG assignment was in Brentwood. It was a French restaurant called L'espace, and it only took me three shifts as the bartender to see that the bar manager, Tony, was skimming a small amount by selling his own booze. He was let go by the manager, Chris, as his shift was ending on a quiet Monday evening. I stood beside Chris at the bar and described the scam after Tony offered a token rebuttal to the accusation of theft. I was backing Chris up because Tony was a big guy who liked to boast about his MMA training. He surprised both of us when he burst into tears and begged to keep his job. Chris rolled his eyes and said to me, "Can you believe this loser?" I leaned in close to Chris and told him loudly and sharply not to be an asshole. The few customers in the place were staring at us. After Tony left, I poured myself three fingers of the most expensive scotch the bar carried and sat down in a booth at the back of the restaurant. Chris eyed me darkly for this transgression but said nothing. He was also glancing nervously towards a table where a woman with dark red hair was sitting by herself.

I'd quickly drunk one finger's worth of scotch when I saw the redheaded woman walking towards me. She was wearing white capris and a pale blue sleeveless blouse under a thin cardigan of the same color. Her face was sharply angled, with cat-like green eyes that made me think she was sizing me up for a swat to the head, but her smile as she sat down across from me in the booth was reassuring.

"You didn't like any part of that scene, did you?" she said, sounding intrigued.

"No, I didn't. But Tony liked it least of all."

"I thought you were going to hit Chris."

"Chris needs hitting *and* firing, but this company is after thieves, not managers who can't keep their hands off the female staff. Do you know Chris? You work here?"

"I don't work here, but I've seen him in action."

"And you are...?"

"Autumn Marsden. My husband owns this place. You must be with that security company he hired."

"That's right. I'm Tom Bridger."

She extended her hand and we shook. Something about this shared gesture made us grin foolishly.

"You know," she said, "you could get Chris fired. I'd back you up."

"It's tempting, but these days I try and keep my habit of ruining people's lives to the minimum necessary."

"That would ruin him?" she said with surprise.

"You never know. The kind of people I get terminated are usually one paycheck away from losing something critical in their lives—a car, an apartment, maybe a daycare space. Even jerks like Chris. And I can't say for sure that fucking him over won't domino badly onto someone else. I've seen it happen."

"You're in the wrong line of work," said Autumn, surprising me because she said it with sympathy, not irony.

"No doubt. That's why I'm quitting."

"Really? When did you decide that?"

"Just now at the bar. But don't count me as noble yet; I need to keep this job for a while more to save some money. And figure out what to do next."

"Any ideas?"

"Only to stop hurting people who don't deserve it. Beyond that, nothing."

"Have you done a lot of that kind of hurting?"

"As much as my cowardice would allow. Are you here with someone? Your husband?"

"No." She wrinkled her nose. "He's entertaining his hunting buddies at the house. The chef here makes a special dish for me, so I drop in from time to time."

"Well, it's a lovely place to hang out."

"You think so?"

"I do."

"I designed it. I designed all the restaurants."

"I'm honestly impressed. Places like this aren't my natural environment, but I've always felt...comfortable in your restaurants, as long as I don't look at the prices."

"That's in the past, though. The restaurants are all done, and now I just eat in them."

"So, what do you do instead?"

"I do what a billionaire's wife is expected to do: I spend stupid amounts of money to make my surroundings match my position; it's a full-time job keeping all my clothes, furnishings and homes up to standard." She said all this in a mocking tone, but became serious when she asked, "What did you mean when you said, 'as much as your cowardice would allow?'"

"That I could have stopped what I was doing at any time. I could have taken a different path, but I let fear and cowardice direct me. Up to a point. For some things I wasn't cowardly enough."

"That means you took a stand?"

"No," I laughed, "that sounds heroic; simply not being a coward was enough. I've only done it a few times. I should have made it a habit. Maybe in my next life."

She sat back in the booth and studied me. "I guess you used to be a cop."

"Well, I wore the uniform. How about you? What were you before you became Mrs. Marsden?"

"I was Autumn Foley and my cowardice only hurt me. It still does." She was poker-faced as she told me this, and I didn't know how to respond. We sat without speaking for a little while until she smiled and said, "Do you find this awkward, us sitting here and not talking, like strangers who've fallen into a serious conversation on a bus and suddenly realize they don't know how to end it?"

"No. I could sit with you like this quite a while longer."

"I could, too. But I have to get up early and go on the maiden voyage of a yacht to Catalina, and, yes, before you say it, the life of a billionaire's wife is truly a hardship."

"No more buses, huh?"

She stood up and leaned on the table, one hand resting gently on mine. "I wouldn't say that. I think you and I live on the same route. Which restaurant do you work at next?"

"I'm appearing nightly at Mescal in Palm Springs next week."

"How about that; it's only a few bus stops from our house there."

She ran her finger quickly and lightly up my forearm, then turned and left. I pushed my drink away. I didn't need it anymore.

The following week in Palm Springs I was so distracted in expectation of Autumn coming through the door that it almost slipped my attention that two female servers were dealing coke to customers along with their bills. Their tips were enormous. I gave them a warning and frightened some of the customers who got testy with the 'poor service' they were getting from their favorite servers.

It was my second to last day in Palm Springs when I pulled into Mescal's parking lot at eleven o'clock, a half hour before opening, and saw Autumn leaning against a gray Audi in the shade of a jacaranda tree ablaze with purple blooms. I put my Civic into the spot one away from her. She was in matching pale-pink shorts and T-shirt, and her smile, which looked newly minted for me, immediately cleared my mind of the dread I was feeling about another day of spying and eavesdropping.

"I think," she said, "you could use a day off."

"Are you leading me into temptation?"

"I am. Does that sound like a place you'd care to enter?"

"Oh, yes. Your car or mine?"

"You choose."

"Yours, definitely. Judging by the smell, there are some stray fries under my seat that have started a new life on their own."

As we drove away from Mescal she said, "I thought we could talk some more while we do something touristy. Have you been to Palm Springs before?"

"I've passed through, but never stayed. You like it here?"

"We live in the next city over, Rancho Vista. It's all Palm Springs, really. This place is okay if you don't mind all the conversations that begin with someone saying, 'Do you know who used to own our house back in the day?' I play tennis, do some hiking, swim, and hang out at the art museum when I get tired of listening to people talk. I only come here because of Enoch and his golf addiction. It's all an exercise in managing my sanity. What do you do to keep from screaming on street corners?"

"I run. I read. Play some poker and try not to think about the past. Where are we going?"

"The aerial tramway. It's a cable car ride to San Jacinto Peak. You can buy souvenir hats and everything."

It was mid-June, the heat was swiftly approaching painful, and there was only a handful of people on our cable car as it began the ascent up Chino Canyon.

"You know why my husband bought that restaurant chain?"

"Why?"

"As a game farm. You must have noticed by now that the front of house female staff are uniformly gorgeous, or at least adjacent to it. It's basically Hooters in semi-formal wear. He bought it twenty years ago when he was already near enough to being a billionaire that it didn't matter what his investments paid. But he was fifty-four and looking every day of it, and he fancied the idea of having places all over the Southwest where, between golf games and hunting trips, he could wander in and be greeted as a golden prince and then seduce or coerce women into his bed. More of the latter than the former. Like you said, a lot of people are one paycheck away from catastrophe. Sometimes he brought his friends along to share in the sport. That's how I met him, fourteen years ago. I was handing out menus at one of his restaurants in Pasadena. He came in by himself one night and hit on me. And the next night. The third night he wondered how badly I needed to keep my job, and I told him not as badly as he needed to avoid me coming out of the kitchen with a hot pan of grease and chucking it in his face. He didn't know what to say, and I told him he should fire me and then hire me to redecorate his ridiculous-looking restaurants—they really did look awful at the time. He said he'd do it for one date and I said yes."

"What did you do before that?"

"I made an honest living getting naked in cheapo films. Enoch didn't know that at the time, but it pleased him when he found out I had some fame in that field. Anyway, one date led to two to ten, and then I said yes."

The cable car bumped and swayed as it passed over one of the pylons and we held on to each other. The Coachella Valley was spreading out below us, a tan carpet cross-hatched with roads and blocks of housing.

"And that's when," Autumn continued, "I turned coward for the first time. I had other options, but they seemed meager and difficult. Enoch was a sure thing. He was my plush future signed, sealed and delivered with next to no effort from me."

"You could quit."

"I have in my mind a hundred times over. But that's where the cowardice grows sharper and stronger. I need a push."

"I waited too long for a push, and that only added to my regrets."

She turned to look out the window and said, "I'm spoiling your day off. We should be appreciating the view by making awestruck noises."

"Okay. Ooh. Aah."

"That's better," she laughed. "And when we get to the top you have to be properly astonished by how much cooler it is than down in the desert."

We arrived at Mountain Station a few minutes later and went outside to sit at a table overlooking a valley staffed with tall pines and bisected by a transparent creek.

"Well?" said Autumn with a raised eyebrow. "Are you going to say it? Go on."

"It's so much…cooler."

"You see? Now you're enjoying yourself like a proper tourist."

A bird with electric blue plumage landed near us to feed on some peanuts someone had dropped.

"A Steller's jay," I said absently.

"If you tell me you're a nerd birdwatcher, you're going to ruin the flattering image I've built up of you."

"I'll admit to no such thing. I can imitate its mating call, if you'd like."

"Oh, no."

"And what is this flattering image?"

"That you're the wounded, conflicted, sexy samurai of the food services industry."

I laughed so loud the jay took flight with a volley of angry shrieks.

"We should go now," said Autumn after we'd both stopped laughing.

"Already?"

"There's so much more to show you. Have you ever heard of the Capri Inn?"

"No."

"It's on all the architectural tours of Palm Springs—it was designed by Albert Frey—and it has a lovely bar and pool, and a spectacular brunch, but you know what makes it truly wonderful?"

"What?"

"It's absolutely the best place in the world to have sex in the afternoon."

"Do they sell souvenir hats?"

We didn't leave our bungalow at the Capri until the sun was below the horizon, and we only ventured out as far as our patio to eat the dinner sent over from the inn's restaurant. It was the best part of a summer day in the desert: when the heat has become exhausted and bored with its assault on the land and retreated to dream of tomorrow's battle, leaving a dry coolness to creep out and offer comfort.

After dinner, we sat by the pool and let ourselves be mesmerized by the sound of the evening wind hissing through the palm fronds above us.

"How can we make this a regular thing?" I asked. "That's if you want to."

"I do. It won't be hard. Enoch doesn't have a jealous bone in his body, because he doesn't think I would do anything to risk losing the benefits of his wealth. And the pre-nup does me no favors. You'll get to meet him. I usually have lots of guests staying at our houses, so you'll just be one more. Anyway, he'll probably think you're gay. He assumes my male friends are gay because they can't talk about sports or hunting."

"What's he like?"

"Weak. Greedy. Bitter. He used to not care about money as much, but now it's the only thing he can have an iron grip on. Day by day, his body betrays him, and so he punishes the parts of the world he rules for that betrayal. That's why he hired Hessian. MRG makes lots of money, but the idea that people are stealing from him makes him furious. That the thefts are small drives him mad because it tells him his betrayers are nobodies, losers. He only has respect for great thieves. If someone embezzled him for tens of millions, he'd never stop telling his pals at the golf club about it. But when he reads a Hessian report about a busboy stealing tableware, he's in a silent fury for hours."

"I'm familiar with the species. Why don't you leave him?"

"Why didn't you stop hurting people?" she says without recrimination. "It's never the right time, is it? I tell myself he can't live much longer, that I should just wait a little longer, and so every day I hate myself more. I reason that the eventual payoff will be worth all the self-loathing. You have to know that if you want to be with me, I get impulsive, and usually not in a fun way, when the negative feelings pile up too high. You ready for that?"

"You'll have to do better than that if you want to scare me off."

We returned to the bungalow and didn't leave until late the next morning.

Autumn stocked her vast homes in Malibu, Rancho Vista, and Taos with artists, media people, writers, and a nebulous group who described themselves as "creatives," and for the rest of that summer I joined this large and rotating group of her friends. I first met Enoch at the Malibu house. Autumn told him that I worked for Hessian, which surprised him, but then said I did graffiti murals on the side, which immediately glazed his eyes over and made me suppress a laugh. He was tall, slightly stooped, and walked as though being led around by the momentum of his sagging stomach. His eyes were sad and suspicious, and set in a mottled face that the sun hadn't been kind to. Autumn had called him bitter, but what I saw in him was shock over the fact that wealth hadn't granted him an exemption from decay.

At first, I couldn't understand why he tolerated having people filling his homes whom he clearly couldn't stand or was bored by. It was because they allowed him to indulge in his own peculiar sport. Enoch didn't mingle much, but he was always on the alert for a chance to jump into a conversation and cut it down to his size; if a well-known actor was mentioned, Enoch would have played golf with someone far more famous; if something was described as rare or unusual, he would have seen or done something more remarkable; and he could always prove that a thing of beauty or significance actually had feet of clay and money.

I'd stay at one of the houses every second weekend, and Autumn and I would slip off to a hotel whenever Enoch left for his daily round or two of golf. Some weekends Enoch was absent, and we could act like a normal couple, although Autumn was careful about alerting the servants to our relationship—she wasn't certain of their loyalties. Her friends were in on the charade, and I wasn't the first boyfriend she'd brought into her circle like this. In September, she and Enoch left for Europe. He to play golf and kill wild boar from shooting platforms in Hungarian forests, while she went to the Biennele in Venice and the International Art Fair in Zurich.

Autumn returned in mid-October, and we were both surprised by how much we had missed seeing and touching each other. We fell back into the same routine of spending a couple of weekends a month at one of her homes, and maybe a day together at a nearby hotel. She never came to my apartment, saying that it was better to hide in plain sight when it came to Enoch.

One night at the Malibu house, shortly after her return, Autumn and her friends, as they sometimes did, decided to play a board game. I'd never played one as a child or an adult, and the idea of them baffled me. Whenever they dragged one of these entertainments out, I'd go for a run or find something to read. That night I sat down in front of a TV in my bedroom and turned on the Kings' game. Enoch wandered past on the way to his office and noticed me transfixed by the action.

"You watch sports." It was more a surprised statement than a question.

"Hockey mostly. Sometimes football and baseball."

And with that I instantly became Enoch's favorite amongst Autumn's friends. He invited me up to his office, a space he guarded jealously, to watch the game. He had a view over the Pacific, but what held the eye was a collection of mounted trophies on one wall. There was a leopard, a bighorn sheep, and some horned African animals I couldn't put a name to. Another wall held framed photos that chronicled Enoch's life up until he began to look his age. The rest of the house was a testament to Autumn's love of art and design, and was, along with her friends, her intellectual insulation against Enoch. The office, with its seedy, atavistic trophies and narcissistic memory wall, was his revenge for feeling an outcast in his own house.

Enoch loved sports, especially football, and in me he found someone who could speak the same language. And when I told him I was once a cop, he pestered me for anecdotes about my former career, especially the violent ones. The stories I related hadn't actually happened to me— my memories weren't to be dragged into the light for the entertainment of someone like Enoch—so I passed off incidents from the careers of other deputies as my own. He began to crave my companionship for sports viewing and the testosterone-flavored doses of cop life I supplied him with, and he told Autumn to have me over as often as possible. It was an arrangement that worked well for all three of us. Autumn would sometimes call to say that Enoch wanted me for a playdate.

By spring of the next year I'd grown weary of any time spent in Enoch's company. I maintained a pleasant façade with him, but as the intensity of my relationship with Autumn grew, the less I could tolerate being in the same room as the man she hated, but shared, on occasion, a bed with. Like any jealous lover I pictured him touching her, and I let my imagination gnaw on those images as if they were bones that fed me a thin but satisfying diet of resentment. One afternoon in Taos, while we were out hiking, I told Autumn how painful it was to spend time in Enoch's company.

In a cold, mocking voice she said, "Painful. You find a few *hours* painful. Who lives with him?"

I had no reply for her and we marched in silence for nearly an hour until she sat down on a rock, took a sip from her water bottle, and said, "You can't stomach the fact that I have to sleep with him sometimes. Am I right?"

"Yes."

"You're in good company; my last two boyfriends said the same thing. I have no time for male possessiveness anymore. I take my freedom where I can until the day, and I pray it's soon, when Enoch flat-lines. I have the patience—barely—do you?"

"I guess I'll have to as well."

"Glad to hear it. And here's something I never told those boyfriends: seven years ago Enoch gave me syphilis for a birthday present. Since then he only gets to have sex with my right hand."

I took a long drink from my bottle before saying, "Have you thought about just using your feet?"

She squirted water at my head, kissed me lightly and quickly, and said "You're such an idiot."

My patience wasn't as great as Autumn's. As the summer began my annoyance with Enoch turned to hatred. As he began to believe that he and I had something like a friendship, he started to speak disparagingly of Autumn when he was alone with me. It started as lame little jokes about her love of art and architecture, then comments about her being made a fool of by her "parasitic, liberal" friends—excluding me, of course, he would always hasten to add—and finally, one afternoon in early July, he described her life before she met him as being "when she was whoring around in skin flicks." He immediately complimented her looks, but I barely heard it over the blood pounding in my ears. That's when I decided to kill Enoch.

Convincing myself to take his life was easy. I had killed other people for little or no reason, so what was one more body added to a heap I couldn't see the top of? I didn't know what was in Autumn's pre-nup, but I assumed she'd get more from Enoch's death than a divorce, and, if I could manage it, she wouldn't even have to know that I had done it. His death must look accidental or natural, since a murdered billionaire always draws a crowd. He would be, I promised myself, the last person I would ever murder.

A few weeks later I had a half-formed plan for doing something to Enoch's meds—he took a regiment of pills for various ailments—when there was a shift in my relationship with Enoch and Autumn. I had the impression that both had received news that they didn't want to tell me about and dealt with it by drawing away from me. Autumn would become strangely quiet, and then the next minute display the impulsiveness she had warned me about when we first met. One night at the Malibu house, after Enoch and her friends had gone to bed, she suddenly said she was going to go surfing in the dark. Without waking the house up by shouting, I tried to argue with her, but she went ahead and paddled out on the water while I waited on the beach. She came back to shore looking exhilarated and clearly amused by the concern on my face. The next day I asked her if there was something she wasn't telling me, or if Enoch was giving her grief. She answered no to both questions, but she was a poor liar.

I couldn't gauge what was wrong with Enoch, He didn't stop asking me to watch games with him—he needed to demonstrate his encyclopedic knowledge of sports to someone—but he lost interest in stories about Hexum, and, more tellingly, he stopped talking about Autumn. I kept expecting Autumn to tell me that he didn't want me around anymore, but each weekend that summer I was either at the house in Malibu or Rancho Vista.

I was in Hessian's offices on South Broadway a few days before the second weekend in September when I got a call from Enoch.

"Tom," he said abruptly, "you're coming up to Rancho Vista this weekend, aren't you? It's the beginning of the season, lots of good matchups to watch."

"Uh, I guess I could, but I hadn't heard anything from Autumn; she might have an all-girls weekend planned."

Autumn did, from time to time, have weekends with only her female friends around.

"So what?" he barked. "You just have to stay out of their way. C'mon, Tom, it's the best weekend of the year: start of football, pennant races. I'm sure Autumn would want you here anyway."

"Yeah, sure, Enoch. I'll try and get out there Friday night."

Enoch had never phoned me before, and everything about the way he spoke sounded off. I called Autumn immediately afterwards and told her about Enoch's strange call.

"That is weird," she agreed.

"Was he worried you weren't going to invite me?"

"Probably," she said quietly. "Because I did tell him you weren't going to be coming. He asked about you yesterday."

"Girls only this weekend?"

"No. Me only this weekend." There was a long pause. "I planned to Zen out, do some hiking by myself. Normal service will be resumed shortly, as they say. Next weekend, for sure."

I'd never heard her sound so subdued.

"You okay? You don't sound right. You're sure you don't want me up there?"

Another long pause.

"Yeah, why not? I might not be the best company, but I'd like to know you're there. You alright with me being out of sorts?"

"I'm always alright with you."

"You know what, Tom?"

"What?"

"We're too good for each other. We deserve worse. Bye"

Something was very wrong between Autumn and Enoch, but I couldn't fathom what it was. With no other guests cluttering up the house this would be the best opportunity to dispose of him. His meds were the cure for my problem. He left them lying around wherever he was, and over the course of the summer I was able to learn what they were. The most useful for me was Zopiclone, a mild sedative he took to help him sleep when his knees were aching too much. The tablets were flat and small, no larger than the top of a thumbtack. One of his regular medications was a large green capsule he took every night before bed. I would empty out one of the capsules and fill it with five or six Zoplicones. That wouldn't kill him, but it would allow me to take his unconscious body and drop him in the pool. I'd tell the police he'd been complaining about his knees and had probably taken extra pills to get to sleep and then gone out by the pool for a breath of air before going to bed. The optics weren't ideal with Autumn and I being the only other people in the house, but there wouldn't be a shred of evidence against either of us. And I wouldn't move him until Autumn had gone to bed, so even she would believe in the story.

I left work early on Friday and got to Rancho Vista around seven o'clock. As usual, the first sight of the house astonished me as I came up the twisting road from the gatehouse; it's illuminated cubes of glass and white brick lay like a giant's bracelet discarded at the foot of the mountains and made me feel as if I was passing into a world ruled by different laws of physics. Autumn had told Enoch she wouldn't spend time in Rancho Vista unless she had somewhere special to live while he was golfing from dawn to dusk, and he had grudgingly footed the seven-figure bill it took to build it.

Neither of them greeted me normally. Autumn was nervous and curt, and Enoch was all over me with uncharacteristic effusiveness, asking questions about my work and what I thought about the upcoming NFL season. Autumn said she had a headache and was going to bed early. She went down the hall to her room and threw a glance back at me that left me feeling scared. But I was relieved she hadn't gone to the master bedroom, which would have announced that Enoch had asked her to sleep with him that night.

Enoch and I stayed talking in the kitchen. His pill case, divided into the days of the week, was on the kitchen island. The pill bottles were all kept in the fridge. After a few minutes, Enoch hustled me into his office to watch a Dodgers game. I waited an inning before telling him I was starving and had to get something to eat. He was transfixed by the game and grunted a reply. I went to the fridge, took out the pills I needed, and went to a bathroom where I carefully dumped the powder out of the green capsule and inserted six Zopiclones. I returned to the kitchen and switched the green capsule in the pill case with my doctored one, then made a sandwich and rejoined Enoch in his office.

When the game ended at eleven, Enoch was already yawning and rubbing his eyes. I followed him out to the kitchen where he slowly and dutifully swallowed his nightly ration of meds. He said goodnight and lurched back to his office where he would stretch out on the couch under the static gaze of beheaded animals and watch sports until he fell asleep. I went outside to the pool area to escape the house's frigid air conditioning and sat on the end of a lounger. In the distance a rabbit screamed as it was taken by a creature stealthier than it.

After forty minutes I went back into the house and pushed open the partially closed door to Enoch's office. The TV was still on and Enoch was on the couch under the sleeping bag he used for the many nights he slept in the office. His eyes were closed and one hand hung down on the floor.

"Enoch?" I said loudly.

He didn't move a muscle. For a moment I thought he was already dead, but when I turned off the TV, I heard him snoring. I gave his arm a gentle pull and there was no reaction. To be absolutely sure of his unconsciousness I used my thumb to gently push back one of his eyelids. It had no effect on him. I sat down on the couch and mapped out the best route to carry him to the pool that would avoid the security camera in the kitchen. Without the TV on, the room was in semi-darkness, the only illumination coming from yard lights outside the window. The cold, pale light made Enoch's immobile face look even older and grimmer, like something from a tomb in an old black and white horror movie. I kept telling myself that in another few seconds I'd get to my feet and begin carrying him to the pool, but the seconds stretched into minutes. I was a kid standing on a high diving board thinking that he'll jump any second…any second…any second now.

I went effortlessly from visualizing Enoch sliding from my arms and into the pool's calm, blue water with only the smallest splash, to realizing I couldn't kill him. I didn't want to kill him. He was a frail, useless creature whose natural end was undoubtedly near at hand. I didn't need to rush things. What truly stopped me was the knowledge that my decision to murder Enoch had been made for me by Hexum. It had taught me that life was to be taken from others and used, repurposed or discarded. As I sat staring at Enoch's vulnerable body, I thought about how I'd never contacted Jessica after leaving Hexum because I was sure my savage soul would infect or wound her. Killing Enoch would, I wagered, bring the ghosts of Hexum back to life in me, steer me back to what I had once been, and poison Autumn as well. I remembered Monica lying in the tall grass, and then let the shades of my other victims, the intentional and the accidental, leave the sealed rooms of my memory and taunt me. It was the howling arrival of these specters that forced me to my feet and out of Enoch's room.

At the bar in the living room I poured myself some neat vodka, toasted *Standard Station*, knocked back my drink, and briefly considered going into Autumn's room, if only to lie beside her. I retreated to my own room and fell into an unpleasant sleep spiked with Technicolor dreams of chaos.

The next morning, I found Enoch eating breakfast at the island and complaining to Maria that everything tasted bitter. He tried to give me a friendly greeting, but it sounded forced. I got myself a coffee as he pushed away his half-eaten plate of scrambled eggs and went to his office clutching a glass of water.

"You want something, sir?" asked Maria.

"No thanks. And c'mon, Maria, no more 'sirs.'"

She smiled tightly and started cleaning. All of the staff at Enoch's properties were Latino, and I sometimes worried one of them might remember me from elsewhere. Occasionally Maria studied me with an alertness that made me think she had secrets or was keeping one. Oribe, the only other servant at the house, was outside cleaning the pool. He looked fifty with a face the color and complexion of a tobacco leaf and had to be twenty years Maria's senior. He claimed to be her husband, but I knew it was a lie, one I had no interest in exposing. From force of habit I hadn't let either of them know I could speak Spanish.

I took my coffee out to the pool and asked Oribe if he'd seen Autumn.

"Morning, sir. She went for a hike real early." He waved his hand vaguely in the direction of the mountains behind the house. "Mrs. Marsden likes to stays fit."

He laughed for no reason, except possibly to remind me how much I disliked him, especially his fawning smiles and forced laughter. His ersatz good humor seemed extra false that day. I sat by the pool and nursed my drink. After Oribe finished, I went and changed into my swimming shorts and swam lazy laps until my pounding head grew quieter. As I climbed out of the pool, I saw Autumn in the distance climbing down a ridge towards the house. She was wearing tan shorts, hiking boots, a wide-brimmed straw hat and a gray T-shirt that had U's of sweat down the front and back. I got a cold bottle of Perrier from the kitchen and waited for her by the pool. When she arrived, she took it from me and killed it in one go.

"You must be roasted," I said, "it's nearly ninety already."

"It makes the remainder of the day seem cool."

"Any plans?"

"No. Just chill."

She hurried into the house and I tried to work out why both Autumn and Enoch were acting so oddly around me. I could even add Oribe to that equation.

I swam a bit more, then went to my room where I spent most of the afternoon reading *The Baron in the Trees*, the last book Latimer had written down in his journal as something he should recommend to me. He was right. I kept expecting Autumn or Enoch to appear at my door and suggest doing something, but it never happened. The house was filled with a strange silence. On normal weekends there would have been five or six other people staying over, plus Autumn's local friends stopping by for the day. Now the place had the hushed atmosphere of an art gallery, which it mostly was. A low drone of sports chatter escaped from Enoch's office, and occasionally I'd hear Maria doing something in distant parts of the house. I heard nothing from Autumn until she appeared at my door wearing a yellow bikini and, with a nod in the direction of the pool, said, "Swim?"

I followed her outside. Enoch was already by the pool, sitting in the shade of a sun umbrella in a pair of red trunks and studying his skin as if searching for clues on a treasure map. Autumn stretched out on a lounger near him. I took a lounger on the other side of the pool. Although the sun was stalking away behind the mountains, the day's heat had yet to follow and it held me firmly under its paw.

I thought about how the day had passed slowly and quietly, rather than beginning, as it could have, with Enoch being dragged from the bottom of the pool, and I relaxed in a way that felt foreign to me. I'd chosen not to use death to manipulate my world, and it felt good to leave fatal decisions to Nature and Fate, entities that were no kinder or crueler than me, but certainly knew nothing of nightmares.

My reverie was broken by the sound of Enoch scraping his chair across the patio stones as he stood up and walked over to me.

"Tom," he said, "I'd like you to do me a favor."

The Skeleton Palms

I should be amused by the comically stupefied look on Autumn's face as she looks down at Palmyra, but it makes me want to turn around and leave.

"Is it an old film set?" she asks.

"That would make sense, but no."

I don't want to tell Autumn much about Reinhart—that would mean detailing the worst of my many crimes—so I give her a brief history of the place and how Reinhart came to find it.

"Did he buy it in the end?" She asks.

"No. Before the sale was completed, he died in a hunting accident. But he'd already hidden a briefcase full of gold certificates down there for a rainy day. They're payable to the bearer."

"And how did you find out where it was?"

"He told me about it."

Autumn gives me her warmest smile. "You know how I can tell I'm in a serious relationship with someone?"

"How?"

"I care enough about them to study their character and learn how their mind works, and so that's how I know you're lying. I've noticed you always lie, more or less, when you talk about Hexum. Nothing you said just now made sense. Try again."

"Reinhart stole the certificates from a man I killed. I blinded Reinhart and left him to die a few miles from here the day before he was going to use them to buy this atrocity. His dried-out skull might be watching us right now."

She looks at me intently and says, "Did they deserve to die?"

"Many times over."

"I believe you. Let's get this gold and go."

I throw the car in low gear and start down the slope. The surface is loose and rutted, and I have to fight the wheel to keep the heavy vehicle from sliding sideways.

The avenue before us is an exercise in perspective that arrows straight to the house. Everything looks the same until I look at the palm trees. All of them are dead. Their trunks are dirty gray and bent; the canopy of palm fronds that shaded the road is now a series of long, leafless stems that hang down like fleshless fingers; and withered palm leaves the color of bronze litter the ground in all directions. I drive forward slowly and Autumn points to the right.

"What the hell's that?"

It's what's left of the statue of Pan. His head and cock have been broken off, and his headless trunk tagged with spray paint and cratered by bullets.

"That's just the first," I say. "There's plenty more."

The other statues have been tortured and pillaged in a similar fashion, some removed entirely. Autumn mutters "Jesus" as we reach the house and drive around it. The wooden doors are gone, the windows shattered, and the walls wear a luxuriant growth of tags. The iron birds that were perched on the roof have migrated elsewhere. One section of wall on the side of the building looks like it was hit with an explosive charge, leaving behind a charred, star-shaped hole a couple of feet across.

The tree I buried the briefcase under is leaning over at a precarious angle, but the soil at its base is undisturbed. I park beside it and get the shovel out of the back.

Autumn surveys the decaying husk of Reinhart's dream home, and asks, "Why's it called Palmyra?"

"I'm not sure. It was the name of an ancient city in the Middle East."

"It looks the part. Sort of."

"But then someone told me once that it's the name of a villain's place in a Bond movie."

"That works too. It should be bulldozed or left as a warning, but nothing in-between."

A few strokes with the shovel is all it takes to reveal the briefcase. I open it and find the certificates in pristine condition inside their clear plastic bag.

Autumn looks into the briefcase and asks, "Are they all there?"

"Looks like it."

"Why didn't you want to get them? You probably could have used them years before this."

"Caleb, the guy they belonged to, could have taught Gideon a few tricks. Caleb had a family, but it was a combination brothel and slave pen he'd bought and bred for fun and profit, and when he found out that his treasure was gone, he slaughtered them in his rage. There should be a statue of him here; he'd fit in nicely. Reinhart was no better. I was partly—unintentionally—responsible for those deaths. Sometimes I'm convinced it was entirely down to me, so I always thought cashing these would be like bartering with scalps I'd lifted."

"What the fuck was in the water in that town?"

"Nothing special. Just a concentrated form of what you find most everywhere now."

Autumn shakes her head in amazement. This is the first time I've ever told anyone about Caleb and the deaths at the Settlement, and it leaves me feeling wounded.

Autumn takes my hands in hers. "You think you're like those other men, don't you? I've known men like that all my life and you're not one of them. Believe that."

"I want to."

"Let's go."

The track that leaves the valley behind the house is still there, but it looks in poor shape, and I don't know what the rest of that route is like, so we drive back to the front of the house.

"Stop," Autumn says suddenly. "I want to take a picture of this madness so I can always remember why I'm leaving this country."

She hops out of the car and takes a quick picture of the house and then the road that's waiting to lead us away.

Autumn hesitates before getting back in the Yukon and points to the other end of the valley. "What's that?"

A tan cloud is drifting up over the horizon somewhere along the route we took into Palmyra. It's dust from one or more vehicles moving in our direction.

"It's someone coming here. Fast."

"Off-roaders? Dirt bikes? Maybe it's people wanting to do some more tagging and target practice. It can't be Gantry."

"Let's be ready if it is."

We get the rifles out of their cases and attach the magazines and telescopic sights. Autumn bites her lip the whole time, but her hands are steady.

She slides a round into the chamber and gives me a grin. "You do like to get a girl in trouble."

"Don't tell me you wouldn't rather do this than kill time at the airport."

"When you put it like that…"

"When the vehicle comes into view, we'll check it out through the scopes. If it's Gantry, he won't be expecting us to have anything more than handguns, if that, so he'll feel safe at long range. It's got to be more than 400 yards from here to the end of the road, too far for my standard of accuracy. When they've closed to 100 yards we start shooting. We'll both aim for the driver. When he's dead, the car will veer to one side. I'll move out into the valley on that side while you advance up the road. Take cover behind the statues and keep up a steady fire. If there's others in the car they'll think we haven't changed position and they won't see me flanking them until it's too late. You ready?"

"Ready."

We each take cover behind a palm tree on either side of the road. The rising sun is behind us and should help blind Gantry and his men.

"It can't be him," says Autumn. "There's no fucking way he could have tracked us here."

"Shit."

"What?"

"Shout if you see a vehicle on the ridge."

I look underneath the Yukon and find a tracker in virtually the same position as the one that was put on my Honda. Lodestar must have had someone, probably the guy in the Mazda 3 with the bandaged arm, put trackers on Enoch's cars in Rancho Vista. Gantry would have wanted to be able to track any of Enoch's vehicles in case Autumn or myself used one, or in case they needed to follow Enoch to a rendezvous with us. They would have done it after they'd followed me to the Capri Inn. I pull the device off and put it in my pocket.

Autumn shouts, "They're here!"

A white SUV is parked on the road at the top of the ridge.

I take up my position behind the tree. "It'll be Lodestar. They had a tracker on the Yukon."

"Efficient bastards, aren't they?"

"And stupidly vengeful."

A man steps out of the passenger side of the vehicle. I look through the scope at him. It's Gantry. I lower my weapon and hold it behind the tree as he brings a pair of binoculars up to his face.

"Keep your weapon out of sight," I say urgently. "I don't want him to see that we've got rifles."

"Is it Gantry?"

"It is."

The Yukon is blocked from his view, so I lean out from the tree so Gantry can get a glimpse of me. He stays standing beside his car looking through the binoculars, then turns and speaks to someone in the SUV. A moment later I hear the faint sound of a car engine and a cloud of dust rises up behind him. The dust contrail moves to the right, following the edge of the valley but staying out of sight.

"He's brought friends," says Autumn.

"Let's see what they do."

I'm distracted by watching the progress of the second vehicle's dust smearing the blue sky, and when I glance back towards the road there's a third vehicle, a silver sedan, slithering down the road from the ridge.

"Didn't you say something about that gold being cursed?" says Autumn. "This is turning into an absolute clusterfuck."

"I've been in worse jams."

"Liar."

"So much for trying to sound encouraging."

"I'd be encouraged if you told me you have a superpower you've been hiding."

"Sorry."

The silver car is moving slowly along the road towards us, and on the lip of the valley to my right, about two hundred yards distant, a black Jeep pulls to a stop, its attendant swirl of dust drifting to the east.

"Do you think this might be a good time," says Autumn calmly, "to call 911? Let the cops come and cause some confusion we can escape in."

It's not a bad idea, if we can last long enough for them to arrive. I pull my phone out. There's no signal.

"No signal. Try yours."

Autumn looks at her phone. "Nothing. Well, it's remember the Alamo, I guess."

We could make a run for it using the road behind the building, but the Jeep on the ridge will probably be able to cut us off, and we'll have the other vehicles coming up behind.

"We'll take out the first car as planned, but we'll let it get closer, maybe thirty yards. I want Gantry to come down into the valley and get within range. He's sent down the silver car to find out if we're armed or not. If we wait to the last second, he might get impatient."

"What about that Jeep?"

The driver of the Jeep has gotten out and is cradling a rifle.

"Damn. After we stop the first car run to the far side of that statue." I point to a winged lion with a man's head on the left side of the avenue that's as big as an SUV. "Shoot at anything that moves on the road, even if you just see an arm or leg. If the second car is in range fire at it."

"And you?"

"I'm going to make a run for the house and try to get a shot from a window at the guy on the ridge."

"Look."

The silver car is accelerating and suddenly makes a hard turn to our right, darting between the palm trees 200 yards away and speeding across open ground parallel to the road. Three men are in the car, one pointing a shotgun out of the front passenger window. They're between us and the sniper on the ridge, and as soon we fire, he'll have our positions.

"Change of plan," I yell, "three quick rounds at the car, then three each at the guy on the ridge. Then you go to the statue and I'll go into the house if we haven't killed him. Now!"

The car is bouncing over the uneven ground making it a harder target, but Autumn's first shot is squarely in the middle of the front passenger door. The shotgun jerks up and I hear a cry of pain. Our other shots hit the car but don't slow it down. I look through the scope at the ridge where the sniper is prone on the ground taking aim at me. The muzzle flashes and a chunk of tree a foot above my head explodes, which makes me jerk the trigger and send my shot into the grill of his Jeep a good eight feet off target. I hear Autumn fire behind me and see the shot kick up an exclamation point of dust a foot from the man's head. His open-mouthed yell of alarm is silent to me as he raises himself slightly to crawl behind the Jeep. My second shot is no better, but Autumn's hits him in the back. I can hear him screaming now, but the sound is cut off by the shotgun firing from the window of the silver car. The pellets splatter into the statue that Autumn's behind and I fire four times at the car, bursting one of its tires, before it disappears behind the house.

"You okay," shouts Autumn.

"Yeah. You?"

"Thirsty."

On the ridge to our right, the wounded man is crawling towards his Jeep. The back of his white T-shirt is wet with blood and his legs are useless to him as he tries to lever himself up on the running board and reach for the door handle. I decide not to waste bullets on a cripple.

"One of us has to go after that car before they come up behind us," says Autumn.

"I'll do it. You're a better shot, so stay here and watch out for Gantry."

We both look up the road where the white SUV is still sitting on the ridge. Three other men have gotten out of the vehicle and are standing beside Gantry. None of them carry long guns. I grab an extra magazine from the Yukon and run into the house. The ground floor windows let me see out both sides of the house and there's no sign of the car. The back wall is windowless, so the car must be behind the house, and the men will be coming up one or both sides of it to flank us. I kneel beside a shaft of light spearing down from the oculus in the roof and wait.

Autumn shouts from outside, "Gantry's coming!"

I turn and look through the doors and catch a glimpse of the white SUV coming down into the valley. There's a noise to my right and the top of a man's head passes the first of four windows in the southern wall of the house. The windows are high off the ground so he'd need to jump up to see inside. Another head passes the window and I hear a grunt of pain. This must be the man with the shotgun who was wounded by Autumn's shot through the door. They'll have to pass the star-shaped hole in the wall after the second window, which will be at shoulder-height for them. I aim at the gash in the wall. A shadow falls on the edge of the hole and then stops. He's being cautious about passing the opening. Autumn's rifle fires three times and the first man moves forward slightly, his right shoulder and part of his tattooed arm appearing at the edge of the hole. I fire and the bullet rips through his bicep. As he shouts and disappears from view, I sprint to the first window they passed; a hand holding an automatic appears at the hole and shoots wildly into the room, missing me by miles. I lean out the window and see a man on his knees near the hole clutching his arm. His partner is wearing shorts and has blood leaking from a tear in his right calf. He continues shooting through the hole as I lean out the window and drop him with a bullet through the head. His body falls across the other man, whose gun is on the ground a few feet away. His look of horror is terribly familiar, as is his cry of "Don't!" as I swing the barrel towards him and put a round through his heart.

The instant I run out the front doors to the portico Autumn shouts a warning and there's an explosion of sound to my right and I'm hit with shotgun pellets in the arm and shoulder. Autumn is firing rapidly as I throw myself down and roll behind one of the pillars, just in time for another shotgun blast to splatter against a pillar behind me. I chance a look at the corner of the house where the shot came from and see a man running up onto the portico, an empty red shell sailing out of his shotgun as he racks it. Before I can bring my weapon up a bullet from Autumn catches him in the neck and sends him crashing down. He presses his hands to his throat and attempts to stem the blood that's pumping out between his fingers and fanning across the white marble. He understands that he's dying from the way I return his gaze and lower my rifle. His lips form silent words, as if he's trying to give me a message even as his eyes close and his head sinks into the gleaming sheet of his own blood.

I shout, "I'm okay!" before Autumn can ask, then run and join her behind the statue. She's breathing rapidly and sweat runs down her face. She reaches out and touches my bloody shoulder.

"How bad is it?"

"It's only a few pellets; I think they may have been ricochets."

"The three in the car?"

"Dead."

The SUV is stopped on the road over 200 yards away. I look through the scope; there's a bullet hole in the windshield, but no sign of Gantry and his men.

"What happened?" I ask.

"They started to speed up so I fired, then they stopped, dived out, and hid themselves. Now what?"

They'll be in pairs on either side of the road, covering each other as they move slowly and methodically towards us using the palm trees and statues as cover. Our chances of killing them all are virtually non-existent.

"You have to leave right now. There's a road out of the valley behind the house; it's rough, but it's not as steep as the other one. There's an old track up there that should lead back to the road we turned in off."

"Why aren't you coming?" Autumn says with shock.

"When they see our car leaving a back way they didn't know about, they'll give chase and come right past me; it'll be point blank range and I can take them all out."

"I don't like it."

"It's that or we both die. I don't want scum like Gantry being the end of me or you."

"So, I wait for you when I get out of the valley?"

"No. Keep going. Fast, all the way to the airport. We don't know if he has backup coming or if it's already on the road into here, but Vegas is where Lodestar is based so there must be more of them around and on alert. Once I'm done with these bastards, I'll take the car they left at the back of the house. I'll call you when I'm clear, but I want you to take the first flight out of here. Get out of the country, don't wait for me."

"Fuck that."

"I'm going to have to get my arm cleaned up and bandaged before I can walk into an airport. Every minute we're in Vegas is risky, but not as dangerous as standing here talking. Leave now and we both stand a good chance; stay and we almost certainly die."

Autumn hesitates for a moment, but then says, "Alright."

We sprint to the Yukon and Autumn gets behind the wheel after laying her rifle within reach on the passenger seat. I grab my bag from out of the back, some bottles of water, two magazines for my rifle, then take the tracker out of my pocket and hand it to Autumn.

"At the first gas station you come to, stick this on another car; it's got a magnetic base."

"Okay." She puts her hand to my cheek. "You're not staying behind to look noble and brave, are you? You forget that I'm shallow and your good looks are more than enough to impress me."

"Same here; I only fell in love with you because you made me laugh that day on San Jacinto Peak."

"Now's a fine time to tell me that. I'll only say I love you when I see you again somewhere far away, so you'll have to bust your ass for that pleasure. Deal?"

"Deal."

We hold a kiss that's both too short and too long.

"Boot it," I tell Autumn.

She floors it and sends a cloud of noise and dust into the air that announces her departure. I run back to the statue and slap a full 30-round magazine into my rifle and cram the other in my pocket as the Yukon disappears around the back of the house. Shouts comes from up the road and I peek out to see men jumping back into the SUV. I look back as the Yukon emerges briefly on the edge of the valley and then darts out of sight.

The SUV's engine starts and I move behind a tree closer to the house. They'll have to brake and turn sharply at the point where the road meets the house and turn broadside to me, and that's when I'll fire. I hear the SUV approach and put my back to the broad trunk of the palm tree and look up at its thin, lifeless stems reaching down as if straining to catch something living in their grasp. My throat is painfully dry. I haven't had a drink in hours. The sun is full in my face, its heat a reminder of the day I struck down Reinhart.

The SUV's brakes squeal slightly as it passes behind me and I step away from the tree. My first shots are aimed at the driver, who holds a futile hand up in front of his face as if hoping to catch the bullets that strike his chest and face. The bulky vehicle ploughs slowly up the marble steps and is stopped by a column as I follow beside it emptying my magazine into the doors and windows. One man in the car is screeching like an animal, another gets off a shot that punches through the roof of the car. I pop in my second magazine, move to the other side of the car, put a dozen more rounds into it, then fall back and look and listen for movement.

The engine coughs and dies, and out of the corner of my eye I see the cloud of dust from the Yukon moving steadily away. Blood begins to seep out around the bottom edge of a door frame, then becomes a steady stream that worms down the steps.

As I lower my rifle, I hear quick steps behind me. I spin around and Gantry tackles me before I can fire. The rifle has fallen somewhere behind me, and he has a rock in his right hand that he drives down at my head and barely misses with as I roll over and throw an elbow up into his chest. He raises his hand to strike again with the rock, but I block it with my arm and reach with my right hand to grab his balls through his jeans. He makes a hissing sound and head-butts me in the cheek. I'm dazed, but I squeeze harder and he throws himself off me with a shout and tries a two-handed blow with the rock while on his knees that hammers into the ground by my shoulder. I kick him solidly in the chest and knock him onto his back, and as he tries to scramble to his feet I extend my arms to grab the barrel of my rifle and then scythe it around to catch him in the side of the head with the butt. Gantry groans and curls into a ball, his hands clutching his head.

I stand up and step a few feet away. My back is sore from landing on the ground and my cheek throbs from Gantry's blow. He moves into a crouching position and looks at me with defeated eyes as I point my weapon at him.

"What can I give you, Bridger?" he whispers frantically. "Anything is yours."

I hesitate before firing. A strange feeling comes over me—one that I know won't last—that I need a breather between killings, a brief respite from seeing men's bodies become bloody and still.

"Don't even try, Gantry. Why weren't you in the car?"

"The bastards left me. They gave up. They saw your car leaving and said it was time to run before the police turned up." He extends an empty hand toward me. "They took my gun from me, the fuckers, and said I wasn't paying them enough for all this shit."

I laugh. "Finally, the revolt of the henchmen. It looks good on you. Is Enoch dead?"

He nods.

"Accident or murder?"

"He drowned."

"It disgusts me that you and I think alike. Do you have any other teams out there backing you up?"

He shakes his head.

I raise my rifle.

"No, Bridger."

"Why not?"

He struggles to find his next words, a perplexed look coming over his face. "I don't belong here, Bridger. This isn't a place to die."

I prove him wrong with one shot.

The pain in my throat is intense, so I retrieve my bottles of water and chug them all, then climb the steps of the house and look into the windows of the SUV, my gun at the ready, to make sure everyone inside is dead. They are. I go to the rear of the house to the silver car, an older Accord, and find the keys still in the ignition. One of the front tires is flat. I open the trunk expecting my bad luck to continue, but the temporary spare is in place. By the time I've changed the tire my thirst is back with a vengeance and very few parts of my body aren't aching.

The road Autumn left by is too rugged for the small spare tire; I'll have to exit the way we came in and take it slowly. I drive to the front of the house, collect my bag, then continue down the avenue. I keep glancing at the rear-view mirror, my tired mind expecting to see Reinhart step out between the palms and beckon me to return. Near the bottom of the slope I gun the engine and the car leaps up the incline, slows, then creeps over the top with a final tap on the accelerator. I give the wheel a congratulatory slap and get out of the car.

I stand on the edge of the valley and check my phone. I have a signal, but the phone drops out of my hand as I take a monstrous punch to my right thigh and fall on my side, the crackling echo of a rifle shot filling my ears. I crawl to the car as another shot zips over my back. I claw open the rear door and pull my rifle off the back seat, then lever myself up and look through the scope at the Jeep on the edge of the valley, over 200 yards away. The crippled sniper is sitting on the ground and looking in my direction, his back against the fat front tire of his car and his lifeless legs arranged in front of him at odd angles—he's a blood-soaked scarecrow with an agonized face. He's trying to reload but his gun's jammed

He lays his rifle down at his side, shrugs eloquently, then solemnly and repeatedly points to the middle of his chest. A flash of pain goes through my wound and is followed by an almost pleasant wave of fatigue and dizziness. My leg is leaking dark, arterial blood. I look through the scope again and fire a shot that hits the Jeep four feet to the left of the shooter. He gives me a thumbs-up and continues pointing to his heart. He's young, no more than twenty-five, with reddish hair and ivory skin, and I stupidly think he shouldn't be out in this sun. I overcompensate with the second shot and it hits the bumper a foot to the right of him. He nods appreciatively, as if I've made an interesting point, and continues tapping his chest. I try and slow my breathing down like they tell you to do, but it's difficult now, and the next shot goes in his right cheek. The parts of his body that aren't already dead jerk and then slowly stiffen. I would have liked to have done as he asked and hit his heart. He knew when to give up.

My phone glints on the ground, and I hobble over to it, sit down, and call Autumn.

She answers with a shouted, "You made it out!"

"I have. Where are you?"

"The airport."

"Excellent. Any problems?"

"No. I stopped in Boulder City at a Dunkin' Donuts and put the tracker on an ambulance."

"Perfect."

"You alright? You sound tired."

"I've had less strenuous mornings."

"How did things go at your end?"

"All problems solved. What flight did you get?"

"San Francisco, then on to Hong Kong; I don't even have to change planes."

My leg is in a tightening vise and the sun isn't hot enough for me now.

"You should go on to Singapore. I'll meet you there and we can cash those things together."

I can see Autumn's delighted smile in the way she says, "Raffles Hotel! We can meet there. You must have heard of it—it's a landmark."

"Sure. Somerset Maugham stayed there."

"Who?"

"Writer."

"I know what we should do to pass the time when we're settled."

"What?"

"Fill in the blanks in each other's education. You need to learn all about Bauhaus, Art Deco, Figurative Expressionism, the International Style, Postminimalism, Miesian and Brutalist architecture, and so much more; it'll take years, because you're horribly ignorant that way, and I didn't even mention art. What are you going to make me read?"

"How not to be a snob."

"Ha ha."

My body is hollow and light, and the pain is in a distant part of me. A small pool of blood has formed on the ground beside my leg and I dip a finger into it and study its color.

"You there?" asks Autumn.

"Yeah. I should go."

"When do you think you'll leave?"

"Tomorrow, maybe the next day."

"Are you okay? Did you get hurt anymore?"

"No. Just scratches and bruises."

She pauses before saying, "Remember what I said: you'll only hear those three little words when you get the hell over there."

"That's all I needed to know."

"Okay. Bye for now."

"Bye, Autumn."

I slip the phone in my pocket. It takes a while to get to my feet and stagger to the car. As I lean against it, I feel blood moving in gentle waves down my leg. The bullet has probably nicked my femoral artery. If I drive very slowly and avoid hitting potholes or rocks, I might make it to the highway and be able to signal for help before the nick becomes a tear and I bleed out.

But I don't want to.

The task of escaping this place and finding safety seems long and exhausting and futile. Rest is what I want. All my life I've been leading a parade of violence and death, and now I've brought my bloody cavalcade to this valley filled with mad dreams made solid and sowed it with yet more bodies. And all for nothing. There's no comfort in the deaths of Gideon, Enoch, Pinder, and Gantry. The billions that will fall to their heirs will bring them back to life in one form or another.

The sun sits directly overhead, but it might as well be the moon for all the warmth it gives.

If I leave here, the spirits that follow in my train will be hungry to conjure fresh miseries.

I belong with the dead.

I limp away from the car and move gingerly down the steep slope that takes me back to Palmyra. When I reach the bottom, blood starts rushing down my leg.

I'm not thirsty now.

The desert is hot but I'm cold.

I reach the first of the palm trees.
Walking this way is slow and foolish-looking.
My leg doesn't want to move.
I don't hurt anymore, not really.
The desert is hot but I'm cold.
I hop over to a palm tree and sit with my back against it.
I'll rest a while.
Pan is looking at me.
My eyes close.
The desert is hot but I'm cold.
There are things I want to remember. Things I can't forget.
Levi is shaking me awake.
"What?"
"We're going on an adventure, Tom; a big adventure!"

THE END

Printed in Great Britain
by Amazon